THE TRIB_

ALSO BY MICHAEL ARDITTI

The Celibate
Pagan and her Parents
Easter
Unity
Good Clean Fun
A Sea Change
The Enemy of the Good
Jubilate
The Breath of Night
Widows and Orphans
Of Men and Angels
The Anointed
The Young Pretende
The Choice

MICHAEL ARDITTI
The TRIBE

CROMER

PUBLISHED BY SALT PUBLISHING 2026

2 4 6 8 10 9 7 5 3

Copyright © Michael Arditti 2026

Michael Arditti has asserted his right under the Copyright, Designs and Patents Act 1988 to be identified as the author of this work.

This book is sold subject to the condition that it shall not, by way of trade or otherwise, be lent, resold, hired out, or otherwise circulated without the publisher's prior consent in any form of binding or cover other than that in which it is published and without a similar condition including this condition being imposed on the subsequent publisher.

This book is a work of fiction. Any references to historical events, real people or real places are used fictitiously. Other names, characters, places and events are products of the author's imagination, and any resemblance to actual events or places or persons, living or dead, is entirely coincidental.

First published in Great Britain in 2026 by
Salt Publishing Ltd
12 Norwich Road, Cromer, Norfolk NR27 0AX, United Kingdom

GPSR representative
Matt Parsons matt.parsons@upi2mbooks.hr
UPI-2M PLUS d.o.o., Medulićeva 20, 10000 Zagreb, Croatia

www.saltpublishing.com

Salt Publishing Limited Reg. No. 5293401

A CIP catalogue record for this book is available from the British Library

ISBN 978 1 78463 364 6 (Paperback edition)
ISBN 978 1 78463 365 3 (Electronic edition)

Typeset in Neacademia by Salt Publishing

Printed and bound in Great Britain by Clays Ltd, Elcograf S.p.A.

*For Ann Pennington, Jenny Topper
and Timberlake Wertenbaker*

'And the Lord shall scatter you among the peoples, and ye shall be left few in number among the nations, whither the Lord shall lead you away.'

Deuteronomy 4:27

The Carrache Family

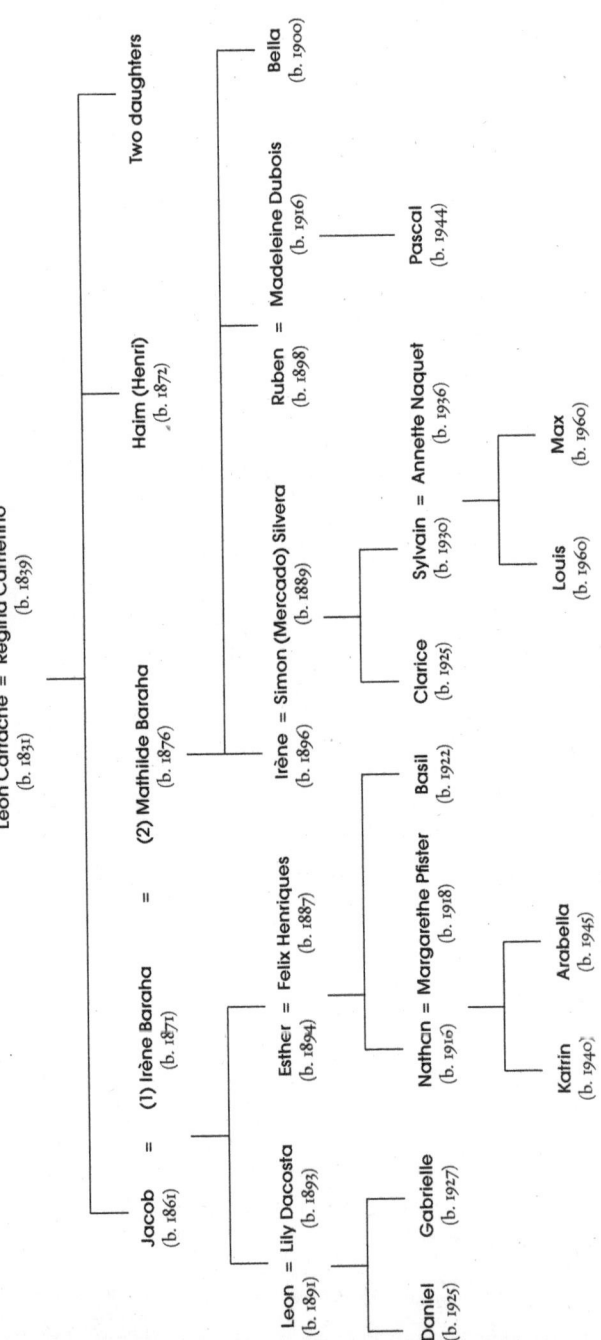

ONE

1

JACOB

SALONICA, JUNE 1911

THE CITY WAS festooned in honour of the Sultan. Every window frame and doorway was wreathed in flowers; every balcony was draped in a blood-red Ottoman flag. Twenty-six ceremonial arches had been erected along the processional route, one of them the gift of the Carrache family. A military band played martial airs in the recently renamed Liberty Square. The fountain in the centre flowed with cherry juice, much to the delight of Jacob's youngest children, Ruben and Bella, and the dismay of their mother, who had issued grave warnings of dysentery and cholera.

The Sultan had entered the harbour the previous day but remained on board his flagship, *Hayrettin Barbaros*, where he received the Governor and provincial representatives, before resting after the two-day voyage from Constantinople, which had been the longest of his life. His loyal subjects had had little chance to rest, as carpenters hammered and sawed through the night, fixing uneven stands and rickety railings; sweeps spread sand to smooth the imperial carriage's path over cobbled streets; and officials bawled commands at underlings during last-minute inspections. Any lull was broken by the snap and sputter of firecrackers, further alarming the jittery gendarmes, although the most incendiary rabble-rousers, the four leaders of the Socialist Federation, had been imprisoned or exiled prior to the visit.

At last, the steamer carrying the Sultan and his entourage pulled away from the flagship and made for the shore. With a raucous whistle, it chugged through the sloops and skiffs that clustered round it like beggars soliciting alms. It was barely fifty years since the first steamship arrived in Salonica. Jacob had been a babe in arms and his father later told him of the panic on the quayside, with frantic calls for fishing boats to sail to the rescue of the seemingly stricken vessel. It was a sign of the city's transformation that the plumes of vapour were now a familiar sight. The crowds on the waterfront were marking the Sultan's arrival not with shrieks of terror but whoops of welcome, although he was too far away to hear.

Jacob gazed at the ship and pictured the scene through the Sultan's eyes. The city was smaller than Constantinople but more cosmopolitan, poised midway between East and West, its skyline adorned with minarets and bell towers. Although the synagogues were less conspicuous, the Jewish influence was no less pronounced. Salonica might belong to the Turks and be claimed by the Greeks and Bulgarians, but Jews made up the majority of its population. And it was Jacob and his coreligionists who had reshaped it in the past thirty years from a sleepy backwater to an economic hub, building the hotels and department stores that bordered the square, building the warehouses that fronted the quay, building pipelines and plants that brought water and electricity into private homes. But even more than electricity, they had brought enlightenment.

The steamer docked to thunderous applause. After a lengthy delay, the Sultan stepped ashore and ascended a specially erected podium. He stood ramrod straight and saluted as the band struck up the updated imperial anthem. Short and stout, with pursy checks, a walrus moustache and a medal-encrusted tunic, he exuded a faintly disgruntled air, either at finding himself in this unknown and, to him, remote outpost of his empire or, simply, at having been plucked from opulent obscurity two years earlier and thrust on the throne after the bloodless coup that deposed his brother. A very different monarch from the despotic Abdul Hamid, he had immediately ratified the new constitution, guaranteeing parliamentary rule and the rights of all his subjects.

While wary of the firebrands from the Committee of Union and Progress who had orchestrated the coup (and, indeed, of firebrands in general), Jacob had broadly supported their aims and applauded their spokesman, Enver Bey, who'd stood in this very square and declared that no longer were there Bulgarians, Greeks, Serbs, Romanians, Jews or Muslims: from now on, all were Ottomans, equal under the same blue sky. Setting caste aside, Jacob had linked arms with Ishak, an elderly waiter at the Club des Intimes, and hummed a few bars of the Marseillaise.

He emerged from his reverie as the final jaunty chords of the anthem faded and the Mufti approached the podium to perform the sacrifice. Tall and turbaned, sporting a full beard and an emerald kaftan, he looked so much more regal than the Sultan that Jacob could imagine Ruben, a youthful devotee of *The Arabian Nights*, confusing them. Four acolytes followed, dragging two rams, their horns painted green and fleeces dyed red, orange and purple, some of which stained the men's white jubbahs, as if the prescient beasts had sought to escape their fate. The Mufti slit the first throat with admirable adroitness, while an acolyte held up a bowl to collect the blood. The second ram, its last steps on earth as tottery as its first, lurched backwards, its desperate bleats accentuating Jacob's horror of a practice long since expunged from his own rites. The Mufti, glaring at the beast as if its recalcitrance were an insult to the hundreds of soldiers lining the square, each of whom had pledged to lay down his life for the Sultan, grabbed one of its horns and hacked at its throat. Making supplication to Allah, he sprinkled the blood on the ground.

The Sultan, accompanied by the Grand Vizier, inspected the rows of assembled dignitaries. Jacob, attending as president of both the Jewish Community Council and the Salonica Chamber of Commerce, felt a twinge of adolescent bashfulness as the Sultan walked past, no trace of curiosity in his hooded gaze. He watched as the Sultan stepped into his carriage to drive to the Konak, where he would reside during the visit. The processional route was flanked by children from the city's various schools – Jewish, Greek, Serbian and Bulgarian – with only the Turkish pupils granted the honour of parading in front of the Sultan at the Konak. The original plan for a broad-based parade had been abandoned, ostensibly to avoid congestion on the narrow streets of the Muslim quarter. Yet Jacob had it on good authority that the true concern was inflaming tensions over the order of precedence among the other ethnic groups.

Ruben and Bella were both taking part in the reception: his son grumbling about his cape, the laurel sprig he was required to wave, and the long wait in the clammy heat; his daughter enraptured by the prospect of throwing a rose at the Sultan's carriage ('Madame Dupont told us to aim at the wheels, or else it will look like a funeral'). They and their classmates from the lycée occupied a prime spot on the quay. Despite his support for universal education, Jacob had dismissed any suggestion of sending his own children either to an Alliance school or the Talmud Torah, where they would receive an unduly vocational or religious training and acquire undesirable habits from their peers, many of whom would in due course work for him.

Muffling the nagging voice accusing him of double standards (which sounded uncomfortably like that of his eldest daughter, Esther), he scanned the quay, in anticipation of Bella's inevitable 'Papa, did you see me?' But at this distance, picking out one white-clad child from the crowd was as hopeless as picking out a pet goose from a gaggle. He prepared himself for the equally inevitable prevarication.

His fellow dignitaries began to disperse: some heading up Sabri Pasha Street to greet the Sultan a second time at the Konak; others, duty done, to join family and friends. Jacob's family was scattered across the city. His wife Mathilde was watching the ceremony alongside both of their mothers and their middle daughter, Irène, from a balcony at the Hotel d'Angleterre. Although the Governor, fearing for the Sultan's safety, had decreed that all balconies remain sealed for the duration of the visit, the edict had been widely ignored. Jacob smiled at the notion of anyone mistaking the eminently respectable Carrache women for insurrectionists.

Irène had protested at being stuck with her mother and grandmothers while her brothers and sisters were out with their friends, prompting Mathilde to remark, with uncharacteristic asperity, that she was free to stay at home. 'It's not fair,' Irène had replied, as she did to countless perceived injustices every day. Despite Jacob's sympathy for his all-too-easily overlooked middle child, he could do little to help. At fifteen, she was too old to throw flowers with Bella, and too young to dispense with adult tutelage. He wished that he might say the same of seventeen-year-old Esther. His parents would never have permitted either of his sisters to go out alone before they were married. But the city's landscape wasn't all that had changed in the past thirty years.

Esther had bought tickets for herself and her friend Leah Sagues to view the proceedings from the vantage point of the Club Nouveau. On the face of it, she couldn't have chosen a more suitable chaperone. Leah was a dedicated, impassioned and highly intelligent teacher at the Alliance girls' school. They'd met when Esther accompanied Mathilde to distribute clothing to the poorer pupils and had since become inseparable. Mathilde had invited Leah to dine and, on learning that she had no family in the city, renewed the invitation at least once a week. Leah made no secret of her radical sentiments, with which he feared she was infecting Esther. She even challenged him at his own table, and Esther, who would never have been so presumptuous herself, egged her on. Although Leah showed him every sign of respect, above and beyond what was due to a major benefactor of the school, he could never shake the suspicion that she was silently laughing at him.

While four of his children were accounted for, he was ignorant of the whereabouts of his elder son. If anyone should have been celebrating the Sultan's visit, it was Leon. Three years earlier, in defiance of his father's express command, the then seventeen-year-old had been among a group of Jewish youths who, with their Greek, Bulgarian and Serbian comrades, marched beside rebels from Abdul Hamid's army to the military headquarters at Monastir and exhorted the soldiers to mutiny. When he returned, flushed with the flame of revolution, Jacob had been so overwhelmed with relief that he neglected to punish him, an act of clemency he had come to regret. For all his qualities – honour, loyalty and compassion chief among them – Leon lacked application. Neither a year at the Sorbonne nor placements at both the tobacco factory and the bank had held his interest. He spent his days hunting and sailing, playing billiards and backgammon. Having declared the visit of the Sultan, for whose accession he had risked his life, to be nothing but 'bread and circuses', he was no doubt drowning his disappointment in a taverna.

The last in the cavalcade of carriages rolled along the quay, its occupants, two elderly beys, chattering animatedly, as if to counter the crowd's indifference. Tired and thirsty, Jacob crossed the square to the Club des Intimes. He handed his fez to the doorman, who informed him that his father and brother were upstairs.

His father had been a founding member of the club, which was modelled on the Jockey Club in Paris, in every respect but for its admittance of Jews. It swiftly became the favoured meeting place of the city's financial and mercantile elite, a place where business and leisure converged – and, on occasion, clashed. For more than thirty years, his father had ended each working day with a visit to the club, to see friends, drink an aperitif and chew over issues of mutual concern, before heading home to his wife. Even after the stroke, which severely restricted his speech and mobility and forced his belated retirement, he maintained his daily visits. Two porters carried him up to his appointed seat at the library window, where he surveyed the passing scene, read the foreign papers, and acknowledged the greetings of members with whom he could no longer converse.

Jacob entered the library, breathing in the congenial aroma of wood polish, cracked leather and citrus beard oil. He found his father sitting with his younger brother Haim, and Baruch ben Yaakov, whose dye house the Carraches had bought at the turn of the century but who continued to think of himself as their associate. Bending to kiss his father's hand, he acknowledged with a familiar pang of guilt that, despite his sympathy for his impairment, he felt more at ease with this snow-bearded husk of a man than the former forbidding patriarch. After taking a seat and ordering a glass of boza, he related his impressions of the ceremony, exaggerating the discomfort of the protracted wait in deference to his chairbound father. To spice up the account, he cracked a joke about the famously greedy Rabbi Sardo's stomach rumbling as the slaughtered rams were dragged away. Haim and ben Yaakov laughed (the latter immoderately), but his father, who disapproved of such irreverence, scratched a fingernail on the table.

'I have to congratulate you on your arch,' ben Yaakov said, as conversation stalled. 'One of the most spectacular in the city, if not the most.'

Jacob could not disagree. The arch, one of only two privately financed by Jews, was magnificent. As well as saluting the Sultan in three languages, French, Turkish and Greek, it listed the multifarious Carrache banking, brokerage and manufacturing enterprises, with pride of place given to the tobacco factory, the principal supplier to the Sublime Porte. Ideally located near the Ayasofya mosque, where the Sultan would attend Friday prayers, the arch was crowned by six giant cigarettes, fashioned from light bulbs, which glowed at night, in turn promoting the Carrache and Mordoh Electricity Supply Company.

A second scratch of the table signalled his father's displeasure at ben Yaakov's remark. Jacob struggled to contain his frustration. The Carraches had lived in Salonica for almost two centuries; they owned large tracts of the city and employed more than a thousand of its inhabitants; yet his father objected to any display of wealth or status lest it stoke resentment. He harboured a constant fear that they would be expelled as brutally as their ancestors had been from

Spain. Jacob was not naïve. He was well aware of the Tsarist pogroms. When two thousand Russian Jews fled here in 1891, he found work for many in his factory and built homes for their families nearby. Three years later, he watched, in even greater consternation, as France, the centre of the civilised world, was consumed by antisemitism over Major Dreyfus's alleged treason. But justice prevailed; the authorities admitted their error. Dreyfus was reinstated and Jacob assured that the country had recovered from its derangement.

His father and brother knew his sentiments without his needing to reiterate them. Instead, he outlined the latest arrangements for Ruben's tefillin celebration, ben Yaakov commending every detail as if angling for an invitation, which he failed to secure. Oozing wounded pride, he took his leave and, with their father's tacit blessing, the brothers made their way to the dining room for lunch. Their father no longer ate anywhere but at his own table, Haim feeding him with boundless patience, while their mother carped either that the heaped forkfuls would choke him or that he was spilling food. Haim was her youngest child by almost a decade and, far from rejoicing at the birth of a Benjamin, she had resigned herself to it as to a disease from which she had thought she was cured. In spite – or because – of her hostility, Haim's abiding wish was to be of service to his parents and, at thirty, he still lived at home. To Jacob's children, 'Le pauvre oncle' was so often attached to his name that it was almost an honorific. Mathilde, an inveterate matchmaker, had introduced him to a string of eligible girls, all of whom he rejected. Jacob, who hated any kind of ambiguity, longed for Haim to regulate his life.

The chef had chosen to celebrate the Sultan's visit with a traditional Turkish menu. Both brothers started with tripe soup; Jacob following it with quince stuffed with minced lamb and pine nuts, and Haim opting for fried anchovies in a cinnamon-and-pomegranate sauce. For dessert, Jacob ordered almond-and-rosewater halva, while the more adventurous Haim settled on sweet chicken pudding. After accompanying him back to their father, Jacob withdrew to the library, where he leafed through the latest issue of Le Charivari, which, thanks to the new fast train service, was on sale in Salonica only three days after appearing in Paris. Though not always abreast of its satire, he admired the comic sketches and took a boyish delight in the caricatures.

A studied harrumph roused him from his doze. Trusting that Mathilde's assurance that he didn't snore was no mere conjugal kindness, he sat up.

'Are you reading that, Monsieur?' asked an unfamiliar man, pointing to the journal lying like a reproach on his knees.

'Not at all,' he replied, briskly smoothing the pages. 'Be my guest.'

'Thank you.'

'A bumper issue, I think you'll find,' he added, lest the man suppose it soporific.

He headed outside but, having granted his coachman leave in the belief that the streets would be thronged, he found them no busier than usual. Nevertheless, he was glad of the long walk home, to digest both his meal and the day's events. The quayside had a deflated, end-of-party air: flags and banners drooped on the walls; fruit rinds and pastry wrappings littered the pavements; wheel tracks crisscrossed the sanded cobbles, splattered with horse dung and strewn with the wilted roses tossed at the Sultan's carriage. He ambled past the tobacco factory, nodding to the people he met – in his own sphere, he too was a sultan – until he reached the White Tower. The trampled sand marked the procession's sharp turn up Union Boulevard, the former Hamidye Avenue, whose renaming came less naturally to him than that of Liberty Square.

His children accused him of living in the past, but his youthful memories remained vivid. For the first decade of his life, this had been the city's eastern boundary, protected by massive, timeworn walls. Every summer, he and his brother and sisters would drive through the heavily guarded gates to picnic in the meadows and, on one thrilling occasion, he and his cousin Nissim accompanied their fathers to the tobacco harvest in Kilkis, with an escort of armed outriders to ward off bandits. But every expedition, however splendid, had been blighted by the corpses strung up outside the gates. He never accustomed himself to the sight and, no matter how carefully he calculated when to close his eyes on the journey home, he always opened them too soon, knowing that the image of their bloated faces, lolling tongues and livid skin would haunt him long into the night.

The walls that had encircled the city for centuries were torn down in the 1870s, once the threat of invasion was finally deemed to have passed. Seizing their opportunity, the Carraches bought up swathes of the surrounding countryside, later selling residential plots to merchants and industrialists who, unlike their predecessors, wished to distance themselves from the source of their wealth. In time, Jacob joined them. While his father and uncles remained in the Jewish quarter, he built a house for his growing family, alongside a garden that ran down to the sea. In a further break with his roots, he welcomed the presence of Greek and Turkish neighbours as a sign of the city's coming of age. He even forced a smile when Esther, doubtless prompted by Leah, argued that the Campania district was as parochial as any other. The only difference was that its presiding deity was not Yahweh or God or Allah but Mammon.

The grandest house in the neighbourhood belonged to Jacob's friend, Charles Allatini. In 1909, he loaned it to the government to accommodate the deposed Sultan, much to the excitement of Irène, Ruben and Bella, who basked in reflected glory. Every afternoon for weeks, they gathered at the railings, eager to spot the erstwhile potentate, until they were warned off by a guard.

'He put a curse on us,' Ruben said.

'How do you know?' Esther asked scornfully. 'You can't speak Turkish.'

'He bared his teeth. They were long and pointy like a tiger's. Then he spat three times on the ground.'

'Four,' Bella corrected.

They lapped up the accounts of Abdul Hamid's activities in the *Journal de Salonique*. Ruben was most taken with his demand for a hammam in place of an 'insanitary Western bathroom', accusing his parents of wanting him to die of plague when they refused to install one. Bella was intrigued by his retinue of twenty servants, compared to their mere six.

'What's a eunuch?' she asked Mathilde, in reference to four of them.

'A man in charge of the treasure.'

'So is Papa a eunuch?'

'Don't be absurd!'

'Why?' she asked in a hurt voice. 'Isn't there treasure in his bank?'

Irène, meanwhile, was exercised by the Sultan's three wives.

'That's nothing,' Ruben said. 'Monsieur Dumain told us that Suleiman the Magnificent had four hundred.'

'And King Solomon had seven hundred wives and three hundred concubines,' Leon added.

'What's a concubine?' Bella asked.

'A laundress,' Mathilde said. 'Now, no more questions.'

The Allatini house may have been the grandest in the Campania, but there was no question which was the most distinctive. Having been dazzled by the *style moderne* buildings during his visit to the 1900 Paris Exposition, Jacob had commissioned a prize-winning young architect to design the house (so much for living in the past!). He had waited four years for him to complete his existing projects and spent far more than he'd admitted even to Mathilde, but it had been worth every piastre. As he walked down the drive and glimpsed the blue and white stonework with the floral medallions, the cantilevered balconies with the wrought-iron grilles, and the gabled portico with the cornucopia pediment, he brimmed with proprietary pride.

The interior was no less striking. The circular entrance hall boasted a variegated mosaic floor with a seashell motif, and four star-patterned stained-glass windows that lent it a quasi-devotional air. The curved marble staircase led to the three upper storeys, supported by columns so slender that impressionable guests feared their imminent collapse. His mother declared that the view made her dizzy, while his mother-in-law visited for several years before she could be coaxed upstairs. His father's protests at the extravagance intensified after Jacob permitted the *Journal de Salonique* to photograph the house for a feature entitled 'The visionaries transforming the face of the city', which credited architect and patron in equal measure.

'It's an open invitation to assassins and thieves,' his mother said.

'And to the new government to tear up the capitulations and compel us to pay tax,' his father added.

Eager to enjoy a final moment of calm before dinner, Jacob wandered through the garden. He savoured the sultry scent of jasmine and frangipani laced with the powdery sweetness of tuberose. He gazed with satisfaction at the ripening apricots, mulberries and figs. He made his way down the pebbled path and scanned the molten-gold sea, streaked with purple in the twilight.

He had every reason to be contented with his lot. At fifty, he was in his prime, with a loving wife and five healthy children. The Carrache businesses were thriving: in the past year, they had doubled their share of the burgeoning Russian tobacco market and set up a brokerage house in New York. The Albanian ports had reopened after the recent revolt, and goods left to gather dust at the docks were at last being shipped . . . Before he knew it, he had reached into his pocket and clasped the protective cloves that Mathilde had sewn into the lining. He felt a fleeting irritation at both her credulity and his compliance, which was swiftly subsumed in a surge of tenderness.

Hearing footsteps, he retreated to the shadows and watched as Leon unlocked the door to the ground-floor apartment. He had made it over to him on his last birthday, in the hope, as yet unrealised, that an element of independence would foster his sense of responsibility. His vantage point gave him no clue as to his son's mood, purpose or even sobriety. Mathilde maintained that every twenty-year-old was a mystery to his parents, in which case he himself must have been the exception. In awe of his father, he had striven above all else to gain his approval. It had been his good fortune to come of age alongside the railways and steamships, and he had taken full advantage of the opportunities they presented. With no similar advancements in view, he feared that, far from wanting to build on his success, Leon felt daunted by it.

Mathilde's remedy for Leon's malaise was marriage. She was apt to prescribe it for every uncommitted bachelor, but, in this case, Jacob agreed. He had been twenty-three at the time of his marriage to his first wife Irène, although, unlike Leon, he'd dedicated the years since leaving school to mastering his profession. There was no currency richer than reputation and none so easily devalued. While they might overlook Leon's youthful indiscretions for the sake of an alliance with the Carraches, no notable family would countenance a wastrel.

One misgiving spawned another. At seventeen, Esther was the same age as Irène when she married. With girls enjoying a degree of latitude inconceivable to previous generations, he had trusted that Leah would serve as a moderating influence. Unsuitable ideas, however, were as harmful as unsuitable attachments. No one could accuse a staunch advocate of girls' education of trying to silence them. All he asked was that they kept their opinions to themselves. Esther made herself ridiculous by pronouncing on matters far beyond her experience. The condition of the poor in the city might well be deplorable, but how would it be improved by offering them pipe dreams and pamphlets? If she genuinely wished to help, she should join her stepmother's sewing circle or assist with the weekly pitta distribution: supplying them with bread, rather than half-baked ideas.

As a twenty-four-year-old spinster who affirmed her independence, Leah set a dangerous example to Esther, who, for months, had been cajoling him to send her to train as a teacher in Paris. But what did she know of the realities of such a life: the candlelit reading in garret rooms that would destroy her eyes; the unresponsive pupils, indifferent parents and fractious colleagues that would destroy her morale; the gruelling obligations that would plunder her youth until, when she at last came to her senses, any prospective husband would have taken fright?

He had neglected his paternal duty. Finding a match for Esther was an even more pressing task than finding one for Leon. Nevertheless, he must proceed with care. She was wilful and volatile and he dreaded provoking a permanent rift. She had been outraged when her sixteen-year-old cousin Ida married their uncle Salvator, and not just because of Salvator's overfamiliarity towards his other nieces. The very notion of such a youthful bride offended her. Irène had died giving birth to her and, although she had been ripe for childbearing, Esther blamed her death on the strain of undergoing five pregnancies – three of which miscarried – by the age of twenty-two. He knew that she viewed his remarriage the following year as evidence of his callousness, whereas the truth was that, heartbroken, he had sought a mother for his infant son and daughter, and his parents-in-law had proposed that Mathilde should take her older sister's place.

They were so alike in looks, voice and disposition that his second marriage seemed almost an extension of the first. Some nights, the scent and touch of Mathilde's flesh were as redolent of Irène's as if she had assumed her body as well as her bed. Having feared that their union was a betrayal of both women's singularity, he had come to see it as a way to keep Irène's spirit alive. Far from resenting his enduring affection for her sister, Mathilde had suggested that they name their first daughter after her, and when he'd once called out 'Irène' while making love, he was able to ascribe it to the baby's wail, rather than his dead wife's memory.

Sustained introspection unnerved him, so he headed to the house. He walked round to the portico, narrowly avoiding a lizard soaking up the last ray of sunlight on the steps. With a glance at the now dimmed cornucopia, he touched a finger to the mezuzah, brought it to his lips and entered the hall.

2

LEON

SALONICA, JUNE 1911

THE GREEK CEREMONIAL arch was no more. According to the *Journal de Salonique*, it had collapsed during Monday night's storm. If so, the turbulence must have been localised, since there'd barely been a rustle in the Campania.

Leon stretched, yawned, put down the paper, nudged the breakfast tray along the bed and wiped a crumb of feta from his pillow. The *Journal* was edited by Sadi Levy, one of his father's closest friends, so its relentless positivity came as no surprise. The Sultan's visit was accounted a success. He had received officials, delivered speeches, inspected the troops and distributed 4,500 lira to the poor after Friday prayers. Yet no sooner had his train left Pristina station for the second leg of the imperial tour than tensions between Greeks and Bulgarians within the city had reignited, ending with chunks of lath and plaster strewn along Union Boulevard. But in the judgement of the *Journal* and to the relief of its readers, who could rest secure in the goodwill of their fellow citizens, the sole culprit was Nature. No doubt in Saturday's edition, the *Journal* would attribute the boulders, which had blocked the track as the Sultan's train steamed northwards, to an avalanche.

Papa accused him of bad faith for failing to honour the Sultan after agitating for his accession. The charge was predictable but unjust. How could a man who eschewed politics understand disenchantment? Three years earlier, while still at school, he had been inspired by the vision of universal brotherhood proclaimed by the Committee of Union and Progress. He and his two best friends, Aron Sides and Ettore Defano, had joined the outlawed society. With no concessions made to their youth, they were directed to meet their contacts in Beschinar Gardens at dead of night, where they were blindfolded, bundled into a cart and hidden beneath an oilcloth. After juddering through the streets, they were whisked into a house, in what from the mingled sounds and scents he took to be the Muslim quarter, and led down a flight of slippery steps, which would have been hazardous even with unimpeded vision. Their blindfolds removed, they found themselves in a grim basement, opposite two unsmiling men, with several others lurking in the shadows. When Ettore glanced round, he was ordered to face the front as brusquely as if he were on parade.

Leon's immediate concern was to stop himself shivering, which, given the muggy room, he could no longer blame on the cold. One of the men read out the Committee's aims, which, with the Torah in their left hand and a revolver in their right, they each swore to obey. It was hard to credit that, two hours before, he had been lying in bed, albeit fully clothed, and now he was pledging to kill not only proven traitors but anyone whom the Committee decreed, even his father or brother. While more disturbed by the prospect than Ettore, who regularly professed his willingness to shoot his brutal father, he was eager to demonstrate his commitment.

It was put to the test a few weeks later when, with protests sweeping through Macedonia, the three young men were instructed to join the scores of Salonicans marching to Monastir to incite the army to revolt. Flouting Papa's injunction, Leon crept out of the house in the early hours, taking nothing but his game gun and a small sack of provisions. At the Arch of Galerius, he met up with Aron and Ettore and a motley band of volunteers. They set off in ragged formation, halting only for the Turks' dawn prayers. Leon, who regarded his own scriptures as ancestral history, watched with awe as they bent, knelt and prostrated themselves on the ground.

While better equipped and shod than most of the men (some of whom, he noted with shame, were barefoot), Leon was hungry, thirsty and stiff after the day-long trek. They camped overnight in a meadow and, with no well in sight, filled their water bottles from a brackish river. Leon's sweat-stained shirt clung to his back and he longed to wash, but he feared the mockery of his less fastidious companions. The Turks recited their evening prayers and the Greeks, not to be outdone, loudly invoked the Virgin Mary. Leon and his friends lay on the bare ground, which was warm and dry, but, with mosquitoes and ants swarming over them, foxes and possibly jackals howling nearby, and men evidently inured to the harsh conditions snoring all around, they struggled to sleep.

Aching and bleary-eyed, Leon was roused by a marshal at daybreak. Word of their mission had spread and, as they tramped through hamlets and villages, priests waited at crossroads to bless them, old women brought them balls of yoghurt, mekitsi, apricots and peaches, and young men toiling in the fields ran out to join them, turning their ploughshares and sickles into swords and spears with biblical fervour. As they approached Vodena, six Albanian bandits drew up on horseback, rifles slung over their shoulders and cartridge belts looped around their waists. To Leon's amazement, far from confronting them, they came to swell their ranks and, although he took care not to look them in the eyes, he was elated to find his childhood ogres become his comrades.

On the fifth afternoon, when the Monastir clock tower appeared on the horizon, Leon's fantasy of himself as a latter-day Davy Crockett gave way to fears of what awaited them. They were fewer than two hundred men facing the might of the Ottoman Third Army. What if the soldiers stood by the Sultan to whom they had sworn an oath as sacred as the one he had sworn to the CUP? Would they slaughter the insurgents on the spot or subject them to protracted torture? As he weighed up the horrors, news reached them that, shortly before their arrival, both the citizens and the garrison had renounced their allegiance to the Sultan. Nevertheless, they entered the town like conquerors. Girls – including Jewish girls, reputed to be even more modest than their Salonican counterparts – lined the streets to kiss them. Innkeepers offered them food and soldiers offered them billets. But, as the company dispersed, Leon and his friends found more congenial lodgings with Ettore's uncle, a mill owner who, though as law-abiding as Papa, welcomed the three young men, before seeing them off by train the following day.

Thus ended Leon's military adventure: the sole adventure of his life to date. Although his wounds amounted to no more than mosquito bites and blisters, and his terror of torture made him feel a fraud, he found himself hailed as a hero by both his schoolfellows and his younger brother and sisters (always excepting Esther, his only full sibling yet his fiercest critic). The adults were less impressed. Papa, who rarely raised a hand to his children, announced his intention to beat him in front of the entire family, relenting only when Leon declared, with strained bravado, that, having defied the Sultan's bullets, he could withstand his father's cane. Moreover, subsequent events vindicated his stance, when a weakened Abdul Hamid agreed to restore the suspended constitution, triggering a wave of euphoria across the Empire.

Within a year, however, egged on by traditionalist clerics, the Sultan attempted to reimpose the caliphate, in accordance with strict Islamic law. The CUP launched an effective counterstrike and Abdul Hamid was deposed and exiled, not to a remote island in the South Atlantic but across the Aegean to Salonica. Installed in the Allatini house, he had yet to step outside its gates, even to attend the mosque. It was unclear whether this stemmed from disillusion with Allah, who had allowed his deposition, or fear of an assassin's blade.

Disillusion was something Leon understood. While stung by Papa's jibe that he had milk in his moustache, he acknowledged that, at twenty, he lacked experience. The transformation of the CUP after the Sultan's failed fightback had been a painful lesson.

The new government passed a series of laws that were as repressive as those of the previous regime: banning unauthorised gatherings; expanding the police's powers of arrest; tightening censorship and curtailing press freedom. While those around him acquiesced in the measures, Leon felt as betrayed as if he'd discovered that Papa kept a mistress. Why strive for anything when everything remained the same?

Bumps and bangs resounded through the house in preparation for the evening's festivities. He burrowed down in bed, but the sheets, so cosy an hour earlier, now felt as constricting as a shroud. The day stretched emptily before him, and he half wished he were a tobacco cutter starting his shift at the factory. He knew better than to say so (especially in Esther's hearing), but there were reasons to envy the poor. They didn't agonise over the meaning of life; for them it was simply making a living. There was something noble - indeed, pure - about an existence bounded by the bare essentials of food, clothing and shelter.

His, on the other hand, was shaped by his family's expectations. At first he had endeavoured to meet them. On leaving school, he had spent six months at the factory, observing its operations, only to conclude that it operated better without him. His grandfather, who had lost the ability to speak but not to command, decided that he would be more suited to a position in the bank. That was the domain of Grand-Oncle Lazar and Cousin Nissim, who appointed him cashier of the Marseille branch, a title that belied his inconsequence. Every minor transaction had to be authorised in Salonica, and he did little more than send telegrams and validate documents, with a signature that grew more and more ornate until one day a bill of sale was returned as counterfeit.

After three months he resigned and returned home, waiting for his father to find him a more purposeful role. Esther, who credited him with meagre intelligence but limitless cunning, accused him of making himself unemployable. 'You're a hedonist, a sybarite, an epicurean,' she scoffed. 'Do you intend to devote yourself entirely to pleasure?'

'Here's hoping!'

For months, his aimlessness appeared to warrant Esther's sneers, but then he met Xenia. 'Xee-nee-ah.' He savoured each syllable, sending a rush of blood, like molten lava, through his veins. Who would have thought that a chance visit to an out-of-the-way taverna would change his life? He'd spent the evening with Aron at the Pathé Frères's new electric theatre, but the programme had lasted less than an hour. Reluctant to head home so early – and inspired by the cinematographic explorers – they ventured into the port area and spotted the weathered Praxidike sign. Descending into a dingy cellar, they were hit by the sweet and spicy fragrance of a row of hookahs and the acrid tang of the all-male clientele. A glance revealed that they'd stumbled on a group of *mangas* in their distinctive one-sleeved jackets, striped trousers, woollen hats and pointed shoes. Strings of worry beads snaked around their left arms and daggers gleamed in their belts.

Never had Leon been so conscious of his tailored clothes. A hasty retreat might have saved his skin but would have injured his pride. So, with a feigned smile, he led Aron to a side table and ordered drinks from the barman, who was scarcely less hostile than his customers. A rebetiko trio was playing at the far end of the room, and he listened to the plaintive strumming of the bouzouki, the resonant wheeze of the accordion and the rattle of the tambourine. After several minutes, the musicians were joined by a short, dark woman with a slight stoop, in a red tunic and white pantaloons. Her features were hard to make out in the gloom, but her voice was strong and clear, alternately crackling like blazing firewood and caressing like a velvet mitten. Despite his rudimentary Greek, Leon grasped the essence of the song, which told of a village girl fated to give her heart to a man whom she knew would betray her. By the final chord, his own fate had been sealed.

After two more songs, Aron was ready to leave. Eager to untangle his emotions, Leon agreed, only to return on the following three evenings. He sat alone, ignoring the glares from men who would have slit his throat without a qualm, and wondered whether that hint of danger formed part of his attraction to the chanteuse. Her set varied little, but judging by the whoops that greeted each opening phrase, the audience welcomed the familiarity. She sang of one mother seeing her son off to war and another vowing to win back the children she'd been forced to surrender; of an innocent man dancing his way to the gallows; and of the joys of hashish. Above all, she sang of love: of first love and true love; of abandoned love and abused love; of foolish love and faithless love. What was more, Leon learnt from the bouzouki player that she had written several of the songs herself. It grieved him to think of the pain she must have endured.

Once or twice in each show, she stepped off the cramped stage and crossed the floor towards the flustered, flattered audience. Having ignored Leon on his first three visits, she singled him out on the fourth, fixing him with a gaze at once amused, provocative and surprisingly vulnerable. She slid behind him, twined a lock of his hair around her finger and tugged it, to the mirth of a group of watchful *mangas*. Next, she snatched a tambourine and, like a lioness toying with her prey, shook it as she circled him. Unsure whether she were mocking or wooing him, he applauded wildly as she returned to the stage, where she sang three more songs, without so much as a peek in his direction. At the end of her performance, she drank a shot of ouzo and moved back to his table, pulling out a chair as if it were hers by right.

'Shouldn't you be in bed, young man?' she asked pertly.

'Is that an invitation?' he replied, seeking to match her tone.

'So you speak Greek?'

'Not well enough for everything I'd like to say to you.'

'And Turkish?'

'Much better.'

'What are you doing here?' she asked, in what would become their common tongue. 'Look at them!' Her gesture encompassed the room. 'Their cheeks all swarthy and scarred. While yours are pink,' she added, turning them red. 'Your hair's like silk.'

'You grabbed it.'

'Not a line on your face! Has life left no mark on you?'

He strove to conceal his confusion. 'I was attacked by a gang of Bulgarians on the way to school.'

'In other words, no,' she said, with a smile.

Leon longed to lavish her with compliments, but her beauty wasn't easy to define. Everything about her – her eyes, her hair, her complexion – was dark. She was sharp-jawed, with heavy brows and a narrow forehead, each of which might have been deemed a defect but combined to give her an extraordinary allure. Hers was the heart-stopping beauty of a storm at sea – the pitch-black waves burnished by bolts of lightning – and it was a sea in which he would have happily drowned. They talked until the early hours. Then, when the taverna closed, to the teasing glances of her fellow musicians and the studied indifference of the *mangas*, she invited him home.

Leon had never made love outside a brothel and, as Xenia steered him through a warren of streets in the Christian quarter, he trembled at the new responsibility. To both his shame and relief, she mistook his nervousness for innocence and, clasping his wrist, assured him that there was nothing to fear. Reaching the house, she kissed him full on the lips before ushering him up the spindly stairs.

'It's snug,' he said, as she lit a candle, illuminating the sparsely furnished room with its wooden dresser, overflowing trunk and single bed beneath a gaudy icon of the Virgin Mary.

'You mean boxy,' she replied. 'But it's mine. I'm beholden to no one.'

He trusted she wouldn't object when he showered her with jewels.

Given that she was several years older and, if her songs were any indication, far more experienced, he expected her to guide his hand, but, to his delight, she deferred to him. He slowly undressed her, struggling with the buttons on her pantaloons and discovering, to his surprise, that she wore no drawers. He was transfixed by her naked body: her breasts as full as a nursing mother's; her slender waist, wide hips and wispy pubic hair. He realised that the women in the brothels had shaved and longed to erase their memory. For the first time in his adult life, his pleasure was shared.

Since that initial encounter, they had rarely spent a day apart. Leon told his family that he was with friends and his friends that he was under a strict curfew. For her part, Xenia was subject to no constraints but Nature: her 'the Furies have called' expressing his own sense of exclusion more accurately than Esther's 'Eve's curse'. He became such a familiar figure at the taverna that certain of the *mangas* acknowledged his greetings even before he bought them drinks. He watched every performance and, although she had barely altered her repertoire in the four months that he'd known her, he marvelled at her ability to keep the sentiments fresh. He no longer felt threatened when she chatted, laughed and even flirted with the customers, since he knew that they would end the evening together. He no longer questioned why so accomplished and desirable a woman should have fallen for him. It was one of life's mysteries . . . or, rather, one of its miracles.

'Will you write a song for me?' he asked shyly one afternoon, as she worked on a new composition.

'I already have,' she said, her voice tightening.

'What? When? I've not heard it.'

'It's your favourite: the girl who promises to keep faith with a man she knows will desert her.'

'But you sang it on my first visit to the Praxidike. You wrote it before we met.'

'True.'

Desolation swept over him. He ached to assure her of his lifelong devotion, but generations of Carraches contrived to stop his mouth. Instead, he took her in his arms, pressing her to his chest, so as not to dampen her cheeks.

The memory of his tears revived them, and he hastily wiped his eyes as Ruben burst into his room and flung himself down on a chair.

'Why are you still in bed? It's gone ten thirty.'

'Why aren't you at school?' Leon asked, struggling to regain his composure.

'I'm excused. Rabbi Pardon-Me is coming to run through the prayers for tonight.'

'Don't you know them yet?'

'Of course. The Shema and the Kaddish Shalem. I can recite them now if you like.'

'And ruin the surprise? No thanks.'

Ruben jumped off the chair and prowled around the room, rummaging through Leon's cufflink drawer and sniffing a bottle of cologne with an exaggerated grimace.

'Can I help you with something?' Leon asked.

'Yes, actually. Now that I'm becoming a man, will you let me live down here with you? It's not fair to leave me alone with those three girls.'

'I doubt that Papa would agree. He thinks I'm a bad influence.'

'Then I can reform you. I know you sneak home at four . . . five . . . six o'clock in the morning. Everyone wonders where you've been.'

'Let them!' Leon said. 'I don't want to dishearten you, but in my experience the manhood is strictly symbolic. Not much more than the right to lay tefillin. Though tonight, it will be Papa and Grand-Oncle Lazar who do it for you. Then tomorrow, we'll escort you to the synagogue to read your Torah portion and make your speech. I trust you're well prepared.'

'As much as I'll ever be. It's about how the sacrifice of Isaac was the first tefillin ceremony.'

'Was he thirteen? I don't remember that.'

'No one knows exactly. But, like you said, it's symbolic. He was just as dutiful as Abraham. He asked one question about the lamb for the burnt offering. Then, when he found out it was him, he didn't plead or argue or try to escape. He accepted the cords that his father laid on him. Which, as I say at the end, is an example to us all. I can already hear the purrs of approval.'

'So young yet so cynical!'

'Along with the clink of the gold and silver when I walk through the congregation, holding out my bag.'

'I hate to disillusion you, but you don't get to keep it. You have to present it to Rabbi Pardo.'

'I know that,' Ruben said, with a grin.

Like every boy who performed the rite, he had no doubt been told of some sleight of hand with which to dupe the rabbi. Leon himself had made a false lining for his bag, but, at the last minute, his nerve had failed and he handed it over intact. He had never heard of anyone, however brazen, who'd managed to secure a single coin.

'When did you last open these?' Ruben asked, blowing non-existent dust off one of the gold tefillin cases their grandfather had given Leon.

'I'm a bad Jew.'

'So's Papa. So's everyone we know. Rabbi Pardon-Me says laying tefillin is an obligation.'

'There are other obligations: prayer; studying Torah (don't say anything!); charity. You can't fault Papa or anyone in the family on that score.'

'But do you believe in God?'

Leon groaned. 'It's too early in the morning.'

'I'm not sure that I do . . . believe in God, I mean. What kind of God would order Abraham to kill his son?'

'It was a test. He saved him.'

'It was still cruel. Just like rescuing the Jews from Egypt and leaving them to wander in the wilderness for forty years.'

'That's ancient history.'

'What about letting us settle in Spain and doing nothing when we were driven into exile? That wasn't so long ago – at least not to hear people speak. How can I believe in a God who allowed that?'

'You'd do better to ask Rabbi Pardo,' Leon said, both moved and disconcerted by Ruben's newfound earnestness.

'I'm asking you! Nothing makes any sense. All the women in

our family are far more devout than the men, yet it's the men who go to the synagogue.'

'But that's not only about God; it's about tradition and community. It's about worshipping where our forefathers have done for the past 250 years. To honour that, I can spare an hour every Sabbath.'

'Not every Sabbath! And an hour is as much as it is. You and Papa join in the prayers and leave before the rabbi's sermon.'

'It's a neat compromise.'

'Why must everything be a compromise? Why can nothing be pure?' He picked up Leon's two ivory hairbrushes, banging them together in anguish.

'Take care! There'll be pure hell to pay if you break them,' Leon said, attempting to lighten the atmosphere.

A knock at the door made him start. 'Come in! What is it?' he asked, slipping into Ladino as Rachel, the new maid, hovered at the threshold.

'Have you finished with your breakfast tray, Señor Leon?' she asked. 'Only Maryam says— Oh!' she stuttered on spotting Ruben.

'Have you met my brother?' Leon said, winking at him.

'Yes, yes, of course. But only upstairs. I wasn't expecting . . . I'll come back.'

'There's nothing to be scared of. Come in!' She edged into the room. 'Yes, you can take away the tray. Then please come back and draw me a bath.'

'In the bathroom?'

Ruben snickered.

'No, the kitchen,' Leon said, gritting his teeth. 'Yes, of course.'

She picked up the tray as if it were a bedpan. 'What's that?' she screamed, dropping it and spilling coffee and sugar on the coverlet.

'What's what?'

'That thing . . . that yellow, crawly thing!' She retreated to the door.

'It's just a centipede. It must have come in through the French windows.'

Ruben ran up and stamped on it. '*Sic semper tyrannis!*' he shouted, digging his shoe into the remains.

'Oh, I feel . . . I'll fetch Maryam.'

'She's even worse than the others,' Leon said, as she fled the room. 'I shouldn't be surprised if Maman gets them straight from the asylum.'

'You'd think she'd find someone who spoke basic French.'

'Then she wouldn't be a maid.'

With language divisions among Jews as marked as religious divisions in the wider city, the Carraches spoke French among themselves and their peers and Ladino to servants and subordinates.

'Still, she's quite pretty.'

'She can't be more than ten or eleven,' Leon said, scenting danger.

'She doesn't know how old she is. I asked. And Esther says she's small because she's never had enough food or sunlight.'

'Rubbish! That's Esther all over. The other day she said that the children in Vardar were left to play in the streets because their homes were so poky. In which case, they'd get more sunlight than us. She can't have it both ways.'

'That's never stopped her trying.' They exchanged a smile. 'Besides, I heard Maryam telling Maman that they'd have to watch out because Rachel was an early bloomer.'

'Well, that's not your problem,' Leon said pointedly.

'Isn't it? You'd think – that is if you think it through – that becoming a man means you're ready to have a woman.'

Leon saw where the conversation was headed and longed for the refuge of his bath.

'How old were you when you first made love?' Ruben asked.

'Nineteen.'

'I don't believe you.'

'Then why ask?'

'If I were hungry, you'd give me something to eat, wouldn't you?'

'Looks like I'll have to draw my own bath. You seem to have scared the girl away.'

'Well, I am hungry. Just not in my gut.'

'Take it from me. Feeding that sort of hunger only makes it worse. If you're desperate, you can always whip up your own snacks.' He jerked his hand up and down.

'You're disgusting!'

'All the more reason to keep out of my way. Rabbi Pardo will be here soon. Now scram, or I'll be late for Aron! We're playing billiards this afternoon, but I'll be back in good time for your party.'

Leon bustled him out and entered the bathroom. For all his flippancy, he felt for Ruben as he recalled his own tefillin ceremony. The rite of passage, just when his body had begun to assert itself, might have been expressly designed to mock his inability to satisfy it. Until he met Xenia, the ordinary run of women had been as mysterious to him as an order of nuns. He knew more about Catherine de Medici and Marie Antoinette than about his friends' sisters or his sisters' friends. Papa maintained that his generation enjoyed unprecedented freedom. In the face of fierce opposition, the Lycée and the Alliance had instituted a joint programme of social events for alumni. In the clubhouse on Parallel Street, young men and women waltzed to the strains of Strauss and Offenbach, chaperoned only by their consciences. But even with his partners pressed tightly to his chest, Leon felt as though he were dancing with dolls. Xenia had changed that. After their first intoxicating intimacies, he had set out to discover every detail of her life. He was jealous of her entire past (not merely the men), entreating as exhaustive an account as if she'd kept a diary from birth. She insisted that anything of consequence was in her songs, adding only that she was the eldest child of a fisherman who drowned when she was ten, after which her destitute mother turned her out to fend for herself. For once, Leon was glad that his mother had died young, bequeathing him a comparable tragedy.

On their three-month anniversary, he bought Xenia a sapphire ring. 'You shouldn't have,' she said, covering his face with kisses, each one of which was more precious to him than the jewel. 'Such extravagance will come between us.'

'Nothing will ever come between us.'

'Oh my love,' she replied, so sadly that he wept.

He soaked in the bath, but the warmth brought little solace. He wondered if it would be simpler . . . wiser . . . fairer to them both to end the relationship. He could ask Papa to find him a bride: exchanging passion for domesticity; parcelling out his love between a wife and children. In time, he would take his place as director of the company, elder of the synagogue, member of the Community Council, stalwart of the Club des Intimes. He pictured a life of consummate respectability, uncertain whether he was looking to embrace it or to escape. Was Papa happy? In his private moments, did he pick up a favourite volume of Casanova's *Memoirs* and lament lost opportunities, or was his leather-bound library just for show?

Washed, shaved and dressed, he left to meet Aron at the Café Colombo. Friends from boyhood, they had caught their first fish, hunted their first woodcock and smoked their first cigarette together. Along with Ettore, they'd formed an inseparable trio, whom Aron's mother dubbed The Three Musketeers. The departure of their Aramis for Rome, closely followed by Leon's encounter with Xenia, put an end to their youthful antics. He'd initially hidden the affair from Aron, afraid to cheapen it by equating Xenia with the women they'd known – and, on one occasion, shared – in the past. He'd finally relented, rhapsodising over her beauty, charm and talent, but he'd still not fulfilled his promise to introduce them. He valued Aron's judgement, and the thought that he might not approve of her dismayed him.

After a quick lunch, they headed to the Association for their game.

'Come on, Carrache, concentrate!' Aron said, after he missed a second straight shot.

'Apologies! I don't know why, but I'm worn out.'

'Really?' Aron replied, with a ribald laugh. 'Still, you know where to send for reinforcements.'

Leon checked his irritation and chalked his cue, but after losing three racks and parting with fifty kuruş, he admitted defeat and took the tram home. His grandparents' carriage stood in the forecourt, its early arrival enabling his grandfather to shuffle indoors unwitnessed. Eager to avoid his mute reproach, somehow more painful than verbal censure, he sneaked round the house to the garden entrance. Formally attired, he walked into the hall, where Papa, Maman and Ruben were greeting their guests. Papa was in his element, showing Sadi Levy his newly acquired death mask of Voltaire. Maman exuded elegance in a floral evening dress with a low-cut bodice, which reminded Leon, to his slight unease, that she was as close in age to him as to Papa. Ruben seemed more jittery than this morning, which was no surprise given the giant bow tied to his right arm that made him look like an expensive hatbox.

Shooting him a supportive smile, from which he couldn't efface a hint of mockery, Leon walked into the crowded salon. He kissed Grandpapa's hand, a custom that felt even more archaic when the fingers were permanently clenched, and Grandmaman Regina's violet-scented cheek. He listened politely as she deplored his father's profligacy in serving vintage champagne before the toasts. When she summoned a maid to replenish her glass, he escaped to greet Grandmaman Falcona.

His two grandmothers were polar opposites in fashion as in everything else. They had been born into a world where women were veiled in public. Regina had broken conclusively with the past: tonight, she wore a gold-and-white silk gown with a high waist and cylindrical skirt, which, she explained, had been inspired by the Parthenon columns and which he suspected had been designed for a less monumental figure. Falcona, on the other hand, favoured the traditional Sephardic costume of pearl-encrusted toque, fur-collared mantle and embroidered robe. As she fussed over him, he felt a pang of guilt at his preference for this gentle, whimsical, unworldly grandmother, which faded when he recalled Regina's oft-stated preference for his 'dutiful, well-behaved' cousins.

He stood beside Falcona as Papa advanced into the centre of the room and, tapping his glass, thanked his guests for joining him on this auspicious day. He singled out the four rabbis, eliciting sly smiles from those who knew of his steadfast resistance to religious authority. The Chief Rabbi, the first to be appointed from abroad and thus unscarred by ancient quarrels, proposed a toast to Ruben. He then called on Papa and Grand-Oncle Lazar to lay the tefillin on Ruben's arm, before laying them himself on his head. Ruben spoke his prayers faultlessly, in contrast to Papa, who stumbled over the Hebrew blessing before gratefully reverting to French.

'It's an auspicious day for Ruben but also for me, since, as the rabbis teach us, I'm no longer liable for his sins. Sadly, there's no such exemption from his debts.' Although he studiously avoided meeting his gaze, Leon was convinced that the quip, which drew a rumble of laughter, was aimed at him. With no further ado, Papa led Ruben around a ring of well-wishers who, pinching his cheeks and ruffling his hair, infantilised him at the very moment of his coming of age.

Conversation resumed, and the maids brought in salvers of champagne, pastries and haminados eggs. Leon glanced at Esther, who was deep in discussion with Leah Sagues, a woman for whom he'd conceived an instant dislike and whose presence at the ceremony he resented. Papa and Maman had been wrong to accede to Esther's demand to include her. He might as well have insisted they invite Xenia.

The comparison made him uneasy.

As if reading his thoughts, Grandmaman Regina approached. 'Esther and that schoolmistress appear to be inseparable. She should be assisting Mathilde with the guests.'

'Aren't you glad she's made such a sensible friend?' Falcona asked.

'She harangued me earlier about the state of the girls' washrooms! She has an unhealthy obsession with sanitation. Still, what can you expect of someone from Smyrna?'

Irène stomped past them, only to be detained by Regina. 'Must you tramp through your father's salon like a peasant treading grapes?'

'I wish I was, Grandmaman. I wish I was the poorest peasant in the whole of the Empire. At least someone in the village would remember my name.'

'Dear heart, what's wrong?' Falcona asked.

'Three people – three! – have forgotten it. One said, "I know there's Esther and Bella, but you . . . it's on the tip of my tongue." How I hate them!'

'Nonsense!' Regina said. 'No young girl should want to make an impression. If they remember Esther, it's because she's headstrong.'

'What about Bella?'

'Don't be pert!'

'But they have twice the reason to remember *Irène*, because of Leon and Esther's mother.'

'My darling daughter,' Falcona said tearfully.

'Now look what you've done!' Regina said. 'Falcona, please! This is supposed to be a celebration.'

'Then I heard Papa telling a fat man I've never seen before that he had three daughters: Esther the scholar; Bella the dreamer; and Irène the homemaker.'

'There you are,' Regina said.

'What did he mean? I gave Bella my doll's house two years ago.'

'Your father was paying you a compliment. What more can any woman want than to make a home for her husband and children? When I married your—'

'Besides, when Bella and I tell each other our dreams, mine are much more interesting.'

'You exhaust me!' Regina said, moving away just as Maman drew near.

'Didn't Ruben do splendidly?' she said.

'Where's he gone?' Falcona asked her. 'I want to give him a big kiss.'

'He's in the study with Jacob and a photographer Monsieur Levy brought.'

'Don't let Grandmaman Regina hear,' Irène said. 'She told Tante Amada that you couldn't make a casserole without putting a notice in the *Journal*.'

'You shouldn't tell tales, Irène,' Maman said sadly. 'It's not kind.'

'But it's true, I promise!'

'That's not the point. Has anyone seen Bella? I can't find her anywhere.'

'I expect she's in bed,' Irène said.

'Was she feeling poorly?'

'She's a dreamer, isn't she?'

'What?'

'Don't ask!' Leon said. 'I'll take a look outside.'

'Would you? She's probably contemplating the mountain as usual.' She sighed. 'Then come straight back. There's someone I want you to meet.'

'Oh no! Really? No matchmaking please.'

'I never said that it was a girl.'

'You didn't have to.'

He walked out and into the hall, almost colliding with Mercado Silvera.

'A thousand apologies!' Mercado said, flashing a sickly smile. 'I trust I didn't give you a shock.'

'No, just a jolt,' Leon replied, since it was no surprise to find Mercado skulking in the shadows. Try as he might, he couldn't warm to the man. He knew that he ought to make allowances for his wretched childhood, but no one could have turned it to greater advantage. Having ingratiated himself first with Grandpapa Beraha and then with Papa, he was now chief bookkeeper at the tobacco factory and, by all reports, a model of efficiency. There again, he treated the whole of life as a ledger. It was a grave mistake to have placed himself in his debt, but he had set his heart on buying Xenia the sapphire and, lacking ready money, secured a clandestine loan from Mercado, who had access to the factory's funds. The humiliation of their interview was seared on his memory. That he, a Carrache, had been forced to go cap in hand to a man who'd been all but sold in a bazaar! It was painfully clear that Mercado's aid sprang from a desire for dominance rather than goodwill.

He had promised to reimburse the cash before the quarterly accounts were due, but that prospect was fast receding. Aron had refused to help him fake his own kidnap and his fabled luck at belote had deserted him. Even without Mercado's prompting, he knew that he would soon have no choice but to confess. He envisaged the conversation as Papa, by turns enraged and wounded, accused him of recklessness, dishonesty and suborning a trusted assistant, without any admission that his parsimony was largely to blame. Although he paid Leon's tailoring, club and restaurant bills, Papa gave him a paltry allowance, just as he only permitted him his own apartment provided it was under the paternal roof. He was as subservient as one of the maids – or, more pertinently, 'Le pauvre Oncle Haim'. He must warn Ruben. Far from becoming a man at thirteen, he would still be a boy at twenty.

'Hell!' he exclaimed.

Sensing Mercado's confusion, he asked him quickly whether he'd seen Bella.

'Now you mention it, not once all evening. Is she missing? Should I help you look for her? I must just tell Monsieur Lazar. He wanted a word.'

'No need, thank you. Go back in and enjoy the party.' He knew that there was nothing Mercado would relish more than to be seen in the Carraches' orbit. He hurried through the hall and into the garden, drinking in the cool evening air, as welcome after the heavily perfumed salon as the crickets' chirping after the idle chatter. He crossed the parterre and strode down the gravel path to Bella's preferred vantage point, opposite Mount Olympus. As predicted, she was perched on the granite bench, staring at the peak.

'What are you doing out here?' he asked. 'You're meant to be mingling with the guests.'

'Watching. Come and sit down.'

'Maman was worried.'

'In a minute. Don't spoil it, please! This is the most perfect place in the whole world – and the most perfect time of day . . . the sun hovering behind the mountain, as if Zeus can't decide whether to let it set or to hurl it back into the sky, sending all of Nature into a spin!'

'How many times do I have to tell you? There is no Zeus.'

'Shush! Take care! He'll be in his palace right now. It's hidden beneath the clouds, but I swear it's there.'

'You're ten years old . . . old enough to know it's a myth.'

'What does that matter, as long as it's a true one? Zeus on his throne of gold and Hera on her throne of ivory will be feasting with their fellow gods. The meal is always the same – ambrosia and nectar – but the taste is so delicious that they never get bored.'

The Carraches had their own myths, one of which was that Bella's eccentricity stemmed from a fall from her cot during the earthquake of 1902. Papa had sent for a specialist from Constantinople, who diagnosed a mild concussion. Observing that babies were remarkably resilient, he promised she would make a full recovery. Ruben and Irène, however, insisted, regardless of reprimands, that the fall had addled her brain. Abandoning the role of responsible older brother, Leon wondered whether they might have a point.

'How can you be so sure they're there?' he asked. 'Has anyone ever seen them?'

'No ordinary mortal,' she replied, impassively. 'A few favoured kings were invited to the palace hundreds of years ago. But Zeus would make it vanish before anyone got close to it now. That's if Heracles and his sons didn't kill them first.'

'Well, it's a great story. But please don't repeat it, not least when we have four rabbis in the house. They believe in the God of Abraham and Sarah, not Zeus and Hera.'

'Do I have to believe in Him, just because He's the God of our people?'

'Not necessarily, but you shouldn't offend anyone, tonight of all nights. So if they ask, say you were gazing at the stars.'

'But that's a lie.'

'It's a kindness. Now come inside. See, the sun has set completely. Nature – if nothing else – is sticking to the rules.'

Leon led Bella into the house, where Maman greeted her with a weary smile. He chatted to several guests, but, surrounded by his 'people', as Bella had dubbed them, he felt more downcast than ever about his future. Papa maintained that the different faiths should be separated only at prayer and that this would be the century of religious tolerance. Yet he and his friends distrusted all outsiders, even Ashkenazim. How would they react if Leon announced his intention to marry a Greek rebetiko singer of humble origins? Would they regard him as a pioneer or as an apostate? And if, as he feared, they were to close ranks, should he stand fast or bow to the pressure, like the doomed lovers in Xenia's songs?

3

ESTHER

SALONICA, NOVEMBER 1911

THE CARRACHE FAMILY held dual allegiances. Though subjects of the Sultan, they were under the protection of the Italian consul. Years earlier, when Esther asked Maman why this was, she had likened it to Esther herself having both a father and a mother (as ever, she omitted the *step*). In which case, since September when Italy declared war on the Empire, they had all, Maman and Papa included, been children of divorce.

The family's ties with Italy stretched back to the 1500s, when one Bonomo Carrache was personal physician to the Duke of Milan. Oncle Haim had discovered a letter from the Duke to his 'full trusty servant', approving his request for his brother Jacobo to set up as a moneylender in the city. Over the centuries, their descendants engaged in finance and commerce rather than medicine. They travelled to Pisa and Genoa before settling in Livorno, where they forged strong trading links with the Ottomans. In the 1750s, the senior branch of the family – by which Haim meant their own – moved to Salonica, swiftly consolidating its wealth. The Italian – or, as it was then, Tuscan – flag proved to be invaluable, since the Sublime Porte granted foreign merchants capitulations that exempted them from local taxes. Even before meeting Leah, Esther deplored the injustice, but Papa assured her that what they saved in tax, they disbursed in charity, witness the various Carrache foundations. 'And doesn't it make sense, little one,' he asked tenderly, 'that I should know better how to help those less fortunate in my own community than the Sultan, far away in Constantinople?'

Papa had another reason to be grateful for consular protection, which freed the family not just from Ottoman taxation but from rabbinical authority. In recent years that authority had waned, but, during his boyhood, it had been absolute. He had frequently fallen foul of the Beth Din and, although he taught his children to respect the law, he enjoyed regaling them with tales of his youthful transgressions. One such, which became a firm favourite, involved his being caught swimming on the Sabbath. After a public uproar, the rabbi's minions chased him through the streets (Esther always wondered whether he'd had time to dress, but it felt improper to ask). He outran them all and, as soon as he reached home, his father raised the Italian flag to remind his pursuers that their writ no longer prevailed.

'Then he whipped me,' he added, much to Ruben's glee. 'It wasn't that he didn't want me to be punished but that he didn't want the rabbi usurping his rights.'

Now, for the first time, the flag was a liability. In the name of preserving the balance of power in the Mediterranean, Italy had invaded Ottoman Tripolitania, a coastal region of North Africa which Esther had secretly needed to look up on the map. Leah maintained that the actual power it wished to preserve was economic, quoting widespread reports in the Italian press that the land was rich in minerals. In the event of victory, it wouldn't be the masses who profited. While the financiers, suppliers, munition makers and, indeed, newspaper owners prospered, working people would suffer: the men dying in the field, and the women left to bring up their fatherless children.

Although loath to challenge Leah, Esther pointed out that she would be wrong to include the Carraches among the financiers and suppliers set to prosper. On the outbreak of war, the Sultan stripped the Italians of their long-held privileges and imposed a prohibitive tariff on their exports. Furthermore, he defaulted on a debt of one hundred thousand lira to the Carrache bank. Grand-Oncle Lazar reassured the family that the bank had survived an equal loss in 1826, when Sultan Mahmud II abolished the janissaries and its loan to the corps fell forfeit. He and Nissim journeyed to Rome to negotiate a guarantee from the Bank of Italy, leaving Papa to manage the crisis at home.

Unlike Ruben who kept up with every skirmish, cheering for the Italians in defiance of Papa's edict of neutrality, Esther noted only the key battles – and gravest atrocities. Italy's hopes of a rapid victory were dashed since, despite its superiority at sea, its attacks on the hinterland met with stiff resistance. As the fighting dragged on, the Sultan intensified measures against enemy nationals and, in late February, almost five months since the conflict began, he decreed that all Italian males over the age of sixteen must quit the realm within twenty-four hours.

After a direct appeal to the Governor, citing the disruption it would cause in the city were he to relinquish his affairs without putting the necessary safeguards in place, Papa secured a two-week deferral for himself, Leon and Oncle Haim, together with a dispensation for Grandpapa, who was unfit to travel. Then, on a suitably grey morning, the family, including both of Esther's grandmothers and two of her aunts, gathered at the railway station to say their farewells. Oncle Haim was as buoyant as if he were embarking on one of his genealogical research trips; Papa, however, looked sombre and Leon sour. It was on his account that they were heading to Paris, rather than to Venice or Brindisi like most of their compatriots. Despite the widely alleged venality of Italian officials, Papa feared that a twenty-one-year-old risked conscription. Yet even while making the arrangements, he was unable to resist a barb at Leon, who'd been in disgrace since the summer for an undisclosed offence. 'I should let fate take its course. A spell under enemy fire might do you some good.'

The stationmaster announced the train's imminent departure, and the three men entered their compartment. Esther felt sorry for Oncle Haim, trapped for three days with his feuding brother and nephew – although maybe they would use the time to settle their differences. The guard blew his whistle; Maman grabbed Bella away from the platform edge; and the onlookers prepared to wave. Just before the train pulled out, Grandmaman Falcona rushed forward and rapped on the window. As Leon opened it, she thrust a package into his hands.

'They provide perfectly palatable meals on the train – or so I'm told,' said Grandmaman Regina, who spurned any means of transport other than her own horse and carriage.

'It wasn't food . . . amulets to protect them on the journey.'

Grandmaman Regina sighed and addressed herself to Maman, who was softly weeping.

'Pull yourself together, my dear. Think of the children.'

'I am. How will they fare without a father?'

'Don't be ridiculous! This footling war can't last much longer. Jacob will be home within weeks.'

The weeks turned into months, without any sign of the war ending or of Papa's return. Despite Maman's concerns, no one in the family – not even Ruben, who made little attempt to conceal his Italian sympathies – faced hostility from their Turkish neighbours. For his part, Ruben was outraged that the government failed to acknowledge his recent coming of age and classify him as a threat. He followed the campaign more avidly than ever, relishing reports that the Italians were using flying machines to drop bombs, an innovation that horrified Esther. He idolised Leon and blamed Papa for keeping him away from the front, where his prowess as a huntsman would have been harnessed. He repeated his complaints at dinner to Leah, one of the few guests Maman continued to welcome.

'He's well out of it,' Leah replied. 'Jews aren't soldiers. They're scholars and thinkers.'

'And merchants and bankers,' Irène said, with inopportune loyalty.

'That's a lie!' Ruben said to Leah. 'What about Samson and David and Joshua?'

'They're the stuff of legend.'

'They're in the Bible!'

'Which is a compendium of legends.'

'Let's save this conversation for when your father's back,' Maman said.

'They may derive from sagas of tribal warlords,' Leah added. 'But they're no more historical than Odysseus and Achilles or Hector and Priam.'

Esther gulped, while Bella bristled.

'Odysseus and Achilles are real, and Hector and Priam and Hecuba, and Paris and Helen. Archae . . . people have dug up the foundations of Troy.'

'They've dug up the foundations of an ancient Anatolian settlement. That doesn't make it Troy.'

'I'm glad you're not my teacher,' Bella said, pushing away her plate.

'That's extremely rude,' Maman said. 'Apologise at once!'

Bella's perfunctory 'Sorry' fooled no one. Although in full agreement with Leah, Esther wished that she'd expressed herself more delicately. At a stroke, she'd antagonised both Ruben and Bella. She longed for them to appreciate her brilliance . . . she longed for everyone to appreciate her brilliance. It was no exaggeration to say that Leah had changed her life.

They had met the previous year at the annual *albasha* on the Sabbath before Passover. As usual, Maman had collected sackfuls of clothing for the children of Vardar and Kalamaria. While she admired her acts of charity, Esther was embarrassed by all the fanfare. The forced gratitude of girls who lacked her advantages filled her with unease, even shame, and she had initially resolved to skip the ceremony. The thought of what she would have missed made her shudder.

She'd sat in the airless hall of the Talmud Torah, discreetly surveying the company. One tall, plainly dressed woman stood out from a group of fidgety girls in their shabby finery. She was noticeably older than her companions - she wore her hair in a bun, whereas they wore theirs either loose, like Esther herself, or in doorknocker plaits - but she looked too young to be a teacher, let alone a parent. Esther, who liked to fit everyone into place, supposed that she was the older sister of one of the girls, perhaps a seamstress or assistant in a department store. But there was nothing servile in her frown when the various rabbis and officials heaped praise on their patrons' castoffs. As the afternoon wore on, Esther found herself increasingly intrigued by her. Then immediately the speeches ended, the directress of the Alliance girls' school brought her over to meet Maman.

Her supposition had been wrong. Leah was, indeed, a teacher, newly arrived from Paris and, according to the garrulous directress, renting an attic room in the house of a widowed dressmaker. Maman, ever solicitous, invited her to dinner the following Wednesday. While she couldn't be sure that she hadn't imagined it, Esther felt Leah give her an appraising glance before accepting. She was astounded to hear Maman describe her later as pallid and in need of a good meal. Hadn't she seen the fire in her eyes? Even though they'd exchanged nothing more than their names, Esther was convinced that she'd found the bosom friend - the soulmate - for whom she had yearned all her life.

Either in disdain for fashion or because she had nothing else to wear, Leah arrived dressed in the same blouse and skirt as at the *albasha*. Maman introduced her to the family, augmented for the occasion by both her grandmothers and Tante Amada. She apologised for burdening her with so many new names, to which Leah replied that she was accustomed to classes of sixty. Esther's fears that her siblings would disgrace her proved to be unfounded. Leon ignored Leah as soon as he realised that she had no interest in flirting; Irène and Ruben were subdued in the presence of a teacher; and Bella, chuckling to herself behind a napkin, was as ever in a world of her own. The only irritants were Maman and Papa:

Maman plying Leah with food as if she were at a soup kitchen; Papa interrogating her as intently as if he were at the bank.

'Jacob dear,' Maman said mildly, 'you're not giving the poor girl a chance to eat.'

'I'm sorry. I'm curious to hear what she has to say. After all, I'm both a governor and a donor to the school,' he added, with a twinkle, which Esther trusted that Leah would detect. 'Don't I have a right to know the sort of teacher it employs?'

'Indeed you do,' Leah replied. 'For now.'

In one respect, Esther was grateful for Papa's persistence, which coaxed far more from Leah than she would have dared ask herself. She was twenty-two years old (so there was a mere five-year gap between them). She came from Smyrna in Anatolia, where her father was a pharmacist, and she had four younger brothers. Her parents had encouraged her desire to teach and, while not wealthy, had subsidised her four-year training at ENIO in Paris ('the École Normale Israélite Orientale' she clarified). The work had been tough but inspiring, with classes in the many different subjects that the students would go on to teach. Nor had their leisure activities been neglected, with twice-weekly walks to the Jardin de Luxembourg and the Jardin des Plantes, and frequent visits to the Comédie Française and the Louvre.

'Did you see *The Raft of the Medusa?*' Esther asked.

'Yes, of course,' Leah replied. 'Along with room after room of masterpieces. You must go.'

'There'll be plenty of opportunity for that once she's married,' Papa said.

'Papa took his honeymoon in Paris,' Esther said, as if to justify his remark.

'Both times,' Leon interjected.

'Were you chaperoned?' Maman asked.

'Constantly,' Leah replied. 'We were so closely guarded that one of my friends said we might as well be in Saint-Lazare . . . that's the prison.'

'Heaven forbid!' Maman murmured.

'Like Monsieur Carrache, the Alliance directors are eager to protect their investment. I've had to sign a contract committing myself to working for them for ten years. I'm not even allowed to marry without their permission.'

'So will they find you a husband?' Irène asked, as ever perking up at the mention of marriage.

'No, or I'd never have signed. I presume they want to ensure that we do nothing to tarnish their reputation. Most of the women teachers marry their counterparts in the boys' schools. But that's not for me.'

Esther couldn't fathom why Leah's resolution to stay single made her so happy, except that she wouldn't want to share her new best friend with anyone, not even a husband. One day, if she could win over Papa, they might become colleagues as well as friends.

'You've chosen a difficult path,' Papa said, as if reading her thoughts. 'It's not one that I'd wish for any of my daughters.'

No, he would prefer her to follow the same path as her stepmother and grandmothers and no doubt her mother too if she hadn't died (she was tempted to think *escaped*) – having children; keeping house; planning meals; overseeing servants – while her husband ventured out into the world.

She was dismayed when, with dinner barely over, Leah cited her eight o'clock class the next morning and stood up to leave. Fearing that the early start was a ploy, Esther's spirits soared when Leah accepted Maman's invitation to dine again on the last day of Passover, only to sink back when, the moment she left the house, the family set about dissecting her character.

'I suppose she's what's known as a new woman,' Grandmaman Regina said.

'Aren't we all born anew every day?' Grandmaman Falcona said, eliciting one of Regina's most sardonic smiles.

'She certainly has newfangled ideas,' Maman said. 'Especially about marriage. Though it can't be easy for her with her parents so far away. Do you think she might suit Monsieur Farragi?'

'Who?' Papa asked.

'Bella's drawing master.'

'Save yourself the trouble! I know the type. No to any hint of a husband! Trying to impress us all with her self-denial.'

Esther felt a stab of hatred for him. She pushed back her chair with a satisfying scrape and quit the room without a word, which she hoped he would take as a reproach but feared he would dismiss as impertinence.

Her friendship with Leah blossomed. She herself was granted so little freedom (the students at ENIO weren't alone in feeling confined) that, more often than not, Leah visited her at home, enduring the assorted horrors of family meals for the sake of intimate conversations as they strolled arm in arm in the garden or sat in her bedroom, smoking Leah's lemon-scented cigarettes, which were not a Carrache brand. She sensed that Maman, who charged Esther with neglecting her old friends, was beginning to regret issuing Leah with an open invitation. But prattle about hobble skirts and French perfume and which of the Nahmias brothers was the best-looking could never compare with exhilarating discussions about literature and art. Papa, meanwhile, despite clinging to beliefs as rigid as the Torah, gave every impression of enjoying their debates.

'Best to get these foolish ideas out of your system while you're young,' he said, when Leah challenged him on the need for equal pay for men and women. Esther, fearful that she would lose patience, apologised for his condescension as soon as they left the room.

'Know your enemy,' she replied.

If Esther had her way, Leah would move into one of their empty bedrooms (not *spare* so much as *wasted*, now that her eyes had been opened to the overcrowding in the city's poorer districts). If she had her way entirely, she and Leah would share an apartment in Paris, but she knew better than to entertain such fantasies. What with her political campaigns and a raft of new lessons to prepare each day, it was a wonder that Leah had any time at all to spare for her.

Unlike the specialist teachers at her own school, where there were only thirteen girls in her class and sixty overall, teachers at the Alliance school, with more than six hundred pupils on the register, were required to cover the whole curriculum. Leah had dreamt of nurturing generations of intelligent, well-informed young women, but, after only a few months in the post, she had to acknowledge that the most valuable lessons were not academic but practical: needlework, millinery and weaving, which would help the girls to secure employment; childcare and bookkeeping, which would help them to manage their lives; and – with a sigh of resignation – moral and personal hygiene.

The one subject forbidden to a woman teacher was Hebrew. The girls received two hours' instruction a week, as against the boys' ten, but then they would never be called up to chant the Torah. Their teacher was the elderly, cross-eyed Rabbi Hazan. For once, Leah and Papa concurred in their contempt for his cant. He had protested against the secular education of boys and preached that the fire that consumed vast stretches of the city in 1890 was God's judgement on its deviation from the true path of Judaism. While even more bitterly opposed to the education of girls, he waived his objections for the sake of his fee. Nonetheless, he constantly complained of their laziness, ignorance and skimped homework. Goaded beyond endurance, Leah retorted that their so-called laziness was exhaustion. If they skimped on their homework, it was because they lacked proper homes, living in shacks and sheds, where they were beaten for every trifling offence by beleaguered parents. His sole response was to quote her most loathed proverb: 'He who withholds his stick hates his child.'

Although Papa was a governor of both Alliance schools, he hadn't sent his children to either. 'What would it serve you to learn dressmaking or laundering?' he asked Esther, rhetorically as always. Instead, she attended the Samuel Modiano, where she learnt the socially useful skills of singing and sightreading, and enjoyed a two-hour break each day for the lunch that a porter brought from home. At least Grandmaman Regina was honest when she declared that 'No granddaughter of mine is going to consort with the children of street vendors. Lice would be the least of it!'

In the year since they met, Leah had opened Esther's eyes to a world of possibilities. On discovering that all she'd read of the French Revolution was Madame de la Tour du Pin's *Journal* and Dickens's *Le Conte de Deux Villes*, she lent her de Tocqueville's *L'Ancien Régime et la Révolution*. On discovering that her favourite novels were Pierre Loti's *Aziyadé* and *Madame Chrysanthème*, she gave her Balzac's *Illusions Perdues*, Maupassant's *Bel Ami* and Zola's *Germinal*. Even so, she was taken aback when, five weeks after Papa and Leon's departure, Leah announced that she had bought them tickets for Racine's *Esther* at the Eden Theatre.

The only plays that Esther had seen were at Purim, when the whole household, including Maryam and the maids, gathered in the salon to watch a makeshift company enact the biblical story of her namesake. Even at six, she had been disheartened by the crudity of the spectacle – bearded, big-bellied men playing Esther and Vashti, since women weren't allowed to assume the sacred roles – and the rowdiness of the audience, who booed and waved rattles at every mention of Haman's name. She longed to see Racine's classic version: to hear his stately verse spoken aloud rather than in her head. But she feared that her four years in Paris, with her visits to the Comédie Française, had blinded Leah to the realities of life in Salonica.

'I can't think of anything – anything at all – that I'd rather do,' she said. 'But it's simply not feasible. Unless it's a charity gala, respectable women here don't go to the theatre.'

'Are you so intent on being respectable?'

Esther was shocked by the question but even more so by her own response. Only a few months before, she would have replied with an affronted 'yes'. Now she was harbouring thoughts that would make Aziyadé blush.

'A Jewish queen who saves her people: what could be more laudable?' Leah asked. 'And it was first performed by the girls of an aristocratic boarding school at the request of Madame de Maintenon. I rest my case.'

'Even so, I'm quite sure that Maman won't permit me to go. She's determined to do everything Papa's way.'

'Then why not just sneak out?'

'Without telling anyone?'

'That's what *sneak out* usually means. Say that you're feeling ill ... no, tired, so they won't check up on you. Put a dummy in your bed. It worked for King David! Or else, bend the truth. Tell her that you're going to a lecture on women in the Bible. Just don't tell her where it's taking place.'

Esther doubted that Papa would have been so easily deceived, but Maman, weighed down by familial responsibilities, was happy for her to attend the lecture, on condition that she asked no questions. Esther's guilt at playing on her credulity, which resurged with every jolt of the tram that took her to the theatre, vanished as soon as she arrived and watched the audience streaming through its doors.

'Are all the women Greeks and foreigners?' she asked Leah.

'Take a look at the posters! What languages are they in?'

'French and Ladino.'

'And what does that tell you? They may not be your friends the notables, but they're Jews: educated Jewish women ... *respectable* Jewish women, who refuse to adhere to antiquated, bigoted rules.'

Esther followed Leah up the winding steps to the gallery, lowering her gaze and praying that she wouldn't chance on anyone she knew. She had hardly sat down when the lights dimmed and the curtain rose on a chamber in Assuérus's palace. It was less sumptuous than she'd expected: a pair of flimsy fluted columns, four gold-painted side chairs, and a low divan covered in tattered skins. The deficiency of the décor was offset, however, by the grandeur of the performances. The actors addressed the audience as much as each other, savouring every emphasis, their inflections more akin to music than to speech. Esther was so overawed that for two hours she abandoned all thought of teaching in favour of the stage, laughing at the most inappropriate moment as she pictured Papa's reaction. It was true that Rachel, the greatest actress of her age, had been Jewish. Then again, she had also been the mistress of Napoleon III, and she doubted that Papa would have approved of that either.

At breakfast the next morning, she was both impressed and dismayed by the ease with which she gave a convincing account of the lecture. It helped that Maman was distracted by a letter from Papa. In a digest of news, he wrote that Grand-Oncle Lazar and Nissim had arrived in Paris after a successful trip to Rome; he himself had made several important contacts in the city and been invited to dine by Baron Édouard de Rothschild; Leon was learning to fence. With an end to the war in sight, he was confident that they would soon be back in Salonica, at which Ruben, listening to Maman read out the letter for the third time, snorted. Although his loyalties hadn't wavered, he declared that the Ottomans were holding their ground throughout Tripolitania, and the Italian generals, having squandered the advantage, should be court-martialled and shot.

While Ruben expounded on the boost that the latter-day Buonaparte, Major Leon Carrache, would give to the flagging Italian offensive, Esther returned to her bedroom. She opened her edition of *Esther* and, acknowledging the applause of the rustling leaves, stood at the open window to deliver the great speech in which the Queen acquainted Assuérus with the history of her people. She declaimed the incantatory Alexandrines, trusting that her Salonican cadences would not offend the playwright's ghost, when a faint knock and an even fainter 'Mam'selle' cut her short. Withdrawing from ancient Persia, she admitted the maid.

Rosa had joined them the previous October and never ceased thanking the Lord – volubly – for her good fortune. 'It's so lovely here . . . and warm . . . and quiet. The looms at the mill used to clatter so loud, I couldn't used to hear myself think. My sister, she's not worked there more than six years and she's deaf as a mole in her right ear. It could be where my dad threw the lamp at her, but he swears that was on the left.'

Rosa, usually so ebullient, was red-eyed and subdued. Presuming that she'd had crossed swords with Maryam, Esther thought it wiser not to press for details. While forbearing to a fault with the family, the housekeeper was a termagant with the maids. She had a particular animus against Rosa who, as she'd explained in graphic detail, had arrived wearing filthy underlinen and questioned the need to change it every day. 'She says that it's unhealthy,' Maryam declared, in tones worthy of Grandmaman Regina, obliging Maman to overcome her squeamishness and intervene. But when she mentioned the issue to Leah, Esther found herself rebuked for naïvety.

'Did you never consider that the girl might have a point? The wells in Vardar are contaminated by cesspits. Washing her underclothes might have infected her with God knows what.'

'But isn't that the same water they drink?'

'Yes, sometimes, I'm ashamed to say. When they can, they haul their pails to the standpipes at the train station.'

Rosa's strangled sobs as she changed the sheets were impossible to ignore.

'What's the matter?' Esther asked.

'Nothing, Mam'selle. I couldn't . . . not to you.'

'If you have a problem, I'll do my best to help.'

'No, you can't. No one can.'

'Is it Maryam?'

'No, don't say anything to her, please. Promise me!'

'Promise you what? What is there to say? You can tell me.' Esther sat on the bed and patted the mattress. Rosa perched rigidly beside her.

'I haven't had my nuisance now for three months.'

'Oh! Have you been eating properly?' Esther asked, seizing on the doctor's explanation of her own irregularity the year before.

'More than that. I've been eating for two,' Rosa said, subsiding in sobs. 'That's what my sister Ada called it.'

'What?'

'But it was different for her. She was cooking for three.'

'I'm afraid I don't follow.'

'Married.'

'Oh, I see.' Esther felt stupid. Despite all she'd heard about the immorality of the poor, she would never have imagined that Rosa, a girl younger than herself, could sink so low. 'How old are you?'

'Fourteen.'

'And your . . . friend?'

'Fifteen, I think. Jacob, that's his name. Same as the master. He works on the quays. He can lift two bales of tobacco in one load. There's not many as can say that. But he stands up straight . . . straight as the White Tower. He loves me. We were promised last year.'

'If he loved you, he'd have taken care not to get you in this condition.'

'We thought we'd be safe if we kept our clothes on.'

Esther bit her lip. While their ingenuousness made her want to scream, she realised that she knew even less about what was euphemistically termed 'the cabbages and the roses' than her maid. 'Jacob will have to accept his responsibilities. The marriage must be brought forward.'

'The rabbis in the Beth Din won't never allow it.'

'Don't be silly! Do you suppose they'd rather the child grew up a . . . ?' She shrank from the word.

'They won't give no one a licence till you show them your dowry chest. It took Ada ten years to buy everything to fill it. And Sara . . . she's the one with the ear: she's still saving for hers.'

'Let me speak to Señora Carrache and see what we can do.'

'No, Mam'selle, you promised . . . you promised!'

'Don't worry, I won't if you don't want me to,' Esther said, anxious to quell Rosa's rising distress.

'She'll turn me out. And she'll have every right. I've brought shame on the house. And what about Mam'selle Irène and Mam'selle Bella? They're so clean.'

'Then what's the alternative?' Esther asked, baulking at the description of her sisters.

'The what?'

'What do you intend to do?'

'It doesn't show yet, does it?'

Esther scrutinised her scrawny figure and shook her head.

'I'll stay until it does . . . so long as you don't tell. And you promised. And then I'll go home. My dad . . . oh the good Lord! But if he kills me, then he kills the baby too. So that's the end of the problem.'

'Stop that! I won't listen to such wickedness.' However hard people tried to console her, Esther bore a lifelong burden of guilt for her mother's death. Leon's jibe that 'Maman took one look at you and decided to die' had stung long past childhood. 'I promise I'll help you all I can. Now wipe your eyes and get on with your work. Or Maryam will have something to say.'

Although Leah acted as though employing servants were little different from owning slaves, there was no one else with whom Esther could discuss Rosa's plight. Leah was horrified, in part by the ignorance of procreation (which Esther was too ashamed to admit that she shared) and in part by the system that obliged girls to sacrifice their youth to amass linen, bedding and pots, along with a dress to wear under the canopy. 'It's as if the rabbis, who hold that our monthly flow is a punishment for Eve's disobedience, have chosen to aggravate it by making us - or at least the poorest of us - work for eight . . . nine . . . sometimes ten years, just so we can become our husbands' chattels, rather than our fathers'. Behold the essence of Jewish capitalism!'

'I don't think Rosa sees it that way.'

'Of course she doesn't. Generations of women have been persuaded that it's in their best interest. You'll find it's what drives half the workforce in your father's factory: girls of eleven or twelve, who've never heard a whisper of a husband, scraping together a few kuruş each month to furnish their dowry chests. But why? In the Torah, it's Jacob who works for seven years to marry Rachel and, when he finds out that Laban has tricked him, he works for another seven. Yet in twentieth-century Salonica, it would be Rachel and Leah who worked for the privilege of marrying him. Why?'

The question was too weighty for Esther to contemplate. While Leah was intent on changing the world, she aimed, more modestly, to save one girl from disaster. The six gold lira, which for Rosa might as well have been six thousand, were sitting in her bank account, accumulated gifts from her father, grandparents and Uncle Salvator, who liked to tuck coins in his nieces' bodices. Relieved that in Papa's absence there was no one to question the withdrawal, she presented the money to Rosa, who dissolved in tears, fell to her knees and kissed her hand with effusive gratitude. Three days later, telling Maman and Maryam that she was visiting a sick classmate, she took Rosa to meet Leah at the entrance to the Stein Palace store in Liberty Square.

No sooner had Rosa begun to thank her, in another lachrymose display, than Leah, ever the schoolmistress, berated her for her folly.

'Jacob's a good man,' Rosa said haplessly. 'We're promised in marriage.'

'Promises don't make you pregnant.'

Not for the first time Esther wished that someone would give her a clearer understanding of what did.

Rosa guided them through the Plaza Judea, past the Talmud Torah, where a scowling rabbi ordered a group of boys to turn away at their approach. They ventured down the dank and grimy alleyways of Vardar, stagnant water spilling from open gutters and splashing at their feet. Esther shielded her face from the stinging swirls of grit, but there was no escaping the pungent, sickly-sweet smell which she preferred not to identify. Two urchins, who looked as if they should be swept clean themselves, tried to sell them a broom. Ignoring their refusal, they followed, first begging and then taunting them. When Leah threatened to call the gendarmes, one spat and called them 'dirty Jews'. Esther was aghast. For the first time in her life, she was the target of a slur which she knew to be commonplace elsewhere. What made it more painful – and perverse – was that the boy was Jewish himself.

Rosa, too preoccupied to take offence, led them not to her own house but to Jacob's. Esther had seen booths, erected for the seven days of Sukkot, which were more substantial than this ramshackle hovel, its walls made of crooked boards and roof a patchwork of corrugated iron and straw. Rosa drew back the scrap of cloth that passed for a door and ushered them into a stale, asymmetrical room. The only light seeped through the cracks in the boards, but once her eyes adjusted, Esther saw that there was no furniture (not even a bed), only crates and sacks on the dirt floor. A ragged woman nursing a baby made no attempt to cover herself as they entered. Two small boys, sitting on their haunches, gaped at them. The woman greeted Rosa with a nod, as if lacking the energy to speak, and looked vacantly at Esther and Leah when Rosa introduced them. Evincing no curiosity when Rosa explained that they had come to see Jacob and his father, she sent one of the boys to fetch them. By any measure he was too young to wander the city alone, but Esther knew that it wasn't her place to protest.

The poverty here was of a different order from that she'd witnessed on her charitable visits with Maman. Moreover, she was accustomed to a degree of deference, and however awkward that had been, its absence was disconcerting. Even the most penurious of their hosts would insist on serving meagre refreshments. This woman didn't offer them so much as a glass of tea. She smiled wearily at Rosa, while Leah questioned the boy about school.

Trusting that if she could adapt to the gloom, she could adapt to the stench, Esther waited for Jacob and his father, whose arrival brought a fresh assault of odours. Rosa and Jacob greeted each other so shyly that Esther wondered whether they were inhibited by the visitors or less intimate than the pregnancy would suggest. Jacob was as handsome and well-built as Rosa had described, while his father was leathery, bent and wheezing. In spite of his ailments, he remained capable of delivering a hefty blow, as he did to the stupefied Jacob after Rosa imparted her news.

With the father cursing his cowering son, Leah, a practised peacemaker, intervened. 'Hold out your purse,' she instructed Rosa, who opened it and let the coins drop into her hand. While it was too dark to discern anyone's expression, Esther felt the atmosphere lift, as if the gold itself had curative properties. 'Señorita Carrache will take Rosa to buy everything needed for her dower chest. Then Jacob can apply to the Beth Din for the marriage licence. Congratulations, you're about to have a grandchild.'

The baby, unimpressed by its prospective niece or nephew, bawled.

Leaving Rosa to reconcile Jacob to his unforeseen fatherhood, Esther and Leah walked back. Even the muggy, miry streets were a relief from the squalid interior. Papa had horrified the family with his account of a Turkish lavatory which, while carefully oriented away from Mecca, had no seat. But Jacob's shack had no sanitation of any sort, prompting Esther to reappraise the faecal smell that pervaded the district.

'How can people live like that?' she asked Leah.

'They live in poverty, so that you can live in splendour. It's a simple equation.'

'That's not true,' Esther replied boldly. 'My father may not be religious, but, as a boy, he studied Torah. He likes to quote Moses's precept about the poor being always with us, so we should open our hands to them. Which he – Papa – does. Not just through his foundations, but when the Jews fled here from Russia, he built them homes . . .' She paused, recalling the slum they had just left. 'Gave them jobs in his factory.'

'Undercutting the wages of local workers.'

'You've met him. You know he's not like that.'

'I'm not saying that was his motive – at least not his primary one. But it was the result. Besides, it's merely a sop . . . a salve to his conscience. Charity is part of the problem, not the solution. The whole system needs to change.'

'If it weren't for charity, we'd never have met.'

'That's not worthy of you,' Leah replied, to Esther's consternation. 'But if you're genuinely concerned, come to one of our meetings.'

Leah's political meetings, to which she made frequent reference, had fascinated and alarmed Esther more than ever since she read *Germinal*. She pictured the participants being harangued by anarchists and extremists, much as the miners in the novel were by the rabble-rousing Souvarine. Her initial sympathy for Zola's oppressed workers had dwindled after the mob marched on the pit manager's house and the women mutilated the grocer's corpse. Was it that her reading of Madame de la Tour du Pin, and even of Monsieur de Tocqueville, had taught her that, no matter the cause, violence was never justified? Or was it rather, as Leah would say, that she clung to her class privilege?

'On Thursday evening, we have a speaker coming all the way from Berlin.'

'A German?'

'No, Swiss. She was a delegate to the Second International Socialist Women's Conference in Copenhagen two summers ago. She's talking about the role of women in the movement.'

While eager to share all Leah's interests, Esther couldn't help wishing that, as with her schoolfriends, they consisted of sketching, needlework and playing duets. Nevertheless, she told Maman another white – albeit greyer – lie, and took the tram to the Jewish quarter. Leah met her at the stop, steering her down a narrow street to the Socialist Federation building. Esther faltered on finding that it was shared with the Tobacco Workers' Union. Whatever Leah might say, she knew Papa to be a model employer, and it came as no surprise that the recent trouble at the factory had occurred during his exile. Even so, she suspected that the Carrache name might not be welcome and wondered whether she should choose an alias.

'Such as what? Sarah Bernhardt? Don't be absurd. Come on!'

Following Leah up a rickety staircase, Esther entered a large room, whose stark décor signalled its serious purpose. Rows of bentwood chairs were set before a small podium, beneath a banner depicting a bare-chested worker throttling a snake. Flanking it were two photographic portraits of pensive, bewhiskered men. One, in three-quarter view, was white-haired, with his right hand tucked in his jacket like Napoleon's. The other, in profile, was dark-haired and better groomed.

The room gradually filled up, mostly with staid young men, who looked more like clerks, railwaymen and pharmacists than the labourers and porters she had expected. Notwithstanding the speaker, there was a mere handful of women, soberly dressed in brown or grey jackets and skirts, and plain caps or headscarves. As Leah smiled and waved at several newcomers, Esther longed to be less conspicuous.

'Shall we sit down? Not that the chairs look too comfortable. I suppose it's one way to stop people dozing off.'

'Which may well be necessary, given that many of them have worked a twelve-hour day,' Leah said sternly. 'Not everyone can spend their afternoons lazing on a swing-seat, eating pumpkin seeds and reading novels . . . Don't look so affronted! There's someone I'd like you to meet.'

She escorted Esther to an intense young man, with beetle brows and a receding hairline, who was mopping his forehead despite the draught.

'Esther, this is Maurice Saltiel, my friend, comrade and opposite number at the boys' school. Maurice . . . Esther Carrache.'

'Ah, the famous Esther,' Maurice said. 'Leah told me she was hoping to lure you here.'

It took a moment for the full import of the epithet to hit Esther. 'I'm excited to come,' she said, gazing gratefully at Leah. 'Tell me, are all teachers socialists?'

'Isn't everyone of good faith?' Maurice replied. However unprepossessing his looks, his smile was most endearing.

'Maurice runs our drama group,' Leah said. 'Actor, writer, producer extraordinaire.'

'You put on plays?' Esther asked.

'Raising money and consciousness at the same time,' Maurice said. 'What could be better?'

'And raising our own spirits,' Leah added. 'Maurice has translated Molière's *L'Avare* into Ladino.'

'Why?'

'To reach the widest possible audience,' Maurice replied. 'I've also transplanted it from Paris to Salonica.'

'Is that allowed?'

'Molière's in no position to object. Besides, he stole vast chunks of the plot from Plautus. Do you know the play?'

'We read it at school,' Esther said, her memory suddenly blank.

'It's about an autocratic father, Harpagon, who compels his children, Cléante and Élise, to marry in order to enhance both his fortune and his social status. That money can't buy happiness is a truism, but I've tailored it to our circumstances by turning Harpagon into a factory owner. Don't worry, his wares aren't specified.'

'Esther's father is a well-known liberal who would never compel his children to do anything against their will.'

'We aren't talking about my father,' Esther said, uncertain of Leah's tone.

'Whatever the setting, we'd have had to make some changes,' Maurice said. 'I doubt that our audience would welcome Cléante's description of a usurer as a Jew, or the Ottoman authorities brook Harpagon's boast that he'd even marry a Turk with a big enough dowry.'

'Those are just minor adjustments,' Leah said. 'Maurice's masterstroke is that instead of La Flèche stealing Harpagon's cashbox—'

'He's Cléante's valet, by the way,' Maurice interjected.

'I'm sorry. I should have made that clear.'

'You're not in the classroom now.'

Leah laughed, and Esher forced a smile.

'Well, instead of La Flèche stealing Harpagon's cashbox, he and Frosine, the matchmaker, tell the workers that Harpagon is planning to cut their wages, inciting them to call a strike.'

'Just when the factory has received a huge order from the Sultan,' Maurice chimed in, bubbling with enthusiasm for his own creation, 'Harpagon tries – and fails – to persuade the Governor to break the strike. The workers will only agree to return if he permits Cléante and Élise to marry Mariane and Valère, who turn out to be brother and sister, the children of Anselme, an exiled social philosopher. Fearing ruin, Harpagon reluctantly agrees.'

'Isn't that rather far-fetched?' Esther asked. 'I can't imagine anyone at my father's factory showing such concern for me or my brother Leon.'

'Is it any more far-fetched than the original,' Maurice replied sharply, 'where Anselme is separated from his children during a shipwreck and, presuming them dead, lives under a false name to forget his loss?'

'I suppose . . . I'm sure not.'

'You should play one of the women,' Maurice said, changing tack.

'I couldn't possibly . . . I couldn't begin . . . I wouldn't know how. My father would never allow it.'

'I thought he was a liberal.'

'But on a stage . . . in front of an audience.'

'Pity. You'd be a perfect Mariane. Leah has already bagged Élise.'

'You're going to act?' Esther asked.

'Why not? Don't you think I could convince as a rich man's daughter?'

'I think you could do anything,' she said, remembering to smile. 'Why not? May I read the play? Do you have a spare copy?'

'Dozens. For the past few weeks, I've been giving it to the boys as dictation. I'll fetch you one after the talk.'

Esther felt her heart flutter. Who would have thought that her theatrical dreams would be kindled at a political meeting? Papa would never countenance her performing in public, let alone under a socialist banner (she averted her eyes from the opposite wall), but he was a thousand miles away and, if Ruben were to be believed, wouldn't be returning for some time yet. She'd have to win Maman over, since it was one thing to attend a play in secret, quite another to act in one. The key points in her favour were that the performance was for charity and the play itself a classic . . . it would be best not to mention the adaptation. The presence of two teachers in the cast must offer a measure of respectability. She turned to see Maurice whispering to Leah and hoped that he wouldn't be playing Valère.

Their friendship was both unexpected and unnerving. She had assumed Leah's life to be as austere as her lodgings, her visits to the Carraches her sole respite from work. But her closeness to Maurice, exceeding any professional requirement, painted a different picture. Her defence of the single state had struck a chord with Esther, who despaired of her schoolfriends' fixation on marriage, oblivious of the fact that they would be subservient to their husbands and risked dying in childbirth. But what if the truth were not that Leah saw educating children as an honourable alternative to having them but, rather, as a way to meet like-minded men?

'What part will you be playing?' she asked Maurice.

'Cléante,' he replied, with a grin. 'Mariane's lover.'

'Time to sit down,' Leah said. 'They're ready to start.'

The chairman introduced the speaker, Emma Weinrich, a portly, middle-aged woman with a pince-nez and her hair in a straggly pompadour. Apologising for her lack of Ladino, she spoke in French, which a show of hands revealed that only half the audience understood. With her thoughts racing ahead to rehearsals, costumes and profound conversations with Leah about Molière's intentions, Esther struggled to concentrate on the speech, but several of Frau Weinrich's remarks hit home. She asserted that male dominance was the product of history, not biology; that women were doubly oppressed in a world of patriarchal capitalism (words that Esther had never before heard coupled); and that Marx's claim that gender oppression would vanish alongside class oppression was naïve, whereupon she gave the portrait of the white-haired man a jaunty nod. When she turned to marital matters, however, Esther was shocked. She demanded the abolition of sexual slavery, as if all men – not just Turks – locked up their wives in harems, before assuring the women in the audience that they had as much right to sexual satisfaction as men. This prompted several – although not Leah – to applaud. Esther, warier than ever of male kisses after Rosa's pregnancy, kept her hands clasped in her lap.

After Frau Weinrich answered questions, most of which were thinly veiled compliments, the chairman asked the audience to stand and sing the workers' anthem. Esther, moving her lips in a bid to blend in, felt as great an imposter as if she had kissed an icon of Saint Demetrios during a Greek festal procession.

After a final burst of applause, the atmosphere in the room changed as people stacked their chairs against the walls and the speakers were replaced on the podium by four musicians: two playing guitars, the third a harmonica, and the fourth a pair of spoons. As couples took to the floor with far more abandon than the girls in Madame Tiano's dance class, Esther edged towards the shadows and prayed that she would escape notice. She might have countenanced dancing with Maurice, if only to keep him away from Leah, but it was too late for that. As she watched them polka, a large man in soiled shirtsleeves, with a red kerchief round his neck, approached and silently held out his hand.

'Thank you so much,' she replied, trying not to breathe in his wet-leather smell. 'But I don't dance.'

'I won't bite,' he said, with a jagged grin.

'I never imagined . . . but I'm really not up to it.'

'Aren't I good enough for you?' he asked, with a faint air of menace.

'Of course. It's just . . . I'm with child,' she said, triumphantly. 'I feel a little nauseous.'

'Oh, would you like some water . . . or a chair?'

'It'll pass. I just need a moment to myself.'

He nodded and moved away. The music stopped and Esther

headed for the door, where she was intercepted by Leah.

'I saw you spurn Moïse.'

'I didn't want to wound his pride.'

'Is that the first time you've ever spoken to a cobbler, except to ask him to mend your shoes?'

'I haven't. Maryam takes care of all that. Oh!' she broke off, as Leah laughed. 'It's not fair. I can't help who I am.'

'That's a moot point. But I'm sorry you won't dance. I remember you waltzing very elegantly with Irène around the garden.'

'That was in the garden. And there was nobody watching but you.'

'Would you dance with me?'

'Here?'

'Yes.'

'Now?'

'Yes.'

'But there are so many men without partners.'

'Equal rights. Weren't you listening to the talk?'

A smile playing on her lips, Leah reached out her hand and, after a momentary hesitation, Esther took it. She followed her onto the floor, where five couples were dancing in a mishmash of styles that would have horrified Madame Tiano. Though no words passed between them, Esther knew instinctively that Leah must take the lead and, sensing a warmth in the small of her back, placed her left hand on her partner's shoulder. As they strove to match the band's dissonant rhythms, Esther's blood rushed, her skin tingled and her feet twirled as effortlessly as the ballerina's in her music box. She caught sight of the cobbler's astonished face, but she no longer cared about offending his - or anyone's - sensibilities. Never before had she felt so free. If this were what it was to dance with a woman, no wonder there were so many prohibitions against her dancing with a man.

4

MERCADO

SALONICA, MARCH 1912

ALLAHU AKBAR RENT the air and Mercado Silvera, always a light sleeper, wakened. The thin light of dawn crept through the window which, mindful of nocturnal odours, he kept open summer and winter alike. With the lengthening days, there were two hours between the Adhan and his starting work, but, resisting any slothful impulse, he leapt out of bed and began his morning callisthenics. For the past two years, he had diligently followed the Müller system, doubling the standard fifteen-minute routine, building up a sweat which he pumiced away at the basin.

After dousing himself in eau de cologne - the genuine article and a rare indulgence - he headed downstairs to breakfast with Falcona. It was one of life's quirks that she should have settled in the Muslim quarter and another that he should once again be lodging with her. He would have preferred to eat alone, but that would be to offend a woman who, as no one let him forget, had shown him unflagging kindness.

Wearing a voluminous green and gold robe and a brimless cap that lent her face a strangely masculine cast, she clasped his arm as he bent to kiss her cheek. 'If only all men smelt as sweet as you, we wouldn't need to plant flowers,' she said, with characteristic whimsy.

'Where would bees find the nectar to make honey?' he asked, conscious of the smirking maid.

'Why, you would exude it,' she said, which made him feel queasy.

'Did you sleep well?' he asked, changing the subject.

'Oh, at my age, there's little time for sleep. Too many old friends come back to reminisce. Hannah, pass Señor Mercado the olive bread . . . Your ears must have been burning yesterday evening. I was at Mathilde's for dinner and Regina Carrache - she's not an easy woman to please, as you know - was heaping praise on the way you've held things together at the factory.'

'Really?'

'All the more impressive, she said, given that you weren't born to it.'

'How gracious of her!' he replied coldly. Was there some mystical property in a Carrache cradle, akin to the chrism used to anoint the kings of France? 'Yes, please.' He thrust out his cup so abruptly that Hannah spilt coffee on his cuff.

'Take care!' he snapped.

'Not to worry.' Falcona stood up and, waving away the flustered maid, dabbed her napkin first in the water jug and then on the cuff. 'There, good as new! Besides, I know you'll laugh, but a coffee stain is a sign of impending wealth.'

'Where did you hear that?' Mercado asked, recovering his composure.

'My grandmother, from her grandmother, and her grandmother before her. Or so I'm told.'

'Aunt Falcona!' He sprang up and kissed her on the cheek. 'I sometimes think there's no one in the world I love but you.'

'What?' She looked alarmed.

'I mean as much as you.' He sat down and reached for a bowl of fig jam.

Returning to his room, he wondered whether for once her superstitions might have some substance. Along with the majority of his male compatriots, Jacob Carrache had been exiled. For all his tributes to the city's diversity, he remained intrinsically tribal, trusting few people outside the family circle, which, by a twist of fate or, more precisely, an ancient custom, included Mercado. So with no blood relatives left behind except for his stroke-afflicted father and thirteen-year-old son, Jacob had placed him in charge of the tobacco factory. In barely four years, he had risen from clerk to bookkeeper to overseer to manager. The position was strictly temporary, and would end on Jacob's homecoming. But the French and the English had once waged war for a hundred years. Surely he might be forgiven the hope that the current conflict would last for ten?

He retrieved his bicycle from the courtyard and rode slowly through the neighbourhood, alert to the faintest hint of sweat. He weaved through the early morning bustle, as peasants brought in barrowloads of fruit and vegetables from outlying villages; sweetmeat vendors set up booths of baklava, lokma and lokum; and the toothless tinsmith, Haji Ghazi, kindled his brazier. He turned into Sabri Pasha Street, exchanging the cheap market stalls of the city's fringes for the elegant fashion and furniture shops at its centre. He reached the quayside, pausing to savour the briny sting of the breeze, before continuing to the factory.

The crowd at the gate was visible from a distance of several blocks. As overseer, he had drawn up a memorandum for the directors, questioning the need for three separate gates, which made it harder to monitor what was taken in and, more to the purpose, smuggled out. His concerns had gone unheeded, but one of his first acts as manager had been to lock the two side gates and post male and female guards to frisk the workforce on both arrival and departure. The resulting delays had reignited claims for payment by the hour rather than the piece, which he had flatly refused.

Extending greetings, which were grudgingly returned, he entered the building. He called into the depot, less the heart of the operation than its belly, where bales of raw tobacco waited to be taken up to the factory floor, and processed bales and crates of cigarettes to be taken down to the barges. He made his way to his office, where his first task was to telegraph the previous day's production figures to Paris. At noon, he made his regular circuit of the factory, starting in the softly lit sorting room and following the path of the leaves to the cutting room, where, in a configuration that never failed to delight him, sixty master cutters sat facing their apprentices on neat rows of mats, like Muslims at prayer.

He headed into the women's workshops, where they sieved the low-grade leaves to remove impurities and rolled the cigarettes. As a newcomer, he had been shocked to find that the women were more militant than the men, indeed the union leader was a woman, Raşel Surashi, albeit one with the belligerence – and build – of a Turkish wrestler. While most female workers left to marry in their early twenties, Raşel, notorious far beyond the factory gates for having set up house with a Greek fisherman, stayed on. Taking advantage of Jacob's absence, she had presented Mercado with an extensive list of demands. In addition to the perennial calls for guaranteed employment during the winter months when production was halved, shorter hours and payment on religious holidays, she was now pressing for women to receive the same rate as men, at which the two male delegates had clucked like capons.

He had sent her away with a flea in her ear. While under no illusions that he'd seen the last of her, he hadn't expected her to return so soon. Yet in the early afternoon, she appeared unannounced in his office. This time her posse of three was exclusively female, one of whom brought a baby, a flagrant infringement of workplace rules which, for the moment, he chose to disregard.

'Ladies, welcome. Please, take a seat. Tell me, what can I do for you?'

Ignoring both the chairs and the false bonhomie, Raşel slammed a pamphlet on his desk. 'Read this!'

'What is it?' he asked, bristling at the bluntness with which she would never have addressed Jacob.

'*Pregnancy and Pregnancy Management.* Or don't you speak Turkish?'

'*Konuşurum da, okurum da,*' he replied, surprised to discover that she did.

'It was sent me by the tobacco union in Smyrna.'

Mercado seethed. It was bad enough that the union was active in Salonica without its corresponding with similar saboteurs across the Empire.

'Don't you want to know what it says?' she asked.

'Not in the least,' he said, feeling a deep repugnance that people were publishing treatises on matters that ought to be left to providence. Resisting a strong urge to toss it in the basket, he slipped it into a drawer. 'I'll glance at it later.'

'Then I'll summarise it for you.'

'You tell him, missus,' said the woman with the baby, while her companions stood as stiff as a guard of honour.

'We all know the damage breathing in tobacco dust can do. Eyes weeping like wounds; non-stop coughing and wheezing; headaches—'

'Stabbing pains up and down your spine,' a third woman interjected.

'We're talking about the dust,' Raşel reminded her.

'But sitting twelve hours on the floor—'

'The dust! Now we learn what it does to our insides.'

'Whose insides?'

'Ours . . . women's. It's all there in black and white. Written by a doctor. So damning that you're already trying to hide it away.'

Mercado wished that he'd left the pamphlet in plain sight. 'Why have I had six babies - six - and not one of them lived long enough to be born? Why has Rivka - go on, show him . . . why is her baby like this?'

Rivka laid the child on his desk. She slowly uncovered him, revealing first his harelip and then his scalp, which looked to have been sliced at the back like a wedge of cheese.

'I really don't see what this has to do with—'

'Show him more!' Raşel ordered, and Rivka pulled up the baby's frayed smock to expose a hollow chest with a single nipple.

'Dust!' Raşel pointed to the deformity. 'Dust!'

'Utter nonsense!' Mercado said. 'On the strength of a single leaflet written by an ill-informed woman—'

'Man,' Raşel shouted triumphantly. 'Besim Omer, a man!'

'Man or woman: it's one person's opinion.' Although he didn't smoke himself and regarded the factory solely as a stepping stone to his ambitions, he refused to sit back and hear it traduced. 'The medicinal benefits of tobacco are universally acknowledged. It relieves pain, calms nerves, unblocks the throat and chest. What's true of the smoke must be equally true of the dust.' He turned to Rivka. 'As for you, I have no idea when you last worked here, but I suggest you remove your brat before I summon one of the guards to remove you.'

'Three weeks! Three weeks before I gave birth, I was rolling cigarettes.'

'Exactly. What other company would have kept you on, when you should have been at home rather than flaunting your condition? Yet you dare—' He broke off as he felt the sweat beading on his brow. 'Please leave my office. You,' he said to Rivka, 'leave the building. And the rest of you return to work, unless you'd rather go with her.'

'Is that a threat?' Raşel asked.

'It's a warning.'

'We'll see about that. Come on!' She moved to the door, followed by her minions.

'Just a moment!' Mercado faltered. 'You come in here . . . you bring this unfortunate child . . . you hand me this unfounded document. You haven't said what it is you want.'

'You gave us no chance,' Raşel said. 'So quick to defend yourself and attack us.'

'Then tell me.'

'Here!' She handed him a sheet of paper which, to his disgust, was moist. 'Better ventilated rooms with drinking water. Longer breaks. A pharmacy—'

'What?'

'On the premises.'

'Yes, and I'd like six months' annual holiday, but it's not going to happen.'

'And equal wages with the men,' Raşel continued relentlessly. 'After all, we're the ones who have the babies. We're the ones at risk.'

There was a simple answer to that, but Mercado bit his tongue. 'You can't be that concerned about the risks,' he said, 'if all you want is to be better recompensed for taking them.'

'We have to live.'

'In which case, I advise you once again to return to work. Unless, of course, you'd prefer to try your luck at the mill, along with the cotton dust; or the tannery, with the burns and the stench; or the laundry, with the damp; or . . . well, when you find somewhere free from risks, be sure to tell me. I'd love to know.'

'This isn't the end of it,' Raşel said, as she walked out.

For the remainder of the afternoon, he addressed the logistical tasks at which, though he said so himself, he excelled. He returned home, but, instead of a quiet evening studying English grammar, he was obliged to dine with his parents. Falcona, the unwitting cause of the estrangement, insisted on his seeing them regularly, sending him with parcels of clothes and food for Maman and Mari, and bottles of raki for Papa. The gifts made his visits feel even more like acts of charity.

Struggling to steady his overladen bicycle, he headed to Kamara, where his family occupied three rooms in the house of a Bulgarian spice merchant's widow. With his customary distaste, he called on her to pay the rent, listening to the familiar plaint that, if only she had a son as devoted as him, she wouldn't need to take in lodgers to eke out her meagre savings. Sickened by her insensitivity, he gulped down the mandatory glass of xinomavro and escaped. Whatever loss of status she had suffered, it was nothing compared to Papa's.

Elie Silvera had farmed silkworms. The last time Mercado recalled being happy – actively happy, not merely free from discontent – was at the age of five, when Papa gave him two trays of the insects to raise himself. As they audibly munched mulberry leaves, he watched them grow from eggs the size of poppy seeds until they were plump and ready to spin their own cocoons, which Papa and his team plunged into boiling water to extract the thread. The following year, disaster struck both farm and family: a fungal infection destroyed two successive crops, while Mercado's four elder siblings died of cholera. In an effort to console him, Papa quoted an ancient Turkish proverb: *Eternal sunshine makes a desert.* He had failed to detect a single ray of light.

He had been standing beside the last of the four coffins when Papa grabbed him by the waist, hoisted him high above his head, and called out to the assembled mourners: 'I have a young slave for sale. Who wants to buy him?' He squealed and squirmed, doubly terrified after Maman's bedtime reading of *Uncle Tom's Cabin*. Whether by prior arrangement or from sheer goodwill, Avram Beraha shouted: 'I do!' and, at the end of the vigil, he took home a frantically protesting Mercado – except that he hadn't been Mercado then but Shimon. He had lost his brother and sisters, and nothing that Avram or his wife, Falcona, said could convince him that he wasn't also losing his parents. Although he returned to them after the statutory three days, with new clothes and toys and, most precious of all, the recollection of Falcona's kindness, he never recovered his name. Wherever he went, he bore the stamp of his purchase, *Mercado*, like a permanent price tag.

For years, he'd presumed that the fantastical interlude was unique to him, until Falcona recounted the age-old belief that, when several siblings died precipitately, it was to atone for their parents' sins. Selling a surviving child freed him from further liability, while changing his name duped the Angel of Death. It came as little surprise that Falcona clung to such arcane notions, but it made no sense that, even in extremis, forward-looking men like Avram and Papa gave them credence. Nevertheless, he couldn't have hoped for more generous benefactors than the Berahas, who continued to support him, allowing him to finish his schooling rather than being sent out to work at twelve. They included him in family gatherings and introduced him to the Carraches, in whose house he became a frequent guest. When Avram died, three months after securing him his post at the factory, Falcona suggested he move out of his parents' cramped lodgings and live with her.

Although he relished the extra space (and freedom), his primary reason for accepting the offer had been to strengthen his bond with Jacob, whose routine inquiries after his parents' health was an added incentive to visit them. Yet he struggled not to turn on his heel as the reek of Papa's failure, more pungent even than that of Mama's cooking, seeped down the dilapidated stairway. Papa opened the door, shaming them both by stooping to kiss his hand. Maman rushed up and fluttered kisses on his cheeks, drawing him into the salon, where his urge to flee intensified. Although Falcona's mistrust of electricity had accustomed him to shadowy rooms, his parents' single candle was a stark reminder of their poverty or, rather, improvidence, since Papa's flushed face and slurred speech betrayed how he spent every kuru.

Refusing to relinquish his hand, Maman led him to the table and proudly announced that she'd made his favourite childhood dish of aubergine pie. She disappeared into the kitchen, leaving him to make stilted conversation with Papa, who, in spite of his fading memory, never once let slip a *Shimon*. After ten torturous minutes, Maman returned, carrying a casserole, followed by his Mongolian sister Mari, who, to cap the family's misfortunes, had been born the year after Mercado's 'sale'.

Falcona, predictably dewy-eyed, claimed that children like Mari were noble souls sent by God to test a family's faith. He was tempted to ask whether the Silveras' faith hadn't already been tested enough. As ever, he fought against his revulsion as Mari lumbered towards him, her right hand limp, the fingers hanging like tassels, and nestled her face against his chest. Having promised his parents to take care of her after their deaths, he'd been heartened to learn that Mongolians rarely lived past the age of ten. Mari was fifteen.

After a meal which, in its way, was as trying as his encounter with Raşel, he cycled home, taking a lengthy detour through Bara, lingering on Afroditi Street, both to bait the prostitutes who emerged from their doorways, toying with their dishabille each time he came to a halt, and to prove to himself that he could resist their tawdry allure.

The mood in the factory the next day perturbed him. Although it remained unspoken, he sensed the discontent simmering in the sorting room, and even more palpably in the rolling and packing rooms. Believing it best ignored, he withdrew to his office, only to be confronted with a severe supply crisis. Karanos Milev, their agent in Berea, had telegraphed that, due to further sabotage of the railways, he was transporting the crop by buffalo. After cabling back his approval, he began working through his mail when the reception clerk brought word of a visitor. 'She says you know her. She wouldn't give her name.'

'Show her in,' he replied, irked by the clerk's grin when he returned two minutes later with a visibly pregnant Xenia. Dismissing him, Mercado invited her to sit down.

He noted the sapphire ring on her finger. He had been in two minds when Leon asked him for a loan with which to buy it: a sum that any reasonable man would hesitate to spend on a wife of twenty-five years, let alone a mistress of a few months. He'd balanced the prospect of gaining Leon's favour against the danger of losing Jacob's. In the event, neither hope nor fear was realised. Leon confirmed the maxim that indebtedness was not the same as gratitude, while Jacob, having heard his son's confession, acknowledged that Mercado had been coerced and thanked him for his discretion.

As the price of his pardon, Jacob exacted Leon's promise to cease all communication with Xenia – a promise that he broke within hours. On the eve of his departure for Paris, he entreated Mercado to act as courier, receiving and redirecting their mail.

'Why the subterfuge? You've been ordered to leave the city, not to sever all contact with it.'

'But I have been ordered to sever all contact with Xenia. Who knows if I can rely on the hotel's cooperation?'

'It's the Ritz!'

'And it's my father! What if he takes it into his head to have my letters brought to him, spots one in an unfamiliar hand and opens it?'

'That's a lot of "ifs". Even so, that doesn't stop you writing directly to Xenia.'

'No, but she lives in one of the narrowest, most obscure alleyways in the entire city. It doesn't have even a name: just "the street with the withered fig tree". A letter might not reach her.'

'So you're at an impasse?'

'Not if you help us.'

Mercado agreed to the request, flattered that Leon should have entrusted him with such a delicate task. Then it struck him that the reason he hadn't asked any of his friends was the fear that they might proposition Xenia during his absence, whereas he considered him to be no threat.

For two months he fulfilled his charge, a regular presence at the French post office, dispatching Xenia's letters to Paris and delivering the replies to her lodgings, where her landlady lauded Leon's charm, good looks and generosity, as if Mercado were no more than an errand boy. Since neither correspondent thought to seal the envelopes, he steamed them open, both rapt and repelled by their romantic effusions. Then in December, Xenia disclosed that she was pregnant. He never forwarded the letter.

He had harboured many resentments over the years, but none with the venom he bore Leon Carrache, whose privilege and presumption had humbled him since childhood. One incident, in particular, he could never forgive. He was nine and Leon seven; they were sitting at table, listening to the adults discussing slavery.

'We had several slaves when I was young,' Leon's Carrache grandfather said. 'They came from Circassia and the Ukraine. Of course, it was all very discreet. My father would go down to Beschinar

Gardens at dawn when the ships landed their cargo and bring back a choice specimen. No one thought anything of it.'

'Shameful!' Jacob said. 'Thank the Lord those days are over.'

'But they're not,' Leon piped up. 'Are they?' He turned slyly to his Beraha grandfather. 'You said Mercado's father sold him as a slave.'

'I said nothing of the sort.'

'You did too! You said his father sold him and you bought him and he's your slave, which means he's mine too.'

'Don't talk nonsense!' Mathilde interposed. 'Eat your pie.'

'You've got everything muddled,' Jacob said. 'Mercado's father had been dealt a series of blows – not literally, like the smack you'll get if you don't behave,' he added, as Leon stuck out his tongue at Mercado. 'Your grandfather was doing him a favour. It's a tradition: the sale was a form of words. Though it's high time such traditions were laid to rest.'

Mercado had waited fifteen years for the chance of revenge, and now it had fallen into his lap. It was not without risk, since at any moment peace might break out, exposing his treachery, but his close study of reports from Tripolitania suggested that he would have enough time to implement his plan before Leon's return. Since her initial announcement, Xenia had sent him seven letters, while Leon had sent her three. Each wrote in mounting desperation. She, on paper streaked with tears, accused him of abandoning her and their unborn child. He, in surprisingly fluent Turkish, accused her of taking another lover. Both repeatedly sought his pledge that he'd passed on the mail, which he gave, along with regret that he lacked the power to conjure a reply.

For nine weeks he had played the supportive friend, assuring Xenia that Leon's silence didn't signify rejection, and Leon that Xenia's disappearance wasn't sinister. All had gone better than he dared hope, but he couldn't afford the slightest slip. Meeting Xenia for only the third time, he had to remind himself that he knew nothing of her plight. But as soon as she sat down, refusing all refreshment, she revealed – or, rather, reiterated – the truth.

'Pregnant?' he asked, in an astonished tone. 'My congratulations.'

'Are you mad? I'm sorry, I didn't mean . . . But do you think I want the child?'

'Then have you tried . . . ? I'm no expert, but I understand that there are ways to resolve the problem.'

'Oh yes, the famous tincture of oleander. It worked for two of my friends, but not for me.'

'A baby as tenacious as its mother.'

'I'm not asking anything for myself, but for the child . . . Do you think he's met another woman?'

'He's young,' he said, twisting the knife. 'And I hear that the women in Paris are the most beautiful in the world.'

'So what am I to do? I can't go on working much longer. You know I sing?'

'Does pregnancy affect the voice?' he asked innocently.

'Not that I know. But tiredness does. And heartburn does. And cramps do. And taunts from the audience that I'm putting on weight. Not to mention being fired when the manager finds out why I'm putting on weight. How are we to live?'

'I promise I'll do what I can. I'm no Leon Carrache, but I have some savings.'

'No! That's very kind, but I couldn't . . . I didn't mean . . .'

'Of course not. But Leon's my friend. We grew up together. I regard it as my duty. Not that I believe he would ever behave dishonourably. I'll write to him again this evening and tell you the moment I hear back.'

He tried to engage her in conversation, but, her mission accomplished, she declared that she had imposed on him long enough and hurried out. Left alone, he considered his options. Would it serve him better to inform Leon that he was to father a child: a half-Greek bastard whom, for all his vaunted liberalism, Jacob would never acknowledge? Or should he keep him in the dark and seek to eliminate Xenia from the picture, before presenting the story - carefully expurgated - to Jacob, who was sure to commend him for preserving the family's good name, further cementing their bond?

He pondered the matter throughout the day without reaching a conclusion. The following morning, he cycled to the factory, where, instead of the usual two ragged lines at the gate, he was met by a rowdy mob, brandishing scrawled placards, haranguing any worker who ventured inside.

'What's going on?' he asked a porter.

'We're withdrawing our labour,' the man replied, as though it were a commodity to be traded.

'Get to work now and we'll say no more about it,' he said, addressing everyone within earshot.

'We have our rights,' an unidentified man said. 'We're all God's creatures.'

'You'll be poor and hungry ones, unless you stop this foolishness.'

'We have our legitimate demands,' Raşel said, bludgeoning her way forward.

'In what way legitimate?' Mercado asked, locking eyes with her.

'Here,' she said, thrusting a sheet of paper at him. 'We're not all the halfwits you take us for. Some of us can read and write.'

'Thank you. I'll give it all the attention it merits.' He smiled at her confusion. 'Now shall we get to work and discuss this when our heads are cooler?'

'Our heads are cool now. You're the one who's sweating,' Raşel retorted, to his mortification.

'I don't propose to bandy words with you in the street. We'll speak inside or not at all.'

'Not at all then,' she said, leaving him to jostle his way through the crowd. Some shouted slogans; some booed; others wore anxious expressions that offered him hope.

He had not shared Jacob's delight in Abdul Hamid's abdication, suspecting that, once the natural order was overturned, there would be clamour for further changes. Sure enough, within months of the Revolution, Salonica had been riven by a series of strikes: dockers; draymen; brickmakers; carpenters; tailors; foundrymen; and, inevitably, tobacco workers. This was not the freedom envisaged by the CUP leaders, who swiftly outlawed such subversion. They failed, however, to outlaw the unions, forcing the employers to take action themselves. The previous March, the Central Court had granted Jacob an injunction against the Tobacco Workers' Union, only to revoke it when hundreds of protesters besieged the building. Having tasted blood, they thirsted for more. On 1 May, a day they commandeered and celebrated as if it were Purim or Easter, several thousand, among them women and girls, marched through the streets, chanting, waving banners and intimidating passers-by. He would have preferred a detachment of enemy soldiers to swoop down on the city than to see it overrun by such a rabble.

Fate had placed him in command of the factory, and he had no intention of loosening his grip. He skimmed through Raşel's 'legitimate demands', which amounted to the usual petty grievances. He might have had more respect for her if she'd called for radical reform, such as turning the factory into a workers' cooperative, as had happened in France. There was no reference to the dust problem that had exercised her earlier in the week, proving that it had been a distraction. He flung the paper into the basket before fishing it out to tear it into shreds. The longer he refused to engage with them, the sooner they would come crawling back. A day or two's lost production was a small price to pay.

He made a rapid tour of the factory, praising – but not unduly – the hundred or so honourable workers who remained at their posts. Returning to the office, he telegraphed Jacob, making no mention of what was merely a temporary nuisance and which, in any case, he had under control. Now that the *Journal de Salonique* had ceased publication, the dispute would be resolved long before it was reported.

A small but menacing crowd lingered by the gate when he left for the evening. Like a knight errant on his horse, he mounted his bicycle, swerving perilously when a lout hurled a lemon at the wheel. He wobbled away to a chorus of jeers. Once at home, he scrubbed himself in near-scalding water before accompanying Falcona to dinner at the Carraches, which, with Mathilde struggling to restrain the children, would have been an ordeal even on a frictionless day. At least he was spared Esther, whom her censorious friend, Leah, had taken to a lecture on women in the Bible.

'I bet it's all the boring ones,' Ruben said. 'Sarah and Rachel and Rebecca. Why don't they give a talk about Delilah and Jezebel and Gomer? She was Hosea's *wife of great whoredoms*. Did you know that, Grandmaman?'

'I'm sure she had some redeeming qualities,' Falcona replied indulgently.

'God Himself told him to marry her. I wish He'd tell me to marry a *wife of great whoredoms*.'

'Stop showing off,' Mathilde said. 'When the time comes, it will be Papa who tells you who to marry, not God. And it certainly won't be a . . . a woman of that stamp. Now be quick and wash your hands. Maryam's waiting to serve.'

Ruben's mischief-making wasn't over. At dinner, he read out a newspaper article about a Greek timber merchant's concession to chop down the trees at the base of Mount Olympus. Bella screamed that Zeus would prevent it, sending gadflies to unhorse them, just as he had done Bellerophon.

'They won't be on horseback, stupid!' Ruben said.

'Behave yourself! Why must you torment her?' Mathilde asked. 'It will only be on the lowest slopes,' she said to Bella. 'The very bottom.'

'I must write to the Sultan at once,' Bella said, jumping up from her chair. 'Will you take it to the Turkish post office in the morning?' she asked Mercado.

'Yes, of course,' he replied in surprise, as she scuttled from the room.

He was further surprised at the end of the meal, when Irène accosted him in the hall.

'We're reading *Robinson Crusoe* at school,' she said.

'You are?'

'Have you read it?'

'Years ago. I find real life more interesting than books.'

'Madame Streicher has set us an essay on the person we'd most like to be marooned with on a desert island. Who do you think I chose?'

'I honestly have no idea.'

'Guess!'

'Alexander the Great?'

'No! You . . . you, you silly!' She shook her head in frustration and ran off so fast that he wondered whether he'd heard her correctly. And if he had, what was it that she meant? How old was she? Fifteen? No, sixteen. He had been at her birthday party in January. Was she attracted to him? Or was it simply that of all the men of her acquaintance – and there couldn't be many – he was the one most likely to know how to build a shelter and catch fish?

On the carriage ride home, while Falcona fretted over Bella's fragility, he steered the conversation towards Irène.

'She feels neglected,' Falcona said. 'It's understandable. When Mathilde married Jacob, she was determined not to favour her own children over her sister's. Between ourselves, she may have tipped the scales too far the other way. As the first of the younger ones, Irène resents it more than Ruben and Bella. But you need have no worries on her account. She can look to a golden future. Whenever I read her coffee grinds, I see good things: long life, beautiful children and a large fortune.'

'How about a happy marriage?'

She stared at him strangely. 'We can't have everything.'

The next morning, with no sign of the strikers' resolve crumbling, Mercado could no longer delay notifying Jacob. He dispatched a telegraph to Paris and, an hour later, received a reply which, far from delivering the anticipated reprimand, expressed support for his position (as far as succinctness allowed). *Understood. Expected workers flex muscle during absence. SS Galant due Odessa 2 April. Full cargo vital. Settlement vital. Offer + 8 kuruş week.*

A further exchange of cables confirmed that Jacob wished the increase to be applied across the board. With a bulging order book, his sole concern was to resume production. Refusing to cede victory to Raşel, Mercado made a series of calculations. Jacob's offer of an extra eight kuruş a week across the workforce left him with eight thousand kuruş at his disposal. If he were to allocate the entire sum to the 250 men, he could give them each thirty-two kuruş, equivalent to a day and a half's wages. Moreover, he would drive a wedge between men and women as great as – if not greater than – that between workers and management, strengthening his hand for the future.

Eager to bypass the union, he summoned five of the senior men and submitted the offer. They left to put it to their *comrades* – he winced at the word – and returned within the hour, raising only token objections.

'We accept, but is it fair on the women?' the spokesman asked.

'Sorting and cutting are highly skilled jobs,' Mercado replied smoothly. 'Whereas a child can handle rolling and packing – and many do! Besides, you men remain with us all your lives, while the women leave to get married. We wish to reward your loyalty.'

'True,' the man said, 'but they may not see it that way.'

'Then it's up to you to make them – by any means necessary. Señor Carrache was adamant that his offer was only open for a day.'

Unlike Leon, he was no gambler, yet once again he was courting danger. Should the men fail to convince – or coerce – the women to return and Jacob find out that he'd disobeyed instructions, not even Falcona's intercession would save him. The next morning, he steeped himself in cologne in preparation for a gruelling day and cycled to the factory. To his profound relief, two orderly lines of workers stood at the gate, with a mere handful of agitators hovering nearby. As he approached, he noticed two women with blackened eyes, one with a split lip, and another wearing an improvised sling.

'What happened to your arm?' he asked her.

'I slipped, Señor, but I can pack just as well with one, by my life!'

'Let's hope so,' he said magnanimously. 'Don't dawdle! We have two days' output to make up.'

He spotted Raşel, skulking behind a bollard.

'Not going in?' he asked. 'You'll be late.'

'I'd rather sell my bones in Bara.'

'That's your privilege,' he said, choking back the obvious riposte. 'There are plenty of women who'll be glad of the job.'

She drew her face close to him. He strained not to shrink from her breath. 'You think you're one of them, but you'll never be . . . Señor Merchandise!' she spat, snapping her fingers. 'And when they've done with you, they'll toss you into the wolf's mouth. And I'll be there, laughing.'

'From your doorway in Bara?' he asked, with a show of nonchalance. 'Excuse me, I'm needed inside.'

He entered his office and telegraphed news of the agreement to Jacob. The following week, with the Russian shipment dispatched and production levels restored, he turned his attention to Xenia. Rather than call on her at her lodgings or arrange to meet in a café, he decided to visit the Praxidike. Its location in the city's most unsavoury district could not have been more dispiriting. The clutter of feral cats, hissing at his approach, compounded his unease. Bracing himself, he walked warily down the precipitous steps and into the musty, smoke-filled cellar. As his vision adjusted, he was startled to see four flamboyantly dressed men, bristling with weapons, who puffed on hookahs. He skirted around them, threading through the tables of drinkers and smokers (and one audible snorer) with what he trusted would pass for insouciance. Two young men, with the cropped hair and guarded gaze of newly released prisoners, returned his nod, but the rest ignored him. He ordered a glass of raki and sat, listening to the music and observing the clientele, several of whom were openly taking drugs. At one table, two middle-aged men and a boy, whom he assumed to be their catamite, sniffed powdered cocaine, and, at another, three boisterous men shared a gourd, which emitted the unmistakeable compost-like smell of hashish.

As mindful of the time as the others were oblivious to its passing, he sat nursing his drink and waiting for Xenia to appear, which at last she did, joining the musicians on the minuscule dais. With her dark tresses tumbling about her shoulders and wearing a scarlet tunic, white blouse and white bloomers, she cut a striking figure, although it was unclear whether the strip of pink flesh between blouse and bloomers was intentional or the effect of her swollen belly. Accustomed to the fanfares that heralded the performers at the Odeon music hall, he was surprised – embarrassed even – by the silence that greeted Xenia. As the trio struck up her opening song, she lifted her head to survey the room. Spotting him, she gave a visible start, followed by a quick bow, prompting the two former prisoners (the pervasive criminality had turned supposition into fact) to stare at him with a mixture of circumspection and respect.

That first song extolled the joys of hashish, drawing raucous cheers from those who were smoking it. The second lamented a girl's frenzied search across the city for the lover who'd deserted her, its cheap sentiment finding favour with an audience doubtless recalling their own jilted sweethearts. The third, more mawkish still, recounted the plight of a mother who chose to drown the children she was too destitute to feed. And although she stood next to the hookahs, snatching an occasional puff between verses, Mercado was convinced that she was aiming it at him. The fourth song, displaying her full register from metallic rasp to plaintive whine, described the pain of exile (which, if his plan succeeded, she would soon know for herself), and the fifth a woman's farewell visit to a lover condemned to hang. Halfway through, a short, malformed man leapt up and gyrated about the room, his limbs flailing so wildly that, despite himself, Mercado felt a flicker of pity and longed for one of his companions to drag him back to his seat. Then, as Xenia sang of the victim's last gasp, he stood stock-still, mimed a noose tightening around his neck and dropped his head to his chest with eerie finality.

After acknowledging the applause, Xenia joined Mercado at his table. 'I wasn't expecting to see you.'

'I have news.'

'You do?' Xenia's eyes glistened. 'Not here please. Come with me.'

She ushered him across the floor, through a torn curtain and up three steps to a cubbyhole barely bigger than a cupboard. Casks of beer and bottles of raki lined the walls, with at one end a scratched spindle chair and side table, crammed with pots of powder, rouge and lip stain, bangles and pendants, brushes and combs, a broken-handled mirror, and a prayer rope.

'This is where I dress,' Xenia said, with a sweeping gesture at the scramble of clothes on a crate.

Achingly aware of her body heat in the confined space, Mercado was desperate to escape. 'I fear I'm the bearer of bad tidings,' he said, sprinkling sensitivity like scent. 'I've received a letter from Paris. Leon won't be returning to Salonica. He's engaged - not to a French girl, as you might have supposed - but the daughter of his father's Dutch business associate. Won't you sit down?'

'No,' she said, sinking onto the chair. 'I always knew this would happen. I told him from the start that our love' - she laughed bitterly - 'was impossible. But he insisted that once his father knew me, he'd love me as much as he did.'

'Which wasn't enough.'

'Don't say that! Don't make me hate him! I could never hate him.'

'And I admire you for that. The worst that can be said of him is that he's weak ... not heartless and faithless. Not really. Just weak.'

'Is that why he stopped writing to me?'

'I presume so.'

'Did you tell him about the child?'

'Of course. But then he'd already had all your letters.'

'He promised to marry me!'

'You know that could never be.'

'Because I'm a Christian?'

'Because you're a whore.'

'What?' she screeched.

'Forgive me, but I'm only repeating his words. He could never be certain that the child was his.'

'No, you're lying! I don't believe you.'

'Men!' he declared, as if he were sexless rather than chaste.

'What am I going to do?' she asked, starting to weep.

'That's where I can help,' he said, eager to convince her of the merits of his plan. The longer she remained in the city, the greater the risk of Leon's returning and discovering his deceit. 'I haven't told you everything. I'm afraid there's worse.'

'Worse? What could possibly be worse?'

'Leon confessed everything to his father, who blames the taverna as much as you for his son's corruption—'

'What corruption? I never—'

'That's not the issue. His agents have given evidence of illegal drug activity to the Governor. They're partners in some land development scheme. No war can stand in the way of commerce! The Governor has promised him to shut this place down. Everyone involved can expect lengthy spells in Yedi Kule.'

'But not me? I'm only a singer.'

'Some of your songs, I'm afraid, could be construed as encouraging drug use ... even drumming up trade.' She moaned. 'Of course, if you're able to hire a first-class lawyer ...'

'I can't have my baby in prison!'

'Señor Carrache agrees. Which is why he's authorised me to offer you a generous settlement on condition that you leave the city permanently. It will be enough to establish you and the child back in Greece. I'd suggest you try Piraeus. A bustling port. Plenty of opportunities for a woman like you.'

'A singer,' she said coldly.

'A singer, of course. But you must make up your mind quickly. I don't expect an instant answer. Unless ... ?' His hopeful look drew no response. 'But within the next forty-eight hours. You can send word to me at the factory.'

'Very well.'

His return to the bar triggered a barrage of glares. When one of the hashish smokers spat in his path, he realised with horror what his fellow customers had pictured taking place behind the curtain. Was that Xenia's regular practice? Had he unwittingly done Leon a service? The irony was too painful to bear. His sole concern now had to be ensuring her compliance.

He cycled home furiously. Even his sweat smelt fresh after the foulness of the Praxidike. He slept so soundly that, for the first time in months, he didn't wake until the *La ilaha illa Allah* at the end of the Adhan. He performed his morning exercises and ablutions, then, judging that the moment was right, extracted two boxes from the bottom of his chest.

He made his way downstairs for breakfast.

'Is that a new tie?' asked Falcona, whose keen eyes missed nothing.

'Do you think it's too bold?'

'It's navy blue! You look dashing.'

'Wait till you see this,' he said, taking out his new pocket watch.

'Very smart,' she said, cradling it in the palm of her hand.

'It's solid gold.'

'Quite the thing for the up-and-coming young manager.'

'Interim manager.'

'Maybe just interim for the interim.' She turned the watch over. 'Oh no! Look! They've got your initials wrong. S.L.S. instead of M.L.S.'

'Have they?' he said, with a smile. 'Never mind.'

5

MATHILDE

SALONICA, OCTOBER 1912

MATHILDE TURNED AWAY from Maryam and discreetly dabbed her forehead. Even with the door propped open, the kitchen was blisteringly hot. The thick, mellow, woody aroma of boiling tomatoes wafted from the range, where Rachel stirred a large pan, while another simmered beside it. Malka sat at the table, sluggishly chopping a fresh batch of the fruit, and Maryam stood at the sink, rinsing two dozen jars, which would soon be filled, labelled and stored. She herself grated a knob of the ginger which her mother had declared the key ingredient in the cherished family recipe. The irony was that no one in the household much liked the jam, and several unopened jars were gathering dust in the cellar. Yet she made it religiously every autumn, just as her mother and grandmother and generations of Beraha women had done before her.

The porter arrived to collect the children's lunches, his rhythmic tap on the door amusing Rachel and Malka but infuriating Maryam, who ordered him to scrub his hands before touching the tightly sealed containers. It was almost noon: another morning of her life – her one and only life – had slipped past. It would shortly be time for a strained lunch with Esther, who made no secret of her discomfort at being waited on at table. At three o'clock, her cousin Elvira was coming for coffee. Then at five, the children would return from school, full of rambling stories which she would struggle to follow, while ensuring that Irène and Ruben gave the more pensive Bella a chance to speak. They would head to their rooms to do homework until the gong summoned them to dinner. Before she knew it, she'd be sending them back upstairs, accompanied by the usual grumbles from Irène, two years older than Ruben, and Ruben, two years older than Bella, about the injustice of a common bedtime. With nothing to keep her in the salon, she would soon follow suit, slipping between the cold sheets and thinking of Jacob.

She had still been in mourning for her beloved sister when Papa broke the news that she was to marry him. It was as if the Carraches held Papa liable for supplying Jacob with a defective bride and expected him to find a replacement. And as it happened, he had another daughter of marriageable age. She was horrified. She'd always liked Jacob and, from everything Irène had told her, he was a kind and considerate man. But for five years she had known him as a brother; all at once, she had to think of him as a husband. The rabbi at their betrothal ceremony even likened him to his biblical namesake, who had married two sisters, Leah and Rachel, which did little to reassure her.

Her mother asked her to honour Irène's memory by wearing her wedding dress. It fitted perfectly, which, needless to say, both families regarded as auspicious. It was a beautiful dress and, though she knew that she should be happy to give her grief-stricken mother that solace, she longed for one that was hers alone. Her friend Adela Andjel, who'd herself married a widower the previous year, complained that he constantly judged her against his dead wife. Jacob did the opposite. He revelled in her resemblance to Irène, claiming that her manner was so like her sister's that they might have been twins. When he told her that they had the same smile, she'd practised a new one, until four-year-old Leon asked why she was pulling faces. Over time, however, rather than questioning her composite identity, she had come to embrace it. She was Madame Jacob Carrache, which was distinction enough.

At long last, Jacob was returning home. The warring parties in Tripolitania had agreed to a ceasefire, and although as yet there'd been no word from the Sublime Porte, the Governor of Salonica, of his own volition, had invited the Carraches back. Mathilde saw this as evidence of his respect for Jacob, but Esther, who took a closer interest in such matters than was proper for a girl of her age (or, indeed, of any age), maintained that it was because they were associates in a property deal. 'They have their fingers in the same pie,' she said, adopting one of the vulgar expressions she'd picked up at Leah's theatre group.

Amid the joy, relief and excitement that swept through Mathilde at the prospect of Jacob's homecoming, there was a touch of dread. Until his exile eighteen months earlier, they had rarely spent more than a few days apart. They were each other's second skin, and never more so than at night. His absence would have been easier to bear had they been an orthodox couple, accustomed to a cycle of separation and reunion every month. But Jacob had never shrunk from her, either when she was bleeding or heavy with child. Her mother, who had prepared her for the marriage bed with what sounded like a series of riddles, insisted that it was a wife's duty to meet her husband's needs, as if it were no more than ensuring that he had a clean shirt every morning. Her recent hint that Mathilde must be enjoying the respite from her marital obligations could not have been further from the truth. But what of Jacob? Had he too endured eleven months of sleeping alone? Or had he sought one of the many consolations for which Paris was famed?

Like Mount Olympus for Bella, Paris had acquired an almost mythic status for Mathilde. Every June, Jacob took the family to Vichy, to the marked disapproval of his mother, who had listed the various spas within easy reach of Salonica. Attending a concert, strolling through the Parc des Sources and hearing French spoken by the locals made it the high point of Mathilde's year. But despite repeated promises, he had yet to take her to the capital. He explained that he wanted to wait until he was free of commitments and could introduce her to the city's attractions at leisure. Might one of those attractions be the lingerie model she'd seen in the latest issue of *L'Art et la Mode*? Or were she and her ilk precisely why he wished to keep her away?

Ruben's spirited 'hello' cut short her conjecture, reminding her that, whatever else, she was the mother of Jacob's children. He hurtled into the salon, followed by an equally ebullient Irène, and a moment later by Bella, who entered even the most familiar room as if for the first time.

'The gates to the Allatini house are wide open,' Ruben said. 'The guards have gone.'

'Anybody could walk in,' Irène said.

'We did,' Ruben said.

'If you both talk at once, I can't hear you.'

'The Sultan's left,' Ruben said, 'along with all his wives.'

'Don't exaggerate. There were only three.'

'His sons and his servants and his eunuchs.'

'Which is a good sign. The war's over and the whole household has returned to Constantinople.'

'Think, Maman,' Irène said, with heavy forbearance, 'why would they want him back? The new Sultan didn't even visit him when he came here last year. His own brother! He's been moved away because there's another war.'

'I told you that,' Ruben said. 'Didn't I tell you that?' he asked Bella, who ignored him. 'You should have let me tell her.'

'That's nonsense,' Mathilde replied uneasily. 'The Ottomans have sued for peace. They're signing a treaty as we speak.'

'We know that,' Ruben said impatiently. 'They've been forced to give up Tripolitania. All they're being allowed to keep are a few paltry islands in the Aegean. Islands! It's not the Italians fighting them this time but the Balkan League. That's the Serbs, the Bulgarians and the Greeks. Monsieur Dumain said that they've sniffed out the Empire's weakness, set aside their differences, and declared war.'

'He shouldn't have discussed it with you,' said Mathilde, fearful that this new conflict would delay Jacob's return.

'Why not, when it's the truth?' Ruben said. 'Teachers are supposed to tell us the truth.'

'So are parents,' Irène added.

'Well, this parent's telling you to take off your coats. If you're hungry, ask Maryam for some honey cakes. Then go upstairs and do your homework. You don't want Papa to think you've been slacking.'

'You don't want Papa to think you've let us slack,' Irène said pertly.

'Very clever, but not very kind,' Mathilde replied. 'What is it, Bella?' she asked her younger daughter, who was gazing into the garden.

'Has Esther had a baby?'

'Whatever do you mean?' Mathilde asked, joining her at the window.

'Mad!' Ruben said. 'She gets worse every day.'

'It's all very well for you,' Irène said. 'You've never had to share a room with her.'

Mathilde kissed the crown of Bella's head. 'No, of course not. Don't be silly,' she said, comforted nonetheless by her innocence. 'She's just holding him. It's Rosa's baby. Don't you remember? She left to get married last winter. She's come back to see us.'

She swallowed her annoyance at Esther, who'd brought mother and child to spend the day without so much as a by-your-leave or a thought for the example it set to her sisters, to say nothing of the two impressionable maids.

'Can I hold him too?'

'Go and ask. I'm sure she won't mind, as long as you're gentle. What about you, Irène?'

'I may as well. It's useful experience,' she replied, following her sister through the French doors.

'And you?' Mathilde asked Ruben.

'Babies are for girls.'

'Boys have a part to play too,' she said, glancing apprehensively at the down on his upper lip.

'Not this one,' Ruben said, clomping towards the kitchen.

Although the children's information was correct, the fresh outbreak of hostilities didn't disrupt Jacob's return. He telegraphed the news of the Governor's invitation on 18 October and booked a sleeping car for himself and Leon, scheduled to arrive in Salonica three days later. That morning, Mathilde packed the children off to school and, unable to settle, wandered the house, adjusting ornaments and almost knocking over a Meissen candleholder when she twisted it round to favour a reclining shepherd. After an interminable lunch during which Esther, as if sensing her agitation, was uncharacteristically chatty, she installed herself at an upstairs window and kept watch on the drive.

In mid-afternoon, a trolley trundled up, loaded not only with cases and trunks but with crates of Parisian purchases. One of the porters handed her a note in which Jacob scribbled that he was paying his respects to his father and would call in at the factory and bank but be home in time for tea. She strove to quell her disappointment, telling herself that he was right to put duty first. The visits meant that the children returned before he did. Fearing that they would clutter the pristine rooms – and intrude on the marital reunion – she dispatched them, protesting, into the garden, her paean to the virtues of fresh air undermined by the overcast sky.

Just when she'd decided to call them indoors, she heard the scrape of carriage wheels on the gravel, followed by the scuffle of feet on the front steps, which Jacob bounded up like a man ten . . . twenty . . . thirty years his junior.

'Mathilde!' he exclaimed breathlessly, clasping her to his chest and kissing her. 'You haven't changed a bit,' he added, looking her up and down as intently as her dressmaker.

'How could I on my own?' The uneventfulness of her life at last felt like a blessing. 'You, on the other hand . . .' she said, registering the strange pair of spectacles without sidepieces propped precariously on the bridge of his nose, and the high starched collar with protruding wings, which served to conceal his jowls.

'Papa!' Esther cried from the top of the stairs, sweeping down them as if on a stage before yielding to her emotions and running to kiss him.

'Who is this elegant young lady? Where's the gawky girl I left behind?'

Esther blushed, and Mathilde prayed that he would approve of the rest of her transformation. She summoned the younger children and, after the initial flurry of embraces, followed by an awkward moment when he struggled to lift Bella, Jacob led them to his study for the distribution of gifts.

For Irène and Bella, he'd bought matching powder-blue frocks with ruffled bodices, large bows and tiered skirts from Paquin 'the most chic couturier in Paris'. Setting aside their reluctance to be coupled ('like bookends', Irène had once complained), it was clear at a glance that both garments were too small. Mathilde forestalled the girls' objections by invoking Madame Naar's wizardry with a needle. The dress he'd chosen for Esther was more exotic: purple and gold silk, with an irregular geometric pattern and fur-trimmed sleeves, based on a design for the Russian ballet. Thankfully, the theatrical association eclipsed her growing distaste for anything she regarded as frippery. Ruben, who dreaded presents of clothes, was thrilled to be given the manual for the latest Labor racing bicycle, which was being shipped from France. Mathilde barely had time to reflect on the potential perils when Jacob handed her a velvet box. She opened it to reveal an emerald and diamond pendant on a white gold chain.

'No,' she said, clutching her throat as if she could already feel the chain. 'This is too much. You should give it to your mother.'

'Nonsense. It's no more than you deserve. Isn't that right, children?'

'She definitely deserves it more than Grandmaman,' Esther said.

Jacob insisted that she wore it that evening, when it drew a pursed-lipped 'Very pretty' from her mother-in-law, who shared Esther's horror of extravagance, albeit for different reasons. Her father-in-law remained at home, his health having declined so markedly that even an intimate gathering exhausted him. Her mother arrived, accompanied by Mercado, whose presence had an unsettling effect on the usually self-possessed Irène. Her blushes and simpers betrayed a fondness for him which, to Mathilde's relief, showed no sign of being reciprocated. Notwithstanding his kindness to her mother, she felt an instinctive mistrust of the man and regretted having welcomed him into the family circle. Besides, however much he admired his proficiency, Jacob would never permit him to marry one of his daughters. She must speak to Irène before she was hurt.

'Here we all are, together again,' her mother said, as they sat down to eat, 'except for your Leon,' she said to Regina, who gave her a long-suffering smile, 'and my Leon,' she said, at which Regina's smile soured.

'Didn't he take the train with you, Jacob?' she asked.

'Yes of course. I knew better than to leave him in Paris on his own! But he had to meet a friend . . . some urgent business,' he added, seeing her frown.

'Understandable,' her mother said. 'At his age, he'll want to catch up with his friends before his family.'

'Is that so?' Regina asked. 'I care nothing for my own sake, but I'd have thought he'd have had the courtesy to visit his grandfather.'

'I'll make sure he calls round first thing in the morning,' Jacob said.

'Too late!'

Bella's knife clattered to the floor.

'Leave it,' Jacob said, as she leant to retrieve it.

'But it's just—'

'Leave it for the maid.' He motioned to Rachel, who slid between the chairs and under the table.

'Ow!' she yelped, backing out. 'My head!'

Mathilde trusted that she was alone in seeing Ruben pinch her bottom.

'We must be on our guard,' her mother said. 'A dropped knife heralds a quarrel.'

'Really, Falcona,' Regina said, 'must you fill the children's heads with fairy tales?'

'Not mine,' Ruben said. 'I'm living in the twentieth century.'

'Fate is fate,' her mother said. 'It will be the same come the thirtieth century.'

'Except that there'll be no knives . . . and certainly no dinner tables,' Mercado said. 'I read once that in a hundred years' time, people will live on pastilles. A single one will feed them for weeks.'

'I want one!' Ruben said. 'No more boring meals.'

'Not that I read that sort of thing now. Or any sort of thing, really,' Mercado added, as if afraid that Jacob would judge him frivolous. 'I was just a boy.'

The exchange was interrupted by Leon's arrival. Travel-stained and unkempt, he ignored everyone but Mercado. 'I've been looking for you all day,' he said, in a strangely pinched voice. 'We have to talk.'

'You forget yourself!' Jacob said. 'Where are your manners?' As if catching sight of the company, Leon ran his fingers through his hair and moved to Regina, who grimaced at his kiss.

'Did they have no soap on the train?' she asked.

'I'm sorry. I've been rushing all over the city.'

'Not in your grandfather's direction.'

'It's very remiss of me, I know . . . You look well, Grandmaman.' He bent to kiss his other grandmother, who petted his perspiring cheek, then crossed to kiss Mathilde. 'Maman.'

'Have you eaten?' she asked. 'Rachel, fetch Señor Leon a plate of fish.'

'I don't want any food!' He took a deep breath. 'Not now, thank you.'

'Not until he's had a chance to wash,' Regina said.

'Not until he's greeted his adored sisters and brother, whom he hasn't set eyes on for almost a year,' Esther interjected tartly.

'I know, I'm sorry . . . Later . . . Mercado, I really need to speak to you.'

'Yes, of course. What is it?'

'In private.'

'Let Mercado eat his food before it gets cold,' her mother said.

'I'm sorry to disturb you all. I really am,' he said, fixing his gaze on Mercado. 'But it's a matter of life and death. I'm looking for a musician friend . . . he - yes, he - used to play in a taverna near the port.'

'Oh, I wouldn't go into one of those, dear heart,' her mother said. 'You hear such dreadful things.'

'That's just it. I can't! It's been boarded up. Did the Governor introduce new laws while we were away?'

'Let's not spoil everyone's meal,' Mercado said, following Leon out with a pointed glance at Jacob. At a nod from Mathilde, Rachel started to clear the plates, when Malka burst into the room.

'Beg pardon, Señora, Señor . . . beg pardon, but there's a giant bird . . . a monster, giant bird flying over the mountain.'

'It's Zeus turned into a swan!' Bella dashed to the window and slipped behind the curtain.

'She's unhinged!' Ruben said, squeezing in beside her, as Mathilde wondered whether Bella believed half the stories she concocted or if they were a stratagem to keep the world at bay. 'It's a flying machine. A flying machine coming here. Look!' He tore the curtains open.

'Will you both sit down!' Jacob thundered, in a voice that would have given Zeus pause. 'I'm beginning to think I've come home to a madhouse.'

'No wonder when Bella lives here,' Ruben said.

'Sit down now!'

'Your children are not conducive to sound digestion,' Regina said to Mathilde.

'It must be a Greek or Serbian pilot on a reconnaissance mission,' Ruben said, as he and Bella returned reluctantly to the table.

'And you're glad about that?' Jacob asked incredulously.

'It's the first flying machine that's ever come to the city.'

'What if that pilot is preparing the way for an invasion?' Jacob said. 'There'll be bloodshed on the streets, where for years we've lived in harmony.'

'Please Lord, don't let it disrupt the play!' Esther murmured.

'What play?' Jacob asked sharply.

Esther looked startled at having spoken aloud.

'I'll tell you about it later,' said Mathilde, who had been waiting for the right moment to broach the subject. As much as she'd longed for his return, the one – the only – reason for wanting a brief postponement was for the play to be safely over.

'I've joined Leah's drama group,' Esther said, taking it upon herself to explain. 'We've been rehearsing Molière's *L'Avare* since March. The performances are next week.'

'At the school?' Jacob asked.

'The producer's an Alliance teacher,' Esther said, sidestepping his more contentious affiliation.

'It's for charity,' Mathilde said. 'Which is why I gave my consent.'

'Where's it being staged? The Union Park or the Eden?'

'Neither,' Esther replied hesitantly. 'The Paradise Hall.'

'Rachel, will you serve the *bourekas*?' Mathilde said.

'Isn't that a workers' club?' Jacob asked. 'The Socialist Federation or some such outfit?'

'Forget the Greeks and the Serbs,' Regina said, waving away the dish. 'The reds are the ones who'll bring carnage to the streets.'

'What's wrong with our playing there?' Esther asked defiantly. 'Are only the notables allowed to be philanthropic?'

'How dare you talk back to your father!' Regina said.

'I wouldn't mind if she were talking sense,' Jacob said. 'There's no question of your acting in that hall. And that's that.'

'They'll never find another Marianne in a week!'

'That's their problem.'

'Maybe since the opening's so close . . .' Mathilde said.

'And whose fault is that?' Jacob asked.

'You're worse than Harpagon,' Esther said.

'Who?'

'The father – the tyrant – in the play.' She broke down in tears. 'We've been so happy here without you. Why did you have to come home?'

'Apologise to Papa at once,' Mathilde said. 'You don't mean that.'

'Yes, I do. Every word.'

'Come with me, dear heart,' her mother said, casting a reproachful look at Mathilde. 'You're just upsetting yourself. Let's go and wipe your face.'

'I wish I'd never been born,' Esther whimpered, as her mother led her away.

'Well, that was a performance and a half,' Jacob said. 'No need to go to the theatre. How could you have agreed to it?' he asked Mathilde.

'I know how much you admire Molière.'

'At least it's in French,' Regina said. 'Which rules out the rabble.'

'No, it's in Ladino,' Irène interjected. 'I've been helping Esther learn her lines.'

'But it's Molière!' Jacob said.

'They've translated it. So that the rabble understand,' Irène said, with a smirk.

'It's not fair,' Ruben said. 'We're forbidden to speak a word of Ladino at school. They give us detention if they catch us. Monsieur Bruton threw the board rubber at Henri in geography.'

'You see,' Bella said. 'Grandmaman Falcona told us there'd be a quarrel. She was right.'

Mathilde insisted that a frank exchange of views did not constitute a quarrel, but Regina's harrumph, Irène's snort and, most of all, Jacob's silence refuted her. Regina consoled Jacob on the state of his homecoming (and, implicitly, Mathilde suspected, on the state of his home). The children wolfed down their puddings, and even Ruben declined a second *boureka*. When her mother and Mercado returned from their respective charges, the visitors left and the children went to bed. With the evening's tensions clinging to them like burrs, Mathilde and Jacob made their way upstairs. While he disappeared into the bathroom, locking the door with newfound modesty, she sat at her dressing table and unfastened her necklace, the emerald seeming to stare at her in reproach. She took her turn in the bathroom, lingering over her toilette, before slipping into bed, where he was annotating a report, his spectacles perched more perilously than ever. No sooner had she lain down than, to her dismay, she found herself sobbing.

Jacob removed his spectacles and leant towards her. He kissed and caressed her face and breasts, before lifting her nightgown and pressing his lips to her thighs. She wrapped him in her arms and felt the distance between them dissolve. She quivered and moaned; he panted and laughed; and in the phrase that had baffled her as a girl, they 'made up on the pillow'.

The next day, he had an early meeting with the Governor, who, confirming Esther's suspicions, was eager to discuss a building project on the last parcel of land that Jacob's father and uncle had bought after the demolition of the city walls. The plans, finalised after years of obfuscation from the Sublime Porte, had been stalled by the fighting in Tripolitania, and now faced further delays following the Balkan League's declaration of war. Moreover, the Sultan's repayment of a loan from the Carrache bank, which was crucial to the project's finance, would be in jeopardy if Salonica were to fall into enemy hands. Indeed, Oncle Lazar and Nissim reckoned that the Governor's haste to bring them home was in order to raise funds to bolster the city's defences.

After Jacob's departure, Mathilde luxuriated in bed while Maryam brought her the first cup of coffee of the day. She savoured each bittersweet drop before heading downstairs to supervise the younger children's breakfast and wave them off to school. She longed to check on Esther, but, with her door firmly shut and an ominous silence in place of the muffled Ladino speeches of recent weeks, she lost heart and, instead, looked in on Leon.

'Good morning,' she whispered as, her knock drawing no reply, she entered the musty room.

'No need to creep about. I'm wide awake.'

'So why are you lying here in the dark?' she asked, opening the curtains to reveal his shrouded shape on the bed.

'What's the point of getting up?'

'How about breakfast?'

'Sheep, goats, cattle: all eat. So what else?'

'Go upstairs and talk to Esther. She's very upset about ... I'll leave her to explain. Besides, you haven't seen each other in almost a year.'

'Ten years would be too soon for her.'

'Don't be ridiculous! She's your sister.'

'That doesn't mean we have anything to say to each other.'

'What about me then? Have you nothing to say to me? I can tell something's troubling you.'

'You wouldn't understand.'

'I'm not your grandmother! In your last letter, you wrote that you were desperate to come home.'

'So I was, but everything's changed.'

'I don't und—' she faltered. 'I've no wish to pry, but did you meet a girl in Paris?'

'Why Paris? Why must it always be Paris? Are there no girls here?'

She thought back to the friction between Leon and Jacob in the autumn. She had presumed it was a question of money and resolved not to interfere. What if it had concerned an ill-suited attachment?

'So were there ... girls – a girl – in Salonica?'

'Yes ... yes. The most wonderful girl in the world.' His eyes glistened with both joy and sorrow. 'She was a nobody ... a shopgirl. That's right, she worked in a shop. Not Carrache material, of course. But we fell in love ... swore that it was the real thing. When I left for France, we wrote to each other every week. I longed to hear her voice – her voice was special ... truly special. But how, in this godforsaken city, with barely a telephone to its name? Then she stopped writing. A well-meaning friend told me she'd gone home to nurse her dying mother. But that's not true. It turns out she's met someone else and run off with him. She's having his baby.'

'The musician?'

'What?'

'The man she met: was he the musician you were searching for last night?'

'Oh, what does it matter!'

'You're right, it doesn't. I know that it hurts, and I'll do anything I can to help. But you must realise that it was never going to last. You'd have had to say goodbye eventually, when your father found you a bride.'

'I shall never marry.'

'Of course you will. And it'll be someone who'll stay true to you for life.'

'You're making it worse!' He threw his head back on the pillow and pulled the covers over it. 'Just leave me alone!'

Stung by his rebuff, she made her way to the kitchen to alert Maryam to the stream of visitors arriving to welcome the returning exiles. Regina and Tante Amada were planning a formal celebration at the Club des Intimes, but they were waiting for Haim, who had been detained in France. In recent months he'd undergone a radical transformation. Having taken no interest in any of the family enterprises, he'd been persuaded by a young silk manufacturer to invest in a factory in Lyon. Jacob was as scathing about his brother's late-life entrepreneurship as he had been about his lifelong aimlessness. 'As if there aren't enough silk factories in Lyon already!' he complained to Mathilde. 'The difference, according to Haim's new partner (a smooth operator if ever I saw one), is that he's employing the brightest young artists from the Left Bank to create his fabrics.'

'What Left Bank?' Mathilde asked.

'It's the Vardar of Paris. They can't sell their paintings, so what makes him think he'll sell their designs? He seems to have bewitched

Haim. He won't listen to reason. There's nothing we can do, short of having him declared incapable.'

'You wouldn't!'

'It did cross my mind. Then I thought of Papa . . . the scandal. And I suppose he has the right to do as he pleases with his own money – that is, the money he inherited from Grandpapa.'

Mathilde longed for him to extend the same indulgence to Esther. Yet, despite her tears and tantrums and refusal to eat, and despite the pleas from her sisters and brothers, with even Leon reminding him of their visits to *Tartuffe* and *L'École des Femmes* at the Comédie Française, Jacob wouldn't budge. Leah wrote him an impassioned letter, citing a Shakespeare play in which a browbeaten Jewish girl abandoned her home to live with her lover, and begging him not to force Esther to make a similar choice.

'What lover? What choice? Does she think she'll induce me to allow my daughter to act by naming an unnatural daughter in another play?' Jacob asked, ripping up the letter.

Relief came from an unexpected quarter. Mercado showed Jacob a pamphlet, circulating in the factory, which alleged that he would rather sacrifice his own daughter – a latter-day Louise Michel – than let her side with the workers. Beneath a fuzzy silhouette of a bonneted woman, which looked to have been stencilled from a Stein Palace catalogue, it reported that, even though he was keeping Esther locked up and half starved, he had failed to break her spirit. Jacob, outraged as much by the impudence as the calumny, proposed to ignore it, but Mercado, on whose advice he increasingly relied, convinced him of the need to disprove it by permitting Esther to perform.

Esther's revival on hearing the news was so abrupt that, had she not spent three days sobbing in her room, Mathilde might have thought she was shamming. Within the hour, she'd sent word of her reprieve to Leah and enlisted the ever-obliging Irène to practise her lines. Taking a basket of provisions for the cast, which for once Maryam didn't begrudge them, she passed the evening rehearsing, returning to announce that she'd reserved seats for the entire family at the last of the three performances.

'Why not the first?' Bella asked.

'I'll be nervous enough without knowing that you'll all be watching me. I want you to see me at my best.'

Mathilde suspected that the real reason was Esther's fear that, if her father disapproved of the first performance, he would put a stop to the second and third. Nonetheless, she was looking forward to it. As a girl, she had read Molière's plays with relish, even *Dom Juan*, which she'd sneaked from her father's shelves after her teacher banned it from the classroom, yet she had never seen a single one on stage. In recent years, several French theatre companies had visited Salonica, and a Viennese troupe brought operetta to the White Tower. She'd watched scenes from Marivaux and Racine at her friends' receptions and heard airs from *The Merry Widow* and *The Dollar Princess* at her own. But Regina considered it improper for women to be present at public entertainment, a rule that she'd dared to flout in Vichy but not at home.

Regina's refusal to attend her granddaughter's debut – and, as Jacob drily remarked, valedictory – performance was a blessing. Leon also declined the invitation, and Mathilde argued that it would be unfair to press him – not least to Esther, whom he was bound to offend with either an empty compliment or a self-absorbed silence. The three younger children were going, despite their father's reservations, along with her mother and Mercado, whom Esther now regarded as her champion. The seven-strong party required two carriages and, if their silk dresses and tailored suits weren't enough to mark them out from the sea of coarse woollen skirts and shapeless trousers, their mode of transport was. Their arrival sparked a cacophony of catcalls and derisive cheers, which alarmed Bella and enraged Jacob.

Mathilde sought to distract him from the large red banners flanking the entrance, emblazoned with the words *Socialist Federation*, but her assumption that they would deter any of her acquaintances was confounded when she was hailed in the vestibule by Joya Kastro.

'My dear!' she cried. 'What an adventure! I haven't felt this out of place since Monsieur Diehl showed us the Byzantine mosaics he'd uncovered in the Ayasofya.'

'How did you hear about the play?' Mathilde asked, striving to conceal her disquiet.

'Your Esther told my Esther. She and Albert are already in their seats. I stayed behind in the hope of catching you. I must admit I was surprised – stunned, you might say – that you'd allowed her to take part at all, let alone with a group of anarchists. Albert says they're biding their time until they set up a guillotine in Liberty Square. But I told him that Mathilde Carrache's stamp of approval was enough for me. You must have a very accommodating husband lined up for her. I've been racking my brains to think who it might be.' Mathilde forced a smile. 'Still, we mustn't linger. Heaven knows what they'll do to us if we're late!'

More apprehensive than ever, Mathilde rejoined her family, taking a seat whose very rigidity felt like a reproof. The curtain rose on a plain, poorly furnished room, which struck her as perfect for Harpagon, a man who preferred to accumulate wealth than to spend it. Jacob, however, thought otherwise. 'Ridiculous!' he huffed. 'How could they be so lax? Not one of those chairs dates from the seventeenth century!' It soon became clear that the choice of furniture was neither anachronistic nor random since, in addition to being translated into the idiom of their city, the play had been transposed into its world.

'What on earth! She never mentioned this,' Jacob muttered to Mathilde, prompting a loud 'Shush' that made him seethe.

Although the audience greeted the local references with knowing laughter, Mathilde took issue with the transposition. Even with the shift in social attitudes, it would be impossible for a notable's daughter such as Élise (played with rouged cheeks and ringlets by a barely recognisable Leah) to meet secretly – much less exchange vows – with her father's steward. And while the Salonican Harpagon, played by the head waiter at the Café Bekchinar (an establishment she had hitherto regarded as exemplary), kept faith with the original character, he domineered his workers as well as his servants, which was savage rather than comic.

Esther's entrance instantly captured her attention. Betraying no trace of nervousness, she delivered her lines with a passion and poise which, in other circumstances, would augur well for a career on the stage. She – or, rather, Marianne – was in love with Harpagon's son, Cléante, but Harpagon had his own designs on her – or, rather, her estate. After their first meeting, in which she was repulsed by both Harpagon's appearance and manner, La Flèche, a revolutionary posing as Cléante's valet, informed the highly partisan audience that 'capitalism poisons all human relationships'.

That neatly packaged moral concluded the first half. Mathilde, eager to avoid Joya, and Jacob, eager to avoid Albert, stayed in their seats while Ruben and Mercado went to the foyer for refreshments. They returned with glasses of apple tea and lemonade, and a plate of *marochinos*, which put Jacob in a better mood for the second half. It was swiftly dispelled. After two slapstick scenes, in which first Harpagon and then Valère rained down blows on the cook, La Flèche stepped forward to declaim another maxim: that young or old, the rich were as one in exploiting the poor. He then conspired with Frosine, a matchmaker and clandestine activist, to organise a strike at Harpagon's factory. Harpagon appealed to the Governor to order the workers' return, only to be told that no authority on earth had the right to prevent a man withdrawing his labour.

Left with an unfulfilled order from the Sultan, Harpagon sank into despair. La Flèche and Frosine, showing their true colours, promised to call off the strike on condition that he consented to Valère's marriage to Élise and Cléante's to Marianne, doubled the workers' wages and gave them all a month's paid holiday. With the rest of the company clustered around him, La Flèche assured the audience that he hadn't grown soft. While he was happy to see true love prevail, his primary concern remained the common good. Addressing the four lovers, he advised them to enjoy their honeymoons, since, on their return, they would be stripped of their privilege and set to work alongside everyone else. At this, Harpagon threw his head in his hands, La Flèche kissed Frosine, Valère kissed Élise and, to Mathilde's horror, Cléante kissed Marianne.

The curtain fell to clamorous applause, rising again to reveal the cast lined up to bow (which exposed the immodesty of Esther's bodice). Jacob sat clenching his hands, and Mathilde felt the heat radiating from him. The curtain fell for a third and final time and, while an ardent coterie clapped and stamped, the rest of the audience made for the exit.

'Wait!' Jacob called to Ruben, who was hustling Bella into the aisle. 'Remember who you are!' He turned to Mathilde. 'Are we supposed to meet Esther here, or will she be leading a mob to burn down the bank and the factory?'

'It was a play, Jacob.'

'So I thought. Molière . . . for charity . . . in support of workers' education. Well, what did they learn tonight?'

'That freedom is a right, not a gift,' Bella replied.

'Not now, Bella,' Mathilde said.

'But Papa asked what they'd learnt. That's what the man with the brown teeth told us.'

'Not now, dear . . . She thought we might like to go to the changing room and be introduced to the cast.'

'How kind! Perhaps we should invite them back to dine?'

'Yes,' Bella said.

'No!' Jacob retorted. 'Your grandmother and Mercado will take you children home. Mathilde, fetch Esther from wherever it is she changes. I intend to wait in the carriage.'

'Irène, you stay with Papa,' Mathilde said, anxious to avert any more doting glances at Mercado.

'That's not fair!'

'It'll give the others more space.'

A diffident young man led Mathilde down a warren of murky corridors to the women's dressing room, scowling as he declined the proffered tip. Finding to her relief that the room was full of visitors, she crossed unnoticed to Esther, who was deep in conversation with Leah.

'Maman,' she said, clasping her clammily. 'What did you think? Did you like it? Tell me the truth.'

'You were very ... yes, of course. I don't know how you remembered all those lines.'

To her surprise, both women laughed.

'Where's everyone else?' Esther asked.

'Grandmaman took Bella and Ruben home. Papa's waiting with Irène in the carriage. So gather your things and come along.'

'But the cast are having a party.'

'Not tonight, Esther. Papa's very ... tired.'

'Did Monsieur Carrache enjoy the play?' Leah asked coolly.

'You'll have to ask him yourself. He was taken aback by the adaptation.'

'But he always advocates fresh approaches ... urges us not to be slaves to convention.'

'Not to be slaves, no. But not to be saboteurs either.'

'Well, to quote another of his favourite expressions, we must agree to differ.'

'That's one thing at the dinner table, quite another on a public stage, when his own daughter makes a mockery of everything he holds dear,' Mathilde said, angered by Leah's disingenuousness. 'Hurry up, Esther! We must go.'

Esther said a perfunctory goodbye to her companions and led the way back through the hall. Mathilde tried to prepare her for her father's reaction, but she underestimated the intensity of his rage. The moment they stepped inside the carriage, he signalled to the coachman to set off. As they drove through the sombre streets in silence, she sensed Esther choking back her tears. In an effort to console her, she turned to Irène. 'You thought Esther was very good, didn't you?'

'Were you meant to drop the key at the end?'

'Nobody noticed,' Mathilde said.

'I noticed,' Irène insisted, as silence descended once more.

'What did you think of the play, Papa?' Esther asked, with a catch in her voice.

'Is that a serious question? I was humiliated. You insulted me . . . you insulted Molière . . . then you insulted yourself by kissing that young man.'

'That wasn't me, Papa, it was Marianne.'

'Did you hear that, Mathilde, did you?'

'Try not to upset yourself!'

'I didn't steal that purse, Monsieur; it was my right hand! Are you stupid as well as shameless?'

Esther's tears flowed freely now. 'It wasn't just me. Everyone kissed at the end.'

'I don't give a fig for anyone else. They can kiss each other till their lips bleed. It's you I care about. What will people say?'

'It was the Paradise Hall, Jacob. Nobody we know will have seen it,' Mathilde said.

'How about Albert Kastro and his wife? And who knows who might have come on the previous two nights? They were promised a light-hearted comedy . . . a piece of buffoonery, not some travesty where they're denounced as ruthless exploiters. These are the very people who've brought wealth to this city – and work to the ingrates who sat there cheering.'

'Don't you think that, given the chance, they might find work for themselves?' Esther asked.

'No, to be frank. No! And you and your friends do them no favours by encouraging them to strike.'

'Mercado broke the strike at the factory all by himself,' Irène said. 'He had a plan to dress up some small men as Turkish women so you could only see their eyes and . . . I don't remember the rest.'

'How vile!' Esther said, her distaste for him resurfacing.

'Mercado has this family's interests at heart,' Jacob replied, 'which is more than can be said for some of my children.'

'This family's interests can be summed up in one word,' Esther said. 'Money! And who invented it? The Babylonians. The same people who forced the ancient Israelites into slavery.'

'I suppose it's Leah Sagues who gave you that nugget of information.'

'No, Maurice Saltiel,' Esther replied truculently.

'Maurice who?'

'The man Esther kissed at the end,' Irène said. Mathilde shot her a look, which was lost in the dark.

'Shameful!' Jacob exclaimed.

'So you said, but the true shame is the condition in which half the population of Salonica is forced to live.'

'What condition? What do you know about it?'

'I've been to Vardar.'

'When? Did you give her permission?' Jacob asked Mathilde.

'She went to visit Rosa.'

'Another name that means nothing to me.'

'One of the maids. She left to have a baby.'

'Is it Leon's?' Jacob asked hoarsely.

'No!' Mathilde said.

'No!' Esther echoed. 'Is that all that worries you: that we might be implicated? Well, we already are. There are people sleeping ten or twelve to a room. Remember how Irène complained when she had to share with Bella in Vichy?'

'I'd like to see you try it! She spent half the night staring out of the window.'

'Their homes are insanitary,' Esther continued. 'No wonder there was another cholera outbreak this spring!'

'And you went there? If you choose to put yourself at risk, that's your affair, but you've no right to endanger anybody else. No family has done more than ours to improve the lives of the poor in this city. Who is the new wing of the hospital named after? Your great-grandmother.'

'That's just papering over the cracks.'

'No doubt that's this Maurice again.'

'No, it's me. I have a brain. I am able to think for myself.'

'Would you like me to give away everything I possess? How would you feel if I had no money for your dowry?'

'Ecstatic!'

'That's enough, Esther,' Mathilde said. 'You shouldn't talk to your father like that.'

'Such ingratitude! After everything your mother and I have done for you.'

'Stepmother! She's my stepmother. Why can't you be honest about anything?'

Mathilde felt as though a rod had fallen from the carriage roof and struck her in the face.

'She's your aunt as well, so she's two things,' said Irène, punctilious as ever, while Jacob, either mindful of Mathilde's hurt or furious at Esther's defiance, fell silent.

Reaching home, Esther ran straight to her room, without a word to Maryam, who had waited up for a report on the performance. Mathilde sent Irène to bed and checked on Ruben, already asleep, and Bella, who was writing her journal. Although she longed to rest, she went down to the salon, where Jacob, wreathed in cigar smoke, sat leafing through a volume of Molière.

'You know I've always supported education for girls as well as boys,' he said, shutting the book. 'A skilled workforce is essential for a strong economy. But it can be taken too far. "I am able to think for myself." You heard her! I dread to think how my father would have reacted if either of my sisters had said that to him.'

'Times have changed, and you're not your father.'

'No, but I won't be played for a fool. The truth is that she hasn't thought for herself since Mademoiselle Sagues arrived.'

'You approved her appointment.'

'And in fairness to her, she's proved her worth. She's raised standards – of conduct as well as learning. But she's achieved all she can here. She needs a fresh challenge. I shall convene my fellow governors and propose that we ask the Alliance directors to transfer her to a school in a less advanced city – Edirne or Damascus, perhaps – where her talents would be put to better use.'

'Esther won't thank you.'

'That will no longer be an issue. How old were you when we married?'

'Nineteen,' she said, saddened that he needed to ask.

'And Irène was seventeen. Esther's already eighteen. What does that tell you?'

'Do you have someone in mind for her?'

'Among the guests at the Ritz was Alfred Henriques, a cotton manufacturer with one of the largest mills in Europe.'

'And he's a bachelor?'

'He's older than me!'

'A widower?'

'He has a wife, who's very much alive, two sons and a daughter, Milly . . . Molly . . . something. She's at a finishing school in Fontainebleau. They were there to visit her.'

'But what's that to do with Esther?'

'The sons are both in their early twenties. Basil and Felix, charming young men, personable . . . presentable. They work for their father, though they spend every spare minute motor racing.'

'Surely that's dangerous?'

'Which is why Henriques is anxious to see them settled. When I mentioned Esther, he said she sounded like the answer to his prayers.'

'But there are two of them!'

'So she'll have a choice. Isn't that what I've always promised her? They got on splendidly with Leon. I've invited them to stay.'

'And they're French?'

'Not at all. When did I say that? They're English, though the family comes from Aleppo. They live in Manchester.'

'Where's that? In England?'

[112]

'Don't you remember? Maman's cousins, the Moïse Koens, moved there from Ruschuk twenty years ago.'

'I meant where on the map.'

'Isn't family the only map we need?'

6

RUBEN

SALONICA, OCTOBER 1912

SLEEP BROUGHT LITTLE solace to Ruben. As a boy, he had suffered nightly assaults from mythical beasts and demons and, worse, shapeshifting family and friends. Now, the monsters and fiends had been replaced by sirens, whose ravishments left him drained, with no more control over his body than a baby. Scarcely a day dawned when he wasn't confronted by the evidence of his frailty, and this one was no exception. He tentatively slipped his hand down the bed, snatching it back, sticky and, in a painful irony, smelling like the laundry blue the maids used to whiten the sheets. At a rap on the door, he hurriedly wiped it on his nightgown. 'Come in!' he called, praying that it was Malka rather than Rachel, since, in a transformation that made no sense, the girl he scorned and taunted during the day consumed his fantasies at night.

He blamed his best friend, Ephraim, who, after their Greek classmate, Platon, impugned Turkish virility, told them of a sultan – Ahmed I – who'd fathered a son at fourteen. Their history teacher Monsieur Dumain grimly corroborated the story, adding that his death from typhus at the early age of twenty-seven showed that precocious passion had sapped his strength, and the key to a long and healthy life was youthful continence. But while the waking Ruben concurred, the sleeping Ruben found himself summoning Rachel from his harem and ordering her to strip naked, before burying his face in her breasts, which were fuller and softer than he'd imagined. When she refused to lick his toes, he instructed a eunuch to drown her in a barrel of boiling oil. But, as he had already discovered, the punishment was his.

His prayer went unanswered, since Rachel entered and set down a bowl of water on the washstand, before opening the curtains.

'It's all right for some,' she said, with a brazenness that confirmed Ruben's worst fears. While she might not be able to read his thoughts (he made sure to greet her with a scowl), she and Malka were the ones who changed his sheets. He had begged Maman to let him do it himself, claiming that Monsieur Bruton had recommended it to the class as a useful discipline. Looking quizzical, she agreed, but Maryam, to whom she deferred almost as routinely as she did to Papa, pronounced it unseemly. At least during the summer, the residue dried overnight, imperceptible to the eye if not the touch, but in the autumn, the air was damp and so was the sheet. He had twice spilt a glass of water on the mattress, but not even the dimmest maid would be fooled a third time. Was it worse to be mocked for wetting the bed or for sullying it?

'Does Señor have everything he wants?' she asked, her posture a deliberate provocation.

'Go away,' he replied, just as Maman appeared at the door.

'Still in bed, sleepyhead?' she asked. 'It's high time you were up. And Rachel has work to do.'

'Señora,' Rachel said, bobbing as she left the room.

'Come on, or you'll be late for school.'

'Will you pass me my dressing gown?' he asked, mortified by the reflex Rachel had triggered.

'You must get ready.'

'I need to use the closet . . . and I'm cold,' he said plaintively.

'Here then, you silly boy,' she said, handing it to him with a kiss on his brow. 'Now hurry up.'

She left and he jumped out of bed, wrapping the gown around

him, the cord double-knotted for good measure. After washing and dressing, he headed down to the breakfast room, entering alongside Bella.

'Did you sleep well, darling?' Maman asked her.

'Like a baby.'

'How do you know?' Ruben said. 'My memory's easily as good as yours, and I don't remember anything before I was four.'

'Eat your breakfast,' Papa said, from behind his newspaper. 'Leave your sister in peace.'

'Besides, when you were a baby, you didn't sleep "like a baby",' Ruben added, defiantly. 'You screamed and screamed. I remember.'

'How?' Irène, sitting next to him, quibbled. 'You've just said you can't remember anything before you were four. When Bella was a baby, you were two.'

He opened his mouth to reply, but no words came out. So he reached across her plate and grabbed two hard boiled eggs and a *boyoz*. As he ate, he felt a pang of regret that he hadn't been raised Orthodox, with a stipulation to thank God daily for not making him a girl.

He had grown up with three sisters and, throughout his childhood, he'd treated girls with the same condescension as he did his sickly cousin Salomon. But lately, changing his tone, he had started trading tales of erotic exploits with his schoolfriends. His own account of stumbling on Rachel and Malka bathing in the nude led him to doubt the veracity of several others, but there could be no argument about Jovan Lazović's visit to the Eden Theatre to see a French vaudeville about a warm-hearted prostitute. He had shown them a programme signed by the leading actress, above an imprint of her lips. In the second act, she – the prostitute – had been discovered in bed with her lover's best friend, although they'd drunk so much champagne the previous night that they couldn't recollect whether they'd coupled. After a series of comic reversals, she was reconciled with her lover, but not before spending the greater part of the play in her underwear. Jovan's description almost broke

Ruben's resolve never to set foot in a theatre again, after enduring Esther's performance in *L'Avare*.

He was certain that if he'd passed the night with a prostitute, he would recall every moment the next day . . . he would recall it for the rest of his life. He was equally certain that if he could once couple with a woman – any woman, although for a fourteen-year-old schoolboy a prostitute appeared to be the only option – he would regain his peace of mind. He would no longer fall prey to the phantasms that assailed him, and not just in the dark. The previous week, Grandmaman Regina had held a dinner to celebrate her sons' safe return from exile. As he entered the Club des Intimes, a coat-stand with a feathered hat perched on top, and a fur cape draped across two hooks, aroused him so violently that he had to rush to the nearest closet. To add to his discomfiture, he learnt later that they belonged to the Chief Rabbi's wife.

The manhood conferred on him at the tefillin ceremony may have been symbolic, as Leon had warned, but the scribble of hair on his upper lip, under his arms, and in his private places, which filled him with both pride and shame, was real. Herr Heilbut, who taught natural history, had explained that body hair, although now covered out of modesty, had originally served as a signal to potential mates. So where were they? The closest he had come to a naked woman was in the anatomical charts Herr Heilbut pinned on the classroom wall, and the albums of classical statuary on Papa's shelves. It was difficult to say which were the more disconcerting: the former, with bodies split down the middle and organs in contrasting colours like countries on a map; or the latter, with their frozen poses, flawless skin and breasts as hard and cold as mountain peaks.

There was no one to whom to vent his frustrations but Ephraim, who was similarly afflicted, having abandoned the pretence that his father, a director of the Ottoman Railway Company, possessed any kind of harem, much less one to which he invited his son. The natural history lessons, a bold innovation at the lycée, which taught Western theories of evolution, while the Talmud Torah and even the Alliance school remained stuck in the Garden of Eden, raised as many questions as they answered. One, above all, exercised Ruben. To the fascination of some of his pupils, the shock of others and the ribaldry of still more, Herr Heilbut had explained that human beings shared a common ancestor with apes. But having outlined the sexual swellings by which female primates indicated fertility and attracted partners, he neglected to mention whether their human cousins experienced comparable changes and, if so, whether they were modest like those of gorillas or blatant like those of baboons. To ask risked courting the derision of the class and the disdain of Herr Heilbut, who had already accused Dymek Galanis of dragging science into the sewer.

The only solution Ruben could see was to visit a prostitute. Ephraim agreed to join him, expressing the hope that she would be as pretty and compliant as the one Joran had described.

'Maybe in Paris! We're left with the women in Bara.'

'Where?'

Ruben related how, in her self-appointed role as family conscience, Esther had lectured them on the fate of Ashkenazim who'd fled persecution in Russia with nothing but the clothes on their backs. Destitute, the men sold their wives, their sisters, their daughters, even their mothers.

'This is not a suitable subject for the dinner table,' Maman had said.

'It's not a suitable subject at all,' Papa had added.

No matter how impoverished the family might become, Ruben couldn't conceive of selling Irène or Esther, let alone Maman (the thought made him shudder!). No wonder Papa had told them to keep away from Ashkenazim. On the other hand, their venality would work to his advantage, since the sin of visiting a prostitute would surely be mitigated if she were a fellow Jew.

For weeks, he and Ephraim plotted their visit to a brothel, devoting every free moment to the practicalities, chief among them being price. Ruben, who'd heard Papa rail against the tobacco union's wage demands, noted that he paid his female workers between eight and ten kuruş a day.

'Prostitutes can't expect as much for simply dropping their drawers and lying down.'

'And it won't last all day,' Ephraim said.

'So let's reckon on one or two kuruş but bring ten just to be safe.'

'We should put five in our socks,' Ephraim said.

'Won't we take them off?'

'Why?'

'When they want to kiss our feet,' Ruben said. 'They're completely shameless,' he added, as Ephraim stared at him in disgust.

Against all odds, Ruben had retained one gold lira from the bag he presented to Rabbi Pardo. Although at times the prospect of using money from the tefillin ceremony for his initiation weighed on him, at others, it felt strangely fitting. Ephraim, meanwhile, was confident that he could obtain the cash from their housekeeper's coffer, since his parents already suspected her of stealing.

They planned their venture for Friday afternoon, when school finished early. What neither had anticipated was the Balkan League's military success. With Serbian troops advancing on Monastir and the Greeks laying siege to Ioannina, tensions in Salonica ran high. The threat of harassment along the way emboldened them (there had been no reports of actual violence), yet in the event the only hostility came from their classmates, Platon Florakis and Michalis Lykaios, who, buoyed by their countrymen's victories, hurled insults at the vanquished Turks.

They made their way to the city centre, averting their eyes from both sets of their coreligionists heading to Friday prayers. They crossed Sabri Pasha Street and entered Bara, a foray that would have horrified their parents, irrespective of its purpose. They walked down Afroditi Street, which Ruben remembered Monsieur Bruton denouncing for its obscene display, but, with most doors barred and windows shuttered, he searched in vain for any trace of obscenity. A few houses had awnings, beneath which traders sold grain, candles, cabbages and baklava, while one heavily sweating old man fried sausages on a griddle. Keen to break his first taboo, Ruben approached him and bought two.

'Here!' He handed the scandalised Ephraim a sausage with the same bravado as when, three years earlier, he'd handed him his first cigarette.

'They'll smell it on my breath,' Ephraim said, making the same excuse.

'So brush your teeth,' Ruben replied. 'Mmm!' He exaggerated the pleasure of biting into the heavy, salty meat, its grease smearing his lips.

The sausages devoured, they ambled past a trio of women chattering in a doorway. All wore matching white cotton shifts, black woollen stockings, and shawls wrapped slackly around their elbows.

'Do you think they're . . . you know?' Ephraim asked.

'No,' Ruben replied. Although he suspected otherwise, his pride refused to admit it, since, after a passing glance, the women had dismissed them as prospective clients and resumed their conversation. 'Come on,' he said, leading Ephraim deeper into the hinterland. Within a few steps, the pavement abruptly gave way to loose boards, mud oozing over the sides.

'My shoes!' Ephraim moaned.

'Don't be such a baby!' Ruben said, thinking that the barefoot children who featured in Esther's tirades would be at an advantage. 'Through here!' He turned into a narrow, malodorous alley.

'It's so dark.'

'Exactly. Do you expect the prostitutes to flaunt themselves in broad daylight?'

They walked on, past an old woman slumped on a step in a flimsy smock rucked up over flabby, mottled thighs. She might have been a prostitute, beggar or drunkard, but Ruben had no desire to find out. He steered Ephraim past a pair of women, both with the same thick raven hair, pinched cheeks and deep-set brown eyes. One beckoned him with a long white finger, while the other stuck her thumb in her mouth like Rosa's baby, only lewdly. Their air of desperation repelled him. He quickened his pace, forcing a flustered Ephraim to scramble after him.

'Aren't we going to speak to anyone?' he asked. Before Ruben could answer, a woman hailed them from a balcony. He looked up to see her sprawled on a crate, her legs splayed to expose a triangle of darkness.

'That's revolting,' Ruben said, pulling Ephraim away.

'But she's a prostitute!'

'Even so.'

'Shall we turn back?' Ephraim asked eagerly.

'Of course not.' Ruben was emphatic, as though they would be turning their backs on manhood itself. 'We'll find the right women. You'll see.'

Just then, they were accosted by a gaunt youth, prematurely balding, with sad eyes and an angry burn on his cheek. 'You look lost, messieurs.'

'Yes,' Ephraim said.

'No,' Ruben said.

'I understand. You know where you are, but not where you're going.' He spoke in halting, Russian-accented Ladino. 'May I be of assistance?'

'No,' Ephraim said.

'Yes,' Ruben said.

'I expect you fine gentlemen are looking to relax after a hard week's work.'

'We don't work,' Ephraim said. 'We're still at school.'

'In our final year,' Ruben said, glowering at him.

'Still at school? What luxury! I'm sure that my sister would be honoured to meet – to entertain – two such educated men.'

'We'd need more than one ... sister, that is,' Ruben said, relieved to find him acting true to type.

'Don't worry,' he replied, smiling to reveal a mouth full of broken teeth. 'I have several.'

Ruben looked at him with a mixture of gratitude and disgust. Whatever transgression he and Ephraim might commit with the sisters would be nothing compared to their brother's offering them for sale.

'How much?' Ephraim asked, so bluntly that the man looked nonplussed.

'How much for an hour of paradise?'

'Two kuruş,' Ephraim replied, taking the question at face value.

'In this world, paradise isn't so cheap.'

'Three kuruş then.'

'Ten. Not a para less. They're my sisters.'

'That's too much,' Ephraim said.

'We don't know the basic rate,' Ruben hissed at him.

'I don't have enough money. Let's go.'

Ruben, aware of the lie, feared that Ephraim had lost his nerve. 'Come on,' he pleaded. 'It's all we've talked about for months. Who knows when we'll have another chance?'

'Let's go, Ruben. I don't trust him,' Ephraim whispered.

'What do you expect? He's a pimp, not a rabbi or . . . or an imam,' Ruben replied, glancing round quickly in case his voice had carried, but the man stood by with apparent indifference.

'No! You can do what you like. I'm going home.'

'Then go! But if you breathe a word of this, I'll tell your father you ate a sausage.'

The feebleness of the threat would have been clear to him even without the pimp's laugh. He watched Ephraim scurry away, his retreat hampered by the unsteady boards.

'I'm Yossel. You're Ruben . . . I heard your friend say. Now we've exchanged names, we too are friends, right? Forget him, it's his loss. To tell you the truth, only one of my sisters is worth the price. The others, ha! Too bony. But the one I have for you is a real beauty. Plump as a *knaidel*.' He kissed his fingertips. 'Let's go.'

Yossel ushered him down an even dingier alley to a house so silent that it seemed to be deserted. They entered a frowsty foyer, where four women sat, restless yet resigned, like passengers waiting for a long-delayed train. His arrival might have been marked by a jet of steam and a high-pitched whistle, since they sprang to life with smiles as painted as their faces. Two leant towards him, offering tantalising glimpses of bosom, until Yossel addressed them curtly and they fell back. 'Give me a moment,' he said to Ruben, no longer seeking to conceal his mangled teeth. 'I must prepare my sister to welcome a visitor.' He bounded up the creaking stairs, leaving Ruben with the women, one of whom flicked out her tongue like a lizard and squeezed her spongy breasts, making him nostalgic for Aphrodite's marble cleavage. He felt his cheeks flush and stared at the floor, prompting her to laugh as if she'd merely been kneading dough, before she turned back to her companions. Unheeded, he was left to study the drab décor: threadbare carpet, mismatched furniture and peeling walls festooned with frayed red-and-white bunting, which looked to have been salvaged from the Sultan's visit the previous year.

'Chana will soon be ready,' Yossel called, as he came downstairs. 'Meanwhile, let's toast our friendship.' He poured two glasses of a cloudy liquor. 'It will make you like a bull all night long,' he said, flexing his forearm and clenching his fist.

'But I can't stay all night. In fact, I really should go now.'

'Nonsense. Drink! Drink!' The women looked round as he raised his voice. 'Have a cigarette.' He held out a packet.

'Those are my father's . . . that is, his factory makes them,' Ruben said, keen to assert himself. Yossel examined the label.

'You are Carrache?'

'Well, I'm his son . . . or rather, one of them,' Ruben replied, instantly regretting the disclosure.

'We are honoured, my prince.'

'Oh, I'm not a prince.'

'Finish your drink and then we will go to see Chana.' Gently but firmly, Yossel pressed the glass to Ruben's lips. He gulped the sharp, fiery liquid, which filled his head with stars. 'Good, come!'

He led him up the stairs to a cubicle off a bleak corridor. He drew back a makeshift curtain to reveal a girl in a thin chemise lying on a bare mattress, the single candle too far away to illuminate her face. He spoke to her in what sounded like Yiddish, and she replied in a whisper that would have been unintelligible, no matter the language.

'I'm not feeling well,' Ruben said, chastened by both her listless manner and the dismal setting. 'I'll give you the ten kuruş we agreed.' He looked down at his right shoe, in which half of it was hidden. 'But I want to . . . I need to go home.'

'Nonsense,' Yossel said, with a cavernous smile. 'It's your first time. It's natural to feel nervous.'

'I've made a mistake. I'm not ready for this.'

'A hot-blooded young man like you? Take off these clothes.' He tugged at Ruben's jacket. 'Then wash yourself.' He pointed to a bowl on the stand.

'My hands?' Ruben gazed at the flakes of mud on his palms.

'Your parts,' Yossel said flatly. 'You must be clean.'

'Is she clean?' Ruben asked, peering into the shadows.

'She's my sister!' Yossel replied, in a voice thick with menace. 'Stop wasting time!'

Ruben turned his back on both Yossel and Chana and, after fumbling with his flies, splashed icy water on his shrivelled penis. With no towel, he dabbed himself dry on the tail of his shirt.

'Good! Now I shall leave you two to get acquainted.' Yossel went out, closing the curtain behind him, and Ruben strained to catch the fading echo of his footsteps. He felt queasy and faint and, with no chair available, slumped at the foot of the bed. Without a word, Chana rose to her knees and laid him down. As she leant over him, he saw that she was very young, with girlish freckles, narrow shoulders and a chest as flat as his own. He braced himself for a kiss but, to his astonishment, she began to lick his cheek. He struggled to check his biliousness as she went on to lick his ears and neck and then up to his forehead and down his nose, scrupulously avoiding his lips. Nothing in his schoolfriends' stories had prepared him for such preliminaries. Struggling with both his confusion and intense fatigue, he gingerly placed his hand on her calf and slid it up her leg, only for her to push it away.

He wondered if it were some deficiency in him that she should be licking so vigorously to so little effect. Not only did he feel no arousal, but he was starting to lose sensation of any sort. His body was leaden and, when he tried to lift himself up, his fingers were left clutching at air. He knew that he was dying and his last thought was of the shame he would bring on his parents, forced to redeem his corpse from a brothel.

'I should kill you now!'

Yossel's roar jolted him back to consciousness. The words swirled round the cavity in his head. A blade glinted at the edge of his vision.

'No, I want to squeeze . . . to twist . . . to feel your bones crack.' He flung the knife to the floor with a piercing clatter.

'I don't . . . I don't understand.'

'Look at her!'

Blinking into the blaze of three newly lit candles, Ruben discerned the girl, now stark naked, cowering in the furthest corner of the bed, welts and scars across her arms, shoulders and undeveloped chest, and streaks of blood on her parts and thighs, the same blood that glistened on the buckle of his belt, coiled beside her.

'She's ten years old. Ten! I should . . . but no, let the law take its course.'

Ruben grabbed at the bowl on the washstand but was sick before he could reach it.

'I'm sorry,' he stuttered, unsure how much the apology encompassed. He turned back to Chana, pained that her brother made no attempt to cover her.

'You think that we're nothing . . . expendable. Poor Jews, forever grateful to our benefactors, who can use and discard us at will.'

'No, not at all. I don't understand . . . Is that my belt?'

'Yes, it's yours.' He seized it and swung it through the air, spraying droplets. 'You think you can behave like a beast and your money will protect you.'

'I don't have any money. Just the ten kuruş.'

'But you can get some.' Yossel's tone mellowed. 'You must write and ask your father to send some.'

'But I can't!' How would he ever explain this to Papa, who thought he was having dinner with Ephraim . . . Ephraim, who'd had the sense to escape? Prison or even the hangman's noose would be preferable. He had never felt so alone. But there was one person who might save him. 'Leon . . . you could try my brother.'

'Where do we find him?' Yossel asked fiercely.

'Is it six o'clock yet? He should be playing billiards at the Association des Anciens Élèves.'

'Six? It's almost ten.'

'It can't be. I've only just arrived.'

'You beat and brutalised this little girl for four hours.'

'No!' He looked at his hands as if they belonged to someone else. Had he been so repulsed by his brutishness that he'd blacked it out? Why hadn't she screamed? Why hadn't her brother come to her rescue? Why didn't he . . . 'Why don't you give her some clothes?'

'What's the matter? Ashamed to look at your handiwork?'

'She'll catch cold.'

'Now you care?' He spoke a few words to Chana, who, wincing, pulled her chemise over her head and chest, leaving her lower body exposed. 'How much do you think her suffering is worth?'

'I don't know . . . one gold lira?'

'Prison! Prison!' Yossel's violence made Ruben shudder for his own.

'More? Two or three?' Leon frequently complained about the paucity of his allowance. How much money did he have and would he be willing to spend it on him?

'Ten, at the very least. Here's pen and paper. Write and tell him that you half killed a girl in a debauched attack.'

'He won't believe—'

'Just write! You need him to send ten gold lira with this letter or else you'll be handed over to the authorities.'

Ruben wrote at Yossel's dictation. No sooner had he scratched his signature than Yossel snatched the paper, blowing on it like a lover.

'Shall we take it to him together?' Ruben asked.

'So that you can run off? No chance! One of my associates will go. Where will he be if he's not playing billiards? At home?'

'No!' What if his mother or sisters overheard what had happened ... what he would never have believed had happened were it not for the injured girl cringing on the bed. He prayed that Leon, who'd been unusually subdued since his return from Paris, had been lured out by some of his friends. 'He's sure to be in one of the cafés ... the Colombo, the Anatolia, the Crystal.'

'Let's hope so, for your sake.'

Yossel went out, showing no qualms at leaving him with Chana, who stared at him impassively.

'I'm so very sorry,' he said, after a while. 'Something – I can't imagine what – must have taken hold of me.' Her silence made him feel like a murderer in Ancient Rome, his victim's corpse strapped to his back.

'Now we wait,' Yossel said, returning.

'In here?' Ruben asked, appalled.

'Why? Would you prefer to quit the scene of the crime?'

'I just thought your sister ... she might want some privacy.'

'Such consideration! Spoken like a true gentleman. Come into the next room.'

Yossel led him into a second cubicle, as cheerless as the first. 'I'll leave you to your conscience. Call me if it hurts.'

He went out, keeping the curtain open. Ruben lay on the bed, hugging his knees, half whimpering, half rocking. The heaviness of his thoughts plunged him into oblivion, from which he was roused by shouting in the foyer. Recognising one of the voices as Leon's, he was gripped by a new terror. What if Yossel should attack him? On his own, he stood no chance, but he'd mentioned an associate and he had a knife. Blocking out the sordid cubicle, he offered a prayer, vowing that he would never touch another girl – not even look on one with desire – as long as Leon was unharmed.

He was repeating the vow when he heard footsteps on the stairs and Leon, without a scratch, entered the cubicle, followed by Yossel.

'You, out!' Leon said.

'You came! I'm so glad . . . I'm so sorry.' He broke down in tears.

'Out!' Leon repeated implacably.

'Am I free to go?' Ruben asked, stifling his sobs. He leapt off the bed and threw his arms around Leon, who stood unmoved, before relenting and rubbing his head.

'Don't forget this,' Yossel said, holding out Ruben's belt, which Leon grasped, and for a moment it looked as though he might bring it down on Yossel's shoulders. Instead, he wrapped it around his fist, propelling Ruben down the stairs and through the foyer, where the one remaining woman gave him a skittish smile.

More confused than ever, he stumbled onto the street, where even the squelch of mud underfoot came as a relief, until he felt a ringing pain, first on one side of his head and then on the other.

'You little fool,' Leon said, boxing his ears. 'I should have left you to rot.'

'I'm sorry,' Ruben said, steadying himself. 'I can't make any sense of it. I don't remember touching her.'

'Of course you didn't. I know it. That slimy whoremonger knows I know it.'

'Then what? Why?'

'He saw at once that you were a simpleton . . . a dupe . . . a soft touch . . . an easy target.' Leon punctuated each epithet with a slap. 'So he drugged you: laced your drink.'

'Ow! Stop, please!' He looked up charily as Leon's rage abated. 'Then what about her scars? The blood?'

'The blood: who knows? A complicit butcher? And the scars: relics of a Cossack's whip or some such savagery. I'd feel sorry for them if they weren't such ingrates, spitting in the soup we gave them.'

Ruben's relief drowned out Leon's words. All he could hear was that he was innocent – reckless, yes; gullible, yes; but innocent. He wanted to kiss his brother, but now wasn't the time.

'What was going through that thick skull of yours?'

'I wanted . . . I needed . . . I thought I'd die if I didn't go with a girl.'

'What a lecherous little boy you are! Don't you know that you're supposed to wait until you're married?'

'You didn't,' Ruben said, his courage returning.

'At least I was seventeen.'

'You said nineteen before.'

'You're in no position to argue!' Leon bellowed, jostling him down the cramped pavement until they arrived at a square, where their coachman was fighting off several urchins who clambered over the carriage. 'Here!' Scattering small change, Leon sent them scrabbling in the mud. Seizing his chance, he pushed Ruben up the steps, before springing after him.

'To the Campania and look sharp!' he ordered the coachman.

'You won't tell Papa, will you?' Ruben asked, as they drove off.

'I haven't decided yet.'

'I'll do anything . . . anything.'

'You can be sure of that. It's too late to discuss it now. And I'm eight lira out of pocket.'

'Only eight?'

'What do you mean "only"?' Leon asked, giving him another slap. 'Come to my room before the service tomorrow and we'll talk.'

'Of course. Whatever you want. I won't be late.'

'You've heard of the sultans who killed their younger brothers when they ascended the throne?'

'Yes,' Ruben replied uneasily.

'I sometimes wonder why they waited so long.'

'That's a horrid thing to say. You don't mean it.'

'No, you're right, I don't. Come here.' He put his arm round

Ruben's shoulders and ruffled his hair. 'I promise I'll always look out for you.'

On reaching home, Leon led him round the back, and he crept up the maids' stairs. The house was quite still, but just as he opened his bedroom door, Maman appeared at hers.

'Ruben, what on earth! The state of you!'

'We were cycling. I fell into the mud.'

'Are you hurt?'

'No, not at all,' he replied, too ashamed to solicit sympathy.

'I told your father that machine was dangerous. Why do you need to change speeds anyway?'

'I'm tired, Maman. I want to go to bed.'

'You'll filthy your sheets. I'll call Rachel to draw you a bath.'

'No!' Ruben replied, his voice rising an octave. 'It's late. It's not fair on her. I'll do it myself.'

'How thoughtful! You really are growing up.' She moved to kiss him, only to recoil. 'Make sure you have a good soak!'

Rested and refreshed, Ruben woke for the first time in weeks without embarrassment. He dressed quickly and made his way downstairs to Leon's apartment, wary of his reception. But Leon welcomed him warmly and led him to the breakfast table, laid for two.

'Sit, eat!' he said expansively, reminding Ruben of the prisoners in Yedi Kule who were served a lavish meal on the eve of execution.

'I'm not very hungry.'

'I'm not surprised,' Leon said, tearing off a slab of challah. 'Did you sleep well?'

'Yes . . . that is, not badly.' He suspected that he should claim to have tossed and turned, tormented by his depravity. He wanted to thank Leon for coming to his aid; he didn't dare contemplate what might have happened had he still been in exile. But he seemed determined to keep him in suspense. When had he ever cared how he'd slept before?

'You won't tell Papa, will you?' he asked. 'I'll do anything . . . anything you want.'

'Yes, well, we'll come to that. First you must tell me why. No, not the obvious . . . "Too much blood," as Grandmaman Regina would say. But why that squalid, verminous place? Would you eat a meal in a café that filthy?' Ruben shook his head. 'No. If you're that desperate, there are houses: clean, safe . . . or as safe as can be.'

'But how do I know where to find them?'

'How did you find that one?'

'Esther said—'

'Esther!'

'When she talked about the girls who sold themselves in Bara.' He was struck by the realisation that Leon wanted to help, rather than to punish him. 'Will you take me to one of those clean houses?'

'No! No, definitely not. You're fourteen years old. I've told you before, use your right hand.'

'Don't!'

'You wouldn't be the first. Papa . . . Grandpapa . . .'

'Stop it!' He plugged his ears.

'Though, take it from me, you'd be wise to forget all thought of women. The Bible may tell you not to spill your seed, but it should tell you not to give your heart. Since the beginning of time, women have been nothing but deceivers. Eden may be a fantasy, but Eve is real.' He bit into the challah. 'I used to envy my contemporaries in Paris – Jews as well as Christians – who could marry of their own free will. But now I think – no, I know – that we're better off here. Let Papa choose someone for you who'll be a good wife, the mother of your children, a credit to the family. A marriage should be based on something more lasting than passion.'

'Do you want my bicycle?' Ruben interjected.

'What?'

'I owe you eight gold lira. We can tell Papa that the frame's too big for me.'

'What do you think I am?'

'The best brother in the whole world!'

'True.' Leon laughed. 'But you still owe me. And I promise you're going to pay. But not like that. I want to be proud of you, Ruben. At least one of the Carrache brothers has to amount to something. I shan't say a word to Papa.' Ruben felt his anxiety melt away. 'On one condition.'

'Anything.'

'So you said. You know my friend Aron?'

'Aron Sides?'

'Who else? He helps out at a club for Jewish youth. The Maccabi.'

'Like at Hanukkah?'

'Yes, I presume that's what inspired the name. Jewish rebels ... Jewish warriors. It was started by members of the Club Nouveau, who want to establish a Jewish homeland in Palestine. Aron got involved with them when I was in France. If you ask me, they're building castles in the air. But that's their problem. Meanwhile, they're trying to nurture a generation of pioneers. They do gymnastics ... football.'

'What's that to do with me? I've never played football.'

'You can learn.'

'But—'

'But what? Remember: "Anything". Aron asked me if you'd like to join them a while ago. I said I thought not. But I've realised it would do you good. You can ignore the politics. They won't try to indoctrinate you. And it will keep you out of mischief.'

'I can keep out of mischief at home. I don't need nursemaiding,' Ruben said, his resistance creeping back.

'I'll be the judge of that. We'll talk to Aron after the service.'

Ruben was ambivalent about the Sabbath service. Though bored by the impenetrable psalms and prayers, he enjoyed the serenity of the Italia Yashan Synagogue, which had witnessed almost five centuries of worship. He was proud of his father and uncles, who processed with the Torah, but ashamed when, with no attempt at stealth, they hurried out the moment the scroll had been replaced in the Ark, leaving the rabbi to preach to a depleted congregation and the women and girls in the gallery.

This morning was no different. Papa chatted to various acquaintances as the cantor sang a blessing. When Baruch ben Yakov stepped up to read from the Haftarah, Leon signalled to Aron, who extracted himself from a packed pew and met him in the portico. They conferred in a corner, while Ruben idly sought patterns in the veins of a marble pillar. No sooner had he identified a withered olive tree than the two friends approached. Seizing his hand in an iron grip, Aron expressed delight at his wish to join the club.

'There's a practice session tomorrow afternoon. It's at the football ground behind the Baron Hirsch hospital. Don't worry about boots. We'll lend you some for now. I persuaded my father to buy a dozen pairs for the boys from the Talmud Torah. But make sure you wear old clothes. It'll be muddy.'

'Oh, Ruben's used to mud,' Leon said, giving him a gentle cuff, which hurt nothing but his pride.

Straight after lunch on Sunday, he cycled across town to the ground, where an officious keeper agreed to watch over his bicycle after a lengthy demonstration of its mechanism. He entered the clubhouse to find twenty or so boys limbering up before the practice. 'I see you've already built up a sweat,' Aron said, handing him a pair of boots with six studs and laces up to the ankles. He apologised for their condition, suggesting that he buy a pair of his own before next time. He introduced him to the players, some who looked as young as nine or ten and others whom he would have put at twenty, had Leon not told him that the age limit was eighteen. About a third were Ashkenazim, but, at first glance, the Osips and Mendels were as friendly as the Vitalis and Amados.

'My apologies to those of you – all but one of you, in fact – who've heard this before, but it bears repeating,' Aron said, as the boys gathered around him. 'The club was founded just over four years ago, when the Sultan lifted the ban on team sports. What purpose did it serve? I'm no mind reader, but I'd hazard a guess that he was afraid of a population of healthy young men. He wanted us to look like our fathers.' Aron puffed out his cheeks and distended his stomach, to gusts of laughter. 'Well, we intend to prove that those fears were justified. We have an obligation to ourselves and to our nation.' Ruben was perplexed by the idea that he belonged to any nation but the Ottoman. 'We must prepare ourselves for the task of rebuilding our homeland, so that it's as strong as it was in the days of King David. But that's to look into the future. For now, we must show our mettle on the pitch by trouncing teams from Iraklis and the Hellenic Gymnasium.'

With that, Aron divided the group into one team of nine and the other of ten, placing the inexperienced Ruben in the larger. He assured him that he'd pick up the rules as he went along, which turned out to be true, although it would have helped to know that he could only tackle with his feet before he'd knocked down one of the ten-year-olds. At the end of the game, when Aron asked if he'd enjoyed himself and would be coming back, he replied with a resounding 'yes'. After two more practice sessions, Aron decided to try him out on the team to play Iraklis. Having pictured himself as its leading scorer, he had to curb his disappointment when, assessing his skills as strength, not speed, and blocking, not attacking, Aron put him in defence.

He took part in the club's other activities, signing up for a series of lectures which, though in a multiplicity of languages, conveyed the same message: that, having been dispossessed of the land given to them by God, Jews had been living inauthentic, unfulfilled lives. It was both their right and their duty to return to Palestine and rebuild Jerusalem. He sat beside his teammates, Itskhok and Volf, twin sons of a maintenance engineer from Kiev, who, it turned out, worked for Ephraim's father on the Salonica to Monastir railway. Despite their disparate backgrounds, he felt a closeness to them and a new sense of identity, where being a Salonican and even a Carrache was subservient to being a Jew.

To his regret, there was no one in the family with whom he could share his budding commitment. Leon held that the Zionists were hopeless dreamers and Papa that they were dangerous zealots.

'Forget all this nonsense about establishing a Jewish homeland!' he said. 'We're already living in one. There've been Jews in Salonica since the time of Alexander ... some say Darius. Why else did Saul of Tarsus come here to preach? We were here before the Christians and Muslims. We were here before there were Christians and Muslims! Why should we ever want to leave?'

One answer to his question presented itself on 10 November, when the Greek army invaded the city. Intent as ever on preserving the status quo, Papa insisted that his three younger children attend school, although, to mollify Maman, he posted a porter outside both lycées, with orders to bring them home at the first hint of trouble.

Few Greek pupils turned up, and those who did waved miniature blue-and-white flags in the faces of their Turkish classmates. The peaceful transfer of power in the city was not mirrored in the school corridors and, after struggling to uphold discipline, the headmaster cancelled lessons. Ruben walked home to the nonstop ringing of church bells, which had hitherto been restricted to a single peal so as not to drown out the Adhan. He passed, unmolested, through groups of Greeks embracing one another and announcing joyfully, tearfully, and at times drunkenly, that 'Christ is risen.' One particularly befuddled trio, deaf to imprecations from carters and coachmen, stood in the middle of the street, jumping on their fezzes.

'They'll be sorry when it rains,' he said to the porter, who chivvied him along.

Ephraim failed to appear at school that day. For all the horror of the brothel, Ruben resented his desertion, not least his attempt to credit it to conscience rather than cowardice. Nevertheless, he still considered him his best friend and was relieved that he wasn't in class to suffer Platon and Michalis's taunts. On his return home, he learnt that Ephraim's absence would be permanent, when Maryam, holding the receiver as though it might explode, called him to the recently installed telephone. Struggling to make himself heard over the crackling, Ephraim explained that his father, fearing for the family's safety, was taking them back to Anatolia. They arranged to meet to say goodbye.

Ruben recounted their conversation to Papa, who maintained that there was no need to panic. As President of the Jewish Community Council, he had been summoned to talks with Greek officials, who'd assured him of their good faith. Faced with certain defeat, Hasan Tahsin Pasha, the Ottoman commander, had displayed true leadership in surrendering his garrison before a single shot was fired. In return, the Greeks pledged that there would be no reprisals and that both soldiers and civilians would be protected. Under pressure from the Great Powers, they had even undertaken to retain the existing gendarmerie. 'What more proof could anyone want that nothing will change?' Papa asked. From what he had ascertained, their new rulers were less concerned with asserting their authority over their Jewish and Turkish subjects than with ensuring that their Bulgarian allies – only a few hours' march away – didn't launch a rival claim to the city.

For all such professions of tolerance, the following days witnessed a series of brutal attacks on Jews. While Papa insisted that these were isolated incidents, Esther, brandishing a copy of *Avanti*, read out a report that fifty Jewish women had been raped; four hundred Jewish homes and three hundred Jewish shops had been pillaged; dozens of Jewish men had been robbed and beaten in the street, and those who resisted had been slaughtered.

'You mustn't believe all you read in that socialist rag,' Papa said. 'I and the Council have the ear of the authorities. They're doing everything they can to root out the violence. Surely it's better to work with them . . . to show that we're loyal citizens of the new Greek state?'

'Better for whom?' Ruben asked.

'Better for everyone,' Papa replied.

'Better for business,' Esther said.

'Business isn't just about making money, whatever Mademoiselle Sagues might say. It's the glue that binds people and nations together.'

In the face of Papa's acquiescence, Ruben deepened his commitment to the Maccabi. Leon passed on Aron's remark that he was rapidly becoming the club's most dedicated member. He played football every week, the team winning all but one of their fixtures in December and January. After their three-nil victory over Audax, the referee, Mr Jefferson, vice-consul of Great Britain, the birthplace of the game, declared them to be the equal of any youth side he had known.

For all the pleasure he took in sport, it was the lectures that truly engrossed him, even though many of the foreign visitors delivered them in Hebrew. He was eager to master the language, not only to dispense with the need for the twins' translation, but to play his part in building – or, rather, rebuilding – the Jewish homeland. The obvious course was to transfer to a Jewish school. Keenly aware of Papa's opposition, he broached the subject one evening when he appeared to be in better spirits than usual.

'Don't be absurd!' Papa said, his good humour vanishing in the smoke of his cigar. 'You go to the best school in Salonica, if not the entire Empire. What could you possibly gain from switching to the Alliance school?'

'I was thinking more of the Talmud Torah.'

'Are you out of your mind? Don't you realise how lucky you are to live in an age that has shaken off the shackles of religious dogmatism?'

'But you're one of the Talmud Torah's principal donors. You sit on its committees.'

'I sit on the community assembly. And that's the salient word: *community*.'

'Aren't I part of that community?'

'What did you teach your children while I was in Paris?' Papa asked Maman. 'Since when did they all decide that they had the right to defy me?'

'I didn't, Papa,' Irène said.

'It's shameful that I don't speak Hebrew, the language of my forefathers,' Ruben said, glaring at her.

'The language of your forefathers was Italian, dear,' Maman interjected, as if to deflect Papa's charge. 'And before that, Spanish.'

'I had to learn my Torah portion by rote.'

'Then we'll find you a Hebrew tutor,' Papa said. 'An hour every evening if you wish.'

'You used to complain bitterly about Rabbi Pardo,' Maman said. 'I've lost count of the number of times you begged me to write and tell him that you were ill.'

'And I'll have it on my conscience for the rest of my life.'

'Don't exaggerate. He was well rewarded. And Maryam always sent him home with a basket of food.'

'It's our duty to learn Hebrew and move to Palestine,' Ruben said doggedly.

'So you'd be happy to see your mother and sisters living in tents, surrounded by Bedouin bandits?' Papa asked. 'For what earthly reason would we uproot ourselves and go to such a backward, barren land? Let the Ashkenazim settle there if they wish. No doubt anything's better than where they've come from. But we're at home here, honoured by the Sultan—'

'It's the Greek King now.'

'That's enough! I blame you for this,' Papa said, turning to Leon.

'Of course you do,' Leon replied. 'Though I've no idea why.'

'For putting him in touch with that gang of Zionist hotheads. They want to foment strife across the city so that the Jews will feel beleaguered and emigrate to Palestine.'

'What about the Zionists in Austria and Germany and Switzerland and France?' Ruben asked. 'They're not fomenting strife. What about the—'

'I said *enough*! One more word - just one - and it will be the end of that club for you for good. After a trying day, is it too much to ask for a quiet evening in the bosom of my family . . . a chance to smoke a cigar in peace?'

Ruben heard the finality in Papa's voice and knew better than to argue. But there was one place where he could still serve the cause, a place where language was immaterial, and that was the football pitch. The following weekend, the Maccabi were playing Omilos, the finest of the Greek teams. He had invited several schoolfriends, including Platon and Michalis, not in spite – but because – of their support for the opposition. He sat alone in the clubhouse before the match, heedless of his teammates' banter. He listened respectfully to Aron's familiar appeal for sportsmanship, even as he resolved to disregard it. Midway through the first half, he had the ball – and the opportunity he required. The Omilos forward charged towards him. 'Pass!' Shloime shouted from the left wing, but Ruben ignored him. Aron had ruled that he wasn't a good enough shot to be a striker, but he'd reckoned without the power of revenge, as he kicked the ball squarely into his opponent's face.

7

IRÈNE

SALONICA, MARCH 1913

GROWING UP WITH Arabic street signs, Irène had taken the elegant cursive for granted. The sharp, fragmented Greek replacements were both unintelligible and alien.

'What difference does it make if it's White Tower Avenue or Prince Constantine Avenue?' Bella asked, as they walked down the street in question, 'when the pavement, the buildings and the people are the same? We could find the way to Grandmaman's house blindfolded. And now we've started to learn Greek at school, we'll soon be able to read it.'

A glimpse of what Irène continued to regard as the Ayasofya mosque, but which was now the church of Hagia Sophia, made Bella's words ring hollow. In the four months since the Greek invasion, not all the buildings had remained unchanged. She knew from her Turkish classmates, Kadriye and Halme, whose families once worshipped there, that the priests had bricked up the mihrab that pointed towards Mecca, as Christians, like Jews, prayed towards Jerusalem. They had knocked down the fountain in the courtyard, where everyone could wash, and installed a basin that was just for babies. She felt sorry – but not too sorry – for her friends, since what the Christians were doing to the Muslims, the Muslims had done to them first. When the Ottomans captured the city, they'd converted the church into a mosque and painted over the mosaics of Jesus, his mother and the saints.

The Greeks hadn't sequestered any of the city's synagogues, but then the Jews had never sequestered any of their churches. 'So, there's a good side to our always being the conquered rather than the conquerors,' she'd said innocently one dinner, provoking Ruben's wrath.

'Silly, girly rubbish! What about Joshua defeating the Canaanites and Gideon defeating the Midionites and Saul defeating the Ammonites and the Edonites and the Moabites and David defeating the Philistines and—'

'But that was in biblical times,' Papa said. 'Since then we've chosen to excel in other fields.'

'You may have done,' Ruben replied. 'Some of us intend to reclaim what's rightfully ours.'

Irène gripped Bella's hand as they reached the corner, where one of the newly arrived Cretan gendarmes, his pantaloons comically ballooning, ordered them to stay on the kerb. She half expected to see a squad of soldiers, resplendent in their sea-green jackets and sky-blue trousers, marching imperiously down the centre of the road. Instead, a boy in a white robe, carrying a golden cross, led a funeral cortège. When she was younger, a stray glance at the open casket would give her nightmares for months. Now, even a prolonged gaze at the waxy figure, clasping a viper-like rope to his breast, was tempered by the intoxicating scent of the incense the priests were wafting. Behind them came a cluster of black-clad women, whose ululations left her thankful that Jewish women didn't attend funerals. It would be unbearable to witness her mother or grandmothers parading their grief.

'Which of us do you suppose will die first?' Bella said, as if reading her thoughts.

'How should I know! Why not ask when you visit Delphi?' she replied glibly.

Alone of her acquaintances, Bella welcomed the Greek occupation. With travel restrictions lifted, she would be able to head south and consult the Oracle. No matter that Maman told her that no priestess had lived there for more than 1,500 years and the Temple of Apollo lay in ruins; no matter that Papa insisted that it was impossible for anyone – past or present – to divine the future; she was convinced that simply standing on the sacred soil would grant her the answers she sought.

'If it's me,' she replied, deaf to Irène's tone, 'promise you'll put a bell in the coffin, in case I'm only in a trance.'

After the cortège had passed and Irène had restrained Bella from salvaging a sprig of fallen apple blossom to take to Grandmaman Falcona, they proceeded to the Muslim quarter. Grandmaman had never explained why Grandpapa Avram had chosen to live there and, since his death, she had rebuffed all Maman's appeals, perfunctorily seconded by Papa, to move in with them. Irène understood her attachment to the district, which was more vibrant than the Campania, whose houses were occluded down long, tree-lined driveways. The streets, although as cramped as those in Vardar, were far cleaner, no doubt for the sake of the worshippers, who fell to their knees at the wail of the Adhan. For all her fears about her mother's isolation, Maman had to admit that she was fortunate in her neighbours. Nevertheless, she pressed her case, until Grandmaman joked that she didn't dare confess to so much as a cold in case she used it as an excuse to abduct her.

'You ask me to give up my home of forty-five years, the home I made with your father, in which you and your sister were born,' she'd said, in response to Maman's latest entreaty. 'To leave a house full of memories for one that is full of . . . things.'

'What nonsense!' Maman replied.

'This is my world. The children spinning hoops, tossing balls and rolling marbles. Their mothers gossiping and playing cards over cups of *salep*. Gülruch cobbling beneath the window.'

'I thought his hammering gave you a headache.'

'Not since you were a girl. Besides, how would I know the time without the *turkito* calling the faithful to prayer?'

'We have such things as clocks.'

'Clocks stop.'

'There's no arguing with you!'

'Thank you, dear heart,' Grandmaman replied, with a wink at Irène, who said – to herself, not to Maman – that there could be no greater safeguard than having Mercado under her roof.

They arrived at Grandmaman's house and, as usual, made their way to the back entrance: a plain, weathered door in a cracked, lichen-covered wall that betrayed no hint of the delights within. The house occupied three sides of a small courtyard, with an ancient well at its centre (the lack of running water being one of Maman's constant concerns). A pergola soon to be ablaze with pink and red clematis stood alongside jasmine-wreathed trellises and terracotta pots filled with aromatic herbs. Two lemon trees, a pomegranate tree, and a peach tree that bore fruit every other year bordered the lawn. Although their own garden was grander, with its terraces, bowers and lily pond, and the statue of a boy offering a cup to a thirsty eagle, Irène knew of nowhere more tranquil. She loved nothing so much as to watch Grandmaman sitting in the shade, embroidering sheets, towels, nightdresses, and even babies' napkins for her granddaughters' trousseaus.

She relished the invitations to stay the night, when they would gleefully flout all Maman's rules about sweetmeats and bedtime. But she avoided Fridays, when Grandmaman dispensed food to the neighbourhood beggars. Not only did the dirt and the smells and the scars and the clothes and the hair – the matted and verminous hair – turn her stomach, but Grandmaman's insistence that they were 'all God's creatures' made her uneasy. Surely God had created enough gruesome creatures in spiders and scorpions and centipedes and snakes, without including people?

Bella darted through the courtyard and grasped the heavy brass hand on the door, giving it her customary 'how do you do' shake before knocking. In the past, Irène had scrambled to reach it first, but, scorning such childish contests, she now lingered behind. Hannah let them in and led them to the kitchen, where Grandmaman greeted them with a shower of kisses. 'I could eat you up, you're so tender and plump,' she said to Bella, who giggled. Irène, mindful of the anti-Jewish rhetoric in the Greek press, shuddered. She prayed that Grandmaman would never use the expression outside the house.

They moved up to the dining room, where Grandmaman, who liked to say that no one would visit her if it weren't for her food, had laid out a lavish lunch. The first course featured two varieties of *ojaldres* (cheese and potato, and minced beef and herbs) in pastry she'd rolled herself, since Hannah's always turned out too thick. As soon as they had begun to eat – and paid their compliments to the cook, which Esther said were the only ones women over forty could expect – Grandmaman demanded to hear all their news, since she also liked to say that no one in the family told her anything.

'Papa's worried about the Greeks,' Irène said.

'Not true!' Bella interjected. 'He said nothing will change.'

'That was to cheer us up. He's afraid that they'll end the capitulations and make us pay taxes.'

'But wouldn't that be fair? Esther says it's wrong that, just because we came here from Italy long ago, we're let off.'

'Doesn't she know how much your father gives to charity?' Grandmaman asked.

'She says charity is an insult to the poor,' Bella replied.

'We should all be so insulted.'

'Though Papa says that half of what she says is for effect.'

'Three-quarters,' Irène added.

'She's sad,' Bella said. 'The Alliance directors in Paris want to send Leah to a school in Thrace. And she's only been in Salonica for three years! Papa's promised to write and tell them how much she's needed here, but he's warned Esther not to raise her hopes.'

'Anyway, she'll soon have more important things to think about,' Irène said. 'Papa's invited two young Englishmen to stay. They're supposed to be friends of Leon's, but everyone knows they're prospective husbands for Esther. That's why she's angry . . . even angrier than usual.'

'And Ruben?'

'He knows about it too.'

'No, I mean, how is the darling boy?'

'As undarling as ever,' Irène replied resentfully.

'Papa suspects that he's been indoctrinated in the club Leon sent him to,' Bella said.

'I thought they played sports.'

'So did Leon,' Irène said. 'Ruben's become worse than a rabbi. He wanted Papa to put a mezuzah on every doorpost in the house. Of course he refused, though he's allowed him to put one outside his bedroom. We're supposed to kiss it and say *Amen* whenever we go in.'

'I never go in,' Bella said.

'The darling boy,' Grandmaman said. 'I could eat him.'

Hannah cleared their plates and brought in the *sofrito*.

'Why such a big pot, Grandmaman?' Bella asked. 'It isn't Friday night.'

'Just eat what you want, dear heart. We've made extra for Mercado. He doesn't take enough care of himself. He comes home exhausted from the factory and goes straight up to his room to study.'

'But he's twenty-three . . . I think,' Irène said, crumbling a chunk of bread.

'He's been learning English. Now he's started Greek as well . . . Hannah, pass the pot to Señorita Irène. I've told him he needs to keep up his strength . . . is that all you want? It's lamb.'

'I had three *ojaldres*.'

'Well, you can always come back for more . . . Serve yourself, Bella.'

'That's enough!' Irène said. 'You're too fat.'

'It's baby fat,' Grandmaman said. 'Take no notice.'

'She should save some food for other people. How is Mercado? He hasn't been to see us for ages.'

'Grandmaman brought him to dinner two weeks ago,' Bella said.

'He's fine . . . much the same as usual. Though he's anxious, of course.'

'Have there been more strikes?' Irène asked.

'No, about the conscription. Haven't you heard? The Greeks are enlisting all the young men in the city. Jews and Turks too. Mercado says they're preparing for war with Bulgaria.'

'Leon will have to go back to France,' Bella said.

'But they can't enlist Mercado,' Irène said. 'They mustn't.' To her horror, she felt tears pricking her eyes.

'And they won't. Don't worry! He's just been ordered to present himself at the recruitment office for an examination.'

'Then it's decided.'

'Not at all. I shall mix some herbs, which will turn his skin bright red – only for a day or two – so they'll be glad to see the back of him.'

'How can you be sure it'll work?'

'I did the same for my neighbour Nadia last year, when the Ottomans were recruiting. She gave it to her sons and both were declared unfit. They bundled them out double quick in case it was catching.' Grandmaman chuckled.

'May I leave the table?' Irène asked. 'I feel sick.'

'Yes of course, dear heart. Would you like Hannah to make you some lavender tea?'

'I just need a moment . . . some air.'

Undaunted by Maman's misgivings and Papa's mockery, Irène set great store by Grandmaman's herbs, which had cured her of several childhood ailments. Those, however, had been relatively minor: sore throats, stuffed noses and upset stomachs. This was something else entirely. Would the Greek officers be as easily fooled as the Ottomans? What if they were to label Mercado a malingerer? A sea-green jacket and sky-blue trousers would be less resplendent when hacked to pieces and caked in blood.

Appalled by the image she'd evoked, she felt a desperate longing to be near him. She ran up two flights of stairs and entered his bedroom for the first time. The air was fusty but tinged with a whiff of citrus that was distinctly, deliciously Mercado. Even with the shutters open, the small arched window let in little light, and she blamed Grandmaman, whose belief that electricity weakened the blood left Mercado straining to read by a pale oil lamp. As the room gradually slipped into focus, she was struck by its orderliness. Nothing was tossed on a chair, let alone on the floor. The razor, soap, toothbrush and flannel on his washstand and the books, papers and inkwell on his desk were all precisely aligned. Even the pens and pencils were ranged by size. She crossed tremulously to his bed, picking up the book on his night table: *Mémoires du Duc de Saint-Simon*. A feather marked his place, and she resolved never again to dog-ear a page. She was about to peer into a drawer when Hannah walked in with an armful of clean linen.

'Señor Mercado won't like you touching his things, Señorita. He doesn't even let me put these back in the cupboard. So I leave them here.' She laid them on the chair. 'He says if he ever finds out that I've moved anything, he'll whip me.'

'I've come up for some air,' Irène said, unnerved by Hannah's nonchalance.

'Shall I open the window?'

'Then he'll know you've touched it.'

With a sly smile, Hannah turned on her heel and strode out. Irène waited for the sound of her footsteps on the stairs before picking up a shirt and pressing it to her cheek. Freshly laundered, it might have belonged to anyone. Drawn back to the bed, she pulled down the coverlet and ran her fingers lightly over the blanket. Emboldened, she slid her hand between the sheets. Her heart pounding, she lay down and buried her head in the pillow, breathing in a further trace of citrus, mingled with coconut and musk. Lost in the moment, she failed to notice Grandmaman standing at the door.

'What in the world are you doing?'

'I . . . I felt dizzy. I had to lie down.'

'But not on Mercado's bed. It isn't proper.'

'I didn't think . . .'

'I looked for you in the courtyard. I was worried. Come into my room if you're still feeling poorly.'

'I'm much better now. Honestly.'

'Let me see.' She felt her forehead. 'You're very hot.'

'That's just the air.' Irène turned away, fluffing the pillow and smoothing the sheets.

'Leave that. I'll send Hannah up later.'

'It'll only take me a minute,' Irène replied, fearing the maid's scrutiny.

'Then it will take her even less. Come!'

Grandmaman led her across the passage into a room as cluttered as Mercado's was neat. Dresses spilt out of an armoire, while bodices, skirts and stockings were strewn across two slipper chairs and a stool. Beads hung over the corner of an antique gilt mirror, too speckled to reflect more than a silhouette ('A blessing at my age,' according to Grandmaman). Two large brown urns, once used to store honey, were filled with ferns and wild grasses, lending the room a desiccated air, accentuated by the row of tarnished silver photograph frames above the fireplace. Only Maman and Tante Irène, posing together in their teens, were smiling. Grandmaman and Grandpapa looked solemn, even on their wedding day, while all four of her great-grandparents were so grim-faced that she was relieved they had died before she was born.

The fireplace itself was spotless, since Hannah swept the grate and gathered the ashes every morning, ready to scatter them around Grandmaman's bed at night. Any disturbance, let alone the impression of a tail or a footprint, would betray the presence of a demon. Although Esther and her brothers made fun of her, Irène respected the traditions which, Grandmaman explained, had been handed down from mother to daughter since the dawn of time. She wished that Maman had handed them down to her, but, echoing Papa's complaints that Grandmaman was filling his daughters' heads with foolishness, she forbade her to get soot on her bedroom rug. The one occasion that she'd disobeyed her, the only demonic footprint had been Ruben's.

No sooner had Grandmaman settled her on the bed than she felt her defences weaken and tears stream down her cheeks.

'What is it, dear heart? Tell me!'

'You promise you won't say anything.'

'I promise.'

"You swear.'

'I swear.'

'How old were you when you married Grandpapa?'

'Sixteen, I think.'

'How can you just think?'

'In those days, they only registered the birth of boys.'

'Then you've never had a birthday?' It was bad enough that Ruben had been given games and toys when she and Bella were given clothes, but it would have been far, far worse to have had no presents at all. 'That's so unfair.'

'But if you look at it another way, it makes every day special, since – who knows? – it may be the one.'

'Did you never want to find out?'

'When I was younger, yes. But all my mother could remember was that I arrived the summer after Vita. So you see, I might still have been fifteen.'

'I'll be seventeen in May.'

'The twelfth, I know. Times have changed.'

'So I'm old enough to be married.'

'That depends on Papa. First, he'll want to find a husband for Esther.'

'Oh, Esther doesn't want to marry.'

'Nonsense. Every girl wants to marry.'

'But if Esther causes a scandal, it will be harder for me.'

'You must be patient. You haven't been introduced to any young men yet.'

'Yes, I have.'

'Who?' Grandmaman sounded surprised.

'You promised not to tell anyone.'

'And I always keep my promises.'

'Mercado.' Just saying his name thrilled her.

'My Mercado . . . Mercado Silvera?'

'You promised!'

'Yes, of course.' Grandmaman stood up and paced the room. 'Have you spoken to him?'

'No! No, how could I? I couldn't.'

'I think that's best, for now.'

'Will Papa let me marry him? He isn't a notable, but why should that matter? When Papa went to Paris, he trusted him with the factory. And Esther says that he cares more for the factory than he does for us. So he should trust him with me.'

'Esther's not always fair to Papa. But to my mind he couldn't wish for a finer son-in-law. I've seen how loyal he is to his own father, who isn't the easiest of men. And he's devoted to his mother and his sister.'

'His sister? I didn't know he had a sister. He's never said.'

'She's a Mongolian. It's very sad. I've only met her once, when I invited them to dinner as a surprise for Mercado. In fact, that was his birthday. I wanted to ask them again, but he begged me not to. He says it's cruel to give Mari – that's her name, Mari – a taste of a life she'll never enjoy. Children like her die young. He's so considerate.'

'He's too good for me . . . and handsome . . . and clever.' She picked at her cuticle.

'You're a jewel . . . Don't do that! You'll hurt yourself.'

'Is there some way you could find out what he feels about me . . . if he feels anything at all? I don't mean *ask*,' she added, wary of Grandmaman's forthrightness. 'But drop a few hints . . . mention my name . . . say that I'm your favourite granddaughter. You don't have to mean it.'

'If you're serious about this, I can do much more than that. We can make sure he returns your feelings.'

'What? How? Do you have a love charm? A potion? Something our ancestors brought from Spain?'

'The simplest imaginable. We bury an egg. It's many years since I've done it, so I'll need to refresh my memory, but I know that we fill it with blood.'

'My blood?' Irène, who'd fainted when Bella sliced her leg open falling from a tree, felt a stab of dread.

'Don't worry. An animal's. A sheep or goat's, if I remember rightly. We write your two names on the shell and, within weeks, he'll be yours for ever.'

Irène's excitement was offset by doubt. If it were that easy, why didn't every girl use it to ensnare her true love? Or had their mothers and grandmothers lost touch with the old ways?

'Are you certain that it works?'

Grandmaman pointed to her wedding picture. 'There's proof.'

'You used the charm on Grandpapa?' Irène asked, marvelling.

Grandmaman put her finger to her lips. 'It never fails. I wouldn't have suggested it if I weren't sure he'd make you the perfect husband . . . What is it, dear heart?' she asked, as Bella rushed into the room.

'It's the King. He's dead.'

'May his memory be a blessing,' Grandmaman muttered quickly.

'Not just dead . . . murdered. Petros is outside. He told me. Maman's sent the carriage to fetch us home. This is for you.'

Bella handed a note to Grandmaman, who read it and set it aside.

'She urges me to go with you. Tush! I appreciate her concern, but I hope that, when you two girls are grown-up, you'll have more respect for your maman's intelligence than she does for mine. Now shoo! You must hurry. Who knows what new horrors this death will unleash? The poor King . . . Shoo, shoo!' She drove them to the door like stray cats. 'As for the other thing,' she said to Irène, 'rest assured that I'll attend to it.'

Had Grandmaman delivered such an enigmatic message to Bella, Irène would have pressed her for an explanation. Bella, however, never questioned other people's affairs, which Maman maintained was out of respect for their privacy, but Irène reckoned was because she lived in a world of her own.

They settled into the carriage and sped through the Muslim quarter, where it was clear from the customers milling about the stalls and braziers that the *tellal* had yet to announce the death. In contrast, the commercial quarter was almost deserted, with shops shuttered and offices closed. A swarthy man stood in the middle of the street, shaking his fist and spitting out a stream of curses. An elderly woman, routinely dressed in mourning, sat on a low step and keened. They drove on until they reached the White Tower, where the carriage was stopped by two Cretan gendarmes. Faced with a volley of unintelligible questions, Irène could do nothing but smile. Bella, however, replied in French that they had called on their grandmother and returned home on hearing of the outrage. The bemused gendarmes let them pass.

Maman, who was waiting in the hall, hugged them as tightly as if they had survived an attack themselves. Irène, elated by Grandmaman's promise of the love charm, struggled to adopt a suitably grave demeanour. She reminded herself that Papa, once loyal to the Sultan, had been won over by the Greek King. Since transferring the court from Athens, he had granted the Community Council three audiences, expressing his respect for his Jewish subjects and pledging to address their concerns. The Queen, meanwhile, had taken an interest in one of Tante Amada's charities, even visiting Vardar, where, according to Esther, she'd been introduced to a well-scrubbed sample of the poor.

Ruben, darting in and out as if he'd been stung, was convinced that the Greeks would blame the murder on the Jews, a prospect which, perversely, he appeared to relish.

'Remember how the Greek papers accused us of killing babies and using their blood in our rituals? Watch them accuse us of doing the same to the King!'

'That's enough,' Maman said, 'you'll frighten your sisters.'

'We must be ready to defend ourselves. We have the superior manpower. We just need to strengthen our resolve.'

That resolve remained untested, since the assassin turned out to be a Greek by the name of Schinas – a socialist or anarchist, his ideology was unclear. As Papa related on his return, he had made no attempt to escape and was apprehended at the scene.

Maman recited a blessing.

'He's to be tortured,' Papa said. 'To find out whether he acted alone or had accomplices.'

'Poor man,' Esther said.

'You wouldn't say that if he was a monarchist,' Ruben said.

'If he was a monarchist, he wouldn't have killed the King,' Esther replied, with withering scorn.

The revelation of Schinas's identity failed to prevent revenge attacks on Jews by Greeks, who professed – or preferred – not to believe that he was one of their own. Crown Prince Constantine, who had led the triumphant army into Salonica the previous November, succeeded to the throne. Papa, already hit by the closure of Ottoman ports and fearing disruption to the domestic market, commended the smooth transition of power. He therefore assured the Henriques brothers that they had no reason to postpone their visit.

Although he maintained that Leon had met Basil and Felix in Paris, with the three becoming inseparable, Leon told Ruben, who in turn told Irène, that they had spent a single drunken night together in the bohemian quarter of Montmartre, where he found the two motor racing fanatics deadly dull.

'Why are they staying at the Hotel Colombo and not here, Maman?' Bella asked at breakfast on the eve of their arrival.

'Can't have them sleeping under the same roof as their future bride,' Ruben said, in the first open acknowledgement of the trip's true purpose. 'The only question is which one will bag the prize ... Ouch!' he yelped, as Esther leant across the table and slapped him.

'Esther, that's uncalled for,' Maman said. 'Apologise to your brother at once.'

'It's nothing,' Ruben said, regarding Esther coldly. 'What doesn't kill me makes me stronger.'

'You know Nietzsche?' Esther asked in surprise.

'Why shouldn't I?'

'But he's a philosopher.'

'Monsieur Florentin quoted it in a lecture. I thought it came from Proverbs.'

Irène, feverishly awaiting the love charm, struggled to summon interest in the brothers' visit. The following afternoon, while Maman and Maryam were busy preparing their welcome dinner, the precious parcel finally arrived.

'That Hannah brought it an hour ago, Señorita,' Malka said, handing it to her. 'In a carriage, mind you . . . sat there like the Queen of Sheba. I said to Maryam: "Doesn't she have legs?"'

'Thank you, Malka. I'll take it upstairs.'

'Smells off, if you ask me. Bit like her.'

Closeted in her bedroom, Irène tore open the packaging. Inside was a note in Grandmaman's sloping script, along with two vials wrapped in felt, a pipette, and a small box tied with a pink ribbon. Before untying it, she read the note, which explained that the box contained two turtle dove's eggs. With no breed specified, Grandmaman thought a dove's the most fitting. Only one was required for the charm, but, given the delicacy of the operation, she'd included a second. She set out a list of instructions. First, Irène must puncture the egg with a pin and suck out the fluid. Then, she must mix the vials of blood (one from a male calf, the other from a female), and inject the mixture into the pinhole, sealing it with wax. Lastly, she must write both their names – hers and Mercado's – on the egg and bury it. By the next time they met, he would be smitten.

Terrified of cracking the shell, and scarcely less so of spilling the blood, Irène followed the instructions to the letter. She punctured and sucked and injected and sealed so effectively that she considered repeating the process with the second egg but feared that, rather than doubling her chances, one might cancel the other out.

The task completed, she crept into the garden, fetched a spade from the shed and headed to the pond, where she dug a hole beneath the thornapple tree. She placed the egg inside it as tenderly as a baby in its cradle, and covered it with soil. After trampling it flat, she marked the spot with a stone, which she instantly removed since it reminded her of a grave.

She had little time to wash and dress before meeting the brothers. Initially indifferent to their visit, she had come to realise that it might determine her fate. Should Papa consider one of them a suitable husband for Esther, he might be more inclined to agree to a match between her and Mercado. Moreover, there was to be a party in their honour which Mercado would attend, giving her a chance to assess the efficacy of the charm.

The brothers spoke, moved and dressed so alike that Basil's eyeglass and Felix's freckles were the only way she could tell them apart. Their manners were impeccable as they played their allotted roles, addressing polite remarks to Esther, whose terse replies bordered on rudeness. Nevertheless, Leon hadn't exaggerated their obsession with motor racing. They discussed it so relentlessly that even Maman, smiling gaily to compensate for Esther's scowls, stifled a yawn.

'Last year, we entered the Sunbeam in the Grand Prix at Dieppe in June and the Ardennes in July,' Basil said, adjusting his eyeglass. 'We came fifth in Dieppe.'

'What about the Ardennes?' Ruben asked, drawing out Esther's discomfiture.

'We crashed,' he replied, with a debonair laugh.

They failed to understand why there were no cars in Salonica. 'This is the age of the internal combustion engine,' Felix said.

Irène saw Papa's brow furrow at the suggestion that his beloved city might lag behind the times. Maman must have seen it too, since she swiftly intervened. 'Do we really want machines pounding through our tranquil streets . . . all the noise and dust and danger?'

'You can't stand in the way of progress, Madame.'

'Surely progress would be better served by ensuring that everyone had proper housing and sufficient food?' Esther asked. 'Rather than enabling a few dilettantes to get from A to B at twice the speed, only to find that they had nothing worth doing when they arrived?'

Papa, who'd been signalling to her to take part in the conversation, glowered. The strained silence was broken by Basil. 'Really, that's priceless,' he said with a laugh, which first his brother, then Maman, then Leon and finally Papa echoed.

The meal dragged on, with even Maryam's *malabi* failing to raise much cheer. When the last spoon was set down (by Bella, who'd had a second helping), the women and Ruben retired to the salon, leaving the men to their brandy and cigars. Esther declared that she had a headache and needed to lie down.

'No, my dear,' Maman said, with unaccustomed firmness. 'You must stay and entertain our guests.'

'You mean beguile them with my vast knowledge of speed trials and oil spills and tyre changes? I'm sorry, I'm not at my best. It's my time of the month.'

Maman looked pained and Bella concerned, while Ruben, seething at being lumped in with the women, looked blank.

'No, it's not, my dear. That was two weeks ago. I keep a record of these things.'

'Am I never to have any privacy? Why can't you leave me be?' Esther said, fleeing the room.

Later that night, Irène heard Papa upbraiding her, but even when she crept out of bed and opened the door without a squeak, she was unable to make out a word.

All was icily, eerily calm at breakfast, where Leon, who'd reluctantly agreed to be the brothers' guide, announced that he was meeting them at the Colombo for a tour of the city's attractions.

'That should keep them busy for an hour,' Ruben whispered to Irène.

'I thought we'd start at the Acropolis and Yedi Kule, then head down to the Arch of Galerius and the White Tower, of course, before doubling back to the club for lunch. This afternoon, the Talmud Torah and a few of the synagogues. But if anyone has any bright ideas . . .'

'How about the mosaics in the Ayasofya?' Irène said.

'Hagia Sophia,' Bella corrected.

'No,' Papa replied. 'You must all keep well away from there – that includes you, Leon. Hundreds of Bulgarian soldiers have been billeted in the mosque or the church or whatever it is now. There've already been several skirmishes, which the authorities are eager to play down.'

The mention of soldiers put Irène in mind of Mercado, and she gazed intently into the garden, as if it weren't an egg that she'd buried there but a magic bean.

The following day, the household bustled with preparations for the party. Maman warned everyone to stay out of the kitchen, where Maryam was cooking for a hundred guests while trying to keep the peace between Malka, Rivka and the three maids Grandmaman Regina had lent them. Irène took refuge in her room where, at six o'clock, she changed into Esther's old pink taffeta gown, which Madame Naar had shortened, leaving the ruched frill at the hem uneven. For once, however, she knew better than to complain. With a disgruntled glance in the mirror, she crossed the landing to find Esther.

'You look beautiful,' she said to her sister, who stood vacantly at her window in the purple and gold fur-trimmed dress Papa had brought her from Paris.

'I feel like Marie Antoinette being led to the guillotine.'

'She wore nothing but a smock. And her hair had been shorn, whereas yours, piled up like that . . . are those pins diamonds?'

'Maman gave me them this afternoon. They belonged to my . . . her sister.'

'Felix and Basil will be dazzled. One of them is certain to ask Papa for your hand.' Esther made a moue of revulsion, which Irène ignored. 'But they must be as anxious as you – as we all are – to know which you like best.'

'Let's see, the eyeglass or the freckles? Don't act the innocent! I've heard you and Bella talking. It couldn't matter less to me. I might as well pick a name from a hat.'

'Don't you want to be married? To be madame rather than mademoiselle? The mistress of your own household?'

'You mean the mistress of my husband's household? I suppose it's much the same if I'm answerable to Papa or another man. Except at night.' She gulped. 'Painful, wakeful nights.'

Irène accompanied Esther downstairs, where the chatter of guests mingled with the clatter of glasses and the strains of the string quartet. 'No one will hear themselves speak,' she said.

'Be thankful for small mercies,' Esther replied.

Maman intercepted them at the foot of the stairs and, linking arms with Esther, led her to a small group that comprised her friend Fakima Nahum with her daughter Ada; Monsieur Sadi Levy; Oncle Haim; and Felix Henriques. Ada Nahum's simpering showed that, unlike Irène, she would be quite content with one of Esther's castoffs.

Irène made a quick round of the salon, exchanging greetings and kisses and promising Grandmaman Regina to drink no more than a single glass of champagne. She went in search of her other grandmother, finding her in the hall, her toque and robe conspicuous among the French coiffures and gowns, proof that she honoured her heritage in dress as in everything else. Hoping that Mercado would be with her, she was horrified to spot him tête-à-tête with Rebecca Kuenko, one of Esther's former classmates.

It was too soon, of course, for the charm to have taken effect. The watercress she'd grown at school sprouted overnight, but that had been on a cloth, whereas herbs planted in soil took weeks – sometimes months – to germinate. All the same, the wait would be less agonising if he were talking to another man or even a group of girls rather than just one, who was, moreover, exceedingly pretty.

'I've buried the egg,' she said, drawing Grandmaman aside. 'I did everything exactly as you said. The shell didn't break.'

'That's a good sign,' she replied, patting her hand. 'Now you must give it time.'

'But what if he falls for someone else first? What if . . . ?' She couldn't bring herself to say it, but what if Rebecca, assisted by her grandmother or another wise woman, had buried an egg of her own?

'He won't . . . Mercado!' Grandmaman called. 'Don't hide yourself away! Here's someone who wants to talk to you.'

'No, Grandmaman!' Irène said, feeling as if her dress had caught fire.

'Irène, a pleasure,' he said, with such a broad smile that she wondered if, after all, the spell had started to work.

'Yes, it is . . . for me too, I mean.'

They stood for a moment, tongue-tied, before speaking at once.

'Has anyone offered you a drink?'

'That's a lovely dress.'

Their replies also overlapped.

'It's strange, but champagne always makes me sad.'

'It was Esther's. It's been altered to fit me. Not at the bust.'

He looked at her in surprise.

'Irène, why don't you take Mercado for some food?' Grandmaman said, as flames of embarrassment lapped her face. 'The poor boy's been hard at work all day. He must be ravenous.'

'Yes, of course,' she replied, unable to move.

'Now, dear heart,' Grandmaman said, with a knowing smile. 'I don't have a magic carpet to transport you.'

Fearing her indiscretion, Irène whisked him into the dining room.

'I'm sorry to drag you away from Rebecca,' she said.

'There's no one I'd rather talk to . . . than you, that is. But your grandmother's right; I'm as hungry as a wolf. And this looks delicious.' He gazed at the table, where Malka and two of Grandmaman Regina's maids were serving meats, pastries, flans, salads, vegetables, cheeses and dips. Irène, craving only him, took two *keftes* and a spoonful of tabouli. Mercado, however, piled his plate high with slices of beef, *knafeh* and *bottarga*, *borekas* and aubergine.

'Did I take too much?' he asked, comparing their portions.

'Of course not. I'll let you into a secret. I sneaked downstairs before any of the guests arrived and ate two *borekas*.'

They sat in adjacent chairs, Irène stealthily turning hers until they were facing.

'I haven't had a bite to eat since breakfast,' he said. 'I cycled to see my parents straight after work. My mother's sick and my father . . . well, he's not best equipped to look after my sister.'

'Grandmaman told me about Mari. I'd like to meet her.'

'No, you wouldn't.'

'I'm used to unusual sisters.'

'You really wouldn't. She's not charmingly quirky like Bella, her head in the clouds somewhere above Mount Olympus.' He glanced out of the window. 'She's sluggish, lumpen, embarrassing.'

'Grandmaman says you're wonderful with her.'

'I do what I can, but she'd be better off in an infirmary. And what will happen if I'm drafted into the army?'

'You won't be. Grandmaman's potion is guaranteed to make them reject you.'

'Do you believe that?' he asked, forlornly. 'That kind of sorcery only works in folk tales. Army doctors have hearts of stone. One of our porters chopped off his thumb before the examination and they still passed him fit.'

Irène felt her insides melt. 'You must speak to Papa. He'll intercede for you. He has influence.'

'Which he'll need to save for Leon. Even he can't call in too many favours. And family comes first.'

'You're almost family.'

'*Almost*, yes. *Almost* being the key word.'

'It doesn't have to be,' she said boldly.

'How? What do you mean?'

'Can't you tell?' She wanted to dig up the egg and fling it into the sea.

'But Esther's as good as promised to one of the Englishmen.'

[160]

'Not Esther!' She jumped up and strode to the table. 'Here,' she said, thrusting her barely touched plate at Malka. 'I don't know what you put in the *keftes*, but they're inedible.'

Joya Kastro, about to take one, shook her head and pointed instead to the beef. Irène made for the door.

'Wait, please!' Mercado said, following her.

'I'm sorry. I don't know what I'm saying . . . what I was thinking. It just popped into my head. Please forget it.'

'No, I won't, and I don't want to. How can I have been so obtuse?'

'Do you mean that?'

'Is there somewhere we can go . . . somewhere quiet?'

'Like where?'

'Anywhere, as long as it's away from all these people.'

'There's Papa's study. No one will bother us there.'

'Are you sure we're allowed?'

'Who's to stop us?'

She ushered him into the empty, booklined room which, even with the hateful bust of the snake-haired woman, felt more congenial than the teeming party.

'How old are you, Irène?' Mercado asked.

'Seventeen in May.'

'You're very beautiful.'

'You must still be thinking of Esther.'

'No, you. I've always thought so. But I'd never presume . . . Your father would dismiss me on the spot. It would be a worse betrayal than embezzlement.'

'Not at all,' Irène replied, suddenly realising that Grandmaman had given her the wrong charm. She didn't need one to make Mercado love her, but one to make Papa love him. 'He trusts and respects you. And isn't he always saying that everyone should be given the same opportunities? Look at what he does for the Alliance school.'

'He did mention that he might propose me for membership of his club.'

'There you are!'

'Do you really believe it's possible? You're a Carrache!'

'It's just a name.'

'I could change mine. After all, I have done before,' he said with a bitter laugh.

'I love you, Mercado,' she murmured.

'And I you. You're so clever to think of this. Mercado Carrache . . . it alters everything.'

He kissed her hand, and she felt the warmth of his lips suffuse her entire being. She had yearned for his kisses for so long, but the yearning had been accompanied by the fear not only of impropriety but of conception. Bella might talk of Athena being born from Zeus's head and Dionysus from his thigh, but she knew that, in the real world, it was women who gave birth. She had always assumed that they had to be married, but Rosa had proved otherwise. Nevertheless, the mechanics remained a mystery. Having seen her parents kiss, and her grandparents kiss, and Esther kiss Leah's friend in the play, she knew that she couldn't fall pregnant simply from kissing. And even if she could, the risks no longer seemed so terrifying. Papa might denounce her, but he would be compelled to agree to their marriage to avert a scandal. So when Mercado released her hand, she rose on tiptoe and kissed him full on the mouth.

8

BELLA

SALONICA, JUNE 1913

THE LYCÉE HAD been closed for six days. With Greek and Bulgarian soldiers sniping at one other throughout the city, no father would risk his children being caught in the crossfire. 'Remember, it's still term time,' Madame Sapporta said as she set her pupils exercises to do at home. But Bella, who struggled to concentrate in class – long after she'd been moved away from the window – found it even harder in her bedroom. At present, her efforts to master twenty-four basic Greek verbs were thwarted by the sporadic gunshots and muffled cries that rumbled up from nearby streets.

After their defeat of the Ottomans, Greece and Bulgaria were fighting over the spoils. Having entered Salonica a mere eight hours after Prince Constantine, the Bulgarians claimed an equal right to its possession. The majority of their sixteen thousand troops had been recalled to Sofia, but two thousand or so remained, and daily reports of clashes between disaffected soldiers reached even the youngest member of the Carrache family. As a precaution, Papa posted guards at the gates and ran electric wires along the walls, thereby precluding Grandmaman Falcona's seeking shelter with them. Her own defences consisted of hanging garlic bulbs on her doorposts and window frames, as though flesh-and-blood assailants might be deterred as easily as demons. In despair at her mother's stubbornness, Maman reassured herself that any marauder or murderer was more likely to target an isolated mansion in the Campania than the tightly packed houses of the Muslim quarter.

While Papa's main concern was the family's safety, Maman's was its sustenance. When they first made plans for the house, she had suggested planting a kitchen garden. 'We're not peasants,' he'd replied, a rebuff he regretted now that the influx of troops had sent food prices soaring. With farmers afraid to bring their produce to market, staples such as eggs, milk, fruit and vegetables were no longer available, even to those who could afford them. Maman laid in sacks of beans, lentils, chickpeas and rice. The butcher continued to call on favoured customers, but, without regular supplies of ice, the meat had to be salted. Meals were accompanied by apologies from Maryam and inducements from Maman. Papa, attempting to raise everyone's spirits, recounted how, during the Siege of Paris, the starving citizens had been reduced to eating two elephants from the zoo.

'But there is no zoo in Salonica,' Irène said, to a chorus of laughter.

Papa travelled to the factory each morning under armed escort. He forbade anyone else from leaving the grounds, even by the garden path to the shore. Leon withdrew to his apartment, listening to the phonograph and reading poems which he refused to share with Bella, insisting that they only made sense through a haze of absinthe or, in its absence, raki. Esther also shut herself in, writing daily letters to Leah, although, given their enforced seclusion, it was a wonder she had anything to say. After threatening in turn to stow away on a fishing boat, become a salesgirl at the Stein Palace and take poison, with an abandon that Papa attributed to her brush with the theatre and Bella to the horror of being kissed by a bristly chin, she appeared to resign herself to her forthcoming wedding. Yet she openly expressed the hope that the current tension between England and Germany would lead to a war, in which both Henriques brothers would be killed or, as she added at the sight of her family's shocked faces, 'maimed too severely to marry'.

Displaying a newfound fondness for needlework, Irène took her sewing box out to the lily pond, where she embroidered a set of handkerchiefs. Swearing Bella to secrecy, she claimed that they were a birthday present for Maman. Bella nodded dutifully, knowing that, were Maman the intended recipient, the handkerchiefs would be silk, rather than linen, and the initial M entwined in a rose or a lily, rather than framed by a horseshoe.

Instead of practising the Hebrew from which he'd complained that the secular syllabus was a distraction, Ruben clumped about the house, proclaiming his boredom and getting under everybody's feet. When Maman finally banished him to the garden, he fetched his ball and, with dozens of trees to choose from, aimed at the thornapple beside Irène's bench. Regardless of the provocation, her response was unwarranted. Shrieking that he was a self-centred disrespectful pig, among several other epithets that wafted away before reaching Bella's window, she grabbed the ball and flung it over the wall, fully aware that he wasn't permitted to retrieve it. The tree wasn't even a laurel or a sacred oak.

For Bella herself, the mandatory respite offered an opportunity to work on her painting. She was making a frieze of the Marriage of Peleus and Thetis in the style of the Attic amphorae, which had fascinated her ever since she discovered a history of Greek pottery in the lycée library. Even in black and white, the decoration was sublime. In recent months, she'd had the chance to study the original, after Papa procured (a word he reserved for his unlicensed acquisitions) two vases from a contractor in the Cyclades: one depicting Heracles fighting the Amazons and the other Theseus defeating the Minotaur. Her goal was to capture the elegance of the formal composition and the intensity of the stark colour contrast, but on paper rather than clay.

'Very pretty, dear,' Maman said, glancing at the painting, while Bella explained how the apple that Eris, the uninvited goddess of discord, brought as a wedding gift had led inexorably to the Trojan War. 'But if you want to paint apples and discord, why not Adam and Eve in the Garden of Eden? That would be more suitable.'

With a smile as she recalled Maman's bemusement, Bella returned to her Greek verbs: είμαι – to be; έχω – to have; κάνω – to do; έρχομαι – to come; πηγαίνω – to go. It was maddening how, unlike the names of even the most obscure Athenian heroes, they continued to elude her. By mid-morning, the unrelenting gunfire signalled a serious escalation of the conflict. This was confirmed when Papa telephoned with the news that, after the Bulgarian advance into Greek Macedonia, the two countries were at war. The Greek commander in Salonica ordered all Bulgarian citizens to depart by nightfall and, unlike the Ottoman expulsion of the Italians eighteen months earlier, there were to be no exemptions. Papa described the sight from his office window as hundreds of people, weighed down by bundles, bags and cases, hurried along the quay, in search of ships to take them to Burgas or Varna or any friendly port. Meanwhile, the remaining Bulgarian troops in the city were mounting a desperate last stand and, for the rest of the day, both verbs and names were drowned out by the whistle of bullets, the rattle of machine guns, and the roar of canons.

By mid-evening, the guns had fallen silent and, as Bella prepared for bed, the only sound to drift in from outside was the hoot of an owl. Around midnight, she was torn from sleep by a blast so violent that she thought the White Tower had collapsed. Her windows overlooked the sea and the sacred mountain, but Irène's faced inland. She dashed into her room to find her staring at a flame-red sky. Minutes later, Maman came in to chivvy them back to bed, as though they'd been woken by drunken revellers at Purim.

'If you're scared, you can sleep with me,' Irène said, a touch too quickly, and out of kindness Bella agreed. As usual, Irène sprawled across the bed, leaving her squashed at the edge. She had barely settled when Papa peered round the door, telling them to put on their dressing gowns and slippers and come down to the salon. Leon, in mauve silk pyjamas, and Esther, still in evening clothes, were already there. Ruben rushed in, incongruously dressed in his school jacket and trousers over his nightgown. Maman ushered in the maids, each wearing a cream cotton chemise. Maryam's hair hung in a grey-flecked plait down to her waist, Malka's was set in rag rolls, while Rachel's, freed from her cap, was a shock of reddish gold. Despite Maman's coaxing, all three sat bolt upright on their chairs, manifestly ill at ease.

Papa, having sent the head guard to reconnoitre, detailed how a remnant of the Bulgarian force was holding out in the gymnasium. Outnumbered twenty to one by the surrounding Greeks, they had no hope of escape. Nevertheless, he insisted that everyone remain in the salon until he received confirmation that the fighting was over.

'You mean that the Bulgarians are dead?' Esther asked.

'Or they capitulate. Now I suggest that we all have a nip of brandy to calm our nerves.'

'They're not used to it, Señor,' Maryam said, looking at Malka and Rachel.

'Nor is Bella,' Irène said.

'All the better,' Papa replied. 'It'll have more effect.'

Dismissing Maryam's protests, Maman served the drinks herself, while Leon, with Ruben's help, fetched his phonograph. He played some of the love songs he'd brought back from Paris and, though the scratched cylinders were as crackly as a telephone, Maman, who had mused aloud whether music were appropriate at such a moment, dabbed her eyes.

Bella's stomach rumbled, but she feared that to admit to hunger would sound callous when men were breathing their last only a few streets away. Shortly after dawn, the head guard came to the house and reported to Papa. In ringing tones, as if still trying to make himself heard above the fusillade, he announced that the battle had ended and the handful of surviving Bulgarians surrendered. 'It was carnage . . . total carnage. Bodies scattered . . . blood everywhere.'

With a telling glance and a gesture of silence, Papa steered the guard into his study. Before sending everyone to bed, Maman arranged with Maryam to put back breakfast to nine o'clock. Even

Papa took advantage of the two hours' grace, but when the rest of the family gathered, red-eyed at the table, there was no sign of Ruben.

'Typical!' Irène said. 'Lazy toad!'

Malka, dispatched to rouse him, returned with the news that he wasn't in his room. Papa and Esther immediately sought to quell Maman's panic.

'He can't have left the grounds,' Papa said. 'Not with the guards at the gate.'

'Unless he took the path down to the beach,' Irène said.

'Thank you for that,' Papa said, in a voice which suggested the opposite.

'Do you think he might have gone to see what was happening and been taken prisoner . . . or worse?' Maman asked.

'Of course not! I expect that, with all the excitement, he couldn't sleep and is kicking his ball about in the garden,' Leon said, unaware of its fate. 'I'll take a look.'

As he went out, Bella searched her memory for her last words to Ruben, hoping that they had been kind. A tap at the window made her start. She turned to see a tattered Bulgarian army cap, propped on a spade, pop up like a makeshift scarecrow. As Papa growled, Maman gasped and Irène stifled a giggle, the cap slowly sank, and a bloodstained jacket, draped on a garden rake, took its place.

'He's safe,' Maman said, muttering a blessing.

'Not from me!' Papa strode from the room, his face mottled with fury. The unsuspecting Ruben, crouching behind the jacket, waved a grimy, gory sleeve just as Papa appeared and smacked his head. Ruben dropped the rake and Papa, who boasted that, unlike his father, he didn't believe in hitting children, walloped him. Both their lips were moving, but the glass was too thick to hear what was said. With the window framing the altercation like a screen, all it needed was a pianist for Bella to be back in the Pathé Frères electric theatre, watching Max Linder skidding on roller skates or drunkenly dancing with a gendarme.

Ruben, who later described to Bella and Irène how he'd sneaked through the garden and amassed trophies from the deserted battleground, was too proud to admit that Papa's blows had hurt him. It was clear, however, that the most painful blow had been to his pride.

No one appeared more shocked by his loss of control than Papa himself. Although he didn't refer to it directly, when he assembled the family in the salon that evening, he cited 'the tensions and tempers rising in every household in the city' as one of the chief reasons they must move to France.

'You mean for a few months?' Maman asked, as nonplussed as everyone else. 'Until life here returns to normal?'

'It already has,' Leon said. 'Now all the Bulgarians have left.'

'Or been killed,' Ruben interjected.

'They'll be back,' Papa said, glowering at him. 'In greater strength and better armed. Meanwhile, our new masters won't rest until they've tightened their grip on the city. I thought we could live peacefully alongside them; I was wrong. For now, they're preoccupied with the threat from the Bulgarians and the Ottomans. But before long, they'll turn their attention to us. Don't forget, we committed the greatest crime in history when we killed their Christ!'

'I didn't kill anyone,' Irène said.

'How can we leave?' Maman asked. 'Our whole life is here. Our family. Our friends. The factory. The bank. The children's schools—'

'If we don't act at once, we won't have a factory. With supplies and markets disrupted, we're being squeezed at both ends. Every day, I read reports from our agents in Macedonia that the peasants and farmers are rising up against their Muslim overlords, spoiling the crops in fields and barns. At the same time, our ships are denied entry into Ottoman ports, jeopardising the bulk of our trade.'

'Surely we can open up new routes?' Leon said. 'Grandpapa Carrache never tired of telling me how, when Britain closed the Black Sea to foreign shipping during its war with Russia, he and Arrière-Grandpapa negotiated with the Austrians to transport goods through Trieste. Not only did they secure their exports, but they forced the British to pay compensation.'

'Times have changed. I've spoken to your grandfather – or tried to. More to the point, I've spoken to Oncle Lazar and Cousin Nissim. We all agree that in present circumstances the only safe asset is capital. I've struck a deal with one of our competitors – or should I say former competitors? – Yannis Iraklidis, who owns a tobacco factory in Volos. He's keen to consolidate and has offered an excellent price. The increased liquidity will enable us to expand the bank, opening more branches in France and, if all goes well, in Italy and perhaps beyond. True, we'll have to write off a few bad debts here, but nothing substantial; we learnt our lesson after Tripolitania . . . I appreciate that this is a lot to take in, but trust me, it's the way forward.'

'What about this house?' Maman asked, staring at the walls as if for support. 'You're selling the factory, but what about the house? You love it. We all love it. You put your heart and soul into building it.'

'And we shall keep it for when we come back to visit.' Bella detected a note of uncertainty in his voice. 'We're shifting the balance: instead of living here and holidaying in France, we'll be living in France and holidaying here. And we're keeping several other properties in the city, in addition to the land that Papa and Oncle Lazar bought in the west.'

'If we leave, it'll be for ever,' Maman said sadly. 'Look at Maman, treasuring a four-hundred-year-old key in the belief – the delusion – that one day we'll return to Spain and reclaim our ancestral home!'

'It's not the same at all,' Papa said. 'We have deeds, not just a key. Deeds! Besides, haven't you always longed to go to Paris? Leon, tell Maman how wonderful it is. The most beautiful . . . the most modern . . . the most *everything* city in the world.'

'What about Palestine?' Ruben asked. 'Why don't we move there? This is our golden opportunity.'

'You can go to Palestine,' Bella said. 'We'll wave you off at the station.'

'Docks,' Irène quibbled.

'We're going to Paris, and that's the end of it,' Papa said. 'What's more, we're going together, as a family.' He underscored his resolve by quitting the room. Maman hesitated, as though weighing her loyalties, before following him out.

Bella had no memory of the earthquake in which she fell from her cot and, according to her siblings, lost half her wits, but she felt as people must have done when the ground cracked beneath their feet. She walked to the window and gazed at the one thing she had believed would be a constant in her life. She knew as well as anyone that no gods and goddesses lived on its peak, but seeing it every day, shrouded in mystery, allowed her to dream that they might. Stories of the Olympians, with their passions and plots, made more sense of the world than anything she'd been taught in synagogue or at school. Now her universe would be reduced to a single god, whose name she was forbidden to utter.

Expressing hurt at the family's resistance to his plans, Papa revised his approach. Gathering them again in the salon the next evening, he shut both sets of doors and told them that what he was about to say had to remain absolutely secret.

'If we stay in Salonica, it's only a matter of time before I'm arrested.'

'Jacob!' Maman exclaimed.

'I said *time*, not *tomorrow*. Some of you may recall reports that, when the Greek army was poised to capture the city, certain members of the Club des Intimes appealed to the captain of a British warship to intervene on our behalf.'

'I take it you were one of them,' Leon said, to a heavy silence. 'So who were the others?'

'You don't need to know. Nothing came of it, and of course we swore that the reports were false. But during the past few months, even as we've worked alongside the Greeks, some of us have held talks – informally – with representative of the Great Powers about other possibilities, such as designating the city an international free port or even an independent state governed by Jews.'

'Yes,' Ruben said, jumping up and clapping.

'No,' Papa replied. 'At least that was their response. But you must understand, if word of either discussion leaks out – as it surely will – your poor papa might meet the same fate as the unfortunate Schinas.'

'He was brutally tortured,' Esther said, prompting Maman to moan.

'Well, maybe not quite the same,' Papa said soothingly.

'What about Esther's wedding?' Irène asked.

'What does that matter?' Esther said.

'A great deal,' Papa said sternly to his eldest daughter, who, since Leah's departure, had affected a disregard for her future calculated to offend him almost as much as open rebellion. Nevertheless, Bella felt that Esther might have been forgiven for supposing that Papa's promise to consult his children before arranging their marriages would amount to more than a choice between two brothers. Finding them equally tedious, she claimed to have picked Felix because she preferred the name.

'Think of it this way,' Maman had said blithely. 'With Felix taking his beloved Sunbeam around Europe, you'll have more time for yourself. And, of course, for your children.'

'Plus, you never know, his next crash may be fatal,' Ruben added, before being banished to his room.

Assuring Esther disingenuously that the ceremony would be expedited but not rushed, Papa declared that they would celebrate the betrothal in Salonica the following week and the wedding either in Paris or Manchester at the end of the year. Felix, accompanied by Basil, returned to the city and their suite at the Hotel Colombo. His parents sent their regrets, coupled with a diamond and ruby necklace for Esther, which impressed even Grandmaman Regina. Two days later, Bella and Irène joined the *kombidador* as he paraded through the Jewish quarter, stopping in courtyards and doorways to proclaim the occasion and invite the guests. After half a dozen such calls, Bella, abashed by his swagger, persuaded Irène that they should slip away.

Although the family's departure had yet to be confirmed, rumours had spread, and the betrothal party served as their farewell to Salonica. All the notables were present, including Carraches and Berahas so remote that Bella had omitted them from her family tree. Grandpapa Carrache, looking neat as a pin, with a red rosebud in his buttonhole but smelling as though he had stepped in a puddle, was carried into the salon by 'Le pauvre Oncle Haim' and their coachman. Bella kissed his cheek, which felt as brittle as an autumn leaf. He tried to speak, pressing his thumb and forefinger on his brow as if drawing out a thought, but the only sound to emerge was a faint 'eeeh'. Grandmaman Regina, who insisted that she alone could understand him, claimed that he was complimenting her on her dress. But the pain in his eyes, the one spark of expression in his face, said otherwise.

Papa and Maman led Esther into the room to a round of applause. She looked beautiful in the gold-embroidered black velvet dress which her own mother, as well as Maman and Grandmaman Falcona, had worn for their betrothals. She appeared unmoved by the association, having told a dumbfounded Madame Naar, busy altering the bodice, that she felt like a calf adorned for sacrifice. Felix, meanwhile, wore a white tie and tails and, although his good looks and elegance drew widespread admiration, several guests registered disappointment that he had dispensed with the traditional costume. He did honour one tradition: formally presenting Esther with the necklace, along with a jar of perfume and a dish of sugared almonds. Bella couldn't dispel the hope - however unworthy - that Esther's indifference to the ceremony would extend to what were her favourite sweetmeats.

Tradition was further upheld in the music. At Maman's request, Papa had renounced his beloved string quartet for a Ladino trio of clarinet, violin and oud, together with the cantor of the Italia Yashan Synagogue doubling as a balladeer. After a selection of songs, the final one - an impoverished groom's lament for his inability to buy his barefoot bride a pair of shoes - strangely inopportune after Felix's gift of the jewelled necklace, the rabbi drew the music to a close and crossed to the centre of the room. Assembling Papa, Maman and Esther to his left and Felix and Basil to his right, he announced that he would recite the *ketubah*, first in Aramaic and then in Ladino, 'for the benefit of anyone whose Aramaic is out of practice', at which his wife laughed.

Bella had always loved Maman's *ketubah*, not for its wording, which she couldn't read, but for its gloriously illuminated script and exquisite border of birds and flowers. Maman had hung it in pride of place in her bedroom, explaining that it set out Papa's obligation to provide her with food, money, shelter, clothing and affection, the last of which struck Bella as self-evident. Esther had loved it too, but, prompted by Leah (whom, truth be told, Bella hadn't been sorry to see sail for Thrace), she'd horrified Maman by asserting that it 'codified male impurity', since a *ketubah*'s original purpose had been to distinguish between a wife and a concubine – although why anyone should confuse them, unless the wife worked in a laundry, remained unclear.

The recitation over, the cantor launched into a song exhorting a young bride to serve her husband and obey her new mother-in-law, which Bella was grateful that Esther was too busy greeting the guests to hear. She herself was distracted by the maids taking round trays of *masapan manos*, the soft, hand-shaped pastries unique to betrothals. As she weaved through the room, she managed to collect five. Her hopes of doing so unobserved were dashed when, just as she was reaching for the last one on Rachel's tray, she was waylaid by Tante Amada and Irène.

'No more, sweetheart,' Tante Amada said. 'You'll get fat.'

'She's fat already,' Irène said.

'Nonsense. She's just big-boned, like your Great-Aunt Fermoza. Though thank the Lord you don't have her teeth . . . Isn't this splendid? Esther looks radiant. Are you both excited about being bridesmaids?'

'We haven't been asked,' Irène said.

'Because it's understood. Sisters . . . A December wedding. A double celebration with Chanukah.'

'Bella doesn't celebrate Chanukah,' Irène said slyly.

'What nonsense! Of course she does. I remember one year when you came to us and were sick after eating all those *rosquitas*.'

'Things have changed,' Bella said, 'now that Ruben's told me what it commemorates.'

'We know what it commemorates.' Tante Amada's brow puckered. 'We won a victory. I forget which one exactly. Heaven knows, we haven't had that many!'

'When Judah Maccabee recaptured the Temple in Jerusalem.'

'There you are!'

'But he tore down the altars to Zeus and the other gods.'

'I should hope so. They were idols.'

'Not to the Greeks . . . not to me.'

'You're either a very stupid or a very wicked girl.'

'Earthquake!' Irène interjected.

'Yes, of course,' Tante Amada said quickly. With a pitying look at Bella, she walked away.

Felix and Basil took the first train north the following morning, bound for Amiens to compete in the annual Grand Prix. The Carraches' departure was set for 23 July, two weeks later. Each day brought further farewells, none more painful for Bella than those to her grandparents. Even if they returned as regularly as Papa had promised, she knew that she would never see Grandpapa Carrache again. He had taken to his bed straight after the betrothal ceremony and it would be a miracle – as Grandmaman Regina remarked within his hearing – if he were ever to leave it. On their final visit, she summoned her five grandchildren, one by one, to receive his blessing. As the youngest and a girl, Bella was the last. She kissed his hand and prayed for a glimmer of recognition, but his rheumy eyes remained glazed and his swollen lips fluttered in vain.

Despite his father's imminent demise, Papa did not hesitate to leave Grandmaman Regina. Maman, however, was deeply anxious about Grandmaman Falcona. Although she'd accepted the move more calmly than Bella had expected, wishing them well, as if she were waving them off for a fortnight in Vichy, Irène insisted that it was a ploy to reassure Maman, for whose sake she even set aside her fear of deafness and agreed to have a telephone installed. As they said their goodbyes, she gave each of them a hamza pin to wear on the journey.

'What's it for?' Bella asked her dejected mother on the carriage ride home.

'To protect us from the evil eye.'

'Will Leon and Ruben wear them?'

'Of course.'

'And Papa?'

'I'll sew his into his jacket pocket, like the cloves. He'll have no idea.'

Maryam chose to move to Paris with them. As she herself owned, she rarely left the house or spoke to any outsiders but tradesmen, so it made little difference where she lived. 'You're my family. I have no one else,' she said to Bella, which both touched and shamed her. Maman persuaded Grandmaman Falcona to engage Malka as support for Hannah and found Rachel a position as chambermaid at the Hotel d'Angleterre. Bella agonised over her parting gifts for them, before settling on her pearl-and-enamel bracelet for Malka and her silver brush-and-comb set for Rachel.

'They'll only sell them,' Irène said.

Bella forgave her cynicism, which she attributed to her impending separation from Mercado, with whom she was more in love than she cared to admit.

'Papa thinks so highly of him that he advised the new owner to keep him on during the transition,' she declared. 'He knows the business inside out and the workers trust him.'

'Didn't they go on strike when he was in charge last year?'

'What do you know about running a factory?' Irène snapped.

'And that's not all . . . he's appointed him as his agent, to manage his properties in the city.'

'Maman's happy that he's staying with Grandmaman Falcona,' Bella said placatingly.

'He has the sweetest, kindest, tenderest heart. And Papa told him – as good as promised him – that, if everything went well here, there'd be a job waiting for him at the bank in Paris.'

From her tone, it was clear that there would also be a bride.

On the eve of the family's departure, they visited the cemetery, as was their custom before any journey, long or short. It was a custom Bella loathed – not out of squeamishness, as her siblings assumed, but because the cemetery reeked of neglect. Many of the stark, stone slabs had sunk into the ground, while others were so weathered that their epitaphs had been erased. For years, sheep and goats had grazed among the graves, oblivious of the mortality beneath their hooves. Now the desecration had spread, with a flood of refugees from Anatolia and Thrace erecting ramshackle shelters.

'They find a warmer welcome among the dead than the living,' Esther said sourly.

Two *honadjis* greeted them at the entrance, escorting them down a pitted path to the row of family tombs and leading them in a short prayer beside each one. The last was that of Papa's grandfather, another Jacob, and, after the *honadjis* discreetly stepped back, Papa observed a further custom, praising his achievements and reminding the children of their heritage.

'Without him, the Carraches would be a shadow of what we are today. He founded the factory, of course, but he also founded almshouses and a school. He helped rich men in difficulty and poor men in need. He oversaw the refurbishment of the synagogue and commissioned a new Torah. On the day of his funeral, factories, shops and markets across Salonica closed. Schoolchildren – Muslims and Christians as well as Jews – lined the route of his cortège. The docks fell as silent as on the Sabbath.'

'Yet we're leaving it behind,' Leon said.

'We're moving on! Two years ago, I would no more have imagined quitting the city than that the Ottomans would be overthrown. But as the proverb says, and our resident Hebraist will confirm: "Many are the plans of a man's heart, but the Lord's purpose will prevail."' He looked at Ruben, who smiled blankly, before turning to Maman, scrabbling on the ground. 'Mathilde, what in Heaven's name are you doing?'

'I'd like to take a clump of earth – hallowed earth – with us to Paris.'

'Won't we carry it in our hearts?'

'Can't we do both?'

'As you wish,' Papa replied, with a sigh. 'But let Ruben... Ruben, scoop out some soil for your mother.'

Maman stood up as Ruben grabbed a stone from the top of Arrière-Grandpapa Carrache's tomb and hacked at the ground.

'Why all the glum faces?' Papa said. 'We're about to set off on a wonderful adventure. France: the first country in Europe to emancipate the Jews; the birthplace of the Enlightenment; the home of Voltaire and Rousseau.'

'And Dreyfus,' Ruben said, lifting a clod pulsating with worms.

TWO

1

MATHILDE

PARIS, SEPTEMBER 1939

JACOB HAD DREAMT of having a funeral procession as lavish as his grandfather's. Although only eight years old at the time, he had often described how the city came to a halt as the cortège wound its way through the hushed streets to the Jewish cemetery. But that had been in Salonica, where a philanthropic factory owner was accorded the public veneration which, in France, was reserved for a war hero such as Maréchal Foch or a statesman such as President Poincaré. Indeed, even the synagogue promised to be less well attended than if he had died, as the doctors predicted, in early August. Having lingered on until 1 September, the very evening that *Paris-soir* reported Hitler's invasion of Poland, he was to be buried two days later with the country on the brink of war.

After a massive stroke rendered him insensate, Mathilde had sat with him day and night, alert to the slightest spark of awareness in his vacant gaze. Leon and Esther, the one in Marseille and the other in Manchester, hurried to his bedside, only to return home when, defying the augurs, he clung to life. Ruben looked in for half an hour most evenings, and Bella flitted by as erratically as ever. Irène and Simon, near neighbours in the Rue des Martyrs, were regular visitors, with Simon often staying overnight while Irène tended to the children. In a cruel twist of fate, Jacob died during Mathilde's brief absence from the room. Overcome, she declared that, after forty-four years of marriage, her husband hadn't wanted her with him at the end. Simon, who alone had been there, insisted that, on the contrary, he'd instinctually sought to spare her pain. Nevertheless, he acted as though Jacob had chosen him to bear witness, treating anyone who'd listen to an awestruck account of the privilege of sharing his last breath.

The funeral had been delayed by a day to allow Esther and her younger son, Basil, to make the journey from Manchester. Leon had met them at the Gare du Nord the previous evening and driven them back for a late-night supper. All the children were there, apart from Bella who, according to an outraged Irène, had 'an engagement too important to cancel and too complicated to explain'. All the grandchildren were there too, apart from Esther's elder son, Nathan, who'd sent a heartfelt telegram from Buenos Aires. Leon and Lily brought Gabrielle and Daniel. Irène and Simon brought Clarice and Sylvain, at nine the youngest member of the family, whose unease in the presence of his grandfather's coffin was compounded by Daniel's teasing. It was the first such gathering since her ruby wedding and, despite the sadness, the atmosphere was convivial as the children and her brother-in-law, Henri, exchanged memories of Salonica; although Mathilde noted that she was alone in calling it home.

Even as the maids served the traditional delicacies, which her grandchildren regarded with distrust, Mathilde discerned cracks in the conviviality. Leon shook Simon's hand, but he barely concealed his loathing of the man who'd usurped his place at his father's side. Esther kissed Ruben, but she hadn't forgiven him for offering Nathan the post of Argentine representative of Tissus de Lyon without consulting her. Furthermore, there were serious strains in her two oldest children's marriages. Esther had come without Felix, whose drunken overtures towards Bella at the ruby wedding party had horrified the guests and humiliated his wife and sons. And although she was assured that there'd been no impropriety on either side,

Leon and Lily were living apart. Since her two youngest children remained single (Ruben, at forty-one, destined to end up an elderly roué like his Oncle Henri; Bella, at thirty-nine, with no hope of finding a husband, even in the bohemian circles she frequented), the most settled of them all was the unassuming Irène.

Eager to share her thoughts with Jacob, Mathilde glanced across the room, only to be confronted by his empty bed, the absence accentuated by the smiling cherub clasping a horn of plenty on the headboard. Desolation overwhelmed her, and she drained her now tepid coffee in a single gulp. Despite Maryam's exhortation to take her breakfast downstairs, she had stayed in bed. She was happier knowing that the family was close at hand than engaging with them in person. As she sank into a reverie, a knock at the door announced her two granddaughters: fifteen-year-old Clarice and twelve-year-old Gabrielle, whose childhood friendship had survived their fathers' estrangement. She called them in, swallowing a cry when they perched on Jacob's bed as if it were a nondescript divan. Their diffidence confirmed her suspicions that they'd been sent by their parents. In response, she attempted to divert them with a selection of necklaces and brooches to embellish the mourning crepe that they were far too young to wear. But her 'One day, these will be yours to keep' dampened the mood.

While Mathilde promised Gabrielle that she wasn't about to join their grandfather, Clarice replaced the jewellery box in the dresser. After closing the drawer, she smoothed a corner of the cloth that veiled the Venetian mirror, as methodically as she would a skirt over a patch of petticoat. 'Do you realise that you have nineteen mirrors in your house, Grandmaman? Not counting the ones in the maids' rooms.'

'We've checked that they're all covered,' Gabrielle said. 'But we don't know why. Papa says that it's so we don't see our sad faces and feel even sadder, but Oncle Simon says that it's to stop Grandpapa's ghost being trapped in the reflection and haunting us – well, you, since you'll be the only one here.'

'Customs can serve more than one purpose,' Mathilde replied, refusing to favour either of their fathers.

'But Oncle Ruben says it's an old wives' tale that should be laid to rest,' Clarice added.

Mathilde dissolved into tears.

'I'm sure he didn't mean to be rude,' Gabrielle said, rushing over to kiss her.

'And Grandpapa won't be a ghost,' Clarice said. 'His soul's already being purified in . . . I forget the place.'

'Gehenna,' Gabrielle said.

'That's right . . . before going to Heaven.'

Mathilde shook her head. 'Don't worry, I wasn't thinking of Grandpapa.'

'Then who?'

'My maman – your arrière-grandmaman. She treasured all the traditions. I miss her so much.'

'More than Grandpapa?' Gabrielle asked, with a shocked expression.

'Differently. Now run along. It's time for me to have my bath and get ready.'

Their report of the men's dissension deepened Mathilde's reluctance to quit her bed. It wasn't as though there were anything for her to do downstairs. The children had attended to all the day's arrangements, as if the simplest task (which might have afforded a welcome distraction) would intrude on the sanctity of her loss. She understood that the rabbi preferred to discuss the service with her sons, but Irène had even denied her a voice in the reception. Maman had taught her that the appropriate foods for a funeral meal were haminados eggs, bollos loaves, olives, oranges and raisins, the roundness of each symbolising the circle of life. For once, her mother-in-law had agreed. While never one to stint her guests, she'd held that the simplicity catered to the mourners' sentiments rather than their appetites. But Irène and Simon had been appalled, insisting that if Jacob's Parisian associates were served such modest fare, they would assume that his death had exposed the fragility of the family's finances, which might even precipitate a run on the bank. Daunted, Mathilde had acceded to their demand to hire the fashionable Maison Maxime Cohen.

Maryam shuffled in, her face grooved with grief, serenely unaware that Jacob's plight had relieved her own. Increasingly irked by her sluggishness, clumsiness and overfamiliarity, he had proposed to rent her an apartment in Little Turkey, where she could 'enjoy a peaceful old age among her own'. Mathilde successfully pleaded that 'we are her own', but her breaking of his grandfather's Meissen candleholder, accompanied not by an apology but by 'Oops' and a bark of laughter, was the final straw. He instructed Simon to draw up a list of suitable properties, but her departure was deferred by his stroke. Inert in bed, he was reconciled to her soothing presence. She was the only person besides Mathilde herself whom he would allow to feed him, serving him spoonfuls of calf's foot jelly, turtle soup and minced chicken, amid a hotchpotch of Ladino blandishments.

'It's almost noon, Señora,' she said, twenty-seven years in France having failed to accustom her to *Madame*.

'I should get up . . . I should be up already. Have the family all arrived?'

'All except Bella.'

'She was such a dutiful little girl.' Mathilde sighed. 'No arguments?'

'Well . . . Not that I was listening . . .'

'Of course not.' Having repeatedly asked her children to pay more attention to Maryam, she was grateful that for once she had passed among them unremarked.

'But I couldn't help overhearing words between Leon and Esther and Mercado.'

'Simon! It's Simon!' Mathilde wrung her handkerchief. 'How often do I have to tell you?'

'I'm sorry, Señora, this old brain . . .'

'Do try to remember! You know how it offends him. He . . .'

She broke off. Although twenty years Maryam's junior, she was also apt to forget her son-in-law's reversion to his birth name; yet here she was, scolding her like a chastened child smacking her doll. 'So what were they arguing about?'

'I didn't catch all of it – I wasn't trying – but Mer . . . Simon said that they had to consider if this house would be too big for you.'

'Did he now?'

'And Esther said "For Heaven's sake, Papa's not yet in his grave." And Mer – that's to say, Simon – said who knows when they'd all be together again. And Esther said "Bella's not here yet." And Mercado laughed . . . well, not a laugh, more like a sort of snicker.'

'I can imagine.'

'Leon said that, any case, it was something for the children to discuss, not outsiders. And Irène said he was her husband and could speak for her. And Esther said "I'm sure he does." And . . . Simon' – she smiled triumphantly – 'said that it wasn't as if Señor Carrache hadn't left you well provided for, but he didn't think you'd be happy living here all alone. Then everyone looked at me, like if I'd dropped a plate. So I came out.'

'It's very kind of Simon to concern himself with my happiness, but I have no intention of leaving this house. And I won't be alone. Whatever happens, you'll have a home here with me.'

Maryam grinned, revealing the yellow, snaggled teeth that caused her constant pain, although she refused to visit a dentist. She approached the bed, whereupon Mathilde, fearing that she was about to kiss her hand, slid both hands under the covers. Thwarted, Maryam headed to the bathroom to draw her bath, a charge she would never relinquish to either of the maids. Left to herself, Mathilde took stock of what she had heard.

No matter what Simon or anyone else might say, she was determined to remain in the house which, over the years, she had come to love almost as much as the one in the Campania. After their flight from Greek Salonica, it had seemed almost perverse to move to Nouvelle Athènes in Paris, but, from the first, the district enchanted her. Jacob had listed the celebrated writers and artists who'd lived on the Avenue Frochot during the previous century, three of whom – Alexander Dumas, Victor Hugo and Gustave Moreau – she recognised. Moreau had even designed the stained-glass windows of the four seasons that graced, while not illuminating, the library. Everything about the house – from the wisteria on the façade, through the painted dome in the hall, to the Louis XV boiserie in the dining room and the toile de Jouy in her bedroom – signified home. If her family feared that she would be lost or lonely, she might invite Madame Naar to move in. Jacob had often teased her for keeping up the connection, but her former dressmaker was a cherished link to the past. Too blind to continue working and too proud to accept charity, she lived in straitened circumstances in a basement room in the Rue Saint-Maur. Didn't she deserve a little comfort in her old age?

No doubt Simon would voice his objections. For all Jacob's faith in his son-in-law's abilities, she couldn't help wishing he had appointed someone else to oversee her affairs. As his elder son, Leon would have been the obvious choice, had he not moved to Marseille. But his distance from the family was more than geographic. The war had changed him in ways that Mathilde, who'd known nothing more disruptive than Zeppelin raids and food shortages, couldn't begin to comprehend. The failure of his marriage had strengthened his resentment of his father, who'd made no secret of his dislike for Lily's Bordelais family and his conviction that Leon would have been better off wedded to a fellow Salonican.

Even with a mother's fondness, Mathilde understood why Jacob hadn't put his trust in Ruben. While bitterly opposed to his joining an agrarian community in Palestine four years after the war, he'd been dismayed when he abandoned it a mere eighteen months later. Ruben had complained of the closed minds of the community leaders and their insensitivity to their Arab neighbours, but, given his relentless pursuit of pleasure on his return to Paris, it was hard to dispute Jacob's assessment that he had not been equal to the effort.

After a short spell at the bank, he'd taken up Henri's offer to run the Tissus de Lyon showroom in the Faubourg Saint-Honoré. The defection had dealt a double blow to Jacob, who assured Mathilde that he didn't resent Henri's success: 'I just like things to stay the same.' Her own concern was the opportunity it gave Ruben to flirt with the customers, several of whom, as he slyly confided, invited him home to advise on their decorative schemes. No wonder he ignored her invitations to the dances at the Cultuelle Sepharadite.

Whereas both his sons had deserted him, though less brutally than Jacob liked to pretend, Simon remained steadfast. His management of the Carrache interests in Salonica had proved more critical than anyone could have anticipated. Jacob's promise that they would return for holidays had been overtaken by events. He himself had been back only twice: first, three months after leaving, with his brother, uncle and sons for his father's funeral. He had begged his mother to come to Paris, but she was so attached to her native city that she'd even spent her honeymoon at the Hotel Colombo. She died of malaria in 1916, and Maman, who'd escaped the epidemic, died in her sleep the following year. With the war prohibiting foreign travel, Simon organised both funerals and, for all her misgivings about him, Mathilde would always be grateful for his assumption of the task and his detailed accounts of the ceremonies.

Jacob's second and, as it turned out, final visit took place in November 1918, immediately after the Armistice. He was so distressed by the devastation caused by the Great Fire, which had consumed more than three-quarters of the city the preceding year, that he never returned and urged his wife and children to follow suit. Once again, Simon remained on hand, tackling the tortuous compensation procedure for the family's ruined properties and bidding for lucrative building permits in the burnt zone. Throughout their years apart, he and Irène kept in regular contact and, when he moved to Paris in 1921, Jacob gave permission for them to marry. By then, the once impoverished clerk had amassed a considerable fortune. While Leon and Ruben scoffed, Jacob maintained the fiction that he'd inherited valuable assets from his father. In private, he admitted that he must have used the Carrache title deeds as collateral for speculations of his own. 'But what does it matter?' he said, making more allowance for him than for either of his sons. 'Without Simon keeping an eye on them, who knows how the authorities might have swindled us? This way, at least the profits stay in the family!'

As she bathed, dressed and pomaded her hair, she felt a blaze of indignation that such trivial concerns had obtruded into her thoughts. With a fruitless glance at the mirror, she walked out of the room and down the stairs, each hollow step a reminder that Jacob would never tread them again. She crept past the salon, startled by the hum of the wireless amid the murmur of voices, and entered the library, where Jacob lay in a plain wooden coffin. She nodded to Monsieur Laniardo, the *shomer* engaged to keep vigil, who put down his Book of Psalms and drew up a chair for her. Its ornate gilt frame and damask needlework proved that, whatever the simplicity Jacob had embraced in death, he'd eschewed it in life. Monsieur Laniardo retreated to the door as Mathilde took her seat beside her husband. The narrowness of the coffin disturbed her, and she panicked that Jacob, who'd ordered his shirts and jackets with 'room to breathe', might be cramped. She felt a violent impulse to scream and was grateful for the *shomer*'s restraining presence.

The heavy smell of beeswax from the guttering candles conjured up the one smell she would never know again: Jacob's crisp, woody scent, redolent of the ancient volumes lining the walls, just as his mottled hands had resembled their pages. She longed to prise open the coffin to savour it one last time. The notion was absurd . . . obscene . . . deranged. The scent would be no more Jacob than the reek of a compost heap was the fragrance of roses. This time she was unable to suppress her scream, although somewhere at the back of her throat it turned into a snort.

'Is there anything . . . ?' Monsieur Laniardo asked. 'Should I fetch someone . . . one of your daughters?'

'Thank you, no. I'd just like a few minutes alone with my husband.'

'Yes, of course. I'll leave you. But I'll be right outside should you need me.'

Mathilde forced a smile, although the only man she needed was boxed up in front of her. She scoured her memory for her first impression of him. It must have been when he courted Irène, but she could recollect nothing before their betrothal ceremony. They'd made such a handsome couple: Irène in the black velvet *bindalli* with its gold-embroidered tree of life, which she herself wore five years later; Jacob in a brocaded purple kaftan and blue-and-gold *kavese* cap. By rights, it should have been Irène sitting here now. But she couldn't afford to give way to a second sorrow.

Images flickered across her mind as on a cinema screen: not a smart Parisian cinema such as the Grand Rex or the Marivaux, but the Pathé Frères in Salonica, where the projector was prone to break down in the middle of a ten-minute short. Jacob stood smiling, champagne flute in hand, proposing a toast. Was it someone's birthday or anniversary, Esther or Irène's wedding, or was he simply extemporising at the end of a Sabbath meal? Now, the glass had become a telephone and his face was sombre. Had they received word of Leon's wounding at the Aisne? Did his son appreciate how many officials he'd petitioned in order to have him transferred to the Val-de-Grâce? Or was it during those grim months in 1932, when bank after bank had collapsed and he feared that Carrache's would be next? But it had survived and prospered beyond all expectation. Perhaps the toast was to its next ten years of success? Not that he had lived to see them.

She dabbed away a tear and pictured him again: elderly, grizzled, inveighing against an unnatural child, who could only be Bella, the habitual scapegoat for his grey hairs. Had she caused another scandal with her paintings of rabbis frolicking with woodland nymphs? Was he afraid that people might connect it to him, notwithstanding her pseudonym? No, it was worse than that. From a glimpse of the card in his hand, she recalled that they'd been invited to the latest exhibition at Madame Weill's gallery, which, Bella warned them, contained a full-length nude of her by her friend, Robert Delaunay. Jacob had rushed to the gallery, determined to purchase it before it went on display. He'd returned, spirits restored, assuring her that he hadn't had to part with a centime, since the painting was a pattern of circles, squares and triangles, barely identifiable as human, let alone as Bella.

As other images faded, she was left with the most precious: Jacob in his favourite armchair on one of the many evenings when, with no dinner or function to attend, they sat together in the salon, he reading or listening to the wireless, she crocheting or knitting. Perhaps he was about to crack the joke that, given the amount of wool she used, he ought to invest in a herd of alpaca: a joke which, for all its familiarity, never staled. Before she knew it, they had moved upstairs and he was in his pyjamas. The anticipation of intimacy stirred something deep within her. No woman could have wished for a happier ending to the day.

Heartsick at the thought that those days would never return, she bent to kiss the coffin and left the room. She entered the crowded salon, greeting a succession of shapes – not faces, even though her eyes were dry. The two shapes closest to her turned into Cousin Nissim and his wife Luna, whose lace-trimmed mourning gown and wide-brimmed, black-feathered hat made her feel underdressed. Sitting next to them was Henri, who, like Simon, had changed his name on moving to France, while being more indulgent of a forgetful *Haim* than Simon was of a *Mercado*. To Mathilde's surprise, he had been profoundly affected by Jacob's stroke; although given that his father, his uncle and now his brother had all died the same way, his prime concern may well been his own mortality.

The rest of the room slowly shifted into focus. Leon, Irène and Ruben huddled together by the fireplace, the family resemblance more striking than ever when framed in black. Esther and Lily, who'd had little to say to each other for fifteen years, sat side by side on the Aubusson canapé. Clarice, the only musician in the family, squeezed next to Gabrielle on the piano stool, although the lid was closed. Daniel and Sylvain, less companionable than their sisters, perched on the window seat playing draughts. Basil, standing aloof from his younger cousins, was examining a Daumier caricature. Simon, who'd appropriated Jacob's chair, switched off the wireless and sprang to his feet as Mathilde entered.

'Please don't let me interrupt,' she said, disturbed by the sudden silence. 'By all means, listen to the wireless if you wish.'

'Britain has just declared war, Maman,' Esther said.

'On us?' she asked, appalled.

'No, of course not,' Ruben said, covering his testiness with a cough.

'Then we'd have to shoot Basil,' Sylvain said, pointing a finger gun at him.

'On Germany,' Ruben said. 'Chamberlain's ultimatum ran out more than an hour ago – eleven o'clock their time.'

'Yes, of course, I wasn't thinking.'

'You have every right,' Luna said.

'Not really,' Mathilde replied, knowing how Jacob would have despised such self-absorption. 'And Daladier?'

'He's given Hitler a few more hours. Our deadline is five o'clock.'

'Then there's still hope!'

'Of what?' Ruben asked.

'Ruben . . .' Leon muttered.

'Of capitulation?' Ruben added. 'Of allowing Hitler to trample over the Poles like he has over the Czechs and the Jews?'

Mathilde didn't wish to argue (she scarcely wished to talk). She had been horrified by the Nazi race laws and the attacks on Jewish homes, shops and synagogues. She'd engaged a German maid at the request of the Central Consistory, although it had not been a success. But, as ever, she had taken her cue from Jacob, who'd dismissed Hitler as a man of straw. He refused to believe that the land of Goethe and Schiller, Beethoven and Bach, would entrust its fate to such a scoundrel. Moreover, he bitterly condemned the young Pole, Herschel Grynszpan, who'd assassinated Ernst vom Rath at the German embassy, triggering a wave of antisemitic violence at home and abroad. 'So much for diplomatic immunity!' he declared to a jubilant Ruben.

She felt her own loss overshadowed by the looming conflict. She remembered her daily dread of the casualty lists when Leon joined up in 1915, and her relief at the bullet wound that released him from the front for five blessed months, its only lasting legacy a slight stiffness in his right arm. That stiffness, together with his age, would exempt him from having to fight again, just as Ruben's reluctance to apply for French citizenship, a permanent bone of contention with his father, would exempt him from conscription. Daniel and Sylvain were too young to do more than trace battle lines on maps. Her greatest fear was for Basil, who would be eighteen next year. The thought of that clever, sensitive, handsome boy amid the mud and vermin of the trenches terrified her.

'You won't be called on to fight, will you, dear?' she asked him.

'Definitely not,' Esther interjected. 'He takes his Higher Cert in the summer. That's like your Bac,' she explained to his cousins. 'Then he's off to Oxford.'

Basil listened impassively as his mother outlined his future.

'If it comes to it, we'll hide him here,' Irène said. 'His French is so good that, when he stayed with us this summer, one of our friends refused to believe he was English.'

'Would that be Juliette Delfroye?' Clarice asked pertly. 'Basil's special friend.'

'Don't be mean!' Irène said.

'It won't come to that,' Ruben said. 'The war will be sharp and swift. Hitler will be given a bloody nose and slink back to Berlin.'

'I seem to have heard that before,' Leon said. 'Although the Boche in question was the Kaiser.'

'Our troops are the best trained . . . the best equipped in the world,' Ruben said. 'The Maginot line is impregnable. What's he going to do? Invade through the Ardennes?'

Mathilde shared his confidence. Just six weeks earlier, on one of their last outings, she and Jacob had been guests of the Préfecture at the Bastille Day parade. As the troops marched and the tanks rolled down the Champs-Élysées, she'd waved her tricolour as proudly as any native Frenchwoman.

'When will you be joining your regiment, Oncle Ruben?' Sylvain asked.

'Shush!' Irène admonished him.

'What regiment?' Mathilde asked, her throat tightening.

'Nothing, Maman,' Irène said.

Mathilde looked round the room, but nobody met her eye. 'What regiment?' she repeated.

'The Foreign Legion,' Ruben said. 'I volunteered on Friday, when Frenchmen my age were called up. That's why I was late at . . . at Papa's bedside. I'm following in my brother's august footsteps.' He smiled at Leon. 'Now the old chap's past it, I felt there should be another Carrache in uniform.'

'Your father would—'

'Be proud of him, Maman,' Leon cut in.

'It'll be fine, Maman. I'm due to report tomorrow at Sathonay training camp, outside Lyon. I want to fight. For France, yes, but also for our own people.'

Nissim, who had never hidden his disapproval of Ruben's bachelor life, nodded. 'The military may be the making of him.'

'No more of that!' Leon said vehemently. 'He's not eight years old.'

Lucie, the young Breton maid, entered. 'They've come to take Monsieur away,' she said, with a sob that seemed excessive after only two months in their employ. Mathilde's head spun and she feared that she might collapse, until she realised she was sitting down.

'You stay here, Maman,' Leon said, as he led the men from the room.

'Close the door, will you, dear?' Mathilde asked Clarice, dreading a muffled command or, worse, an accidental scrape as the pallbearers manoeuvred the coffin through the hall.

'Are you ready to go, Maman?' Irène asked.

'There's plenty of time,' Luna said. 'The rabbi hasn't arrived.'

'Nor has Bella,' Irène sighed.

'In England, we speak of someone who'd be late for her own funeral,' Esther said.

'Aunt Bella may be late for Grandpapa's.'

'That's not funny, Daniel,' Lily said.

'Yes, it is,' Mathilde said, with a smile at the crushed boy. 'As well as sad.'

'You'd have thought she would have been here to see us last night,' Esther said.

'She had a rendezvous with her prince,' Lily said drily. 'Prince Menshikov.'

'Is he a real prince?' Gabrielle asked.

'And an equally real waiter.'

'We invited him to dinner,' Irène said. 'It seemed only polite. Simon couldn't stop staring at him. Finally, he asked if they'd met before. "Very possibly," he said, cool as anything, "I'm the sommelier at Le Nid. This is my evening off."'

'How mortifying!' Luna said.

'Not for him. We were the ones left floundering.'

'Why?' Esther asked. 'It's an honest job. He should be far more ashamed of his parasitic life before the Revolution.'

'No politics today, Mother, please,' Basil said in English.

'How typical of Bella not to warn you!' Lily said. 'No doubt she thought it amusing.'

At the mention of her youngest daughter, Mathilde gazed instinctively at the picture above the chimney piece. Sentiment alone hadn't granted it pride of place in a room whose artworks would have graced a provincial museum. Over the past decade, Bella had become one of France's most lauded female artists, a designation she deplored, telling one shocked interviewer that 'I paint with my brush in my hand, not in my . . .' Mathilde refused even to formulate the word. It never failed to astound her that Bella's schoolgirl pastime had turned into a serious profession. Shortly after moving to the Avenue

Frochot, Bella had made the acquaintance of Berthe Weill, the owner of a nearby gallery. Against all expectations, Madame Weill charmed Jacob, not only selling him several paintings but persuading him to let Bella, whose talent she quickly recognised, study under her friend Marie Laurencin. Ten years later, she gave her her first solo exhibition, which garnered instant acclaim. Using a basic palette inspired by the ceramics she'd copied in Salonica, she incorporated figures from Greek mythology into scenes of contemporary life, creating her signature style. She even took the name Timarete, after a renowned painter of the ancient world.

The picture above the chimney piece was a double portrait of Jacob and Mathilde as Zeus and Hera. Apart from an unclad Eros hovering overhead, there was nothing in it to which Jacob could object. Mathilde had regularly given thanks for his fading eyesight when, standing back from a canvas to gauge its full effect, the more intimate details escaped his notice. His blushes spared, what offended him most was that Bella's success enabled her to pursue her career independent of his support.

'You must be very proud of her,' friends, whose daughters were safely married, would say with a faintly condescending air.

'It's a mystery where she gets it from,' was Mathilde's stock reply. 'Neither Jacob nor I can draw so much as a straight line.'

Bella finally arrived, wearing a plum velvet cape and a beaded black dress which could at least pass for mourning.

Esther was taken aback by her bob cut. 'You've shorn yourself!' she exclaimed.

'It's more practical when I'm working.'

'Your beautiful hair!'

'Thank you.'

'I meant before you chopped it all off.'

'I realise that. I'm sorry I missed you yesterday. I had a long-standing engagement.'

'I haven't seen you for two years.'

'I'm here now.'

'We live in the same city and we hardly ever see her,' Irène said.

'But do you really want to see me?'

'What kind of a question is that?'

Disdaining to reply, Bella turned to her nephew. 'Basil, I wouldn't have recognised you. Are you too grown-up to give your aunt a kiss?'

'Of course not. He's only seventeen,' Esther said rapidly, as if to distance him from the threat of conscription and the fate of the uncle after whom he was named.

Bella, who was no doubt as oblivious to the prospect of war as to everything else outside her studio, embraced Basil before moving to Mathilde.

'Darling Maman, how are you bearing up?' she asked. She leant over to kiss her, exuding a scent of jasmine and tobacco, with a hint of yesterday's linen.

'I'm very glad to see you, my dear.'

'I know how hard this must be for you. You'll feel much better once today is over.'

'Will I?' Mathilde wanted to ask. 'Are you planning to come and live with me? Are any of your sisters or brothers?' But all she said was 'Thank you, my dear.'

The men returned, accompanied by the rabbi, who, after a further round of condolences, announced that it was time for them to perform *keriah*. He explained that the *shomer* would make a small incision in their upper clothing, which they should then tear a hand's breadth, the children on the left, the widow and other close relatives on the right, since, for reasons Mathilde failed to fathom, she was not required to expose her heart.

'Are we really going to do this?' Bella asked.

'Yes, of course,' Leon said sternly.

'It's a good thing I'm wearing a brassiere.'

As she ripped her bodice, Mathilde felt the strength seep from her hands. She stood numbly until, with everyone ready to depart, Irène helped her on with her coat and hat and adjusted her veil. After checking that Ruben had charge of Maryam, she made her way into the courtyard, where Simon had taken it upon himself to organise the cortège. He escorted her into the first car, with Henri, Leon, Lily and their children. Just as the driver was setting off, she banged on the glass.

'Stop a minute, please! Daniel, there's a small wooden box on my dressing table. Would you be a dear and fetch it?'

'Hurry,' Leon said, as Daniel scrambled out of the car. 'What's in it, Maman?'

'Soil.'

'What?'

'Soil that I brought here from home. I want to sprinkle half of it in Papa's grave. The rest you must keep and do the same for me.'

Daniel returned with the precious box. The cortège trundled down the Rue Blanche, drawing up at the synagogue in the Rue Saint-Lazare, where a small crowd had gathered on the pavement. Conspicuous among them was Madame Naar, who rushed forward, greeting Mathilde in a cloud of camphor.

'Blessed be the true Judge!' she exclaimed.

The blessing was echoed in various tones and accents as Mathilde climbed the stairs to the women's gallery, where she took her seat in the front row between Luna, whose hat obscured her view, and Irène, who pointed out the distinguished figures in the sanctuary, as if they were the audience at an opera gala: the Grand Rabbi; the President of the Amicale Salonicienne; the editors of *Le Judaïsme Sephardi*, *Pax et Droit* and *Les Echos*; together with presidents and directors of banks, trustees of charities, and officials of clubs and societies, many of whom turned out to be Simon's friends.

The rabbi's opening remarks were followed by the cantor's recitation of a sequence of psalms. Mathilde, who knew no Hebrew, surrendered to the melody without having to worry about the words. The rabbi then moved to the head of the coffin to deliver the eulogy.

'We are assembled here to honour the life of Jacob Carrache, husband to Mathilde, father to Leon, Ruben, Esther, Irène and Bella, brother to Henri, and friend to many both in this congregation and beyond.

'Jacob was born seventy-eight years ago in Salonica, the elder son of Leon and Regina, may their memory be a blessing! For fifty years, he resided in his home town, where, in addition to owning one of its largest factories, providing employment for thousands, he was President of the Jewish Community Council, sat on the board of the Talmud Torah, and played an active role in numerous educational and municipal charities.

'After the Greek annexation of the city, he moved to Paris, where he took the helm of the family bank, charting a steady course through the turbulent financial waters of the past decade. He worked unceasingly on behalf of his former compatriots, and it was his diligence that enabled many to retrieve their assets from the now-defunct Ottoman Empire. Meanwhile, he offered generous loans to those less fortunate, to set up new businesses here in France.

'Members of this synagogue have particular reason to celebrate his munificence, since he was the prime mover behind its foundation. A proud Eastern Sephardi, he was dismayed on his arrival in Paris to find that there was nowhere he could worship in his native tradition. There were those who urged him to join the Ashkenazim at the Synagogue de la Victoire, but he chose to remain true to his roots. So, gathering together a group of his fellow Salonicans – I see several of them in front of me, their faces lined with grief but also, I trust, with pride – he bought the building and funded its conversion.'

'Nonsense,' Luna whispered to Mathilde. 'With the utmost respect to Jacob, you know as well as I do that if all he'd wanted was to be true to his roots, he could have gone to the Ottoman synagogue on the Rue Popincourt. But he scorned to rub shoulders with the rabble. And who can blame him?'

Luna's words were blunt and inapposite but hard to deny. Jacob had been as loath to set foot in Little Turkey as he'd once been in Vardar. Indeed, many of its denizens were the same: hawkers, porters, labourers, tailors, seamstresses and even erstwhile tobacco workers, who'd struggled to scrape a living when Piraeus replaced Salonica as the main trading port in the expanded Greek state. Mathilde, however, ventured there on the first Thursday of every month to meet Madame Naar at Chez Sotil, where they would sit and reminisce, sharing a plate of baklava or *tishpisti*, and listening to the Ladino chatter all around them with a joy which Jacob, who'd grown up speaking French, had never understood.

Lost in thought, she was mortified to find that she'd missed much of the eulogy. She rose to her feet as the rabbi returned to the bimah and led them in the Mourner's Kaddish, before pronouncing the final blessing. The pallbearers approached the coffin, which they shouldered and carried through the sanctuary. The men followed them out, and the women left the gallery. Mathilde stood in a knot of family and friends and watched as the coffin was loaded into the hearse. Several men whom she dimly recognised came up and offered their condolences, along with apologies for not accompanying them to the cemetery since, at five o'clock, Daladier was due to address the nation.

'I appreciate that people are anxious,' she said to Lily, 'but can't they spare a couple of hours? Even if war is declared, nothing will happen today.'

'What about a gas attack?'

'In Paris?'

'There are rumours that Hitler has a fleet of planes ready to spray deadly poison on the city. Anyone with transport is preparing to leave. Our driver just told Leon that, while we were in synagogue, a stranger offered him fifty thousand francs – in cash – for the hearse.'

Stupefied, Mathilde stepped into the car. Once everyone was settled, the cortège drove off along the Rue de la Chaussée-d'Antin and into the Boulevard Haussmann.

'There's Grandpapa's bank!' Daniel exclaimed.

'Why's that black book stuck to the door?' Gabrielle asked.

'It's for people to write nice things about Grandpapa,' Leon said.

'Who?' Gabrielle asked.

'Anyone who wants,' he replied.

'Can I?'

'Maybe back at our branch in Marseille.'

Mathilde closed her eyes to blot out the bank, opening them in the Place de la Concorde, where she was shocked to see sandbags, shaped like a giant beehive, piled around the Obelisk. They crossed the river and drove down the Boulevard Saint-Germain, the funereal pace reinforced by the traffic, which, unusually heavy for a Sunday afternoon, bore out Lily's report of a general exodus. They finally arrived at Montparnasse cemetery forty minutes late. Mathilde knew it well since, with her own dead so far away, she had adopted it as a fitting place to commune with them, taking comfort from the jumble of monuments: mausoleums and monoliths, angels and allegories, some well tended, others as decayed as those they memorialised. In contrast, the Jewish tombs stood out as much for their modesty as for their inscriptions. Jacob's plot was close to Oncle Lazar, Tante Amada and Cousin Mazal, and three rows from Alfred Dreyfus. In due course, she would be reunited with him there.

The hearse stopped at a small lodge, and a whiskery old man, in a blue army uniform festooned with medals, shambled out. The driver handed him a document which, despite their late arrival, must have been in order, but he kept shaking his head.

'Let me find out what's happening,' Leon said, jumping out of the car. 'The gates close at six, so we only have half an hour.' He returned a few moments later. 'There's no problem, at least not at this end. The old boy's been listening to Daladier's speech. He's overwhelmed – with grief or anger or something else. All he could say was "Not again! Not again!"'

'It's dreadful, I understand,' Mathilde said, clasping the box of soil. 'But may we bury your father?'

'Strange,' Leon said, as the hearse rolled into the cemetery. 'If we'd arrived on schedule, we'd have been the last burial of peacetime. As it is, we're the first of the war.'

2

RUBEN

PARIS, OCTOBER 1942

THE BELLS OF Notre Dame rang six, in line with those in Munich, Frankfurt and Berlin. Ruben's watch read five, although given that he was an unregistered Jew in Nazi-controlled Paris, his refusal to adapt his timekeeping to that of the enemy was a minor act of resistance.

Fearing the worst, he had chosen not to comply when the German Military Administration ordered all Jews in the occupied zone to register at their local gendarmerie and carry identity cards stamped with their race, even though that was the only communal identity he had left. Unlike the rest of his family, he had never sought French citizenship. As an Ottoman subject under Italian protection who'd emigrated to Palestine and back to France, he had regarded himself as transcending nationality. But when circumstances made it incumbent on him to claim one, he discovered that it was too late. First, an Italian official explained with effusive apologies that his country's consular protection was founded on capitulary agreements which had come to an end along with the Ottoman Empire. Then, a Turkish official took unconcealed delight in explaining that, to be eligible for Turkish citizenship, he should have renewed his passport every year and paid the requisite fee. When he offered to pay retrospectively, the man leapt to his feet, shrieking that he was a deserter and should count himself lucky not to be handed over to the German authorities.

With the aid of a rapacious forger, he had assumed a new identity – that of Jean-Marc Renaud, a chemical engineer from Abbeville – which had thus far gone unchallenged. He'd studied his face as in a police file and judged that it bore no overtly Semitic features. So, in a grim paradox, he owed his safety to the vicious Nazi caricatures: the hooked noses, thick lips and bulging eyes, ubiquitous on posters, in newspapers and, most chillingly, in the Palais Berlitz exhibition, *The Jew and France*, which he'd visited with Madeleine in a bid to ascertain how he and his kind had polluted the nation. He had emerged none the wiser, but the poison had seeped into his innermost self. Somebody long ago – a teacher? Papa? a character in a book? – had distinguished between guilt, which arose from within, and shame, which was imposed from without. Over the past two years, they had become one and the same.

Six o'clock ushered in the nightly Jewish curfew, although the Military Administration was quite capable of bringing it forward unannounced, purely for the pleasure of catching people off guard. Even without the threat of arrest, Jews had little reason to venture out at night, since theatres, cinemas and restaurants were barred to them and shops only permitted to serve them for an hour between three and four in the afternoon. Moreover, as of March this year, they were forbidden to use public shelters during air raids: not just metro stations and garages, but the basements of their own apartment blocks, further confining them to their homes. As a Gentile, Jean-Marc was not bound by the curfew. On the contrary, deeming there to be a greater risk of detection during the day, he rarely went out before dusk. He occupied his time in what, with an ironic nod to the Nazis, he described as self-improvement: reading the classics; teaching himself English; and listening to the wireless (which would have been another offence for Jewish Ruben). Nevertheless, by early evening, he was invariably itching to escape.

This evening, the itch was more insistent than ever, his usual restlessness after a day indoors compounded by hunger. As late as the previous afternoon, he had planned to skip Yom Kippur, fantasising about not just eating, but eating pork, in defiance of a God who'd once again abandoned His chosen people. Yet, in the event, he had been unwilling either to betray his coreligionists, many of whom were suffering far worse hardships than him, or to renounce his vestigial faith, however much it oppressed him. More immediately, he couldn't bring himself to lie to Maman, when he and Madeleine joined her and Maryam to break the fast.

To his dismay, Maman had registered with the authorities immediately the measure was introduced, before he had a chance to dissuade her. She and Maryam presented themselves at the gendarmerie on the Rue de Parme, where, as she reported indignantly, the officer who knew them of old refused to take their names, claiming to lack the necessary forms. 'I may be sixty-three, but there's nothing wrong with my eyesight, and I could see them piled on his desk in front of me. He pretended they were only for men and told us to go home and keep to ourselves.' Ignoring the kindly hint, they went straight to the Préfecture, where they registered successfully. When Ruben remonstrated with her, she insisted that she'd done the right thing. 'The Germans are lumping all Jews together as outcasts and aliens, which will be true if we don't obey the law.'

He might have had more sympathy with her argument had she not conveniently forgotten that, thirty years earlier, they themselves had arrived here as aliens, albeit with more substantial resources. The truth was that his parents had felt as threatened by the influx of German Jews into France as by that of Russian Jews into Salonica. As before, they'd held it their duty to help the new arrivals, taking in Chaya, an eighteen-year-old maid from Breslau. But rather than showing gratitude, she was shocked that they failed to keep a kosher home, complained about wearing a uniform that exposed her calves, and wouldn't lift a finger on the Sabbath. After finding her a more suitable position with an Orthodox family in Saint-Paul, Papa quoted half approvingly a *Figaro* editorial which alleged that, far from seeking a safe haven, the fifty thousand recent German refugees in Paris were part of Hitler's plot to destroy the country from within.

After the Fall of France, Ruben had begged Maman to leave Paris, offering to escort her to Henri and Bella in Lyon or Leon in Marseille, but she refused to quit her home, regarding it as some kind of betrayal of Papa. By the time she accepted the urgency of flight, it was too late. She wouldn't abandon Maryam, whose lameness prevented her from walking more than a few steps, and neither of them was capable of wading waist-deep behind a smuggler across the River Cher. When the military authorities requisitioned her house, she moved into Irène and Simon's empty apartment, where she'd as yet been undisturbed. On the rare occasions that she went out, wearing her yellow star like a sunflower, she encountered no hostility, even remarking on a courteous German soldier who had volunteered to carry her bag, until he was rebuked by his comrades. For safety's sake, Ruben resisted giving her his own new address on the Quai Montebello, but he visited two or three times each week, relieved by the fortitude with which she endured the cold, the rationing, the tedium, the absence of family and friends, and more grateful than ever for Maryam's boundless devotion.

Having promised to be with her by eight o'clock (Occupation time, to avoid confusion), he donned his hat and coat and made his way outside, facing the now windowless cathedral, its buttresses gleaming in the late afternoon sun. He walked along the quay to the Austerlitz bridge, smiling at a lone gendarme, whose nod of acknowledgement brought him a hollow sense of victory. He crossed the Place de la Bastille, jostled by crowds heading home from work or out for the evening. Even so, the absence of cars and the relentless honking by which motorists, himself included, had staked their claims to the clogged Parisian streets, left an eerie silence. Painful as it was to admit, the banning of private vehicles had greatly improved the air, and he took a bracing gulp. He turned into the Rue Sedaine to find the silence yet more pronounced. The once teeming street, where large families had spilt out of small rooms to conduct their lives on the pavement, was virtually deserted. The butchers and grocers, cobblers and tailors, booksellers and moneylenders had shuttered their shops. Chez Sotil and Chez Motola, cafés whose very names evoked the tastes and smells of his childhood, were closed. Le Bosphore alone remained open, a bastion of defiance, although a glance through its smeared window revealed it to be shockingly empty. For a moment, he feared that there had been another wave of arrests; then he remembered it was Yom Kippur. For once, the emptiness was benign.

It was here, among the poor Jews of Little Turkey rather than the rich of Nouvelle Athènes, that he'd redeemed himself on his return from Palestine. Convinced of his failure both as a man and a Jew, he had accepted Papa's offer of a job at the bank, but, whether as a precaution or a punishment, he'd been consigned to the compliance department. He spent his days monitoring transactions, conducting audits and reviewing regulatory changes, until only the thought of another ignominious retreat kept him at his desk. Then, one day, a former Maccabi teammate, whose name he'd spotted on a loan application, mentioned that he was coaching football players for La Fraternité, a Sephardi youth association based in the eleventh. Recalling their glory days in Salonica, he suggested that Ruben join him. He leapt at the chance and, over the next fifteen years, befriended several generations of boys, both on and off the pitch. He helped them to find jobs and put down deposits on rooms, served as a witness at weddings and stood as godfather to two children. Even though he had renounced Zionism, he paid for four of them to travel clandestinely to Palestine.

In July and August, many of the men were arrested, along with their wives, children, parents, siblings, friends and neighbours, and confined in a detention camp in the north of Paris. Ruben knew that, as a good Catholic from an old Abbevillois family, whose records had been conveniently destroyed in the bombing of the town hall, Jean-Marc ought to stay away from the reviled eleventh arrondissement, but he was desperate for news of his former players who, according to rumour, were being sent as forced labourers to Germany. Although perplexed that, as well as able-bodied men and women, the Nazis were taking the elderly, the young and the infirm, he presumed that, despite the brutality of the arrests, they wanted to keep families together or, more cynically, they didn't want them to leave their dependants as a drain on the regime's resources.

'Monsieur Molina!' he called out as a slight figure with tzitzit protruding from his tattered waistcoat crossed the street. The man started and scurried away, without looking round.

'I'm Rub . . . I used to coach your son, Sami, at the Fraternité. I've been wondering . . . have you had any news?'

'Nothing.' Monsieur Molina turned, his long, bearded face hidden in the shadows, but the anguish in his voice unmistakeable. 'All we know is that he's being held in a makeshift prison in Drancy. There has been no charge.'

'And his family?'

'Maxi . . . his son . . . he's six. He's with him in the prison. Also without charge. And Etta – she's two – is at home with my wife. No charge against her yet either.'

'And his wife . . . Forgive me, I forget her name.'

'Better that you should.'

'Why? Did she betray him?'

'Let me ask you. You know how the learned rabbis gave us permission to break the commandments to save a life.'

'Yes,' Ruben said, having broken several with less justification.

'Under such circumstances, we can disregard the Sabbath or eat a forbidden food or even refrain from fasting on this holiest of days. But what would they say of a woman who committed adultery or, more precisely, prostituted herself to feed her family?'

'I'm sure—'

'And even if they pardoned her transgression for the sake of her baby daughter, would they do the same for her aged, wretched, worthless, parasitical parents-in-law?'

'If they were truly learned, they would leave it to God to judge.

And if God were – is – just, He will rule that she has broken no law . . . committed no transgression. Here!' He pulled a bundle of notes from his pocket.

'I am not her pimp!'

'And I'm not a client. Please take it. If nothing else, it should enable her to spend a few more hours with her daughter.'

'Thank you, Monsieur Carrache.'

'You know me?'

'Not if you don't wish me to.'

'Thank you.'

Too dispirited to pursue his inquiries, Ruben headed to the Marais, pausing as ever on the Rue de la Roquette to pay his respects at the plaque commemorating the *Oriental Israelite Soldiers who died for France, 1914-1918*. Paris had become a city of plinths, with Voltaire, Rousseau, Zola, Hugo, Marat and Desmoulins among the scores of those vilified by the Nazis, smashed and melted down. So it was a miracle that the plaque had survived. Perhaps it was too insignificant to attract attention. But it held a deep significance for him. Seven years earlier (although it felt like another lifetime), he had stood beside his parents and sisters to cheer Leon as he paraded with his former comrades-in-arms past the President of the Republic and assorted dignitaries at the memorial's unveiling. The Jews – even the poor Sephardim of the eleventh arrondissement – had been honoured among the heroes of the Great War.

Was it to emulate Leon that he'd signed up to fight? If so, it had been another failure. There would be no monument to the Jewish soldiers fallen in this war, nor, for that matter, to French soldiers of any faith. On completing his army training, he had been assigned to the 13th Legion and stationed in the Ardennes. After the surprise enemy advance through the forest, his unit was deployed to prevent it securing bridgeheads across the Meuse. Beaten back, they withdrew to the hills around Sedan, where his closest friend in the platoon, the scholarly spice-seller Shiloh Abravanel, was killed in an aerial attack. After forty-eight hours without sleep, they were sent to defend the nearby village of Stonne, which, though little more than a cluster of farmsteads, was deemed to be of strategic importance. Over the next three days, it was captured and recaptured almost twenty times. On the third afternoon, Ruben's platoon, exhausted and demoralised, ran out of ammunition. It was then that their sergeant revealed that the company commander, cursing his own men more savagely than the enemy, had abandoned them. When they asked him what they should do, his advice was blunt: 'Surrender to the first Boche you can find!'

After laying down their arms, they were marched halfway across the country to the Satory barracks outside Versailles, a trek which was senseless even by military standards, given their captors' reports that they would soon be heading back east to labour camps in Germany. Ruben was one of half a dozen men dispatched to assist civilian workmen in preparing the dust-coated, water-damaged, verminous palace for a prospective visit by Hitler. In the most intrepid act of his life, he slipped away from the overseer in the Clock Cabinet, put on overalls that a workman had secreted for him beneath the Louis-Philippe Staircase, and strolled out of the palace gates under the eye of the guards. To this day, he agonised over the commandant's threat that three prisoners would be shot for every one who escaped, but he consoled himself with the thought that even the Nazis had to abide by the Laws of War.

Silencing the three shots that echoed in his mind, he crossed the Place des Vosges and threaded his way through the Marais to La Vendangeuse, the dingy wine shop where, for the past eighteen months, he had bought black-market supplies. Before the Occupation, he'd seldom strayed into this heartland of Ashkenazi Paris, finding the heavy, starchy smells of simmering stews and the harsh, guttural snatches of Yiddish less congenial than the spicy, smoky smells of braising tagines and the lilting Ladino chatter of Little Turkey. This evening, however, the districts were equally deserted, although whether the residents here were afraid to venture outside or simply waiting to break the fast was unclear.

Knowing better than to ring the bell, he stepped into the shop, passing shelves bare of all but a handful of bottles, and knocked at a door beside the empty counter. The snap of a peephole was followed by the judder of two bolts as a menacing youth beckoned him into a stale storeroom, where an older man of pugilistic mien sat at a desk illuminated by a solitary candle. Ruben's greeting was met with a grunt. Even if he recognised him as a regular customer, the man wasted no time on pleasantries, inquiring brusquely what he wanted and supplying what he could: two kilos of bread; two hundred grams of butter; a kilo of coffee; a kilo of sugar; a dozen eggs; a wheel of goat's cheese; and a scrawny, unplucked chicken. He asked for eight hundred francs – at a rough estimate, around ten times the authorised price – but Ruben was disinclined to haggle. After all, he was one of those who had created the demand, whereas more principled Parisians saw enduring the privations as a form of resistance. Had he had no ties, he would have done the same, but he refused to deprive Maman, especially now that Irène had stopped sending food parcels from Auvergne. And he longed to pamper Madeleine.

With dusk falling, it was time to collect her from work. He left the shop and took the metro from Saint-Paul to Concorde, which, though not the closest station to the store, avoided the need to change lines and the threat of guards lurking in the corridors. Although Jean-Marc had so far passed every inspection, he had to keep vigilant, not least when carrying two bags of contraband food. He reached the platform just as the train drew up, feeling a pang of shame at the sight of several Jews crowding into the last carriage, while he and his fellow Aryans had their pick of the remaining four. Once seated, he surveyed the carriage with the look he'd honed over the past two years, neither over-confident nor furtive. He averted his gaze from the SS officer who, in a seamless movement, leapt through the closing doors and onto the strapontin. He glanced round, first proudly, as if expecting applause for his athleticism, then plaintively, when everyone – even the hard-faced woman in a mink jacket, clutching a large Bon Marché shopping bag – steadfastly ignored him.

Arriving at Concorde, he sauntered down the Rue Royale, buoyed by the prospect of seeing Madeleine. He had hired her himself four years earlier in spite of her inexperience, assuring a sceptical Jeannette Patenaude, his senior saleswoman, that experience could be gained, but beauty, elegance and charm, all of which Madeleine possessed in abundance, were innate. For years, Maman had chided him, and Irène and Bella teased him, about his dalliances with customers, but employing Madeleine brought that to an end. Danielle Darrieux, Arletty and Simone Simon could have walked in together to inspect the latest silks and he would still have had eyes only for her. Flouting his own rules, he invited her to Lapérouse and the Tour d'Argent, where her appreciation of the food he chose for her delighted him almost as much as if he'd been the one to cook it. He invited her to the cinema and theatre, where, their roles reversed, she regaled him with her intimate knowledge of the actors. Finally, he invited her to his apartment, where, on 5 June 1937, a date forever etched in his memory, to the clinking of champagne glasses and the crooning of Charles Trenet, they first made love.

At forty, he had seen his future mapped out: a series of light-hearted affairs with younger women, the age gap gradually widening until even he had to acknowledge the indignity, before spending his dotage being coddled by a housekeeper, whom he pictured as a more acquiescent Maryam. Since meeting Madeleine, however, that had changed. His one desire was to be with her for the rest of his life – and beyond, if his pillow talk had any substance. A friend to whom he'd bared his soul warned that he was in danger of becoming besotted and advised him to read Proust. Now that he had the time to do so, he was retrospectively offended, finding Swann self-deluding and Odette nothing but a high-class whore.

Within four months of their acquaintance, he had resolved to propose to her, but he dreaded his parents' reaction. While they were sure to frame their objections as religious (with generations of Carrache, Beraha and Camerino ancestors poised to turn in their graves), he suspected that they would be more sympathetic if she were Madeleine de Livet from Normandy rather than Madeleine Dupuis from Belleville. He had finally mustered the courage to introduce her to them when Papa was felled by a stroke, shortly after which he himself enlisted in the army. On his return to Paris, his situation was no easier, since he now bore sole responsibility for his widowed mother. Moreover, given the raft of antisemitic measures, it would have been perverse to ask Madeleine to share his fate. Yet, she vowed that she would never leave him, and he couldn't bring himself to send her away.

Safe in the shadows, he fixed his eyes on the store, impatient for her to come out and dispel his doubts. But when at last a woman appeared, her angular body and long strides immediately identified her as Jeannette. It was she who, from what he took to be jealousy of his relationship with Madeleine but, to be fair, might have been genuine bigotry, had reported him to the authorities for breaking his terms of employment. Although forced to relinquish the business to a provisional administrator, Philippe Charpentier, he had been allowed to remain, provided he had no direct contact with the customers. His own rashness and their repeated requests drew him onto the shop floor, whereupon Jeannette filed her complaint. Charpentier was fired and he himself went into hiding. The Germans installed the Fabrons, a bookkeeper and his wife from Saint-Ouen, as joint managers. According to Madeleine, Jeannette and Madame Fabron got along like thieves at a fair – which, in effect, they were.

The Fabrons hung a red placard in the window, attesting that the store was now *Managed by an Aryan steward*, reminding Ruben of a hygiene certificate in a café. Neither of them knew the first thing about textiles, but, thanks to the systems he'd put in place, the operation ran smoothly. Sales remained steady, although the clientele had changed. Apart from a few well-connected Parisians with dispensation passes, collaborators and profiteers, it consisted of the visiting wives and mistresses of high-ranking German officers and officials. Madeleine, as starstruck as ever, reeled off their names: Emmy Göring; Inga Ley; Baroness Stohrer. Ruben worried that, despite Madeleine's solemn promise that she no longer saw him, a vengeful Jeannette would use her influence with Madame Fabron to have her dismissed. But Madeleine insisted that Monsieur Fabron would never permit it.

'I'm his favourite,' she said. 'Only because so many of the customers ask for me,' she added quickly.

'How do you know you're his favourite? Does he tell you?'

'No, of course not. You're being ridiculous.'

'Does he summon you into the back office – my office – in private?'

'Never. How could he? His wife's always there.'

'What if she weren't? Do you think he would if she weren't?'

'He has two daughters, both older than me. He's almost fifty.'

'I'm forty-four!'

'But I love you.'

Ruben apologised, kissing her wrists until he felt worthy of her lips. He explained that, with so much time on his hands, he couldn't help visualising her with all the men she encountered, although in truth he suspected that he would be just as obsessed if he were fully occupied.

Madeleine's constant presence wasn't the only thing about the store he missed. Who would have thought that selling textiles would turn out to be his métier? He had been sceptical when Henri first mentioned the job, failing to see how a man who'd shown no interest in anything but genealogy could develop a sudden passion for silk manufacture in middle age. It was Bella who explained that his true passion was for Bertrand Viallet, the scion of a long line of Lyonnais weavers. Bertrand had ambitions to transform the industry, but he lacked capital. Henri supplied it, playing a more active role in the company than anyone (including Bertrand) had anticipated. Together, they enjoyed considerable success, expanding into North and South America, where Esther's son, Nathan, was among their representatives. Braving widespread derision, they experimented with artificial silk in the '20s, which not only helped them to weather the Depression but gave them a competitive edge now that Vichy and Berlin were demanding more synthetic materials. Meanwhile, their exclusive contracts with artists such as Raoul Dufy, Sonia Delaunay, Robert Bonfils and, of course, Timarete ensured that their fabrics were the choice of top fashion houses from Worth and Vionnet to Paquin and Patou.

Last March, without telling his mother or warning his sister and uncle, Ruben had journeyed to Lyon. Even with Jean-Marc's papers, he was courting danger, but he felt a deep, almost atavistic need to see other members of what Bella had mordantly dubbed the 'Carrache tribe'. Despite Radio Paris's triumphalist reports of the Luftwaffe's bombardment of towns across England, he felt confident that Esther was safe. His other three siblings were scattered throughout the free zone. After a year in which communication had been limited to ticking boxes on pre-printed postcards, from *In Good Health* and *Slightly Injured* to *Seriously Ill* and *Dead*, a regular – if strictly censored – postal service had resumed between the zones. He'd exchanged coded letters with Leon in Marseille and Irène in Clermont-Ferrand (the latter having twice addressed him as Jean-Luc) and been able to assure Maman that they and their families were well. Meanwhile, by flirting with the delivery drivers, Madeleine had passed on his messages to Bella and Henri.

How had the affronted Monsieur Molina put it? 'I am not her pimp.'

Through a fixer with contacts in the military, he obtained a travel pass and boarded the mid-morning train from the Gare de Lyon. It was surprisingly busy and he secured the last seat in a compartment of six. His fellow passengers were an elderly couple, discreetly holding hands; a young woman whom, from her copy of Rousseau's *Confessions*, he assumed to be a student; and two men of roughly his age. One, with friends in either high or illicit places, devoured a lavish snack of ham, cheese and hard-boiled eggs. The other was engrossed in *Le Franciste*, from which he rarely looked up. Shortly after they crossed the demarcation line at Vierzon, two inspectors entered the compartment. Once again, Jean-Marc raised no suspicions, but the *Franciste* reader was less fortunate. After checking his documents, they tipped the contents of his briefcase onto the floor. Finding nothing untoward, they ripped open the lining of his coat, revealing wads of banknotes. The man stuttered an explanation as they grabbed both him and the money and bundled him out of the door. The elderly couple clutched one another's hands more tightly, and the student set down her book and stared out of the window. As they entered a tunnel, Ruben caught the reflection of her tears.

The picnicker tore off a chunk of baguette, before spitting a single word at Ruben.

'Jew!'

Ruben felt as if he'd been shot. He struggled to breathe, let alone reply, whereupon the man smiled, a crumb wedged between his teeth.

'I smelt it the moment he got on the train.'

'Oh! Oh yes, of course,' Ruben said, suffused with both relief and shame.

On reaching Perrache station, he passed unhindered through the controls and made his way to the old town and Henri and Bertrand's apartment on the Rue de la Fronde. To his surprise, their lift was still in service, as, to his greater surprise, was Nieve, their Catalan maid of twenty years. Even if, like the factory itself, she was assigned to Bertrand alone, it was remarkable that she'd been allowed to remain in a 'non-essential activity'.

'Monsieur Henri!' she called, freeing herself from Ruben's eager handshake and moving to the salon. 'You'll never guess who it is.'

Henri entered the vestibule, stopping short before rushing over to embrace Ruben. 'What are you doing here? You never sent word. We weren't expecting . . .'

'I didn't want to worry you in case I was picked up.'

'But why? Has something happened? Is it your mother?'

'Everything's fine . . . that is, nothing's worse. Aren't I allowed to visit my favourite uncle and my sister?' he asked, managing to keep the tears from his eyes but not from his voice.

'Yes, of course... well no, not when it's so dangerous. I'm furious. Come here!' He hugged him again. 'I'll send Nieve to fetch Bella. She has a place on the Rue de Gadagne. A couple of streets away.'

'By herself?'

'Officially. But who can say?'

Ruben followed Henri into the elegant salon. Amid the judicious blend of Louis XV furniture and paintings by some of their own prize designers, what struck him most was the vase of tulips and forsythia on the secretaire. It had to be eighteen months since he'd seen cut flowers and he leant down to breathe in their scent. He sat in one of the gilded bergères and observed Henri, who had grown to look so like Papa that the joy of reunion was mingled with the pain of loss. Nieve brought in tea and macaroons, another luxury that he hadn't seen – or tasted – since before the war. Despite Henri's request that she fetch Bella at once, she insisted on serving them. 'Monsieur Ruben hasn't come all this way for you to spill the pot over him,' she said sharply. After her departure, uncle and nephew recounted their lives since they'd last met during Ruben's training at Sathonay two years earlier. Ruben put up a brave front as he discussed his newfound leisure, only to lower it as he expressed his fears for Maman.

'She should have come here while she had the chance,' Henri said.

'I begged her. But she believed that keeping up Papa's house was a sacred trust. Soon afterwards, the authorities requisitioned it for some top general.'

'Who's even now pawing Jacob's treasures.'

'If they've not been plundered. There are stories of lorry-loads of pictures, furniture, silver and God knows what being transported to Germany.' Henri glanced round the room, as if in dread of a similar theft. 'I've said nothing to Maman. She regards the current nightmare as a temporary setback: whatever the outcome of the war, justice will prevail, and she'll return home.'

'Poor Mathilde! Jacob was so intent on shielding her from any unpleasantness that she must be utterly adrift.'

'At least Monsieur Druot warned me that our accounts were about to be frozen, so I was able to retrieve the cash.'

'I know that name. Wasn't he one of your father's protégés?'

'He still took a huge risk. But we have enough to live on for several years. Unless of course the Boche trigger another wheelbarrow-level inflation.'

They continued talking, and if Ruben's avid consumption of the biscuits took Henri aback, he had the grace not to show it. He was reaching for another when the door burst open and Bella bounded in, hair tousled, wearing a paint-splattered smock and exuding a powerful odour of linseed oil, turpentine and sweat.

'Ruben, darling!' She cupped his face and gazed into his eyes, reminding him of their staring contests as children, although her gaze now was filled with love rather than rivalry. 'Oh Ruben!' she said, nuzzling his cheek, before Henri, impatient of her idiosyncrasies, instructed her to sit down and offered her some tea.

'Tea?' she scoffed. 'How can you drink tea at a time like this? We must celebrate. Champagne!'

'Tea, my dear,' Henri said firmly.

'Let me look at you!' Bella said to Ruben. 'You've lost weight. And the beard! You look like a philosophy teacher.'

'Not exactly. I'm Jean-Marc Renaud, chemical engineer from Abbeville.'

'You don't sound as though you're from up there. I once had a model from Amiens. Typical ch'ti accent. All *sha va* and *ch'est*.'

'I shall pretend I'm mute.'

'I can't believe it's really you.'

'Ow!' he exclaimed, as she pinched him.

'Yes, it is. It's wonderful to see you. How's Maman?'

'Bearing up ... better than you might have expected. Regularly asking God - through me - what she's done to deserve this in her old age.'

'And Maryam?'

'She's happy as long as she can look after Maman.'

'What about Madeleine? Are you two still together?'

'She's the only thing that keeps me together.'

'You should have taken my advice and married her. Who cares what the parents would have said?'

'Some people do, Bella,' Henri interposed quietly, and Ruben recalled that it wasn't until his own parents' deaths that he acknowledged his relationship with Bertrand.

'Besides, if we'd married, she'd be the wife of a Jew. And if we'd had the children she longs for, they'd have been half-Jews. *Mischlings!*'

'Not if she'd been Madame Jean-Marc . . . what was it?'

'Renaud.'

'There's plenty of time,' Henri said. 'This war . . . the Occupation won't last for ever. And she's how old?'

'Twenty-six.' Ruben was swept up by a wave of melancholy. 'I'm glad to see you're still painting,' he said to Bella, as he struggled not to go under.

'Not really. Just tossing off designs for Bertrand.'

'She's our number one designer.'

'In other words, the cheapest and most readily to hand. It's uninspiring stuff: either milkmaids and cows, as we *Return to the Soil* with Pétain, or simple geometric motifs – spots and stripes and squares – to suit the Boche. They go in for recurring patterns. No variations. There must be a moral in there somewhere.'

'What about your own work?'

'I've put it aside for the present. It seems inappropriate . . . self-indulgent.'

'They say Picasso's busier than ever. Painting and holding court in his studio.'

'Genius sets its own rules. Now may we change the subject?'

They discussed their siblings. Bella had heard from Irène that she and Mercado (she omitted the *Simon* as regularly as Maryam) were preparing to flee to Switzerland, at least that was what she'd understood from her 'hope that restrictions will ease and we'll soon be eating gruyère'. They were debating the merits of the scheme when Nieve called Henri to the phone. He returned to announce that there'd been a change of plan and Ruben would have to stay the night with Bella. He refused to elaborate, and Ruben was both bewildered and hurt until, clearing him a space in her cluttered apartment, Bella explained that Henri was in the Resistance and must have received news of an emergency. Ruben struggled to picture his tender-hearted uncle – a man who paled at the sight of a rare beefsteak – taking militant action.

'You mean he belongs to a cell?'

'Network! Cell sounds as if he's been captured.'

'Since when?'

'Over a year, as far as I know. He and Bertrand adapted one of the roller printing machines at the works to run off copies of *Combat*, the movement's newspaper.'

'Do you belong to it too?'

She shrugged. 'I've passed on the occasional message.'

'Promise me you'll take care!'

'Oh, you know me, I'm beloved of the gods.'

She parried any further questions and Henri failed to reappear before Ruben's departure the next morning. For all the pleasure of seeing them, he returned to Paris consumed by a sense of worthlessness. His uncle was actively working to defeat the Nazis, while he did nothing but nursemaid two old women and encumber a young one.

'Darling!'

All at once, Madeleine was beside him and he had the delightful sensation that he'd conjured her up, though he'd simply been too distracted to register her arrival. He kissed her and buried his face in her hair, breathing in the nutty fragrance of the shampoo he'd procured for her the previous month.

'Oh you poor thing! You must be famished,' she said, as his stomach growled. 'Shall we take the metro?'

'Would you mind if we walked . . . at least as far as Saint-Lazare? I'd like you to myself for a moment.'

'Of course,' she said, looping her arm through his. They strolled down the road like a legitimate couple. Even the poster of the Unknown Soldier rising from his tomb and slitting the throat of a Jew, on the corner of the Rue de Surène, looked less sinister when he was with her. 'Though if you like, we can get a taxi.'

'How thoughtless of me! You've been on your feet all day.'

'I was thinking of your mother. She must be hungry, even if you're not.'

'Now I feel even worse.'

'And my feet are a bit sore,' she added. 'Whatever they say, cork soles aren't as comfortable as leather.'

Ruben hailed a tandem taxi. The seventy-franc fare was as much as it would have been in a car before the Occupation, the cyclists claiming that the cost of replacement tyres matched that of fuel. He squeezed next to Madeleine in the crudely converted trailer and imagined how they might once have ridden in a horse-drawn carriage through Salonica.

'I've brought your mother a scarf,' she said, taking a package out of her bag.

'That's so kind. But you really should save your money.'

'I didn't pay for ... I mean, it wasn't on display. We have hundreds downstairs that we're not allowed to sell. It's hard to see in this light, but the colours are red, white and blue.'

'She'll be thrilled,' Ruben replied. He tuned to kiss her, bumping her chin as they jounced over a pothole.

He wondered whether Madeleine sensed Maman's disapproval or took her chill courtesy as the social norm. For twenty years, she had been urging him to marry, but now that he'd found the love of his life, she'd turned into Grandmaman Regina. 'It would break Papa's heart,' she'd said, 'to know that when we've become second-class citizens, you're living with a Gentile.'

'Then it's a good thing he's dead,' he'd replied, at which her eyes filled with tears, while Maryam's wordless reproach compounded his mortification.

As usual, he gave the cyclists an address several doors down from the building, waiting for them to ride off before entering the courtyard. To his relief, the concierge wasn't at her station. He was resigned to paying an ever-higher price for her 'services', but on this of all nights, he couldn't bear her sanctimonious attempts to justify the extortion.

'I'll definitely have worked up an appetite,' Madeleine said, as they climbed the four flights of stairs.

'It won't be a feast,' Ruben replied quickly. 'Even when food's plentiful, the Yom Kippur meal is supposed to be light and easy to digest.'

'These days, it feels like Lent all year long.'

'I've managed to get hold of a few things – some eggs, butter and sugar – for you and your mother.'

'I didn't mean—'

'Of course not.'

'She'll be very grateful.'

He knew that Madame Dubois, whose chief pleasure in life was poring over murders and scandals in the yellow press, was as opposed to their relationship as Maman. She wouldn't hesitate to betray him to the authorities if she thought it might be to her advantage.

He reached the doorway and kissed the mezuzah.

'I always love to see you do that,' Mathilde said. 'Honouring God's presence at home. We just dip our fingers in the holy water basin at church.'

'It's second nature to me now. When I was thirteen, I went through a religious phase. I read in the Gemara – that's an ancient text – that we should put a mezuzah on the doorpost of every room that measures four square cubits.'

'How big's a cubit?'

'You've got me there. But the house was large. My father emphatically refused, even though I accused him of breaking the commandment (I was such a prig!), but he did allow me to put one outside my bedroom . . . These days, I can't even put one beside my front door.'

'I'm sorry if I've upset you.'

'You haven't.' He kissed her. 'You couldn't.'

'When I was thirteen, I wanted to become a nun.'

'What a waste! No . . . what a crime!'

He rang the bell, and Maryam flung open the door as if she'd been standing behind it. 'What kept you?' she asked. 'Maman is sick. Her chest . . . She hasn't eaten . . . Señorita,' she added, noticing Madeleine.

'You shouldn't have let her fast. At her age – at yours – there's a dispensation.' He seethed, not least at the notion of Maman and Maryam atoning for their sins, when it was the world that ought to atone for its sins against them.

'No, not only today. She hasn't touched a thing for three days, not since she learnt of Madame Naar's death . . . May her memory be a blessing!'

'Madame Naar died? Why didn't you tell me?'

'We don't know where you live.'

Ruben made for Maman's room, with Maryam shuffling behind him. At the door, she turned to Madeleine.

'Not now, Señorita.'

'Please wait for me in the salon,' Ruben said to her. 'Make yourself at home.'

He entered the airless bedroom to find Maman lying flat, her head propped on a pillow, her face grey and gaze blank. She wheezed softly.

'Maman,' he said, pressing a kiss on her damp brow. He knelt at her side and squeezed her hand which, after a faint quiver, hung limp. 'Maman, what's wrong? Can you tell me?' Her wheezing grew louder. 'What's happened, Maryam? This isn't just grief. She's ill.'

'Hush now!' Maryam hobbled towards him, clasped his arm and led him to the door. 'We won't be long, Señora.'

'I'll be right back, Maman.'

He followed Maryam into the salon, where Madeleine was waiting uneasily. 'Is it serious?' she asked. 'Should we send for a doctor?'

'What doctor would come to us?' Maryam replied bitterly.

'Tell me exactly what happened,' Ruben said.

'Maman's been feeling badly for a while. Pains in her chest and stomach.'

'She said nothing on Saturday.'

'She didn't want to worry you. Then on Sunday we heard about poor Madame Naar. It was terrible . . . really terrible.' She wiped her eyes on her apron.

'Was she detained?'

'No, it was in her sleep, or at least at home. The women went to perform *taharah*—'

'When they wash and prepare the body for burial,' Ruben explained to Madeleine.

'Yes. And in the middle of it, the gendarmes broke in and arrested them. All those good women.'

'What about the . . . Madame Naar?' Ruben asked.

'They left her there uncovered, like a baby waiting for clean napkins. A neighbour who witnessed it called the rabbi. He went straight to the gendarmerie to protest. They told him they had orders to arrest all the members of the Chevra Kadisha, but none about removing a dead body.'

'The Boche are swine,' Madeleine said, her eyes welling with tears.

'The gendarmes are French, Señorita.'

'So where is she – Madame Naar – now?' Ruben asked.

'In the ground. They let the rabbi go – they had no orders about him either – and he buried her that day. Then he came here to tell us. It was good of him, but I wish he'd left out the details. That's when Maman collapsed. I put her to bed with a tisane and a mustard compress. I kept saying to her: "Ruben will be here soon."'

'I'm here now, aren't I? I'm here now.'

'Is there anything I can do?' Madeleine asked.

'Wait here with Maryam, while I go and fetch a doctor.'

'Wouldn't it be better if I go? It's dangerous for you.'

'No. I was absent when my father died because I was signing up to fight the Nazis. I won't let my mother die because I'm afraid of them.'

3

LEON

MARSEILLE, FEBRUARY 1943

THE CRACK AND roar of exploding masonry was followed by the crash of flying debris and the rumble of toppling rubble. Even the pall of dust that slowly unfurled across the city emitted an audible rustle as it scraped the treetops of Roucas-Blanc. For the third consecutive night, the Germans were blowing up vast swathes of the Old Port. On the first night, Leon, listening in disbelief, had dared to hope that the Allies had gained control of the Mediterranean and were bombing Marseille from the sea. But by morning, word had spread that Hitler himself had ordered the demolition of what he'd branded 'the dump of Europe', after sabotage strikes on his forces in both the Hôtel Splendide and a military brothel on the Rue Lemaitre. Leon's sole concern had been for the whores.

The Germans had occupied the city for less than three months, and their grip was steadily tightening. For all the regulations and restrictions, the fines and levies, Leon's life had been largely unscathed by Vichy. True, the regime had shut down the bank and claimed the right to expropriate his property, but it had so far made no attempt to exercise it. The large bastide with the abundant garden, perched on the hillside between the basilica and the bay, remained a haven of tranquillity – except on nights such as these, when the air rang with explosions and swirled with grit, stinging his eyes and clogging his throat.

He was heading inside for a cloth and a glass of water, when Daniel intercepted him.

'How long do you think before they dynamite the entire city?'

'Shouldn't you be in bed?' Leon asked, wincing at a further blast.

'Oh yes, while Hitler sings me such a soothing lullaby—'

'Try putting wax in your ears.'

'And you gaze out to sea and dream of being back in Salonica.'

'Some dream! The Nazis are in control there too.'

'Unless they've already razed it to the ground.'

'I doubt it. Vardar - the poor and so-called degenerate district - was destroyed, along with most of the city, in the fire twenty-five years ago.'

'But our family received compensation, didn't we? I've heard Oncle Simon congratulate himself on it often enough. What about the people whose homes have been flattened here? They're poor as Job.'

'Don't always assume the worst! Remember the sinister rumours flying around last week? Now we know the residents were sent to camps to protect them from the detonations.'

'I'm seventeen, Papa. Too old for fairy tales.'

'Don't shout! You'll upset Maman.'

Daniel ground his teeth. 'If only you knew how much I hate that voice.'

'What voice?'

'That "I'm so reasonable and my son's such a hothead" voice. You think because we're up here, surrounded by stone walls and plane trees, with the roads too narrow for tanks and too steep for a surprise ambush - and let's not forget the Madonna guarding the basilica - that they won't come for us.'

'All I want is to keep you and your sister and your mother safe.'

'You treat me like a child, but you're the one putting a bag over your head and pretending that no one can see you.'

Leon felt the weight of Daniel's charge, yet his acute lassitude crushed every impulse to act. Across the country, ordinary men and women were working fearlessly – or, rather, tirelessly – to resist the Nazis. He had never lacked courage and had the medals to prove it, but all he could do was listen surreptitiously to Radio London and pray that right would prevail.

'I'm tired of being afraid, Papa . . . of every scrunch and skid on the gravel, of every knock on the door or, worse, coming home to find it wide open and nobody here.'

'I know how hard it must be at your age.'

'How? You know nothing about me – not the first thing. I can't listen to any more of this. I'm going to Philippe's.'

'It's ten o'clock. You're going nowhere.'

'I'm sorry, Papa. I can't breathe here.'

Leon coughed on a piece of grit. He watched Daniel disappear behind the house. He contemplated following and grabbing him as he jumped onto his bicycle, but, with his son bound to outrun him, it would only give the boy another reason to defy – or worse, to despise – his father.

Lily came out on the terrace, slapping ineffectively at the cloud of gnats attracted by her honey facemask. 'What's all the noise?' she asked.

'The Germans are demolishing more buildings around the Old Port.'

'Don't take me for a fool! I meant the noise out here.'

'Daniel and I were arguing.'

'What about this time?'

'Just father and son things.' How he wished that they were the things he'd argued about with Papa: allowances and late nights and drinking, and even the relatively benign ascendancy of the Turks!

'Where is he?'

'He went to visit Philippe.'

'In the dead of night? Are you mad?'

'How would you have me stop him? Tie him up and lock him

in one of the chambers?' He didn't add that his son could probably outwrestle him too.

'If anything happens to him, I'll never forgive you.'

'When did you last forgive me for anything at all?'

Spurning a reply, she went back inside. Not even the ear-piercing explosions could curb their sniping. Leon knew that he had only himself to blame. He should never have married her when his heart still belonged to the woman who broke it. Though more than twelve years had passed since Xenia vanished from his life, her image remained as vivid as on the day that they'd met. The dream of winning her back had sustained him in the trenches as tangibly as if it had stopped a bullet like his friend Murat's pocket Quran. Six months after his discharge, he returned to Salonica to find her. Having survived the war with only a flesh wound, he counted on a second miracle, whereby he would stroll into the Praxidike (which in his imaginings had escaped the flames) to hear her singing one of his favourite songs. She would spot him from the stage, jump down and smother him in kisses, explaining that she hadn't abandoned him but had been abducted by a *manga*. As soon as she'd escaped, she had scoured the city for him, but he had already left for France. After drying her tears, he'd enfold her in his arms and vow that they would never be parted.

The reality had, of course, been very different. The city, as Papa had warned, was ravaged beyond recognition. The 'street with the withered fig tree' was no longer the only one lost to the map. Even without the barbed wire and trenches, the vista of shattered walls, charred timbers and waterlogged craters resembled nothing so much as no man's land. And having visited every rickety and rebuilt taverna between the docks and the Yedi Kule, he had found no trace of Xenia.

Mercado, Papa's overweening representative, had booked him a room alongside his own at the newly opened Hotel Bristol, but Leon declined to take it. Quite apart from his distaste for the man, he was a constant reminder of Xenia's perfidy. With the Campania house still occupied by British officers, he chose to stay with Aron

Sides and his wife, Mayra. Aron, whose paeans to domestic life were punctuated by three howling infants, was preparing to give up the family flour mill and emigrate to Palestine, where a group of fellow Zionists were founding a collective farm. Convinced that the collapsing Ottoman Empire offered a heaven-sent opportunity to establish a Jewish homeland, he tried to recruit Leon, who demurred but promised to report the venture to Ruben, who, despite not having served in the war, drifted through the peace as aimlessly as any battle-scarred veteran.

Leon left Salonica, vowing never to return, and moved back to Paris, living under the paternal roof and working in the family bank. With more than eight million dead at the front, it felt asinine to remark that the world had changed, but it remained necessary to remind Papa, who acted as if he enjoyed the same authority over his children as before. Then again, given the failure of his marriage to Lily, Papa's match might well have suited him better. At the very least, he would have had someone else to blame.

Even without as diligent a genealogist as Oncle Henri, Lily could trace her ancestors back to Córdoba, where they might have been neighbours of the Berahas. After the expulsion, they settled in Bordeaux, where, classed as 'New Christians', they rose to prominence as lawyers, merchants and shipowners. Granted full citizenship during the Revolution, her great-great-grandfather served as a captain in the National Guard before fighting under Napoleon in Egypt and Italy, for which he was inducted into the Légion d'honneur, the medal still on display in the family chateau. Leon first saw it when he was invited to stay by Lily's brother, Fernand, whom he'd met in Paris at the Cercle Wagram. It was there that he whiled away his evenings playing baccarat, neither running up the losses Papa dreaded nor winning amounts of any consequence, since he scorned to follow a system. 'Leaving everything to chance' had become his creed.

As he would never otherwise have visited Bordeaux, it seemed the merest chance that he should encounter Lily, the first woman since Xenia for whom he felt more than a passing fancy. Delicate and pensive, she was day to Xenia's night, and his nascent attraction to her proved that he was finally free of his grand passion. She read voraciously, played both the piano and violin, and was a keen gardener. She had been engaged to a second cousin who drowned in a German U-boat attack off the coast of Normandy, and, like Leon himself, appeared resigned to remaining single. Compared to the simpering girls whom Maman paraded before him, as desperate to be chosen as tobacco workers during winter, Lily was confident in a way that reminded him of Esther. Trusting that her shrewdness and zest would rouse him from his lethargy, he proposed to her.

After a wedding lavish enough to satisfy both families, they settled in Paris in an apartment Papa bought for them in the Square d'Orléans. Just three streets away from the Avenue Frochot, it allowed Maman, who felt deprived of her grandchildren across the Channel, to pay regular visits. Lily fell pregnant twice within two years, but complications from Gabrielle's birth prompted her prolonged absence from the marriage bed. By the time she returned, his desire for her had waned, never to revive. Retreating into himself, he shouldered the blame for their deepening estrangement.

His family intervened or, in Irène's case, interfered. She treated Lily to the full story of Xenia's betrayal, insisting to a furious Leon that it would help his wife understand him. Instead, it stoked her jealousy and gave her a name on which to heap her rancour. Papa, pragmatic as ever, declared that they would benefit from a change of scene and dispatched Leon to manage the Marseille bank. The move was a success: Leon relished both his professional autonomy and the cosmopolitan port, redolent of Salonica; Lily delighted in the elegant Second Empire bastide, with its hillside gardens and rock chambers; and the children thrived in a city on which the sun shone all year round. But once the novelty wore off, Leon and Lily quarrelled more violently than before. A chill as sharp as the Mistral swept through the Villa Dahlia, and Leon decided to rent an apartment in the city centre, returning home at weekends. He told the children that, after the string of bank failures, he needed to remain close to his desk. Neither challenged the obvious falsehood, as though afraid of provoking a permanent split.

He immersed himself in work. In the evenings, he dined at the Samaritaine, where the proprietress, Madame Imbert, pampered him as no one had since Maryam. Occasionally, he went to a cabaret or nightclub and, after a couple of glasses, imagined that his pastis was raki and the music rebetiko. But in the wake of the antisemitic riots that swept through the city in September 1940, and the Statute on Jews that forced her to give up her maid and gardener the following month, Lily felt threatened and asked him to move back. He set up a bedroom and study on the top floor.

Though eager to head up there now, he knew that he wouldn't sleep until Daniel had safely returned. So after brewing a surprisingly flavourful tea from apple peal and chestnut leaves, he wrapped himself in a blanket and settled in one of the rattan garden chairs, whose disrepair so offended Lily. He dozed off, only to be woken by Daniel shaking his shoulder.

'Papa!'

'My boy, you're back,' he said, drowsily hugging him. 'You must never run off like that again. Not now. No matter what . . . Who?' He blinked, aware of three shadowy figures: a stooped woman carrying an infant and a young boy clinging to her waist.

'This is Madame Esposito, Papa,' Daniel said, respectfully. 'With Antonio and Lucia.'

'Won't you take a seat, Madame?' Leon asked. 'The child looks heavy.' The woman clasped her daughter so tightly that, for a moment, he wondered if she were dead.

'We are thanking you, Monsieur. We are deeply thanking you for your 'ospitality,' she said in her halting French.

'Madame, you look tired. Please, sit down.' She accepted his offer, and Lucia stirred in her lap, revealing the imminence of a fourth Esposito. Leon beckoned Daniel aside. 'How do you know these people? Who are they? Why have you brought them here?'

'I went down to the Old Port—'

'Are you mad?' Leon said. 'The place is swarming with Nazis.'

Antonio emitted a low moan and ran to his mother, who cupped his chin.

'Don't shout, Papa! You'll frighten them. They've been through enough.'

'I'm sorry. Please don't be scared,' Leon said to Antonio. 'Does he speak French?' he asked Madame Esposito.

'He is perfect.'

'Excellent! Then you'll understand, Antonio, that there's nothing to be afraid of. I was just a bit cross with Daniel. Isn't your papa ever cross with you?' The boy's sudden stiffening chastened him.

'His father's interned in Fréjus,' Daniel said. 'The family was taken there in the round-up ten days ago. Madame and the children were released yesterday. They've returned to find their house obliterated.'

'Where will my childs be sleeping?'

'We have plenty of rooms. It won't be a problem.'

'Thank you, Papa,' Daniel said.

'Thank you, Monsieur,' Madame Esposito echoed. 'Daniel said you are a most kind friend.'

'Did you know Madame before?' Leon asked him, sensing a deeper rapport than at a chance meeting.

'Yes, of course. Monsieur Esposito owns the repair shop where I take my bike.'

'My husband . . .' Madame Esposito began to sob. Antonio put his arms round her. '*Non preoccuparti, tesoro*, Papà is coming back with us soon.'

'They have nowhere to go. I knew you'd ask them to stay.'

'Yes of course,' Leon replied, transfixed by Antonio's hair, which he'd thought was glimmering in the moonlight but realised was crawling with lice. 'They can have one of the rock chambers.'

'Not in the house?' Daniel asked.

'They'll have more privacy,' Leon insisted, picturing Lily's response to a lice infestation. 'There are a couple of mattresses left from when you and Sylvain camped out there during his last visit. They'll do for tonight. We'll find something better tomorrow. Now what about food? They must be hungry. Have you eaten, Madame?'

'You are so kind, Monsieur.'

'I'm sorry, is that a yes or a no?'

'What do you think, Papa?' Daniel asked, with a sigh.

Leon went inside and brought out a tray of apples, pears and persimmon, winter fruits from the garden, which, thanks to Lily's expert pruning, were in plentiful supply. Leaving the family to eat undisturbed, he and Daniel descended the stairway to the rock corridor and opened up one of the chambers, which, after months of disuse, smelt not just stale but putrid.

'We can't give them this,' Leon said, flicking his torch across the floor. 'Something must have crept in during the autumn and died.'

'It'll be fine for now,' Daniel said, no longer so fastidious. 'Do you have any idea what conditions were like for them in the camp? Sleeping on straw, alive with vermin,' he said, pulling out three mattresses, which were merely dusty and damp. 'Fifty or sixty people crammed into a tiny hut,' he added, laying the mattresses on the spacious floor. 'The stink of piss and shit and vomit.'

'I don't need details, thank you. How do you know so much about it?'

'I ask. I listen. I keep my eyes open. Honestly, Papa, there's no longer any excuse for standing idly by – if there ever was one. It's time to act.'

'And you have . . . you are by helping these people. That's as much as you can do. I know you don't like hearing it, but you're still a boy.'

As Daniel ran up to the house for blankets, Leon escorted the family into the chamber. Madame Esposito's further expression of gratitude humbled him, and he assured her that the grubby conditions were only temporary. He pointed out the tap in the corner, which, though rusty, was safe to use, along with a bucket whose purpose he signalled with nebulous below-the-waist gestures. Daniel returned with an armful of blankets and pillows and, after he had set them out, Leon drew him away, with a cheery 'Sleep well!' to their guests. No sooner had he closed the door than Antonio let out a piercing yell.

'No, *per favore*, is better it is opening,' Madame Esposito called.

'Yes, yes of course.'

Leon accompanied Daniel back to the house, kissed him and went up to his room. Despite a night of broken sleep, he woke the next morning feeling refreshed. He hurried down to the kitchen to be ready for Lily, who barely acknowledged his greeting.

'I've made a pot of coffee,' he said.

'Hurrah! What is it today? Oak galls or lupin seed or date pips?'

'My own secret recipe. Though I say so myself, it's quite palatable.'

Lily, who resented his refusal to buy coffee off the ration, snorted and went into the hall to summon the children for breakfast. Gabrielle, already halfway down the stairs, entered the kitchen in her school uniform, which, after two years of letting out and patching, looked tighter and shabbier each day.

'How's my favourite daughter this morning?'

'You only have one.'

'You should know by now: your father is the master of empty compliments,' Lily said. 'Which would you rather, apple or pear on your bread?'

'Apple.'

Lily pulled out the fruit basket. 'What?' She looked at Leon. 'Is this you? It was full yesterday.'

'There are crates of fruit in the cellar.'

'That's not the point. It has to last. Or do you want your children to starve?'

Scowling at him, she made a plum jam tartine for Gabrielle, who, with a glance at her indignant mother, chose to eat it outside. As usual when they were alone, Lily busied herself with menial tasks. Leon was wondering how best to break the news of the evacuees when Gabrielle charged into the kitchen, sparing him the need.

'Why is there a boy playing beside the pond?'

'That'll be Antonio.'

'Who?' Lily asked.

'One of the family Daniel brought . . . rescued last night.'

'Why isn't he wearing clothes?'

Without a word, Lily swept through the house and onto the terrace, followed by Leon and Gabrielle. They watched Antonio gaze into the water as intently as Narcissus, his shirt and shorts laid out on the rocks, alongside his mother's and sister's dresses.

'Where's Daniel?' Lily asked Leon.

'Still in bed, I expect. He was up late.'

'Doesn't he have school?'

'It might be best to give them both the day off.'

'May I go down and talk to him?' Gabrielle asked, peering at Antonio, who remained oblivious of their presence.

'Wait!' Lily said. 'How many of them are there?'

'Only three. The boy, his mother and sister. They came back to Marseille to find their home in ruins. They'd been sent to a camp.'

'Why?'

'Why anything these days?'

'But he's not Jewish.'

'How do you know?'

'I have eyes.'

'Maman!' Gabrielle laughed.

'It's not funny,' Lily said. 'Why were they taken if they're not Jews?'

'Because they're poor? Because they're foreign? Because they were in the wrong place at the wrong time?'

'If we're to risk our lives sheltering fugitives, shouldn't they at least be our own?'

'A priest arranged Fernand and Laure's escape from Bordeaux and placed the girls in a convent. Shouldn't we do as much for them?'

As expected, the mention of her brother and his family swayed

Lily, who asked him to take her to Madame Esposito. Seeing them walk down the steps, Antonio ran to his mother, who came out, dressed in a flimsy slip, still holding Lucia. Leon introduced her to Lily and Gabrielle, whom she thanked as profusely as she had him. After introductions to the children, Lily invited them to the house for breakfast, hurrying away as though to avoid a fresh outpouring of gratitude.

'You didn't tell me she was pregnant,' she said to Leon, once they were back in the kitchen. 'It's so irresponsible.'

'Of me?'

'Of her!'

'It may have been an accident,' Gabrielle said, reddening under her parents' gaze.

'The children look like street urchins,' Lily said. 'Go up to the attic, Gabi. There are trunks of clothes from when you and Daniel were small. Bring down whatever looks like it might fit. And wake up your brother. He got us into this.'

'What about the mother?' Leon asked, as Gabrielle went out. 'Have you anything suitable for her?'

'Some maid's overalls . . . What? Don't give me that look! You're surely not suggesting we're the same size?'

'No, of course not.'

'I told you those clothes would come in useful,' Lily said, spreading sheets of *Le Petit Marseillais* on a chair. 'If you'd had your wish, we'd have given them away years ago and those children would remain in rags. And what are they supposed to eat? Three more mouths to feed!'

'Two of them small.'

'And the other eating for two.'

'We'll manage. Who else is as well placed as us? Fruit and vegetables the whole year round. And shelves full of preserves. All thanks to your hard work.' Unlike Papa, he had been keen to have a kitchen garden, although he'd never envisaged its proving such a boon.

'What about eggs and cheese and meat and butter and sugar?

Will Monsieur let me buy them on the black market? Oh no, he's too proud!'

'Pride has nothing to do with it. Rich Jews are being blamed for pushing up prices.'

'Huh! How many still have money?'

'We can't take the risk.'

'I despair!'

Daniel entered in his pyjama bottoms.

'Despair of what, Maman? I can hear you two floors up.'

'Take these!' Lily thrust a stack of newspapers at him. 'Cover all the surfaces! They're your guests. Then get dressed and go to school! Your father may not care about your education, but I do.'

Once she had made it clear that her consent was not to be taken for granted, Lily reconciled herself to the Espositos' presence. She enjoyed having another woman in the house, especially one whose ambiguous status meant that she not only wore the maid's overalls but assumed much of her work. Long accustomed to challenges that were new to the Carraches, she was resourceful and shrewd, enhancing their diet with nettle soup, purslane stew and winter mushrooms; supplementing their meagre supply of soap with an infusion of saponaria and lavender; and fixing carboard soles on the children's shoes. After she'd shorn her irate son's hair, Lily invited her to move the family into the maids' quarters.

The children quickly adjusted to their new surroundings. Antonio was happy as long as he had an audience for his antics, whether climbing to the top of the ancient oak, performing a two-minute headstand or, more disturbingly, beating a lizard to death. Lucia, by contrast, preferred solitude, playing with Gabrielle's old dolls which, for safekeeping, she hid in a different cupboard every night. She showed a particular fondness for Leon, refusing to go to sleep unless he read to her from one of the *Babar* books he'd found in the nursery.

'She's missing her father,' Lily said, piqued.

On Saturday morning, Leon left the house at nine and went

to synagogue. Despite the punitive restrictions imposed on Jews, the authorities had permitted public worship to continue and, as a member of the Consistory, Leon considered it his duty to attend. He entered the sanctuary, taking his allotted pew beside the bimah. While the cantor intoned the opening psalm, he scanned the congregation, nodding to friends and acquaintances and noting absences with apprehension. Nowhere was the perversity of the Nazi project more manifest than here, where scholars scraped a living as copyists, doctors and surgeons worked as hospital orderlies, publishers were demoted to bookbinders, and journalists hawked the papers for which they once wrote.

Lily condemned his profession of a faith that he had long renounced as both reckless and wilful. What she failed to comprehend was that his Judaism wasn't in his heart or his head; it was in his blood and his bones and his sinews. It was inherited from his forefathers in the distant past, when they had not even had a family name but were simply Yitzhak ben Yosef and Rivka bat Yehuda. It was the one part of him that had survived the transition from Ottoman Italian to French. Now that it was under attack, he was all the more determined to affirm it.

Two years before, when the Vichy authorities followed their German counterparts and ordered a census of the Jews, Bella sent him a coded letter urging him not to register: 'Please don't insist on wearing your old coat. Buy yourself a new one. It will fit just as well and, what's more, it's made in France.' She hadn't included an address so he had no means of replying, but if he had, he'd have said that his well-worn coat was made of grey-blue serge and boasted four medals: two for the campaigns in which he'd fought and two for the valour he'd displayed. He had spent three years at the front and, like any soldier wounded in the nation's service, when he applied for naturalisation after the war, he had the right to claim that he was 'French by blood'.

True to Carrache tradition, after four years in Marseille, he had been elected to the Consistory. The previous summer, several of his colleagues had solicited his support for a petition to exempt Sephardim from the anti-Jewish legislation. They claimed that their Iberian ancestry meant that, unlike Ashkenazim, they were not racially Semitic. Moreover, George Montandon, a Parisian professor of anthropology, held in high esteem by both the Commissariat-General for Jewish Affairs in Vichy and the Office of Racial Policy in Berlin, was not unsympathetic to their cause. On receipt of a substantial donation to his research institute, he was prepared to confirm that the blood make-up of Sephardim was, indeed, different from that of Ashkenazim: they were 'Ario-Latins of the Mosaic faith'.

As a boy, Leon had been offended by Papa's mistrust of Ashkenazim and outraged by the contempt with which other notables spoke of them, one even claiming that he'd rather his children 'marry a Turk than a Polack'. While acknowledging that the petition sprang from desperation, not prejudice, he nonetheless refused to sign it. Trusting that his decision would not be relayed to Lily, who would undoubtedly accuse him of choosing his principles over his children, he spelt out his objections. He had known many brave Ashkenazim in the Foreign Legion. They had marched together, slept together, faced the guns together and, at times, wiped each other's innards off their tunics. Given his vehemence, it was no surprise that, shaking hands after the service, two of the petitioners still couldn't look him in the eye.

With an hour to spare before lunch, he decided to stroll back along the Corniche. The Plage du Prophète was strewn with debris, and the mustard-coloured sea vindicated Lily's refusal to let Daniel swim there. On arriving home, he knew that he'd lingered too long. Lucia stood bawling in the hall, but, before he could comfort her, he was distracted by urgent cries from the salon. Rushing towards them, he spied Madame Esposito telling her beads in the library, while Antonio struggled to lift her off the floor. He entered the salon to find Lily clawing at her cheeks with nails which were, thankfully, too cracked and weak to do harm, while Gabrielle pleaded with her to stop.

'You!' Lily screamed at him. 'Where have you been?'

'In synagogue, why? What's happened?'

'Daniel's been arrested, Papa,' Gabrielle said.

'What?' Only his sense of himself as a husband ... a father ... a man ... prevented his drowning out Lily's screams.

'Arrested. He's been arrested,' Lily mumbled, as if her frenzy had burned itself out. She sat moaning, while Gabrielle explained that Julie, one of Daniel's comrades in the Resistance, had come to tell them of his arrest.

'The Resistance? Daniel? That's not possible.'

'And she knew it!' Lily shrieked. 'Your daughter knew all the time and said nothing. Viper!'

'It's not your fault, darling,' Leon assured Gabrielle, as Lily's venom reduced her to tears.

'He said he was just a messenger, carrying documents – forged papers, food coupons, identity cards – hidden in his schoolbooks.'

Leon hugged her, feeling her heart hammer against his own.

'He had a bomb! A bomb! Our son had a bomb!'

'No! How? He can't even mend a puncture.'

'It was Madame Esposito,' Gabrielle whispered.

'She made the bomb?'

'No, of course not! But you know how worried she's been about her husband.'

'Yes.' Dismayed by her persistent questions about his likely fate, Leon had avoided being alone with her. Instead, she'd unburdened herself to Daniel. This was the result.

'Daniel wanted to help her,' Gabrielle said. 'He promised to get news from the camp at Fréjus.'

'It's a prison,' Leon said, clutching the arm of a chair into which he sank. 'How could he get news?'

'I don't know. Someone in the network? A spy among the guards? Anyway, he did. They heard that a unit was being transferred ... not just Jews but Greeks and Corsicans and Italians. I suppose Signor Esposito was one of them. They were being brought back by train to Marseille and then transported up north. Daniel was determined to stop it. They'd find out when the train was due, blow up the track and rescue the captives.'

'Who does he think he is? D'Artagnan? He's only just started shaving!'

'But they were caught laying the bomb. Someone must have betrayed them. Madame Esposito blames herself.'

'Did she tell someone about the plan?'

'No, no, Papa, you're not listening. For loading her problems on Daniel. For getting him involved.'

'I want those people out of my house,' Lily said. 'Today, Leon! Do you hear me?'

'I hear you,' he replied, confident that she would reconsider. 'Does this Julie have any idea where Daniel is?' he asked Gabrielle.

'She thought they'd all been taken to Fort Saint-Nicolas.'

Lily wailed.

'I'll go up there right away.'

'Take gold,' Lily said. 'And my emerald bracelet. And this,' she added, tearing off her wedding ring. 'Give them anything. And offer to take his place. They can shoot you instead of him.'

'Maman!'

'He's my son.'

Leon grabbed a roll of banknotes from his study and left the house, trailed by Madame Esposito, beating her breast like the Greek mourners of his childhood. He assured her curtly that she wasn't to blame and strode towards the gate, where Daniel's bicycle was propped up against the hedge. Taking it as a talisman, he straddled the seat, which was uncomfortably low, and pedalled up the hill. Soaked in sweat, he reached the fort, its stark, windowless walls scarcely distinguishable from the rock on which it stood. He shuddered at the thought of Daniel mewed up inside and prayed that he was sharing a cell, however cramped, rather than languishing alone. Leaving the bicycle at the base of the mound, he approached the two guards at the gate, their faces as stony as the setting. With a faltering smile, he gave his name and begged to spend a few minutes with his son, to reassure them both that he was safe. The request might be irregular, but, if they were fathers themselves, they would understand.

He was met with a flat refusal. 'We have no information on the prisoners,' one of the guards said, 'and, even if we had, we're not allowed to divulge it. Now scram, or you'll find yourself inside for more than a few minutes!' Trembling, less on his own account than from fear that a miscalculation would endanger Gabrielle and Lily, Leon pulled his handkerchief from his pocket, letting the banknotes fall to the ground.

'You've dropped something, Monsieur,' the guard said.

Leon held his gaze. 'I don't think so. It must be yours.'

'That's right,' the second guard said, bending to retrieve it.

'No,' the first guard said, pushing him aside with the butt of his rifle. 'I'm sure it belongs to Monsieur. You should take more care,' he added, handing the money to Leon. 'Someone might suspect it was a bribe.'

Refusing to give up hope, Leon headed back to the city to seek an official permit at the Préfecture. He pedalled furiously, his calves and thighs aching from the strain, his clammy palms struggling to grip the handlebars. Halfway down the Boulevard Garibaldi, his front tyre burst. Passers-by gawked as he flung the bicycle aside and ran the remainder of the way. He arrived at the Préfecture to find every entrance shut. The swastikas draped over the façade mocked his folly. Surely he of all people should have remembered that Saturday was a day of rest? He walked away, sick with self-loathing. Whatever his other failings, he had always protected his children. Yet for months – maybe longer – his son had been risking his life, and he'd had no idea.

He returned home, where Lily greeted his abortive mission with stinging rebukes. Alternately hysterical and listless, she bombarded him with questions which she knew he couldn't answer, as though contempt for his ineptitude were all that kept her from despair. At some point during the evening, Madame Esposito served them apple and tuber soup, which he urged Lily to eat out of courtesy. 'Our son is in mortal danger and you worry about hurting her feelings!' she retorted, prompting Gabrielle to burst into tears. His attempts to comfort her sounded vapid even to himself. More wretched than ever, he retired to his room, where he spent the night fully clothed on his bed, listening to the rustling leaves and wildlife, the hourly chime of the basilica bells, and Lily's footfall on the stairs. Dawn brought no relief, since the Préfecture wouldn't open until Monday. Fortunately, Lily's relentless pacing had exhausted her and, with the aid of Madame Esposito's valerian root tea, she slept for much of the day. To escape from brooding, Gabrielle took Antonio to forage for wild asparagus on the cliffs, while Leon read Lucia her favourite stories, finding almost as much solace in the wise elephant's adventures as she did.

On the dot of eight the next morning, he entered the lobby of the Préfecture, biting his tongue when the supercilious desk clerk told him that, without an appointment, he couldn't say when, by whom or even whether he would be seen. Thanking him fulsomely, he took a seat on an ornate bench facing twin portraits of Hitler and Pétain, evidence that with the Germans now commanding the south, all pretence of autonomy had been dropped. He resisted the urge to address the bustling officials, lest he jeopardise his case, even as he resisted the urge to empty his bladder for fear of missing his slot. Shortly before noon, he was summoned by a junior controller, whose plump cheeks and unblemished skin betrayed no sign of the current privations. After listening wearily to Leon's request, he declared that the government had banned all visits to 'insurrectionists'.

'But he's just a boy!'

'A boy who planted a bomb. Even if I were authorised to give you a pass, it would be of no value since the prisoners are due to be transferred.'

'Where to?'

'Drancy, a holding camp in Paris.'

'Why not Fréjus?' Leon asked anxiously. 'It's closer.'

'I've told you more than you need to know. If you're not happy, you should direct your concerns to Vichy.'

Unknown to the smirking controller, Leon had an ally at the heart of Vichy in his wartime commander, Major Beauchamp, head of the police department in the Commissariat-General for Jewish Affairs. Whether his support for the collaborationist regime was ideological or pragmatic, he had shown himself to be both honourable and just in his leadership of the battalion. Moreover, he had personally recommended Leon for the Military Medal at the Aisne. Until now, Leon had hesitated to approach him for fear of being slighted. But no slight could deter him from saving Daniel.

'Then I shall go to Vichy.'

'You'll need a travel pass, which aren't issued to Jews.'

'Can a Jewish veteran request an exemption?'

'He can, but it will be refused.'

'So the only way I can help my son is by travelling to Vichy. But there's no way you'll give me a pass. What sort of logic is that?'

'The pure sort, unintelligible to Yids.'

Despite all the provocations of the past three years, Leon prided himself on having kept within the law. He now prepared to break it. He left the Préfecture and made his way to the Panier district, where his former secretary, Denise Fournier, lived with her mother. When the Germans first occupied the city, she'd told him that, should he or his family ever need new papers, she had a friend able to procure them. Sitting in her modest apartment, he explained his predicament, whereupon she promised to contact her friend and have the documents ready by evening. She was as good as her word, and Leon returned at nine o'clock to receive an identity card under the impeccable name of Louis Dufresne, along with a travel pass 'signed' by the German commandant, General Mylo. He went straight to Saint-Charles station, bought a third-class ticket for the first time since his army days, and boarded the night train to Lyon.

The compartment was cold, the bench hard, and the train made several unscheduled stops, during which he tried to ignore the distant stomping and muffled thuds and shouts. His own papers passed muster, and he arrived in Lyon at six thirty in the morning. With the Vichy train not due to depart until ten, he had a sudden, overwhelming urge to visit Bella, but even had he known her address, he felt ill-equipped to deal with the emotion that seeing her would stir. So he bought a *pain au lait* at the buffet and a copy of *Le Progrès* at the kiosk and waited opposite a wall neatly plastered with portraits of Pétain, like a giant sheet of postage stamps.

Once on the train, he cast his mind back to his last meeting with Major Beauchamp – since promoted to Colonel – in June 1935, when they had both attended the inauguration of the plaque honouring the Sephardim soldiers killed during the Great War. Although Maman, as proud of his Military Medal as Lily's family were of her great-great-grandfather's Légion d'honneur, claimed that the Major's presence was a testament to Leon, he was in fact representing one of the many veterans' associations which, in happier days, had paid tribute to their Jewish comrades. In retrospect, however, there may have been a hint of his imminent volte-face when, in conversation with Papa, he expressed his surprise at the 'valour and virility' of the Jews under his command.

In 1914, Leon had been living in France for little more than a year. As an Ottoman subject eager to serve his adopted country, he enlisted in the Foreign Legion, where he was thrust into a company of French mercenaries, redeployed from North Africa, who mercilessly bullied the raw recruits. A year later, he was transferred to the 33rd Artillery Regiment, a regular unit, in which he served for eighteen months before being invalided out. He was cited three times in army orders, awarded the Croix de Guerre for his part in capturing a German field gun at Verdun and the Military Medal for crawling through no man's land, his injured arm in a makeshift sling, to rescue his trapped captain at the Aisne. The arm later became gangrenous and only Papa's prompt intervention saved it from amputation. Although he regained most of its use, his left-handedness, which had so disturbed Grandmaman Falcona, turned out to be a blessing.

The memory of his exploits, which steeled him for his mission, would serve as his calling card to the Colonel. Arriving in Vichy, he wasted no time in heading to the Commissariat's offices in the Hôtel Algérie, a building he knew well since it was a stone's throw from the Hôtel du Parc, in which he'd spent several happy childhood holidays. He entered the lobby, where he was interrogated by yet another self-important clerk, who grudgingly agreed to pass on his letter to the Colonel. He summoned a messenger, a fresh-faced boy of about Daniel's age, who smiled at Leon with such unexpected warmth that he almost broke down. He took a seat on a plush circular sofa, watching the various officers and mandarins ascend the sweeping staircase, some bounding up, as if to indicate the urgency of their business, others poring over documents, as if to indicate the complexity of theirs. No one spared him a second glance until Colonel Beauchamp hailed him from the lift.

'Carrache!' Leon sprang to attention, barely suppressing a salute. 'Follow me!' he barked, so anxious to usher him out of the building that they were almost wedged in the revolving door. 'You shouldn't be here. Jews aren't permitted on the premises.'

'Isn't it the Commissariat-General for Jewish Affairs?'

'What does that have to do with anything? Let's walk,' the Colonel said, striding towards the park. 'Keep up, man! I read your letter. I have no idea who you are, but you say I commended you for saving the life of one of my bravest captains, and I have to assume, given the risk you've taken in coming here, that you are who you say you are – whoever that may be. So I told myself, he deserves five minutes of my time. Right?'

'I'm most grateful,' Leon said quietly. 'I know how busy you must be.'

'How do you know? You have no idea. None whatsoever. That's the trouble with you people. You think you know it all. That's what got you into this mess. But I said I'd give you five minutes of my time.' He looked at his watch. 'And I've already given you six . . . no, seven. I must get back to my desk. Appeals, entreaties all day long... immunity from this, indemnity for that! But you've come to speak to me in person, so you expect me to give you an answer. Right?'

'If you please.'

'Well, the answer's no. I've read the report. Your son is a saboteur.'

'He's a boy.'

'Of course he is; he's your son, not your daughter! Besides, he's already been handed over to the Abwehr. The Maréchal himself couldn't secure his release. My advice to you is to go home and keep your head down. Right?'

'Is that all you can say to an old soldier?' Leon asked desperately.

'I'm an old soldier, damn you!' the Colonel boomed, to the alarm of a passing priest.

'Monsieur,' Leon said, 'in the Great War you fought against the Germans. How can you capitulate to them now?'

'I fought for France and I still fight for France! For her spirit... for her survival. For the France that will be reborn when the Germans leave. I fight for the men who gave their lives at my command. I fight for their wives and mothers, their sons and daughters.'

'What about the Jewish men who gave their lives at your command?'

'They deceived me, just as they deceived everyone else. Why did the best-equipped, the best-disciplined army in the world collapse at the sight of a German tank if not for the perfidy of the Jews? Their corruption left it weak and effeminate. Now go before I have you arrested! How dare you weasel your way in here and accuse me?'

He turned back towards the hotel.

'Colonel, may I ask you one final question?' With nothing to lose, Leon found that he had nothing to fear. 'How can you be sure that the Unknown Soldier isn't a Jew?'

4

SIMON

AUBIÈRE, MARCH 1943

THE CELLARS WERE dotted about the hillside like ancient burial chambers. For centuries, Aubière had been a thriving wine-producing region, although, with the river Artière flowing beneath the village, the risk of floods had led the vintners to store their casks on the nearby slopes. But as Monsieur Gaillard, the nonagenarian village patriarch, had told Simon over several glasses of gentian in the *bar-tabac*, cultivation had all but ceased fifty years earlier, when phylloxera and mildew blighted the vines. The labyrinth of chambers had fallen into disuse, except as a site for illicit trysts. Now, as the ransom note indicated, it was serving a more sinister purpose.

Simon had never expected to find himself in such a backwater, but, when the Germans moved into Clermont-Ferrand, he saw fit to abandon urban anonymity for rural obscurity. Conscious that, even in peacetime, villagers viewed strangers with suspicion, he had gone out of his way to win their confidence. In applying for his residence permit, he'd presented the baptismal certificates signed by Father Francis in Clermont. He had donated five thousand francs to Father Loïc of Saint-Martin, even though, as he explained, the family wouldn't be regular worshippers. He had bought drinks at the *bar-tabac* for the locals, young and old, whose conviviality in their cups vanished in the sober light of day. He had informed Madame Serres, on renting her two upper floors, that they had left home rather than live alongside the Wehrmacht officer billeted on them, trusting that their stance would be applauded by her neighbours. But it had all come to nothing due to his son's recklessness. Sylvain, hitherto scared of his own shadow, had turned into Judas Maccabeus, after one of his classmates parroted some of Doriot's antisemitic bile. While his fellow pupils cheered and taunted, he was pushed into a corner and his trousers and drawers pulled down. The ritual humiliation became personal when the 'Jew lover' was exposed as a Jew.

It had been three days since Sylvain came home from school and haltingly described the assault. Irène insisted that, far from doing anything wrong, he had shown admirable courage in confronting bigotry. She looked to Simon for support, but her argument carried little weight with one who had spent a lifetime swallowing his pride. As word spread, he anticipated repercussions but not that they would occur so soon. The previous morning, Irène failed to return from her regular provisioning trip to the Roussel farm. At noon, he called on Madame Roussel, who, invoking 'the Blessed Virgin and all the saints', swore that Irène had left 'with a dozen eggs, some goose fat and a pot of my blue cheese pâté around ten'. Frantic, he ran back to the village, questioning everyone he met, struggling as always to recall the colour of her dress. He paused outside the gendarmerie, but, wary of involving the authorities, he went back to the Rue Pasteur, where the children were waiting, grey-faced on the stairs. 'This is your fault!' he shouted at Sylvain. 'If anything happens to Maman, her blood will be on your hands.'

Clarice hugged her brother, who curled into a ball, crying. 'This came for you,' she said, breaking away to hand Simon a crumpled envelope.

'Who brought it?' he asked, ripping it open.

'It was slipped under the door.'

He skimmed the semi-literate note, which stated that rich Jews who came to the village and bought up supplies, while honest Frenchmen starved, must be held to account. The amount demanded was either ten or a hundred thousand francs, depending on whether the blot on the final zero was accidental or a reduction of the initial demand. Telling himself that there was no price too high for Irène's freedom, he remained determined not to pay it. A man who had overseen the takeover of two rival banks during the Depression was more than a match for a gang of venal peasants.

Ruffling Sylvain's hair by way of apology, he asked Clarice to fetch her freshwater pearls. Promising to replace them with real ones, he tucked them in his jacket pocket, assured the children that he would return with their mother, and set out to meet the kidnappers at the appointed rendezvous. From the bottom of the hill, he spotted a rangy figure whom, on closer inspection, he recognised as Thomas Bonnet, the baker's surly assistant, clamping his muffler to his cheek in a vain attempt at disguise. He followed him down a short flight of steps into a cellar, a trace of vinegar in the foetid air attesting to its former use. As his eyes adjusted to the murk, he made out two men, their thighs spilling over their stools, although their faces remained in shadow. He seethed with fury towards them, as towards all the 'honest Frenchmen' who'd exploited and abused them since they'd joined the desperate caravan fleeing Paris at the German invasion.

Had he possessed a gun, he would have shot all three men without hesitation, but he'd come armed with nothing but the pearls and the desire to outswindle the swindlers. So when one asked, with a cognac-soaked rasp, whether he had the money, he answered with a blunt 'no'.

'Whatever anyone may have told you, I'm destitute.'

'We'll have none of your Jew tricks here.'

'It's the law! Two years ago, our bank accounts were frozen.' There was no call to explain that he'd cleared his before leaving Paris. 'We're permitted only fifteen hundred francs a month for all our needs. But I love my wife, and to thank you gentlemen for looking after her' – he strove to lighten his tone – 'I've brought you the sole treasure we have left: a pearl necklace from the South Seas. You can sell it in the city for twenty . . . thirty . . . forty thousand francs. Or you can give it to one of your wives. Both if you cut it in half,' he added, dismissing Thomas, who was plainly just the errand boy.

One of the men signalled to Thomas to bring him the pearls. 'How do we know we can trust you?'

'It's a small village. You know where we live.'

The two older men conferred in the Auvergnat dialect which, after fifteen months in the region, Simon still found impenetrable.

'You're in luck. We'll take this.'

'And my wife?'

The man signalled once more to Thomas, who ducked beneath a low doorway and disappeared. As the two men passed the pearls between them, with one holding them foppishly to his neck, Simon felt a surge of relief, which vanished at the sound of spluttering and gasping. His fear that Irène had been bound and gagged was confirmed when she staggered into the cellar, red-faced and rubbing her wrists. Despite his resolve to betray no emotion in front of her captors, he scrambled over to kiss her, running his hands through her greasy hair.

'Are you hurt?' he asked her.

'Can we go?'

'Are we free to go?' he asked the men.

'Why? Do you want to stay for soup?' one said, causing his companions to snigger.

With a look of contempt, which he almost wished they could see, Simon steered Irène up the steps and into the sharp afternoon sunlight.

'Are you hurt?' he repeated.

'How are the children?'

'Fine. Worried about you, of course. They'll be fine now. Did they hurt you?'

'I'm tired. I just want to go home.'

'We're going there now.'

'No, home . . . my own home. Not at the mercy of those who hate us. I can't bear any more.'

'Answer me! Did they hurt you?'

'Oh!' She stumbled.

'They did?'

'No, they were perfect gentlemen,' she said sourly. 'They even gave me a piece of sacking for a pillow. It's nothing . . . just my leg gone to sleep.'

'Take my arm.'

'How much did you pay them?' she asked, as they approached the village.

'Not one solitary sou.' His spirits rose at the thought of their credulity. 'Just a trinket. Those artificial pearls Gabrielle gave Clarice. I told them they were priceless.'

'What if they'd found out?'

'How? By rubbing them against their teeth? They're peasants, not Parisian jewellers.'

'But if they take them to Clermont?'

'We won't be here. We must leave Aubière today.'

'And go where? Another village that scorns us?'

'Switzerland. I swear I'll finally get us to Switzerland.'

'Why not Tombouctou?' She sighed. 'I miss my family so much.'

'They're waiting for you at the house.'

'But what of the others? Esther and Bella and Leon and Ruben. And Maman . . . I miss Maman.'

'The Carraches,' he said drily.

'Why say it like that?'

'Like what? *The Carraches* . . . it's their name.'

It was a name that had captivated him ever since Avram and Falcona Beraha took him to the Campania at the age of seven. Irène was still a babe in arms and Ruben and Bella not yet born, but already in Leon and Esther he sensed the unbreakable bond which, petty rivalries apart, would unite all five siblings over the years. As an only child (he discounted Mari, an object of alternate pity and embarrassment), he yearned to be accepted as one of the family. But even after his marriage he remained an outsider, kept at arm's length by everyone but Jacob, whose growing reliance on him fuelled Leon and Ruben's resentment.

'You may see Bella sooner than you think.'

'What do you mean?'

'If we set off for Annecy, we can break the journey in Lyon.'

'Really? And stay with her? That would be wonderful.' She pulled him back and kissed his cheek.

'Not in the street!'

He ushered her down the Rue Pasteur, eager to evade scrutiny, wrenched open the gate and walked up the path to the jasmine-covered porch. As they reached the front door, the children hurled themselves at Irène.

'All's well, I promise,' she said, assuring them both that she was unharmed and a teary-eyed Sylvain that none of it was his fault.

'Leave your mother in peace now,' Simon interjected. 'She said the first thing she wanted when she got back was a bath.'

'I did?' she asked.

'You did,' he insisted. 'Come on upstairs.' He threw a meaningful glance at Madame Serres's doorway. 'Clarice, draw Maman a bath!'

'Are you sure? You know who won't like it.'

'You know who will just have to put up with it.'

As Clarice headed to the bathroom, Simon poured the last of their chartreuse into two glasses. 'Here,' he said, handing one to Irène. 'For your nerves.'

'May I have some?' Sylvain asked.

'How old are you?'

'For my nerves.'

'Children don't have nerves.'

Clarice rejoined them as Irène retrieved her hamza from under her blouse and kissed it.

'You're wearing your lucky charm, Maman,' she said.

'Something made me put it on yesterday. My grandmother promised it would protect me, and it has.'

'Come on!' Simon said, feeling that he deserved a share of the credit. 'If Falcona were here now, she'd write Hitler's name on a scrap of paper, toss it on the fire and claim it would bring about his downfall.'

'Scoff all you like, but the potion she gave you kept you out of the Sultan's army.'

'No wonder! She crushed delphinium seeds in it. I vomited for a week. It's a miracle I didn't die. Next, you'll be telling them I married you because of a buried egg!'

'What?' Clarice asked.

'Has Maman never told you the story? I'm surprised. You may not know this, but she's a witch. At any rate a junior one. She cast a spell on me.' He turned to Irène. 'Well, I'm sorry to disappoint you, but I married you of my own free will . . . for my own reasons.'

'Oh yes?' she asked. 'What were they?'

'Love, of course. Now would you please take your bath, so that we can get ready to leave?'

Her question touched a nerve. She was approaching fifty, but, even when she'd set her heart on him as a schoolgirl, she couldn't have supposed that love was the sole grounds for marriage. After all, her sister had been compelled to marry an Englishman she scarcely knew. It wasn't until he proved his worth in fire-ravaged Salonica, while the Carraches were enjoying the delights of Paris, that Jacob had considered him an acceptable match for his daughter. He took him into the bank, which was far more to his liking than the factory, not least because figures were more dependable than people. Ten years later, he had been appointed deputy director and, were it not for the Nazis, he would have been in line for the chairman's job when Nissim retired. But the Occupation not only stripped him of his authority, it opened his eyes to its insignificance. To his surprise, he found that the most important things in his life were his children: Clarice, who'd inherited his resourcefulness and tenacity, along with her mother's gentleness and grace; Sylvain, by turns excitable and placid, in whom he detected little of either parent but who was his own unique person. If only he hadn't shouted at him earlier . . . if only he could express his feelings for them as openly as Irène. He told himself that it was the difference between men and women, but he suspected that it was the difference between Simon Silvera and the rest of the world.

While Irène took a bath, Simon and the children packed their cases. Unlike the thousands of Parisians who'd fled the advancing Germans with chairs, sofas, beds and mattresses strapped to their vehicles, he'd insisted that they restricted themselves to essentials. Embarrassing as it was to recall, he'd been convinced that, after France fell, the Wehrmacht would reach London within a month; the war would be over, and life would return to normal. So they had brought only clothes, toiletries, a few books and games and, crucially, Irène's jewellery and several wads of thousand-franc notes. Living like gypsies, they were free to move on without fuss. Assigning the newly cleansed and scented Irène to distract Madame Serres, he loaded the car: the cases and boxes in the boot and between the seats; the cash behind the walnut panelling in the driver's door; and the jewellery in a canister welded beneath the running board. With everything in place, there was the usual delay while Sylvain said goodbye to each room in the house, a ritual Simon found dismayingly infantile in a boy of almost thirteen. Since he had also failed to outgrow his childhood motion sickness, the ever-indulgent Irène relinquished the front seat to him.

The drive through teeming rain took nearly five hours. They were stopped once, on the outskirts of Tarare, where a young patrol officer, as gangly as if he'd been made out of yarn, examined the vehicle's documents more intently than their own. Once he'd waved them through, Irène repeated her request that they exchange the Talbot for something less conspicuous, but Simon clung to this last link to their past. They arrived in Old Lyon shortly before midnight, only to cruise around in mounting apprehension. Without street lamps or a map, they had little hope of finding the Rue de Gardagne, until Clarice fortuitously spotted a sign. They parked at the corner of the Place du Change, and Irène entered the building alone. Moments later, she returned to say that Bella was not at home and the concierge, professing ignorance of her whereabouts, refused to let them wait in her apartment.

They sat in the car, their unease increasing by the minute. The strain was compounded by Sylvain's repeated insistence that he needed to pee.

'No, you don't,' Simon retorted. 'If your mother and sister can control their bladders, so can you. Just stop thinking about it.'

'How can I, when the rain's pouring down?'

No sooner had Simon decided to move on than he spotted Bella, beneath a sodden newspaper, running through the square in the company of two men.

'Has she no shame?' he asked. 'The country's under the heel of the Nazis and she's out gallivanting!'

'The children!' Irène said.

'They're old enough to know what's what. Well, aren't you going after her?'

'I don't know . . . I don't want to intrude.'

'For pity's sake!'

The matter was resolved when Bella dashed back down the street to the car, rattling a door handle until Clarice let her in.

'Shift over! I feel like a drowned rat.' She slid onto the seat, crushing the boxes that Simon had meticulously arranged, kissed Clarice and leant across to embrace Irène, who began to cry. 'My darlings, what are you doing here? Why didn't you let me know? Are you all right . . . yes, I can see. Sylvain, don't be shy! Give your aunt a great big kiss!'

Sylvain swivelled round awkwardly and let himself be hugged by Bella.

'Consider yourself kissed, Mercado,' she said, ruffling his hair.

'Simon,' he said shortly.

'We're at war,' she replied, as if that excused everything.

As she cooed over Irène and Clarice, Simon explained their sudden appearance and asked if they could stay with her overnight.

'I wish you could, but it's impossible. I already have a full house.'

'So we saw.'

'Did you?' she replied, with reciprocal bite. 'Let's hope no one else did. We'll go to Henri and Bertrand. They'll be more than happy to have you. It's just round the corner. I'll direct you.'

Despite Bella's 'turn left here ... I mean right', which prompted Irène to declare weepily that she hadn't changed, they reached the building. Bella, worried that a late-night visit would alarm their uncle, went up to alert him.

'I don't give two hoots for myself,' Simon said to Irène, 'but you'd think that, after not seeing you for years, she'd have sent her men friends away.'

'Not now, please! In any case, we'll be far more comfortable here. It's a sumptuous apartment.'

'Does it have a toilet?' Sylvain asked.

'Several.'

Bella came out to say that Henri and Bertrand would be delighted to put them up. Warning that the lift had been out of commission for months, she advised them to take only what they needed for the night. With a promise to return for breakfast, she hurried back to her guests. Sylvain raced up the four flights of stairs, while the others trudged behind. With each step, Simon felt a growing resentment. It was hard enough to beg favours of Bella, far harder to do so of Henri and his friend. It was one of life's many injustices that they should own a flourishing silk factory, when Papa had been unable to sustain a small silkworm farm.

Nevertheless, he couldn't fault their hospitality. Although in their dressing gowns and evidently roused from sleep, they insisted on making supper, heating up a saucepan of soup for which Henri apologised.

'The butcher gives us the bones he used to save for the dogs.'

'But we do have something special for dessert,' Bertrand said, producing a pineapple.

'Where did you get that?' Irène asked, so impressed that she failed to challenge Sylvain's 'Wow!'

'It's one of the perks of having Josée de Chambrun as a client,' Bertrand replied.

'Who?' Clarice asked.

'Laval's daughter. Don't let's talk about her.'

After supper, Simon joined Henri and Bertrand in the salon for coffee – the strongest he'd tasted in months. Irène settled the children, top to tail, on the study divan, before returning to voice her concerns about Bella.

'She's my sister and I love her dearly. I know she has artistic friends, but taking two men home with her . . .'

'What? Oh sweetheart, you're priceless,' Henri said, as Bertrand burst out laughing. 'You always were the family prude.'

'Nonsense!'

'You thought . . . Not at all! She's working for the Resistance. Together with Madame Aguillard, her concierge. Those two men are British undercover agents, here to gather intelligence.'

As Irène blushed, Simon poured himself a second cup of coffee, loath to admit that he had shared – indeed, sparked – her suspicions.

'But she's taking such risks,' Irène said.

'We all are,' Henri said. 'We have no choice.'

He refused to elaborate, but later, lying in bed between the crispest sheets and on the softest pillows that they'd known since leaving Paris, Irène reverted to the theme, contrasting Bella's defiance with her own inaction.

'She's unattached. She doesn't have your responsibilities,' Simon said. He had long hated the way she measured herself against her celebrated younger sister. In the past, he'd assured her that there was nothing more important than nurturing the next generation, but to do so now risked echoing Pétain's exaltation of motherhood or, worse, Hitler's *Kinder, Küche, Kirche*. Besides, he felt himself grudgingly admiring – even proud – of Bella. So he gave his wife a quick peck on the forehead and switched off the light.

Bella's newfound commitment extended to timekeeping, and she arrived for breakfast at eight. The children rushed to greet her, although Simon suspected that much of the attraction lay in the aroma of freshly baked bread wafting from her bag. They'd barely sat down at table when Irène, who had heard nothing from her mother or her brothers in more than a year, pressed Bella for news, which Henri had insisted she would be better able to provide. 'It's very hit-and-miss, but we get messages from Ruben through the store,' Bella said. 'They're as well as they can be, except that Maman contracted pleurisy last autumn.' Irène gasped. 'No need to panic! She recovered, though she's still frail.'

'We should have kept up the food parcels,' Irène said to Simon. 'No matter what, we should have found a way.'

'We agreed it was too dangerous for the children.'

'I don't mind being in danger for Grandmaman's sake,' Clarice said.

'If you've finished your brioche, go and see whether Nieve needs any help in the kitchen,' Simon said.

'What about Sylvain?'

'He can make himself scarce in Oncle Henri's study.'

'It's not fair,' Clarice muttered.

'But I want to hear—' Sylvain said.

'No arguments. Go!'

Once the children had left, Irène asked about Leon, and Bella relayed what she'd gleaned from Gabrielle's cryptic letter: that both Leon and Daniel had been arrested and taken to a labour camp in Germany.

'Will it never end?' Irène asked. 'Leon's fifty-two with a damaged arm. What use will he be to anyone?'

'When they find out, maybe they'll send him home? They won't want any dead weight,' Simon said, anxious both to console her and to silence the small – minuscule – part of himself that welcomed the detention of his arch-rival.

'I tried to persuade Gabi to come to Lyon,' Bella said. 'Of all the children, she's the one I'm closest to.' Simon scowled. 'But she feels she must stay with her mother.'

'Won't she be safer there, given your underground activities?' Irène asked tentatively.

'I had to tell them,' Henri said.

'Who would have thought when we were growing up that you'd become not just a famous artist but a Resistance fighter?' Irène said.

'Who would have thought that Germany would invade France?'

'What about Prince Menshikov?' Simon asked. 'What's his view on all this?'

'I neither know nor care. I haven't heard from him in over a year. He and his Tsarist friends are so consumed with hatred for communists that they've thrown in their lot with the Nazis. He wouldn't think twice about handing me over to the Gestapo.'

'Promise me you'll look after yourself!' Irène said.

'I promise. Besides, there's not just me. I have custody of a little girl.'

'You have a daughter?'

'Darling Irène, the way your mind works!' Bella kissed her. 'No, she's not mine but the child of two comrades, Inès and Yves, who were shot right in front of her. I wasn't there of course, but she was brought to me soaked in blood.'

'Don't!'

'She hasn't spoken a single word since.'

'How long ago was that?'

'Seven weeks.'

'Aren't you putting her in more danger by sheltering English airmen?' Irène asked.

'I don't . . . not regularly. I just pass messages. Far more lowly. But yesterday's safe house fell through. In fact, I must get back to them now. When are you leaving for Annecy?'

'As soon as possible,' Simon said. 'Bertrand's given me the name of a garage in Vaulx-en-Velin that won't fleece us. Half the time I might as well be filling the tank with champagne.'

'If we stay a little longer, can you come back?' Irène asked. 'Who knows when we'll see each other again?' She looked imploringly at both Bella and Simon.

'Once the men are on their way, I can leave Annette with Madame Aguillard.'

'We'll have lunch!' Irène said.

'I'll see if Nieve can get hold of some meat,' Henri said. 'Otherwise, it's turnip and carrot pie.'

Bella went out, and Bertrand, who'd discreetly left the family to themselves, took the children for a tour of the factory. With Henri's assurance that it was 'as safe as anywhere else these days', Simon and Irène strolled through the old city, but the narrow streets and covered passageways, once so full of charm, felt menacing. After an hour, they returned to the apartment to find Nieve in the hall, wringing her apron.

'There's been trouble. I don't know what... I don't want to know what. Sometimes, good people have bad friends. Mademoiselle Bella ... you must go at once.'

'Where are the children?' Simon asked.

'Monsieur Henri went to the factory to fetch them.'

'And Bella?' Irène asked.

'I told you, you must go to her.'

'Yes, but where?' Irène said. 'At her apartment?'

'No!' Nieve shouted. 'Not there. At the museum. Two doors from her building. The Gardagne. She's waiting for you there.'

'We must hurry, Simon,' Irène said.

'What if it's a trap?'

'She's my sister. If you'd rather, I'll go alone.'

'No, of course I'll come. But the children... Nieve, when Henri returns, make sure they're ready to leave. We have two bags. Pack everything. And if we're not back...'

'It will be fine, Monsieur. Quickly! Mademoiselle Bella is waiting.'

Simon followed Irène out of the building and down the street to the museum, where they made their way through rooms devoted to the city's history, from the antiquities of Roman Lugdunum to the textiles and ceramics of medieval Lyon. After climbing a staircase lined with portraits of dour dignitaries, they walked along a corridor filled with weaponry, which the only other visitors, a harassed-looking woman and two small boys, were examining. They entered a room of Renaissance furniture to find Bella lingering in the shadow of a vast armoire, beside a girl of six or seven. She had a mop of curly red hair and a sallow complexion, wore a faded blue dress, and clutched a silver-backed hairbrush.

'What is it? What's wrong?' Irène asked.

'What kept you?' Bella replied. 'Never mind. We don't have much time. There's been a raid.'

'The Englishmen?' Simon asked.

'While we were having breakfast. The Gestapo. Somebody . . . I don't know who or how, but somebody betrayed us. We all have to disappear for a while. That goes for Henri and Bertrand too.'

'Where?' Irène asked. 'How? Henri's seventy-one.'

'Don't ask questions! I'm sorry . . . I'm sorry. The clock's ticking.'

'So what will you do? Do you want to come with us to Annecy and Switzerland?'

'Would you like that, Mer— Simon?' Bella asked, swallowing a laugh.

'Yes . . . yes, if it's necessary. It'll be a squeeze in the car, but we'll manage.'

'Thank you, but it wouldn't be safe – for you, that is. And I have work to do here. But I need you to take Annette. For once, the gods have smiled on us. If we hadn't arranged to have lunch, you'd already have left and she would have no one. You will take her, won't you?'

'Yes, of course,' Irène said, 'if she wants to come.'

'She does.'

'If she doesn't speak, how can you be sure?' Simon asked.

'I've done my best to look after her,' Bella said to Irène. 'Though as we both know, I lack the maternal instinct. But you have it to spare, my darling. And I can't take her with me.'

'We know nothing about her,' Simon said, in desperation.

'It's better that way.'

'We don't have a choice,' Irène said to him.

'We must be practical.'

'A child's life is at stake,' Bella said. 'Is that practical enough for you? Here's her identity card. No incriminating red stamp. And a few food coupons.' She handed them to Irène, while addressing Simon. 'Are they practical enough for you? A couple of hours ago you were telling us how your friends in Annecy would help you. Surely they'll help this little girl you found wandering on the roadside and picked up because you're good people? You are good people, aren't you, Simon?'

'What if she says something different?'

'I told you before, she hasn't spoken since her parents were killed. Look at her!' Simon glanced at the girl, whose vacant expression unnerved him. 'Though it's only fair to warn you, she screams at night. She has bad dreams.'

'So does Simon,' Irène said.

He forced a sullen smile.

'Then he'll sympathise. Goodbye Annette. Be a good girl for Irène and Simon. Do everything they tell you and you'll be safe.' She knelt to hug her and embraced Irène, before kissing Simon lightly on both cheeks.

'Wait!' Irène said, as Bella strode towards the exit.

'I can't. You must do it. There's no one else.'

'Of course we will. Don't worry! But I want you to have this.' She removed the hamza pendant from around her neck and held it out to Bella.

'What is it?'

'Don't you remember? Grandmaman Falcona gave us one each when we left Salonica. It's for protection. I don't expect you've kept yours.'

'I don't remember ever having one.'

'What about you?' Simon asked Irène. 'What will you have to protect you?'

'I thought you said it was nonsense.'

'Even so . . .' Was this what his life had been reduced to: feeling superstitious about a superstition?

'Thank you,' Bella said, slipping the chain over her head. 'I promise I'll never take it off.'

She walked out, leaving Simon and Irène with the impassive girl.

'What just happened?' Simon said. 'Is this the maddest stunt your sister has ever pulled? How can we take charge of a child we've only known for five minutes?'

'I swear, if you fight me on this, I'll go straight to the nearest German and turn myself in.'

'You're being hysterical! I'm not suggesting we abandon her . . . but we could take her to a church or a convent.'

'I mean it, Simon.'

The glint in her eye showed him the folly of arguing. They returned to the apartment, where Henri had delivered the children before seeking refuge with friends, leaving Nieve to convey his goodbyes and emphasise the urgency of their departure. While Irène introduced Annette to Clarice and Sylvain, Simon carried the cases to the car. He hurried back upstairs to gather the family, along with the sparse provisions that Nieve had scraped together for their journey.

'You should think about returning to Spain,' he said to her at the door. 'Whatever else, it's a neutral country.'

'I shall never desert Monsieur Henri and Monsieur Bertrand,' she replied, as if they were her cubs.

They made their way out of Lyon, where Annette's identity card passed its first test on the Quai de la Bibliothèque. Clarice, seated to her left, spent half the journey coaxing her to talk, but she had no more success than Irène in eliciting a glance at the various landmarks. Sylvain, weary of the chatter at the back, began to sing, joined by Irène and Clarice, and, finally, Simon himself, amid the usual protests about his voice. For a moment, it reminded him of their carefree drives from Paris to Annecy before the invasion. Then Sylvain burst into Charles Trenet's 'Boom', a song he'd played so often on the disc's release that he'd worn out the groove. Whether the onomatopoeia echoed gunfire or it held other painful associations, the hitherto silent Annette screamed.

The closer they drew to Annecy, the more Simon relaxed. Switzerland was their goal; meanwhile, he was content to return to a town steeped in memories: boating on the lake; hiking through the canyon; golfing with partners whose friendship would end with the game. He had first visited eight years earlier, when his doctor recommended a course of mud baths to ease his sciatica. On the advice of Claude Joubert, the junior warden of his Masonic lodge, he had brought the family to Annecy, where the manager of the Hôtel Impérial Palace, Georges Legrandin, was a brother. It had been a wise choice, not just for the exceptional rates and service Legrandin provided, but for the fraternal bond cemented during three subsequent visits in as many years. But as they reached the hotel, Simon was struck by the fear that, with the Statute on Jews extended to Masons, Legrandin might have been replaced. Leaving the others in the car, he entered the lobby and felt at once as if he'd stepped back in time. Elegant guests sat at ormolu tables, while a young pianist in a strapless evening gown played tinkling melodies on a white baby grand. Chandeliers, sparkling as if there were no energy controls, cast intricate patterns on the polished marble floor. The only discernible difference from his last visit four years before was that the cohort of bellboys had been reduced to two, both barely in their teens. The unbridled opulence stirred a fresh fear: what if the hotel had been requisitioned as a resort for German officials and their families? But no sooner had he given his name at the reception desk than Legrandin came out of his office.

'I looked out of the window and saw the Talbot. "It can't be!" I said to myself. But it can and it is.' He held out his hand, with the familiar master's grip. 'I've been wondering how you were. And here's my answer.'

'Not an entirely happy one.'

'We weren't expecting you.'

'We don't have reservations.'

'But we have rooms. Plenty of them. Our friends from across the Rhône have made sure of that.'

'Then we'd like two. One for my wife and myself, and one for three children.'

'Three? Have you . . . ?'

'No, definitely not! The daughter of . . . someone we knew. It's a long story.'

'Understood.' Legrandin waved aside the receptionist and consulted the register. 'Let's see, I can give you our second-floor lakeside suite, with a connecting room for the children.'

'That sounds ideal. Just as long as they're facing the mountains.'

'Yes, of course. The view.'

'No, the hope,' Simon said, knowing that this was someone he could trust. 'And the freedom.'

Legrandin followed him outside, kissing Irène on both cheeks and Clarice on the hand (which surprised her), slapping Sylvain on the back (which irked him), and recoiling slightly from Annette's glazed stare. Deputing the bellboys to fetch the luggage, he escorted the family upstairs, suggesting that, after their arduous journey, they might prefer to eat in their rooms, which Irène pronounced 'most thoughtful', though Simon suspected that he didn't want the travel-stained new arrivals alarming his fashionable guests.

'I look forward to catching up in the morning,' he said to Simon. 'And remember, anything . . . anything at all, you need only ask.'

'Thank you. I know.'

Concerned that her fitful sleep would disturb Clarice and Sylvain, Irène prepared a bed for Annette in the salon, where she did, indeed, wake three times that first night. Twice, her nightmares coincided with Simon's, so that, disoriented, he wondered whether he were the one screaming. By day, however, she remained torpid. She made no effort to wash or dress, although she raised no objections to Irène's assistance. She ate what was put in front of her from the hotel's surprisingly extensive menu, but never expressed a preference, even by a gesture. She accompanied Irène and the children on walks in the woods and to the lake, where she refused to paddle. The only thing that roused her was any attempt to remove her hairbrush, to which she clung like one possessed.

While the family was relaxing, Simon arranged for their flight. When he presented himself at the Préfecture for his residence permit, he explained that he was here for a fortnight's cure, but, as he confided in Legrandin, he hoped to get away much sooner.

'I don't want to be discouraging,' Legrandin said. 'If you were a communist or an anti-Francoist, you might have a chance. But the Swiss have closed the doors – or, in their phrase, filled the lifeboat – when it comes to Jews.'

'We have our baptismal certificates. They've worked well so far.'

'Moreover, you have to have a sponsor.'

'We do. Roland Severin.'

'The fraudster?'

'That's a bit harsh. No one called him names when he was offering interest rates five per cent above the odds. He's lived in Geneva ever since leaving prison. I have one letter of recommendation from him and another from Pictet & Cie affirming that we're solvent.'

'I'm sure that will stand you in good stead once you're there, but you still have to cross the border. Trust me, it's pointless going through the official channels. We've had people stuck here for months with perfectly valid visas from, as I recall, Mexico and Cambodia, which the Swiss refused to recognise.'

'So what's the alternative? Staying in France and waiting to be hunted down?'

'No, never lose hope! You must slip across clandestinely. It's too early in the season for the mountain route. The snow won't melt before May and, even then, the passes are treacherous. If it were me, I'd go through Annemasse,' he said, leaning back and cradling his head, inadvertently revealing the gulf between one whose brotherhood had been proscribed and one whose very being was under threat. 'The farmers are more reliable than the *passeurs*, who've been known to rob travellers, desert them, and even hand them over to the Germans. Of course, the land route still poses a challenge. You may not have to negotiate a thousand-metre drop, but there are plenty of guards, ready to shoot on sight.'

Once Simon confirmed his resolve, Legrandin introduced him to Paul Chapal, the Protestant pastor whose support for Jewish fugitives was an open secret in the town, albeit one yet to reach the ears of the authorities. He offered to contact the Annemasse network on their behalf. Three days later, he sent word to Legrandin that everything was in place for their departure the following morning. After dinner that night, Simon gathered Irène and the children in the salon and broke the news.

'Tomorrow, we embark on the last leg of our journey, but it's also the most perilous. We take nothing but the clothes we're wearing ... there's to be no argument (I'm looking at you, Sylvain). We can buy everything we want in Switzerland.'

'What about the Talbot?' Sylvain asked.

'I'm giving it to Monsieur Legrandin.'

'Just like that?' Irène asked.

'He made us a very generous deal on the rooms. Besides, his help has been invaluable. The family couldn't be leaving if it weren't for him.'

While Pastor Chapal had orchestrated the first part of Simon's plan, Legrandin was instrumental in the second, surreptitious part. With a little persuasion, a large incentive and an appeal to his fraternal obligation, he had agreed that, moments before the family set off, he would spirit Annette away. Once they were safely on the train, he would consign her to a convent.

'Please don't think me heartless,' Simon said to him. 'But we've known her for less than a week. She was foisted on us by my unstable sister-in-law. You've seen what the girl's like; absolutely nothing gets through to her. I'm not saying it's her fault. But I refuse to be lumbered with her a day longer. She's not my responsibility.'

'Of course not. You've responsibilities of your own. Madame Silvera . . . your children. You shouldn't feel guilty.'

'I don't.'

'You shouldn't.'

So, straight after breakfast the next morning, when Irène returned to the suite for her usual 'five minutes', Simon led the children out on the terrace for one last glimpse of Mount Veyrier. While Sylvain prattled about the deadly bears emerging from hibernation, the housekeeper approached.

'Monsieur Legrandin thought the children might like to choose some titbits for the picnic,' she said.

'Are we allowed in the kitchen?' Sylvain asked, more excited about the dispensation than the food.

'As a special treat,' she replied.

'You two go ahead,' Simon said, 'while I have a final look in the car.'

'What about Annette?' Clarice asked.

'Do you want to choose something?' he asked Annette, who stared at him blankly. 'I thought not. So wait here, where you won't be in the way.'

The family's dispersal was Legrandin's cue. As Simon headed to the car, greeting two passing gardeners to establish an alibi, he pictured him stealing up the side steps to the terrace, smiling at Annette to gain her trust and bundling her back down the steps into the cellar, where they stored the parasols. For once, her silence would be a blessing, as long as Legrandin remembered to leave on the light. Deeming that sufficient time had elapsed, he returned indoors, where the sight of the perennially flustered receptionist, grinning bellboys and an elderly guest immersed in Le Matin satisfied him that everything had gone according to plan. He wandered around the lobby until Irène came down in the lift, her 'five minutes' having stretched as so often to fifteen.

'Where are the children?' she asked. 'Is it time we made a start?'

'Certainly. Our two are in the kitchen, choosing snacks for the journey. Annette's out on the terrace.'

'You left her alone?'

'It's not the Champs-Élysées!'

Simon followed Irène onto the terrace, which was empty.

'What are you doing?' he asked, as she craned over the balustrade, calling Annette's name. 'Are you afraid she might have jumped?'

'No, of course not! What made you say that?'

He accompanied her into the restaurant, where she questioned the guests. Some showed concern at the disappearance, others annoyance at the disruption, but none had seen Annette. Looking increasingly anxious, she returned to the lobby and demanded that the receptionist conduct a search of the building.

'I'm not going anywhere without her,' she said to Simon, as the receptionist dispatched the bellboys.

'She can't be far. But we need to leave for the station in good time. Undue haste will arouse suspicion.'

'There'll be other trains.'

'Not safe ones. Not today.' He drew her close. 'People – good people – are risking their own and their families' lives to help us. We can't let them down.'

'And I can't let my sister down, or Annette!'

She went back onto the terrace, just as the children came out of the kitchen, wreathed in smiles and flourishing their baskets. Their gaiety evaporated with Simon's news about Annette.

'I thought you didn't like the girl,' he said, wary of Sylvain's trembling lip.

'Of course I do! Lots and lots.'

Irène appeared in the lobby. 'People don't just vanish into thin air,' she said, for once ignoring her son's distress.

'What about Arsène Lupin?' Clarice asked.

'That's not helpful,' Simon replied.

When the bellboys returned empty-handed, the receptionist fetched Legrandin, whose composure as he heard the story reassured both Simon and Irène, though in different ways. He directed the housekeeper to check the bedrooms, in case Annette had sneaked upstairs, and the bellboys to gather the gardeners and comb the grounds.

'Don't worry, Madame,' he said. 'This is a hotel. Children wander off all the time.'

'But she's so . . . fragile.'

'Do you think she might be looking for her parents?' Sylvain asked.

'Don't be silly!' Clarice said. 'She saw them being shot.'

'But she's so little, she might not have understood.'

'Aunt Bella told Maman that she arrived drenched in their blood,' Simon said.

'Must you?' Irène said, as Sylvain began to sniffle.

'How long till we have to set off?' Legrandin asked.

'Now!' Simon replied. 'We're already late.'

'We can't abandon her,' Irène said. 'If people are risking their lives for us, then we'll risk ours for her.'

'I don't want to leave without Annette,' Clarice said.

'You'll do as you're told, Mademoiselle,' Simon said. 'I'm sure that, when she turns up, Monsieur Legrandin will take care of her until we can arrange for her to join us.'

'Absolutely. I promise. It's the least I can do.'

'It won't be for long,' Irène said resignedly. 'As soon as we're in Switzerland, we'll find a way.'

'Of course, Madame. The farmers in Annemasse aren't the only ones willing to risk their lives.'

The receptionist came up to report that neither the housekeeper's nor the gardeners' searches had revealed anything.

Irène moaned.

'We must go,' Simon said to her. 'Besides, if we don't make it across the border, she'll be better off here.'

'Is that supposed to comfort me?'

Legrandin drove them to the station, where he bade them farewell, reiterating his promise to treat Annette like his own daughter. Simon hovered at the booking counter, while the pimply clerk scrutinised his travel pass, as if his officiousness were all that kept him from forced labour service in the Reich. Clutching the tickets, Simon ushered his family onto the platform, where the train was waiting. The Pastor had warned that railway inspections in the forbidden zone were particularly zealous and advised him to use the less closely monitored goods train. It had a single passenger carriage, packed with peasants taking their wares to market, from pungent cheeses to a brace of honking geese. After stops at every village halt, the fifty-kilometre journey took almost four hours. But their documents were checked only once, at La Roche-sur-Foron, by a bored guard who accepted Simon's story that, having recently moved to the region, he was delivering his children to the École Saint-Francois at Ville-la-Grand. No doubt the prospect of being cooped up in boarding school explained Clarice and Sylvain's glum faces, just as the separation from her children explained Irène's. Yet for all their anxiety about Annette, Simon felt that they might have shown more enthusiasm for their impending freedom.

At Annemasse, they followed directions to the Café du Triangle. The only customers were two black-clad old women and a solitary man, but even had the room been crowded, there'd have been no mistaking their contact, whose bulging eyes, bulbous nose and equine teeth bore out the Pastor's description of his striking resemblance to Fernandel.

'My name's Gaspard,' he said, shaking hands, 'but I like to call myself Moses, helping your people to the promised land.' Although the two women were absorbed in conversation, Simon wished he would lower his voice. 'I'll be taking you to a barn on the Cottins's farm, where Jean-Baptiste will meet you. Stick to his instructions and all will be well. Now I must say this . . . I don't want to, but I must. Not everyone manages to get across. Even if they do, the

Swiss guards sometimes send them straight back. In which case, I'll be waiting here, with a glass of genepi, until ten o'clock.'

'We'll be fine,' Simon said, seeing Sylvain's alarm. 'I feel it in my bones.'

'That's the spirit,' Gaspard said. 'Let's be off.'

He refused to let Simon pay for his drinks, just as he refused the two 1,000-franc notes he tried to slip him when, after a long and muddy trek, they reached the barn. 'Please don't insult me, Monsieur. Would you tip Moses?' Then wishing them 'God speed!', he headed back up the path. Simon watched him uneasily. In his experience, altruism was more to be admired than trusted. His unease grew as they waited in the musty, sweet-earth atmosphere of the barn.

'I need to pee,' Sylvain said.

'Go on then, but quickly,' Simon said.

'Promise no one will look!'

'Just go behind that bale, darling,' Irène said. 'How about you?' she asked Clarice.

'The next time I go will be in Switzerland,' she replied.

'Good girl!' Simon said.

After more than twenty minutes, Jean-Baptiste appeared, accompanied by two brawny young men. He apologised for the delay, explaining that there'd been an emergency on the farm, which, judging by the reek of their clothes, involved pigs.

'I'm glad to see you got the message about gloves,' he said, pocketing the envelope Simon gave him. 'Even so, I won't shake hands.' He held up his grimy palms. 'These two rogues are Théo and Berthold, my sons. They'll keep watch for patrols. They pass by every ten minutes, though the bastards sometimes vary them. We have French, Italians and Germans. Touch wood it's the Italians! You can never tell with the French. But the Boche . . . aargh! They don't feed their dogs for days. Then . . .'

'My wife used to be Italian,' Simon interjected swiftly.

With a terse 'Good luck!', Théo scaled a ladder to his lookout post on the roof of the barn and, with a nod, Berthold headed to his on a nearby water tower. Jean-Baptiste led the family to a large, freshly turned field, at the far end of which was a copse.

'Follow me to the trees,' he said. 'Straight below them is a stream and, on the other side, just out of sight, is the border. For the most part, the guards stay on the opposite bank, but from time to time they take it in their heads to come over and we're easy targets crossing the field. So whatever happens, don't stop . . . unless of course they shoot. Then lie flat and, when I give the signal, run like lightning back to the barn.'

A hoot from the water tower alerted Jean-Baptiste. 'Let's go!'

Simon followed him across the field, his feet sinking deep into a furrow. Fixing his gaze on the trees, he trusted that the others were keeping pace until, hearing a yelp, he turned to see Irène stumble. 'Go on, damn you!' he hissed at the faltering children, before running back to his wife and hauling her to her knees. 'Cling to me!' he said, relieved to see Clarice and Sylvain beside Jean-Baptiste in the copse.

'I think I've broken my ankle.'

'Nonsense, you've twisted it, that's all' he said, without looking. 'Put your arms around my neck.'

'I can't. It hurts too much. You go on without me.'

'Tough! I'm not leaving you. It's your choice. Do you want to lose everything after we've come so far . . . turn back and face God knows what from the Nazis?'

'It hurts!'

'Get up!'

'Please!'

Jean-Baptiste darted back and, between them, they dragged her to her feet and into the copse. Bent double, Simon laboured to catch his breath, while Jean-Baptiste ran his hands over Irène's ankle as though she were one of his calves. 'It's just a sprain,' he said, untying his neckerchief and binding the ankle. At any other time, Simon would have shuddered at the sight of such a filthy rag against his wife's skin, but for once he was grateful; just as he was when Jean-Baptiste gulped from his hip flask and, without wiping its neck, passed it first to Irène, then to him.

'How does it feel?' the farmer asked Irène. 'Try to stand, without putting your weight on it.'

'It's fine. I'll be fine. Thank you so much,' she said, panting.

'Not far to go now. Just the other side of the stream. There are stones, but they're slippery, so you'd do best to wade across, especially you, Madame. We've not had much rain, so the water won't reach above your knees. On the bank, you'll come to the first of two barbed wire fences. But directly opposite this tree – this one here – is a section that's been loosened.' He patted an ancient hawthorn, whose gnarled, bark-stripped trunk and warped branches felt like a symbol of survival. 'You'll be able to crawl through the gap and then through another in the second fence two metres along. After that, my friends, you'll be in Switzerland. Shh!' He broke off at the sound of a further hoot, followed by three trills. 'Good . . . very good. That means the Italians. Now's your chance. God be with you!'

For once in his life, Simon wished that he had faith. He clasped Irène's hand and strode through the icy water, desperate to keep her right leg from giving way. After depositing her on the far bank beside a shivering Clarice, he stepped back to help Sylvain who, ignoring the farmer's instructions, was staggering from stone to stone. With his son safely across, he scrabbled up the bank where, seeing no sign of movement, he beckoned the others to join him. A two-metre-high barbed-wire fence stretched before them as far as the eye could see. Choking back his despair, he turned to align the fence with the hawthorn. His head swam and he slapped his cheek, making Sylvain gasp. He wriggled to the wire which, to his elation, he was able to lift sufficiently to squeeze through, holding it up for the others to follow. He repeated the manoeuvre at the second fence where the gap was noticeably lower, and as Clarice slithered after Irène, her plait caught on a spike. Jerking her head in panic, she failed to free herself.

Simon quaked. How many minutes until the patrol returned?

How many minutes until his heart burst? 'Here!' whispered Sylvain, who, with heaven-sent disobedience, had brought his penknife. Moreover, it was a Swiss Army knife, which had to be a good omen. Fumbling furiously with the corkscrew and scissors, Simon pulled out the blade and hacked through Clarice's hair, while she stretched out her neck, her face contorted in a silent scream. Finally, she was clear and under the wire. Seconds later, Sylvain followed.

Incredulously, Simon found himself standing on Swiss soil. At the far end of the field was a row of houses, their deep eaves and wide gables subtly, gloriously different from those across the border. But there was no time to gape; he had to make contact with Roland Severin. 'Come on,' he said. 'There'll be time to rest soon enough. We must get to that village and find a telephone.'

Just as he turned to help Irène, two grey-uniformed guards ran towards them, guns levelled.

'Halt!'

5

ESTHER

DIDSBURY, MAY 1943

EZRA HENRIQUES, FELIX'S great-grandfather, had arrived in Manchester from Aleppo in the mid-1850s, lured by the prospect of cheap, mass-produced cotton to ship back to the Levant. Finding the city to his liking, he built his own mill and sent for his wife and children. It was a family joke – to everyone but Esther – that this archconservative had once entertained Engels, a fellow mill-owner and member of the Royal Exchange. In later life, their paths diverged: Engels retired from his family firm to work alongside Marx, while Ezra transformed his into one of the most prosperous in the north of England. As both manufacturers and merchants, the Henriques weathered the slump in cotton prices in the early 1920s, when many of their rivals foundered, only to be brought down by the Great Depression of 1929. Felix, who'd succeeded his father as director, was forced to liquidate the company. Although she couldn't blame him for the global economic collapse, Esther could – and did – blame him for entrusting what little capital he'd been able to salvage to a confidence trickster at the Midland Hotel.

Facing ruin, Felix urged her to seek help from her father. Though sorely tempted, not least to confront Papa with his misjudgement in yoking her to the Henriques, Esther had been too proud. In the early years of marriage, she'd employed a cook, two housemaids and a nurse for the children. Her father-in-law had even offered her a chauffeur, but Felix, keen for her to share his passion, insisted that she learn to drive. When the money disappeared, so did the servants. By selling her jewellery, she managed to keep up a façade, hiring temporary staff for her parents' sole visit on her twentieth wedding anniversary in 1933, and her siblings' sporadic visits throughout the decade. On their last meeting at Papa's funeral, Leon, Irène and Ruben proposed that, with the Germans on their border, she should bring Maman to England. Loath for her to witness her reduced circumstances, she equivocated, arguing that, without friends and unable to speak the language, she would be wretched in the sleepy suburb. So Felix's credulity and her own pride were equally to blame for her stepmother's plight.

Never in her bleakest moments had she imagined that, at the age of fifty, she would be taking in lodgers, but the house was their only asset and, with Felix mired in recrimination and regret, it fell to her to exploit it. She persuaded the reluctant boys to move in together, freeing up two bedrooms, since under no circumstances would she share again with Felix. She was no longer hurt by his girlfriends – though it came as a surprise to find that his appeal had survived bankruptcy. As for their own lovemaking, that was no more than a dim memory. Besides, by evening, she was too exhausted to care. Had she known the true toll of domestic drudgery when she attended Leah's meetings in Salonica, she would have called not just for social reform but for revolution. Her days passed in a relentless cycle of sweeping, dusting, mopping, polishing and blackleading. The worst was reserved for washday. Hauling water to the copper, scrubbing collars, agitating the dolly peg and feeding the sodden linen through the mangle had left her with chronic backache. Her one satisfaction was that, with their own servants now working in munitions and on the land, her neighbours, who'd expressed such gleeful sympathy over her depleted household, found themselves in the same predicament. The war had restored parity to Elm Road.

Esther herself had been assigned a job at the post office on a salary of £2 12s a week, obviating the need for lodgers. Over almost ten years, she had taken in scores, among them a structural engineer working on the new Wythenshawe Estate, several musicians from the Hallé, an Austrian economics professor and a divorced chemist whom she passed off as a widower. While almost all had been courteous and clean, she had been eager to regain her privacy, until her friend Eileen, at the Wilmslow Road library, asked whether she would rent a room to Jean Ruskin, a teacher at Burnage High School, who'd recently moved from Stoke-on-Trent. Jean, a petite, dark-haired, fine-boned woman in her early forties, whose husband Rodney was serving in the Eighth Army, had returned to the profession with the lifting of the marriage bar. Wary of their demands, Esther had avoided female lodgers, but she'd warmed to Jean at once. Until her arrival, she hadn't realised how much she'd missed the company of her own sex. Within a month, they had forged a friendship deeper than any she had known since Leah.

As usual, she was home before Jean returned from school and Felix from his bridge club, giving her time to freshen up and prepare dinner. Jean was back first, knocking perfunctorily as she entered the kitchen.

'Something smells good!'

'Corned beef hash. I threw in some carrots that were starting to spoil.'

'Rodney used to call it a Tinned Treat. I could never tell if he was joking.'

Esther smiled. It was only right that Jean's thoughts should be with her husband, far away in Africa, but she wished that she had waited a little longer before mentioning him.

'Busy day?' she asked.

'Non-stop. I was in detention all through lunch.'

'What?'

'Taking it.' Jean laughed. 'Some of the fifth form boys sneaked onto the tennis courts – or what used to be the tennis courts – yesterday evening. You'd think that, two years on, rubble would have lost its allure. Then I spent half the afternoon trying to convince 4B that a team of crack German agents hadn't been parachuted into the Lake District. The greater our victories, the wilder the rumours of Nazi plots! How about you . . . your day, I mean?'

'Nothing that exciting . . . No, I tell a lie. One of the sorters spotted a letter to her next-door neighbours from their son, who's a POW. They hadn't heard from him or the Red Cross in months, and of course they feared the worst. Their regular postie had already left, so Mr Stapleton took it round in person.' The front door slammed. 'That'll be Felix. Would you set the table? It's almost ready.'

'Of course. I intended to wash. Still, it will save on soap.'

'I've told you before: pinch some of Felix's shaving soap. A blow for equality! If there were any women in the government, it would be on the ration.'

Felix walked in and, seeing Jean, moved to kiss Esther's cheek.

'Apologies if I've kept you waiting. We played an extra rubber. Will it be long? I'm on duty at seven.'

'Sit down and I'll serve,' Esther said.

'People think that, with the Blitz over, we wardens do nothing but laze around at the post, drinking tea. But the threat hasn't gone away. It's no time to lower our guard.'

'Or raise the blackout curtains,' Jean said, causing Esther to swallow a giggle.

'Quite. Take that tip-and-run raid on Rusholme last month! And the factories are still targets.' He turned to Jean. 'Look what happened when those Jerry bombers strayed off course and hit your school.'

'I heard one of the telegraphists saying the Germans would single out Didsbury because it was "a Jewish ghetto",' Esther said. 'Did you know people call it Yidsbury?'

'How disgusting!' Jean exclaimed.

'That's why I don't like you working there,' Felix said.

'I try to ignore it,' Esther said, dishing out the hash. 'Eat up! I doubt it'll be any better cold.'

'Why bother with that leaflet telling us to get fit not fat?' Felix asked, looking forlornly at his plate. 'We've already got the message.'

'Some of the sorters say their diets haven't changed that much since rationing. It makes you wonder what they were living on before.'

'A bit of a red, my wife. Her brother warned me.'

'Well, this is very tasty,' Jean said, purposefully.

'Yes, you can almost taste the meat,' Felix said, with a laugh.

'You'll have to fend for yourself tomorrow,' Esther told him. 'Mr Stapleton's asked me to stay for some overtime.'

'I trust he'll pay you for the full stint,' Jean said.

'Esther doesn't work there for the money. She's happy to do her bit.'

'Besides, it'll simply be more Post Office credits. I'll be a wealthy woman after the war.'

'Though with all this "overtime", I'm starting to think she's taken a fancy to one of the postmen.'

'Don't be ridiculous!' Esther said, furious at the insinuation in front of Jean. 'Though if I did, we'd have to keep it very quiet,' she added, lightening the mood. 'Mr Stapleton disapproves of fraternisation between indoor and outdoor staff.'

'Rightly so,' Felix said.

'Although one postie, Brian, broke through the class barrier this lunchtime, regaling us with his visit last night to see Phyllis Dixey and her nudes at the Hulme Hippodrome.'

'He talked about that with you?' Felix asked.

'And why not?' Esther replied, although in truth she had been shocked. 'What's more, he said it was a "swizz" – a new word to me – "because they were wearing body stockings. And they didn't even paint them on with gravy browning." Everyone laughed.'

'I admit that's quite funny,' Felix said.

'Really?'

'My wife has many virtues,' Felix told Jean, 'but a sense of humour isn't one of them.'

'In your opinion.'

'And that of the great British public. Case in point: *Band Waggon*.'

'Rodney and I listened to it faithfully every Wednesday.'

'A goat and a camel living in a flat? A fainting young woman called Nausea?' Esther said. 'Maybe my sense of humour is too subtle for the British.'

'Of course, dear, if that's what you want to believe. Now I must love you and leave you.'

'Already?' Esther asked, striving to keep the relief from her voice. 'There are stewed plums.'

'No time, I'm afraid. I have to get changed. Did you take a look at that mark on my jacket?'

'It's gone.'

'Very good.' He left the room, whistling.

'Someone's cheerful,' Jean said.

'He always is when he's on night duty.'

Esther suspected that Felix was one of the few people in the country glad that the war was being fought on the home front, enabling him to wear the uniform (if only in Civil Defence) that his injuries had denied him in 1914.

'Would you like some plums?' she asked Jean.

'Not for me, thanks. Save them for Felix tomorrow. Shall we clear?'

Esther washed the pots and Jean dried them, before they headed into the drawing room, where, mindful of Felix's outrage at any infraction of the rules, Esther double-checked that no sliver of light escaped beneath the curtains. She heaped a scuttle of coal on the fire, explaining that she felt the cold in England, even in May.

'You should try sprinkling the coal with salty water. It retains the heat.'

'Really? I've never heard that before.'

'It's probably an old wives' tale.'

'I grew up on old wives' tales. We called them traditions.'

They sat, each lost in her own thoughts. Whereas, with Felix, any silence was so heavy that it felt almost tangible, with Jean, it was eloquent, speaking of concord and comradeship. For a moment, Esther even forgot about the war.

A barking dog dispelled her reverie. 'Cigarette?' she asked, holding out a box filled with Camel Straights.

'Thanks but no thanks,' Jean said, taking a packet of Craven As from her bag. 'I'll stick to mine. I can't get on with those Turkish things.'

'They remind me of Salonica. My one link to my family. I worry about them all so much.'

'At least you've had the letter from your sister.'

'Yes, though still no reply to mine. But then the post is all over the place these days. I should know!'

Three weeks earlier, Esther received the first communication from her family in almost three years. Irène wrote that she, Simon, Clarice and Sylvain had escaped from France and were living in Lausanne, where the children were already enrolled in school. She hinted at the horrors of the journey, adding that they'd passed through Lyon, where they'd seen Bella and Henri, who, in a somewhat perplexing phrase, were 'very bravely keeping their heads down'. Bella had received word from Gabrielle that Leon and Daniel had been arrested in Marseille and sent to Germany as forced labour, for which one was patently too old and the other too young, but she made no mention of Maman or Ruben, who were presumably still in Paris.

'I'm most concerned about my stepmother, who's spent her life surrounded by servants – how I used to castigate her!' She sighed. 'She won't have the first idea how to fend for herself.'

'I thought she was your mother. You called her *Maman*.'

'She's the only mother I've ever known. She brought me up.'

'So your actual mother died young?'

'In childbirth. Mine. You spoke of old wives' tales. My maternal grandmother knew them all. Apparently, if you put sweets and cakes under a woman's bed during labour, then Lilith and her legion of evil spirits will be so busy gorging themselves that they'll leave the baby unharmed. But the charm didn't extend to the mother.'

'How bizarre . . . the custom, I mean.'

'I have an older brother, Leon. Papa and Maman had three children of their own: Irène, Ruben and Bella - she's the one I'm least worried about, even though she's the most wayward.'

'The painter?'

'Yes. She's shown herself to be infinitely resourceful, capable of meeting every challenge. While I was saddled with domestic responsibilities - towards Felix and the children, to say nothing of my in-laws - she was pursuing her art. The next thing I knew - well, almost - she was holding exhibitions and being lionised in the press, with collectors and galleries clamouring for her work . . . Wait!' She walked over to the bureau, rolled up the top and took out a catalogue, which she handed to Jean. 'Here! As promised. It's of her last exhibition before the war. I couldn't get over there, so she sent it to me.'

'Timarete?'

'Yes. Don't ask me why, except that we grew up in a house that looked out on Mount Olympus and, ever since, she's been infatuated with all things Greek.'

'It may sound odd from a geography teacher, but I'm always amazed to find Mount Olympus on a map.'

'As a girl, Bella insisted that the gods lived in a palace on its peak. The rest of us thought she was deranged. Our housekeeper, Maryam, called her *una loca, una budala*. My Ladino's extremely rusty, but, as I recall, both words mean *crazy*, so she was definitely making her point. Now I wonder if it wasn't a cunning bid for freedom - to escape the double burden of family and culture. In her work, she draws inspiration from ancient Greece, taking the simple colour schemes and formal poses of their pots and vases and making them her own. She's done plenty of portraits and landscapes, but my favourites are her narrative paintings: the processions of war-wounded; the nightclub scenes; the horse races at Saint-Cloud and boat races on the Seine. You'll find several illustrated there, as well as a couple of the pieces that caused such controversy. Let me show you.' She reached for the catalogue, flicked through the pages and handed it back to Jean. 'There!'

'Some highly sexed satyrs chasing nymphs.'

'They may look like satyrs, but, when you examine them closely, you see that those horns on their heads are tefillin – the scrolls that Jewish men wear when they pray – and those bands of cloth are prayer shawls.'

'Now you mention it . . .'

'I've often suspected that, when it came to Bella's paintings, my father's failing eyesight was diplomatic.'

'She certainly has an admirer in Colette,' Jean said, skimming the foreword. '"What the art of Africa is to Picasso, so the art of Greece is to Timarete" . . . if I've translated it right.'

'Perfectly.'

'She couldn't have asked for a more illustrious endorsement.'

'I agree, though when we last met, she said that her greatest accolade hadn't come from a fellow artist or a critic but from Goebbels, since she was one of the few foreign artists included in his exhibition of Degenerate Art.'

Jean stood up, clasping the catalogue. 'May I borrow this? I'd love to read it properly, but I ought to get some sleep. I have an early start. It's my turn to take the meteorological readings for the air ministry.'

'Of course. Sweet dreams!' she said, with a blush.

'Please, tell me if I'm speaking out of turn, but why should the postmen have all the fun? You and I should have an evening out.'

'To see Phyllis Dixie and her not-quite-nudes?'

'Hardly! Though of course, if you want . . .'

'No, thank you.' Esther shuddered.

'I was thinking more of the pictures.'

'I'd like that very much. Just let me know when you're free.'

They made plans for the following Friday. The day began well when Esther received a letter from Nathan. Her elder son had never been an assiduous correspondent, and his short, formal letters from Clifton had only underlined the distance between them. Conscious of her wartime isolation, he wrote regularly and at greater length, even if his matter-of-fact accounts still smacked of the classroom. A sportsman rather than a scholar, he was never going to tread the academic path she'd laid down for his brother. From boyhood, he had been groomed to join the family business, so the closure of the mill when he was fourteen had hit him hard. Leaving school with few prospects, he snapped up Ruben's offer to represent Tissus de Lyon in Buenos Aires. After years of blaming her brother for effecting his removal halfway across the globe, she would be forever in his debt for keeping him out of the war.

Like Esther herself twenty years earlier, Nathan had had to adjust to an unfamiliar environment. He wrote little about his work, but Ruben spoke glowingly of his success in opening up markets, not just in Argentina but in neighbouring Brazil and Venezuela. In his spare time, he played football and table tennis and even took tango classes, which was where he met Margarethe Pfister, whom he married in December 1939. Although she was both German and Catholic, Nathan emphasised the similarities between Margarethe's background and his own. Her ancestors had settled in Russia in the eighteenth century around the time that the Carraches had settled in Salonica. At the end of the nineteenth century, when the Tsar sought to restrict their rights, they emigrated to Argentina, just as the Carraches emigrated to France after the Greek invasion twenty years later. Having expressed disgust at the thousands of Nazi sympathisers in his adopted homeland, he stressed that Margarethe and her parents were staunch anti-fascists, for which they'd been shunned by many of their fellow 'colonists' and her father blacklisted by the German Labour Front.

From their engagement photographs, which Esther studied with a Talmudist's precision, it was clear that Margarethe was very pretty. What was not clear until the wedding photographs, in which she stood beside Nathan (outside a church), was that she was also very small. It was all the more remarkable that the baby she delivered the following year weighed more than four kilos. With their correspondence now confined to aerogrammes, Nathan was unable to send photographs of Katrin, so Esther was left to flesh out his account of a bubbly, mischievous little girl, whom he called Katrin the Terrible, given her propensity to tear apart anything within reach. After she chided him for not providing a detailed description, he replied that she took after her mother, with Margarethe's blond hair, heart-shaped face and button nose, adding, almost as an afterthought, that she had the Carrache hazel eyes.

Esther left today's letter, along with a mock tuna salad, on the kitchen table, ready for Felix's return from the bridge club. With a pang of guilt at abandoning him, she broke off two squares of her Cadbury's ration chocolate and placed them beside his plate. Afraid of being late, she caught the 42 bus, sitting on the upper deck, where the reek of unwashed bodies was masked by cigarette fumes. She alighted on Wilmslow Road and walked the short distance to the Tudor, where Jean was waiting in the café. They had the one-shilling set meal of shepherd's pie, treacle tart and a mug of tea. When the waitress brought the bill, Esther reached for her purse, but Jean stayed her hand.

'My treat.'

'As long as you promise to let me pay next time,' Esther said.

'I look forward to it,' Jean said, at which Esther's pulse quickened.

They headed downstairs to buy tickets. Having explored all the local offerings, they'd decided on *Lady in the Dark*. *Nine Men* was showing at the Scala, but Esther feared that, even after El Alamein, the spectacle of British soldiers under fire in the Libyan desert would be too distressing for Jean. Knowing Esther's antipathy to British humour, Jean in turn rejected Tommy Handley in *It's That Man Again* at the Palatine. Esther's first choice would have been Ronald Colman and Greer Garson in *Random Harvest* at the Essoldo, but Jean had already seen it, with her mother-in-law in Stoke. That left *Lady in the Dark*. Jean had admired Eleanor Powell's tap dancing in a film with Fred Astaire and, though no lover of musicals, Esther would have been happy to sit through a children's matinée, provided she was sitting beside Jean.

'Two one-and-sixes, please,' Jean said at the box office. They took their seats in time for a *Tom and Jerry* cartoon, the bursts of laughter convincing Esther that American humour was as alien to her as British. This was followed by a *Food Flash*, demonstrating how to bone a herring, and the newsreel depicting the surrender of General von Arnim in Tunisia ten days earlier. Cheers and applause rang through the cinema as he stiffly received the British generals outside his headquarters. The cameras caught him again as he took his leave of his staff officers before climbing into an open truck, standing bolt upright and giving the Hitler salute, while being driven through the ranks of his vanquished troops. Esther doubted whether, had their positions been reversed, von Arnim would have shown such courtesy to General Alexander, but that was of little consequence beside the defeat of the Axis forces in Africa. She sneaked a glance at Jean, whose gaze was fixed on the screen, and wondered if she were thinking of Rodney.

After a burst of chatter during the adverts, a charged silence greeted the main feature. Its plot was as nonsensical as Esther had feared. Dixie Donegan, an attractive young lyricist, was seeking a divorce from her composer husband Eddie, whose sole offence appeared to be spending time with his society friends instead of writing songs with Dixie. From her glistening eyes and tremulous voice when she spoke of him, it was obvious that she still loved Eddie and, as the judge granted her petition, Esther felt resentful that in America marriages could be dissolved on grounds of mere incompatibility, whereas in Britain far more stringent conditions applied. The couple were soon reunited and guests of honour at a testimonial dinner, where, in a glittering veil and gown, Dixie sang their latest song, 'The Last Time I Saw Paris'. Her delivery was maudlin, but, to her intense embarrassment, Esther found herself in tears. The more she fought them, the more they flowed. The woman to her left offered her a handkerchief, which she waved away with a spluttered 'thank you'. She was preparing to slip outside when Jean clasped her hand and kissed the crown of her head. Looking up in astonishment, she received a second kiss on the lips.

Astonishment stilled her tears, while Jean, keeping hold of her hand, turned back to the screen. Esther was so confused that, by the time Dixie's friend Marilyn twirled and tap-danced at machine-gun speed in the climactic number, she began to question whether she'd imagined the kiss. The film ended, predictably, with Dixie and Eddie's second reunion, after which the audience rushed for the exit before *God Save The King*. Esther was caught between the happy-ever-after on screen and the what-happens-next in her heart. Unsure of what to think – much less say – she was grateful for the hubbub as people spilt out onto the street. Had Jean intended to kiss her, or simply grazed her lips when she raised her head? If it were an accident, why had she said nothing? They could have laughed it off. Not that she felt like laughing . . . at least not in that way.

They emerged in the aftermath of a downpour, and Jean, professing to love the smell of wet pavements, suggested they walk back. Neither spoke, and for the first time the silence between them felt oppressive.

'That song touched a nerve,' Esther said finally. 'The last time I saw Paris was in September 1939. My whole family had gathered for my father's funeral. I couldn't help thinking of them – and of the city itself. I only lived there for a few months before my marriage, but it still feels part of me.'

'You don't need to explain. It's not healthy to bottle up your feelings,' Jean replied, deepening Esther's confusion. Was she referring to her feelings for her family or something else?

They arrived home to find the house empty. Esther longed to go straight to bed, where she could pretend that kisses in the auditorium were as evanescent as those on screen. 'Goodnight then,' she said. 'Thank you for a lovely evening.'

'You've never shown me your Anderson shelter,' Jean said.

'I beg your pardon?'

'I've seen it from the outside of course, elegantly concealed beneath the rockery. But I've never been in.'

'Have you heard something? Are there warnings of new raids?'

'Nothing specific. But it's as well to be prepared.'

'Now?'

'No time like the present,' Jean said in a schoolmistressy tone.

Fetching a torch from the kitchen, Esther led her through the garden. She lifted the shelter door and crouched to enter. The air was stale and dank. She shone the torch over the furnishings: four bunk beds with neatly folded blankets and rugs, a fire screen to offer a measure of privacy to anyone using the chamber pot, and a Primus stove.

'Ludo?' Jean said, following her inside and picking the box off one of the bunks.

'Don't remind me! For three months the winter before last, we had a guest with us' - she avoided the word *lodger* with Jean - 'I forget his name, but he'd come to run an Emergency Field Kitchen after the Manchester Blitz. He dragged us into endless games to pass the time. I'd rather have stared at the walls.'

'I didn't realise you were such a fan.'

'Of what?'

'Walt Disney.' Jean pointed to the Mickey Mouse wallpaper.

'Oh, we had an old roll, left over from papering Basil's bedroom for his sixth birthday. Needless to say, the seventeen-year-old with a copy of *Health and Efficiency* at the back of his wardrobe was furious that I'd recycled it.'

'And whisky!' Jean said, as Esther illuminated a half-full bottle.

'That's Felix's. He thought we might need "a wee dram" to keep up our spirits.'

'But we don't need one now, do we?'

Esther had forgotten how cramped the shelter was. She was sure that Jean must be able to hear the blood coursing - pounding - through her veins. 'Not at all,' she said. 'Besides, I don't care for the taste.'

'Shall we try something else then?' Jean asked and kissed her again on the lips. To her horror, Esther found herself crying for a second time that evening. 'Forgive me,' Jean said. 'I thought . . . I've misread everything.'

'No, no you haven't. Not at all. Please . . . I don't know what's happening to me. I'm . . .' Unable to complete the sentence and afraid of discouraging Jean, she returned the kiss, which felt more formal and clumsy than the one she'd received. 'I'm sorry. I'm no good at this.'

'Nonsense! You just need practice. Wait and see!'

Gratefully, Esther moved towards her again. This time, the connection felt both spontaneous and true. 'We're married women,' she said, uncertain of what she meant by it but feeling that it had to be acknowledged.

'And?' Jean replied. 'I love Rodney, who's everything a husband should be – except a father, but that's not his fault. He's a good man: decent, clever, funny (in his own dry way). He's a devoted son and son-in-law. But does he touch me here?' She took Esther's hand and pressed it to her heart – and her bosom. 'No. The only person to do that was another woman many years ago.' Esther wanted to know more about her, but not yet. 'And you? Does Felix touch you there?' Jean now placed her hand on Esther's heart – and bosom. If she'd been undecided how to respond before, the charge that ran through her body left no room for doubt.

'No. And he's most definitely not everything a husband should be. Oh, he's not cruel or violent, and he tells jokes or what passes for them. But he's certainly no devoted son – I'm the one who keeps an eye on his mother. And as for a son-in-law . . . all I can say is he's not what my father imagined when he chose him for me.'

'Your father did what? That's medieval!'

'You teach geography. You must know how customs and cultures vary.'

'But that's one that should be consigned to oblivion, along with foot binding and sati.'

'I loved my father and he loved me,' Esther said wretchedly.

'Forgive me, it's not my place to judge . . . So tell me, have you ever felt anything for a woman?'

'Anything romantic?'

'That's right.'

'I'm not sure. Perhaps. It wasn't long before I married. But I couldn't have articulated it, even to myself. It was like a part of the city I never entered.'

'I'm giving you a safe-conduct.'

Jean held her in her arms and kissed her, before gently loosening the buttons on her blouse. Esther felt her touch like a burn and a salve at the same time. She tentatively lifted Jean's jumper, letting her hands roam down her stomach. Not since the boys were toddlers had she known skin so soft. How could a body so similar to her own feel so different?

Her body – her core – was a tangle of contradictions: hot and cold, trembling and tranquil, energised and languid, as she nestled against Jean on a bunk. The shelter had come into its own. To have made love in the house – even in a room that Felix never used – would have felt like a betrayal. This, however, was a space apart, a sanctuary that protected them not just from enemy bombs but from the world at large.

They went down to the shelter at every opportunity. When Felix told her that he'd volunteered for extra shifts, she struggled to contain her joy. She would never have believed such happiness possible. She felt both split in two and uniquely whole. She even found herself dreading the end of the war. Aghast, she blotted the thought from her mind, but its shadow remained. What would become of them when victory was declared? Would the marriage bar on women teachers be restored and Jean return to Rodney? Would she spend the rest of her life tending the plants on the rockery like flowers on a grave?

Her happiness was complete when Basil wrote with the news that he was to be stationed at Ringway airport the following week and would come for lunch on Sunday. While a single visit felt derisory after a nine-month absence, Esther had long been resigned to her separation from her sons. The most perverse of all the perverse practices she'd encountered in England was that of exiling eight-year-old boys from their homes. Felix had quashed her objections, insisting that a public-school education would guarantee their future. He enrolled them at Clifton College, where he and his brother Basil had been pupils. 'It has a Jewish house,' he said, 'so you needn't fear that they'll lose touch with their roots.' What she'd feared was that they would lose touch with her.

In part, those fears had been realised. *Maman* became *Mother* and, on the rare occasions that Felix agreed to make the journey to Bristol, she found that almost as many rules pertained to her as to the boys. She must never compliment them in front of their friends. She must never question their friends about their parents. She must never mention *abroad* except as a travel destination, or reveal that her family lived there. Above all, she must never hug or kiss them in public, let alone spit on a handkerchief to wipe a smut from their cheeks. Even in the holidays, they maintained their reserve. Extracting information from Nathan, in particular, was as tortuous as deciphering a hieroglyph. She had grown up in a household where everyone said what they felt – sometimes too loudly, but that was preferable to English reticence. When she told Felix that she worried that the school was making Nathan aloof, he replied that it was making him a man.

Despite his protests that, with his academic record, it was 'throwing good money after bad', she'd insisted that Nathan stay on in the sixth form. Given that it was her money, raised from the sale of her share of Grandmaman Regina's jewellery, and given the lack of job opportunities in the slump, her voice prevailed. She had no hesitation in invoking her sacrifice to coerce him into working and, although his letters touched on little but rugby and cricket, he scraped through his exams.

Nathan was a popular, outgoing boy who rose to be head of his house; Basil was more withdrawn. His time at the 'Pre' was miserable, and his letters, filled with entreaties to come home and threats of suicide, plunged Esther into despair. Having already moved to Upper School, Nathan could do little to help, but he always looked out for his younger brother, just as Leon had done for Ruben. While on leave from Argentina, he so inspired Basil that he begged to go out and join him. But he was at once more dutiful than Nathan and more sensitive to the strains in his parents' marriage. Aware of the anguish that a second defection would cause her, he remained at Clifton, passed his Higher School Certificate with distinction and won a scholarship to read modern languages at Oxford. Then, at the end of his first year, he defied her wishes and deferred his degree to enlist in the RAF. She blamed Felix for encouraging him as a way to compensate for his brother's death.

Felix had been injured in the French Grand Prix of July 1914. For a time it seemed as if Ruben's facetious prediction of his death at the wheel might be fulfilled. Although he recovered from the fractures to his arms and legs, the nerve damage in his right hand was permanent, preventing him from fighting. Basil, meanwhile, joined the RNAS Armoured Car Division, where his mechanical expertise could be best deployed. He transferred to the fledgling Royal Flying Corps and, in what Esther took to be a positive omen, was stationed in Salonica. Then in June 1916 he was killed in action. His parents were told that he'd been shot down behind enemy lines, but Felix later learnt that his plane spiralled out of control when his machine gun jammed and shot off the propeller. He was buried in the British military cemetery, which Felix, his parents and sister visited in the spring of 1919, although Esther, nursing two-year-old Nathan, had been unable to return to her birthplace.

The Henriques were devastated by Basil's death, and Esther was glad to offer some small consolation by keeping his name alive. She worried, however, that Felix's devotion to his brother's memory had had a damaging effect on their younger son. Her fear that he would meet a similar fate to his uncle was allayed when, having been accepted for pilot training, he was found to have an 'innocent' heart murmur, which kept him out of the cockpit. He qualified, instead, as an engineering officer and served on the ground crew at Biggin Hill. Recently, however, something had changed. After a month on an undisclosed mission in Scotland, he was being posted to Ringway. When she suggested that he seek a permanent transfer to the nearby airbase, he replied that he would be there solely for parachute training. Every night since then, she'd been haunted by visions of the cord twisting, the fabric tearing, and his parachute failing to open. And why was he undergoing the training when he wasn't permitted to fly?

He arrived at noon on Sunday, arrestingly handsome in his uniform, his side cap lending his freckled face a roguish cast. Esther introduced him to Jean, whom he greeted with polite indifference. Reluctant to intrude on the family reunion, she had declined an invitation to lunch while providing the recipe for the main dish: braised rabbit, with apples, onions, mushrooms, half a week's butter ration and a pint of cider. She promised that it tasted exactly like pheasant and, though Esther was unconvinced, Basil and Felix were lavish in their appreciation, each raising a glass of cherry brandy 'to the chef'. Felix coupled his plaudits with a plea for Basil to return home more often and save him from a diet of corned beef fritters and Woolton pie. Esther was angered by the suggestion both that she failed to feed him properly and that the meal was the high point of Basil's visit.

She cleared away the main course and brought in the pudding, together with a single peach.

'Where did you get this?' Basil asked, examining it like a holy relic.

'I won it in our weekly Spitfire fund raffle. I've saved it for you. One of the girls – the sorters – told me to wrap it in cheesecloth and put it in a drawer. It's not rotten, just a bit overripe.'

'It looks perfect. But what about you two? We'll share it.'

'We wouldn't dream of it, would we, Felix?' she replied, in a voice that brooked no contradiction. 'In any case, carrot roly-poly's our favourite.'

Basil devoured it in a few bites. 'It's the sweetest, juiciest peach I've had since I picked them myself in Uncle Leon's garden,' he said, with a smile at Esther.

She made a jug of barely palatable Camp coffee, which Basil gallantly declared to be better than the brew at the base. She seized the opportunity to quiz him on life at Ringway and why he was learning to parachute, but all he would say was that an opening had come up and he'd taken it. When she pressed him further, he asked curtly if she'd joined the Gestapo. She flinched and, in an evident bid to mollify her, he described the experience of plunging through the air.

'I've done three jumps – two from a plane and one from a stationary balloon. The last was only four hundred feet up.'

'That sounds awfully high,' Esther said.

'Quite the opposite. You have to pull your ripcord the instant you bail out. You only have fifteen seconds before you hit the ground. But those fifteen seconds are like nothing on earth.'

'How could they be?' asked Felix, who'd declined coffee in favour of a third glass of cherry brandy. 'You're in the sky.'

'Very good, Father,' Basil replied indulgently. 'It's euphoric! The adrenalin pumping through your bloodstream ... the wind rushing in your ears ... then the deep – the intense – sense of security when the chute opens and weight seeps back into your body.'

'How exactly does this help you to service a plane?' Esther risked another question.

'Aerodynamics,' Basil replied baldly. 'You remember it, don't you, Father, from your racing days?'

'What? Yes, yes, of course.'

After lunch they strolled in the garden, where Basil duly admired his father's vibrant displays of sweet peas and hollyhocks and commiserated on the rapidly wilting peonies. As they passed the dismantled summer house, he reminisced about hiding in it as a boy, which Esther had either not known or forgotten. They approached the shelter and she was gripped by panic lest one or other of them should choose to go inside, where the air itself, charged with passion, would betray her. To her relief, they wandered on to inspect the rows of raspberry canes, which were starting to bloom.

They returned indoors, where Basil squandered their already meagre time together by retreating to his bedroom. She called him downstairs for tea and, at four fifteen, they listened to *The Brains Trust*. Felix displayed his customary scorn for the erstwhile pacifist, Dr Joad, and his 'pussyfooting' replies. 'It all depends what you mean . . .' he mimicked. 'Typical!' Against the incongruously jaunty background of *Forces' Choice*, Basil headed back to base. He couldn't say when he'd next have leave and, for several days, Esther felt his absence so acutely that she almost wished he had never come.

'Like it or not, he's his own man now,' Felix said, dredging up the same platitude as when he'd sent him away to school.

Jean was more sympathetic, even proposing a distraction. 'My aunt has a cottage in the Lakes, which she's put at my disposal. We could go for Whit weekend. Four whole days with not a soul in sight.'

'How would we get there?' Esther asked, both eager and apprehensive.

'By bus to Keswick. Then it's a two-mile hike to Applethwaite, as long as you're up to it.'

'I am. Indeed, I am.'

On the eve of their departure, Esther finished work at six and walked the half-mile from Lapwing Lane to Belfield Road. With Felix claiming that the wall-to-wall cat hair inflamed his chest and his sister Milly living in Bournemouth, it was left to her to pay dutiful visits to her mother-in-law. Her spirits sank on entering the airless, overstuffed house where, in the years since her husband's death, Dina had lived in bitter bereavement with Flori Koen, on paper her companion, in practice her stooge. She leant over her armchair to give – never to receive – the statutory two kisses, while Flori poured her a thimbleful of sherry. She had scarcely sat down when Dina launched into a blistering tirade against the exploitative neighbour with whom she exchanged coupons: bacon and meat for eggs and cheese. Esther nodded and sighed at regular intervals, while daydreaming about a storybook cottage with a thatched roof, wooden beams, a granite fireplace and a snug double bed.

After ninety minutes, she escaped and made her way down Wilmslow Road, where she heard the oscillating wail of an air raid siren, all the more alarming for being the first in months. She considered going back, but preferred to seek shelter from a stranger than be trapped in a cellar with a petulant old woman and her abject dependant. Her chief concern was Jean, in case the bombers had once again targeted the Renold chain factory and veered off-track. But with a surge of relief, she realised that she would have left school hours earlier. She dashed into the nearest driveway, only to fall flat on the ground at a series of thunderclaps. She gazed transfixed when, after a blinding flash, the suburban street became a fairy grotto bathed in an orange glow. She lay still, listening to the bells of the emergency vehicles, and prayed that they would be in time to rescue the injured. When at last the all-clear sounded, she stood up, brushed herself off and resumed walking. Turning into Elm Road, she was met with a scene of devastation. Two fire engines and an ambulance were parked in the midst of billowing smoke and smouldering debris. Flecks of ash pricked her eyes and lodged in her throat as she strode forward, dimly conscious of the scorched trees, scattered rubble and an acrid smell, part-barbecue, part-drain. She reached the head of a small crowd and faced the shell of her home, the half-collapsed rooms exposed, as if the front panel on a giant doll's house had been removed.

Mouth agape, she choked on the dust of her own life. An ARP warden, one of Felix's colleagues whom she recognised but couldn't name, moved to her and put his arm around her shoulder.

'I'm real sorry, missus.'

'Everyone got here so fast. Where's Felix?'

'We were playing poker. He was winning. Threepence . . . The amber warning sounded and we came out on patrol. He saw straight off how it was his house as had caught it. He was all for rushing inside. We told him to wait for the heavy rescue boys. But he heard a woman calling for help.'

'Jean . . . that must have been Jean. Jean, our lodger. Jean . . .'

'He said it was his wife – that's you, missus. He scrambled through the wreckage. You'd never have thought as he had a wonky arm.'

'Did he get her out?' she asked, the words as thick in her throat as the dust.

'We heard a rumble and then—'

Distractedly, she pushed her way behind the ambulance and saw two covered stretchers side by side, like effigies on a tomb.

'No!' she screamed. The warden held her back, as though afraid that she was about to fling herself on one of them, when her first thought had been to pull them apart.

'Drink this, dear.' Mrs Hewitt, her haughtiest neighbour, approached with a mug of tea. 'I've put a little something in it. It'll help.'

Esther looked at her through raw eyes. 'We were going to a cottage in the Lake District tomorrow. No one but us for four whole days.'

'Mr Henriques was a good man. We all thought so.'

'What? Yes, of course,' she said, wishing that her tears were for him.

6

IRÈNE

LAUSANNE, JULY 1943

Hélène Lambert sat behind a heavy desk strewn with paper. An ashtray filled with half-smoked cigarettes and a cup of congealing coffee suggested that Irène wasn't her first visitor of the afternoon, while her weary gaze suggested that she wasn't the first whom she'd had to disappoint. As soon as she was able to negotiate the vertiginous streets of Lausanne's old town, Irène had visited the Red Cross office in the Place de la Palaud to seek help in locating Annette. Having received no word from Legrandin, she feared that his role in their escape had been discovered, resulting in his arrest – or worse. What then had happened to Annette? Might one of the hotel guests or staff – perhaps the prim but motherly housekeeper – have taken her in? There had to be some record of her whereabouts. Hélène had asked one of her fellow tracing officers in Lyon to investigate, but had yet to hear back.

'She may have been given a new identity. But she has frizzy red hair which is instantly recognisable. Plus a silver hairbrush that she never lets out of her hand.'

Hélène, a slight woman of around Irène's age and, to judge by her neat chignon, powder-blue linen suit and gold pendant watch, from a similar milieu, observed her with clinical sympathy. 'We must give it time,' she said, 'which these days is a rare commodity.'

'I should leave you to your work,' Irène said, taking the hint. 'I'll ring the hotel at the first breath of news.'

'I don't want to impose on you. I'll drop in when I'm next passing.' Aware of the contradiction, she added: 'My husband disapproves of these inquiries. He can't bear to be reminded of failure.'

Stepping into the street, she felt faint. Even after four months, she experienced the same disequilibrium when walking through Lausanne as she had when disembarking at Dover to visit Esther. What sparked it here, however, was neither an unfamiliar language nor a return to dry land but rather the sight of ordinary people going about their lives without the need to look over their shoulders. True, they were subject to rations and privations and the threat of Axis troops on their borders; but they remained free: a freedom embodied in the statue of Justice in this very square – not the conventional blindfolded goddess but a determined young woman striding forth, brandishing her sword and scales.

How she envied that confident stride as, her ankle still weak, she limped down the ancient, cobbled Rue du Pont and turned into the wide, tree-lined Rue Centrale. The juxtaposition reminded her of walking from Les Halles to the Boulevard Sebastopol in happier days. From Le Flon, she took the jolting cable car down to Ouchy and made her halting way along the shore to the hotel. Fishermen cast their lines from the jetty; passengers waited for the paddle steamer to make the restricted journey across the lake; a gaggle of screaming children challenged each other to plunge into the water. Across the promenade, a policeman patrolled the park, where the lawns and verges had been dug up and planted with potatoes, cabbages, turnips, carrots and mangolds. What a privilege to live in a country where the police were assigned to guard vegetables!

She passed through the hotel's lakeside portico, collected her key from the front desk and took the lift to the third floor. She felt the usual tinge of disquiet on entering the sumptuously appointed suite. They'd brought nothing from France but banknotes and jewellery. Although Simon had money in Switzerland, she'd questioned how they could afford such opulence for an indefinite period and without Legrandin's favourable rates. Simon explained with customary precision that, ten years earlier, he'd persuaded her father to transfer the greater part of his personal fortune to Pictet & Cie, a private bank in Geneva.

'But why?' Irène asked. 'Wasn't our own bank safe?'

'Perfectly – largely, if I may say so, thanks to my own efforts. But the French economy was in the doldrums and the socialists were threatening to increase inheritance duty, which would have had serious consequences for your father's estate. The two countries have very different financial regulations. In France, banks are required by law to disclose details of accounts to the authorities; in Switzerland, they're required by law to withhold them. Customers are guaranteed total anonymity. They access their funds by a numbered code.'

'And you have Papa's?'

'I was the only other signatory on the account. Not Leon. Not Ruben. Not even Nissim. What does that tell you?'

'But the money isn't ours,' she said, ignoring the question. 'It's Maman's and my brothers' and sisters'. We must find an apartment, somewhere far more modest than this.' She scanned the matching cream sofas, marble-topped mahogany bureau, Savonnerie carpet, Alpine landscapes, and two sprays of white roses and delphiniums. 'In a suburb,' she added, as the lakeside vista compounded the guilt that she was appropriating her family's wealth.

'What would be the good of that?'

'To do right by the others.'

'Who may already be—' He paused mid-sentence as she fixed him with a look of horror. For months, he had assured her that Bella would have escaped arrest in Lyon, that Leon and Daniel would be well treated in Germany, and that Ruben's resourcefulness would have protected both himself and Maman in Paris. Had it all been nothing but empty words?

'We can settle up with them in due course,' he said dismissively. 'And I have some claim to the money too. I may not have been his son, but I was your father's heir apparent. It's no accident that Carraches prospered when the banks around it collapsed like a house of cards. I saved your father and Nissim from some very costly investments.'

'Might one of them have been with Severin?'

'That's not funny. If it weren't for Roland, we wouldn't be here – not just in the hotel, but in Switzerland. You should be more grateful.'

Never had gratitude felt so bitter. Tonight, she would have to swallow her antipathy once again when Severin and his wife Marguerite came to dine. Daunted by the prospect, she headed to the bathroom and mixed a dose of bromide salts. It had been a great comfort when the hotel doctor treated her strained nerves with the same solicitude as her sprained ankle. He advised her to take a month's rest cure in the mountains, but she didn't want to leave Clarice and Sylvain in Simon's charge. She hesitated to articulate her fears to herself, still less to the doctor, but she'd noticed a change in her husband since they crossed the border. He had adopted or absorbed something of Severin's superciliousness – his swagger – and she was afraid of its influence on the children.

The two men met regularly, although, to her relief, Simon travelled to Geneva more often than Severin to Lausanne. Irène knew little of their past association, other than that they'd been members of the same lodge in Paris. Though suspicious of its secrecy, she acknowledged the appeal of the brotherhood to Simon, who regarded himself as an only child. Her father, having encouraged him to join in order to make contacts, had been horrified to find that one of them was Severin, who was later convicted of fraud and embezzlement. She hadn't followed the case in any detail, but knew that it involved buying up ailing companies, issuing bogus valuations and offloading stock at inflated prices, bankrupting thousands of small investors in the process. He was sentenced to five years' imprisonment, reduced to two on appeal, reputedly to avoid his implicating several government ministers. On his release, he moved to Geneva, where, showing no remorse, he resumed both his social life and his business dealings – doubtless on the strength of a numbered bank account.

What she didn't know – and dreaded discovering – was whether he had enmeshed Simon in any of his schemes. He'd gone to great lengths to assist them since their escape, reaching them within an hour of Simon's phone call from the police station at Thônex, where they'd been detained by the border guards. Flourishing four visas in the Silveras' names, along with a letter of authorisation from Heinrich Rothmund, head of the Fremdenpolizei, he overawed the brigadier, who allowed them to leave without further delay. The five of them squeezed into a Volkswagen driven by Severin's doctor, who alone had access to petrol, and made their way to Geneva, where Marguerite provided them with food, baths and a motley change of clothes. The next day, explaining that they had to be at least twelve kilometres from the border to apply for residence, Severin escorted them to Lausanne. They registered with the Fremdenpolizei and the Vaud police, who undertook to forward their application to the municipal council. Confident of success, Severin installed them in the Beau-Rivage Palace hotel.

The arrival of the tolerance permit, granting them indefinite leave to remain, should have alleviated Irène's anxiety. Instead, it had worsened, and the bromide salts were losing their potency. Nevertheless, she measured out another spoonful, before changing into a teal taffeta evening dress, part of the lavish wardrobe that Marguerite had encouraged her to buy as soon as she was fit enough to hobble round the shops. She set it off with Grandmaman Regina's ruby and diamond necklace and teardrop earrings, their first airing after three years concealed in bedframes, cisterns, floorboards and the lining of her coat.

'I approve,' Simon said casually, as he refreshed his eau de cologne.

Primped and primed, Irène crossed the corridor to collect the children. Under normal circumstances, they would have been too old to share a bedroom, as Clarice, craving privacy, regularly reminded her, although the easy-going Sylvain welcomed his sister's company. Severin had pulled strings to have him accepted mid-term by Brillantmont, a school he claimed to be the best in the canton, if not the country. However, three years of fitful education had left Sylvain struggling in several subjects and he'd spent the summer with a tutor. Clarice, meanwhile, was taking twice-weekly piano lessons from a professor at the Conservatoire and practising daily on the Bechstein in the ballroom, leaving her plenty of time to explore the city. As she helped her fasten the clasp of her new pearl necklace, Irène noticed that Clarice had caught the sun. 'I went boating on the lake with a friend,' she explained. Although Sylvain's smirk betrayed the friend's gender, she had no desire to probe. It was enough that her daughter exuded a joyousness she had despaired of ever seeing again.

They went downstairs to the bar, where Severin, in a gold brocade dinner jacket, and Marguerite, in a flesh-coloured sequinned gown, were seated in a booth. No sooner had they exchanged greetings than Severin ordered a second bottle of champagne and four glasses. Irène, protesting that Sylvain was too young to drink, ordered him a *citron pressé*.

'You do know that champagne has medicinal properties?' Severin asked. 'Doctors used to prescribe it for anaemia.'

'Sylvain isn't anaemic,' Irène replied.

'I wouldn't be so sure,' Severin said, with a laugh. 'He looks pretty pasty to me.'

Irène cast a beseeching glance at Simon, who, shrugging it off, proposed that Sylvain be permitted half a glass, which he drained in a single gulp.

'I've got bubbles up my nose,' he said, snuffling.

After twenty minutes of idle conversation, punctuated by Severin's contented puffing on his cigar, Marguerite's pointed coughing and Sylvain's slurping of his *citron pressé*, they moved into the dining room. With its enamelled glass dome, three-tiered chandelier, marble statuary and pastel murals, it was of such grandeur that, on first viewing, Sylvain had instinctively exclaimed: 'Versailles!' Despite food shortages elsewhere, the menu was extensive and the hotel doctor was happy to sign medical certificates exempting guests from the meat ration. Irène felt that she might have been back at Le Nid before the Occupation, were it not for the snatches of German drifting across from nearby tables.

While the diners may have hailed from Zurich or Basle, their accents weren't Swiss. 'I could be wrong,' she said, 'but there seem to be more Germans in the hotel than a month ago.'

'Unsurprisingly,' Severin said. 'The Allied landings in Sicily have made them doubly determined to protect their supplies – and their supply lines.'

'My friend at the Conservatoire tells me more and more German and Italian soldiers are fleeing across the border every day,' Clarice said.

'Here's hoping the guards treat them as mercilessly as they do the Jews,' Irène replied.

'You mustn't take it personally,' Severin said, having discarded his Judaism like an unprofitable investment. 'Neutrality is a dangerous game. This is a small country, surrounded by hostile neighbours. Hitler may have put his invasion plans on hold, but, make no mistake, they'll be filed away in the war ministry in Berlin, ready to be dusted down when needed.'

'They'll never defeat the Swiss,' Clarice said. 'My friend says that, should it come to it, the army will retreat to the Alps and fight to the last man.'

'Which friend is this?' Simon asked suspiciously.

'No doubt a young firebrand,' Severin said. 'Thankfully, wiser heads have prevailed. Never underestimate the power of commerce. The Swiss need coal, steel, oil, gas and fertiliser to keep the economy running. In turn, the Germans need machine tools, chemicals, aluminium, even jewel bearings.'

'All of which can be used to make weapons,' Clarice said.

'I see that your friend has done his homework. As one of our more cynical compatriots quipped, "Six days a week, the Swiss work for Germany and, on the seventh, they pray for an Allied victory.'"

He laughed, giving Irène the chance to put the question that had nagged at her for weeks. 'Are you part of this commerce?'

'Do you expect me to reveal trade secrets?' he replied lightly.

'No, just personal ethics,' she said, striving to match his tone.

'I'm not a manufacturer.'

'But you are a financier.'

'Can we stop this?' Simon asked. 'Roland isn't on trial. I mean ...'

'Don't worry,' Severin said, with a thinner laugh than before. 'In some eyes, I shall be in the dock for the rest of my life. What you have to realise, my dear Irène, is that war is a huge opportunity, this one as much as the last. You come from a great family. Those who are less fortunate, like Simon and myself, have to live by our wits.' Irène was surprised to find that Simon, who was usually quick to embellish his background, had for once laid it bare. 'During the last war I fought at the front, which is not something I'd recommend ... I'm glad none of you ordered tripe.'

'Thank you, Roland,' Marguerite said, pushing her entrecôte aside.

'Unlike my fellow soldiers, I didn't hurry home the minute we were demobilised. Instead, I befriended some British troopers from, as I recall, the 6th and 7th Dragoon Guards. They were left with hundreds of horses, which were too costly to ship back across the Channel. They were due to be shot – a fittingly martial death – but I persuaded the quartermaster to sell them to me for farmwork. Then I transported them to Lille and sold them to butchers for ten times what I paid. So all parties profited.'

'I'm sorry, I need to ...' Clarice said, scraping back her chair and rushing from the room.

'I trust I didn't upset her,' Severin said, unrepentantly. 'Is she fond of horses?'

'She's worried about her boyfriend,' Sylvain said. 'He's been called up in September.'

'What boyfriend? Did you know about this?' Simon asked Irène.

'Please excuse me. I must go and check on her,' she said, seizing the chance to escape.

She found Clarice lying on her bed, hugging a tear-stained pillow. She sat next to her and stroked her hair, eliciting a further flurry of sobs. Slowly composing herself, Clarice told her about Francisque, 'the sweetest, kindest, handsomest boy in the world', whom she'd met at the Conservatoire.

'He passed his *maturité gymnasiale* (that's like their Bac) and wants to be a professional violinist. He's really good. The other students call him Paganini – his father's Italian, but that's not why. His dream is to play in the Orchestre de la Suisse Romande. It used to be the Berliner Philharmoniker, but he says he'd refuse them now, even if they offered him the Beethoven concerto. And who knows when he'll play again? He's eighteen on 16 September, so he has to join the army.'

'You told Monsieur Severin that he wants to defend the country.'

'But I don't want him to! Can't you remember your Grandmaman's spell that made the Turks turn down Papa?'

'I never knew it. Besides, didn't you hear what he told us in Aubière? The crushed seeds very nearly killed him.'

'Francisque may be killed here.'

'Nonsense! The Swiss aren't under attack. He won't be sent into battle.'

'What if the Germans invade to secure a safe route into Italy? Francisque said he'd blow up the tunnels himself.'

'If the Germans invade, we'll all be in trouble. But they won't.'

'If anything happens to him, I'll kill myself.'

'Do you think he'd want that?'

'I love him.'

'Oh my darling, you're very young,' Irène said, clasping her in her arms.

'You were younger than me when you fell in love with Papa. You told us about burying the egg.'

Irène, all too aware of the power and pitfalls of first love, loosened her hold. 'Girls got married younger then. You're lucky to live when you do.' She bit her lip. 'At least in some respects. Over the years, you'll get to know all sorts of boys.'

'Why are you trying to hurt me? I only want to know him.'

'And that's fine. When his military service is over, Francisque will return to the Conservatoire and you'll pick up where you left off. Meanwhile, you have August together. Enjoy it!'

With a tentative knock, Sylvain poked his head around the door. Irène was touched by the way he first checked that he wasn't intruding and then apologised to Clarice for blurting out her secret. Smiling ruefully, she told him that he'd always had a big mouth, which was as close to a pardon as he could expect. Irène kissed them both goodnight and went to her room. She mixed a dose of salts, surprised by how little she had left. After draining the glass, she stood at the mirror, telling herself – and rehearsing for the doctor – how she had spilt the bottle on the floor.

She climbed into bed and opened her book, but Simon returned before she'd had time to turn the page. He tore off his jacket and tie and flung them on a chair.

'Don't look at me! I'm drenched in sweat.'

'It's a hot night.'

'I could see that Marguerite was disgusted. And it's your fault. Why did you have to lash out at Roland?'

'Why does he have to do business with Nazis?'

'He didn't say that he did.'

'He didn't have to.'

'May I remind you—'

'No need. I'm eternally in his debt. But may I remind you of the old saying: "In the company of wolves, we need to howl"?'

'And in the company of birds, we need to sing! So what? I'm taking a shower.'

He spent so long in the bathroom that she'd dozed off by the time he came to bed. She was dimly aware of his snoring until, in the early hours, she was roused as so often by his muffled cries, his coughing, choking and thrashing about. As she shook him gently, he didn't wake, but sank into a deeper sleep, leaving her brooding on the one word she recognised: Mari.

Fearful of trying Hélène Lambert's patience, she waited nine days before returning to the Red Cross office. After apologising for the lack of information, Hélène explained that she wouldn't be available for the rest of the week. 'I have to tour some of our detention camps. We send inspectors into camps all over the world – at least where we can. It's only right that we should check on our own.'

'They must be holiday resorts compared to the ones in France.'

Hélène gave her a probing look. 'Would you like to come with me?'

'To a camp?' Irène asked, the mere word making her shudder.

'Forgive me, but you seem quite on edge. It might put your problems in perspective.'

'Where would it be?'

'Geneva. On Thursday, I'm going to the women's camp at Charmilles.'

'What would I have to do?'

'Nothing you don't want to. Just talk to people. And, more to the point, listen. The women might find it easier to open up to someone of their own faith.'

'They're all Jewish?'

'By and large.'

'Are you sure it's allowed? Won't I need to be vetted?'

'You've been vetted by me.'

Two days later, they met at Lausanne station and took the train to Geneva. During the cramped journey, Hélène described Charmilles, which housed around two hundred women and children. The commandant, Captain Rehfus, imposed a harsh and often arbitrary code of conduct, with the women subjected to regular roll calls and hut searches. When Hélène asked him if they were necessary, he replied that Jews respected discipline.

'Is that true?' she asked Irène.

'The ones I know respect decency and kindness.'

'I'm afraid you'll find those in short supply.'

She explained that, on her last visit, she had received numerous complaints about the guards: their pettiness and cruelty; their routine mockery of the women's appearance and hygiene; their pilfering of food parcels. Worst of all were the sexual offences. One young woman had been raped by four or five drunken sentinels (their repeated assaults made precision impossible). She'd lodged a formal protest, but, rather than the men being dismissed, she was deported for immorality.

'Was there nothing you could do?'

'I and my superiors did everything in our power, appealing to Refugee Commissioner Wildbolz himself, but without success. I understand why most of the women choose to stay silent.'

From Geneva station, they took the bus to Charmilles. Hélène had called it a reception camp, but, to Irène's eyes, this converted football stadium was a prison, with a barbed wire fence and heavy iron gates, where she and Hélène were frisked with excessive rigour, as if to demonstrate who was in charge. They walked through a concrete tunnel and emerged on the former pitch, now dotted with huts. Women as sombre as their surroundings sat on the steps, leant against the walls, or squatted on the ground. Some were knitting, and as Hélène and Irène approached, a couple came to blows. Others gathered round, egging them on. A guard parted them with the butt of his rifle, and peace was grudgingly restored.

'What was that all about?' Hélène asked him, as he returned to his post.

'Wool! The redhead claimed that glasses tore her ball. Would you credit it?'

'It'll make a difference if they're getting paid by the piece,' Irène said, vaguely recalling the tobacco factory.

'They're not,' Hélène replied, leading her away. 'They knit socks and mufflers for the troops for a franc a day, a few centimes more once they've been here several months. But there are cultural . . .

national . . . ethnic rivalries at work here, just like everywhere else. Someone shifts a bed a couple of centimetres to the left or right, and it's war! After a day at a camp, I'm less inclined to grumble when Étienne - my husband - commandeers the quilt.'

As they made their way round, a woman intercepted Hélène to ask if she had any news of her children. She promised her that she was investigating, but the woman, in deep distress, refused to believe it. 'You're lying!' she shrieked. 'They're dead and you won't tell me!' Deaf to Hélène's assurances, she unleashed a torrent of abuse and fled into a hut, while an elderly onlooker tutted at her loss of control. Briskly withdrawing, Hélène guided Irène down a miry passage between two huts, where an Austrian woman begged her help on behalf of her husband, who had been sent from the men's camp at Varembé to dig ditches in the Alps.

'In Villach, he never even dug the garden. We have a *sheigetz* for that.'

They reached the perimeter fence, where a woman stood alone, gazing at an empty stand, as if waiting for a crowd of spectators. Spotting Hélène, she asked if there were any progress on her transfer. Once again, Hélène promised that she was doing what she could, at which the woman smiled wearily and resumed her solitary vigil.

'It's unbearably sad,' Hélène explained to Irène. 'She complained to the commandant that a boy stole her mirror. Rehfus's response was to have him, his mother and baby sister sent back to France. Since then, all the other women have ostracised her. They blame her; she blames herself; I blame my countrymen.'

Only the children, ragged, unkempt and, in several cases, unshod, looked cheerful. They had the run of the camp - literally, in the case of three girls playing tag. Two small boys bounced a ball off the wall of a hut, while another kicked an imaginary one into touch. A more studious group sat cross-legged on the turf, where a spirited woman led them in a recital of the capital cities of Europe, at least as they had been in 1939. One towheaded toddler wandered off by herself, squatted and pissed. A guard, observing it, rushed into a hut and dragged out a woman, presumably her mother, who glanced at her indifferently and returned inside, to the visible disgust of the guard.

A protracted whistle signalled lunch, which was a kind of porridge cake.

'It's more appetising than it looks, or so I'm told,' Hélène said. 'And it's kosher. They've had problems with that in the past.'

A second whistle, consisting of three short blasts, sent the women scrambling into line, while the children clustered in front of them. The commandant, his bullwhip hanging menacingly from his belt, arrived with a pair of thickset men, dressed in leather jerkins, moleskin trousers and heavy boots, despite the August heat. They walked up and down the rows, occasionally stopping to speak to a woman before conferring with the commandant, who dispatched a guard to fetch two of them.

'What's happening?' Irène asked Hélène. 'Are they being punished?'

'On the contrary. The men are farmers, choosing pickers for the fruit harvest. They take women who are willing, strong and childless. Free labour.'

The words Beschinar Gardens flashed through Irène's mind. 'And they want to go?' she asked.

'Wouldn't you?'

After another hour of smiling fixedly, like Maman on a visit to Vardar, Irène followed Hélène out of the camp. On the train back to Lausanne, she asked about the detainees' prospects.

'Is there any hope of release or will they be locked up till the end of the war?'

'There's always hope. The Federal Assembly has passed legislation permitting the children to go into foster care and the women to work as maids or farmhands, as you saw.'

'So why are the children still here? Is it prejudice?'

'No, money. We're a frugal people. The authorities require potential hosts to provide a surety of between three and four thousand francs per child. Many of them don't have it.'

'But we do,' Irène said, delighted to learn of a way to contribute. 'We may not be allowed to foster anyone ourselves, but we can assist other families. I'll speak to my husband as soon as we get back.'

She found him on the terrace, drink in hand, staring into space. How ironic that, after years of his ignoring doctors' advice, it had taken a war to teach him to relax!

Gallant as ever, he rose to greet her. Refusing a glass of vermouth, she drew up a chair and described her visit to the camp and how they might help the children.

'Your compassion is admirable,' he replied evenly. 'But it's not as simple as you think. I don't wish to alarm you, but the Swiss have imposed a hefty mutual aid tax on Jews - only Jews, mind! - with assets over twenty thousand francs. It's unjust and discriminatory, yet we pay it. In addition, they've decreed that refugees from any German-occupied country - which means us - can withdraw no more than three thousand francs a month.'

'So how can we afford all this?'

'Our friend Roland has uncovered a loophole.'

'Then we'll be able to help with the sureties?' she replied, wincing at the epithet.

'I'm afraid not. We have to be provident. Who knows what new ways they'll find to bleed us dry?'

'Sometimes I don't think I know you at all.'

'No,' he replied, his voice and gaze both distant. 'Though that may be for the best.'

Lying awake that night, Irène dreamt up a scheme to circumvent him. The next morning, leaving only her gold blessing necklace and Grandmaman Regina's betrothal ring, she retrieved her jewellery from the hotel safe, took it to the Red Cross office and tipped it triumphantly onto Hélène's desk.

'Have you robbed Bucherer?' Hélène asked.

'Don't worry, it's all legitimate. I'd like you to sell it and use the proceeds as sureties for the children at Charmilles.'

'These are exquisite,' Hélène said, fingering the coral and diamond necklace that had been a wedding present from her parents. 'Do you have any idea what they're worth?'

'Not a clue.' She picked up a sapphire brooch. 'But knowing my father and grandfather, never mind my husband . . .' She faltered. 'They won't have been cheap. I don't mean to malign your compatriots—'

'Please, feel free!'

'But they may take advantage of a foreigner. You should be able to get a better price.'

Hélène promised to consult her brother-in-law, who had recently settled his late mother's estate. After four days, she sent word that Valorum had offered forty-two thousand francs, enough to provide sureties for ten or eleven children. She would contact the Jewish Refugee Aid organisation to oversee the arrangements, in conjunction with the ZLA, the Civilian Directorate of Homes and Camps.

'Once the paperwork's complete, I'm sure they'll be in touch to thank you.'

'Heavens, no! That's the last thing I want. I only wish I could take in a child myself.'

Ignorant of Swiss law on marital property, she made no mention of the sale to Simon. In the evenings, she wore the blessing necklace, which he deemed sufficiently smart for the hotel dining room. But the following Sunday, they were invited to Geneva to celebrate Marguerite Severin's birthday. She put on the ivory velvet wrap dress, which Marguerite had insisted was perfect for her colouring. When Simon told her that her emeralds would set it off, she was forced to confess the truth.

'Is this your revenge?' he asked bitterly.

'What? No. Why?'

'For my using your father's account.'

'Not at all. I just want to support the children.'

'And pauperise your own?'

Declaring that it was solely out of respect for the Severins that he hadn't called to cancel, he led her along the promenade in silence, onto the cable car in silence, and into the trains to Geneva and Eaux-Vives in silence, breaking it only on the doorstep to remind her that 'We're here for a party'. Their hosts greeted them in the hall, Severin kissing her provocatively on the lips and Marguerite handing their gift (a Cartier toothpick, chosen by Simon) straight to a maid to 'put on the pile'. Judging by the sounds emerging from nearby rooms, the party was in full swing, with guests as intent on shutting out the war as soldiers on leave. Severin took Simon to join the men in the gallery, while Marguerite slipped her arm through Irène's and escorted her into the richly perfumed salon. Praising her 'heroic escape from France', she introduced her to a group of elegant women, who, after stock expressions of horror at the Nazis and admiration for her courage, quizzed her about life at the Beau-Rivage Palace and whether conscription had led to a drop in standards.

'Will you excuse me?' Irène said, swallowing hard. 'I need to have a word with my husband.'

She entered the picture gallery, Severin's pride and joy, although, on her previous tour, his emphasis on the history, rarity and value of each work had put her in mind of Bella's disdain for men who collected art like postage stamps. She edged though a fug of cigar smoke, only to stop dead in front of a new addition, a canvas with a terracotta background and red and black figures, instantly identifiable as Bella's. Her surprise at Severin's eclecticism was swiftly eclipsed by the shock of confronting her parents in the guise of Greek gods. She struggled to steady herself as the room blurred. Had her parents' house been looted as well as requisitioned? She'd heard rumours of Jewish art treasures being shipped to Germany, but how had the picture ended up here, unless her suspicions were correct and Severin was colluding with the Nazis?

Dimly aware of Simon drawing on a cigar (which he loathed), she marched up to Severin, who was holding court beside a stormy seascape. 'What is my parents' picture doing on your wall?'

'My dear, I'm mystified. What picture? Where?'

'The Timarete portrait behind you.'

'Those are your parents?' he asked, turning to look at it.

'And Timarete's my sister.'

'Small world!' he said, eliciting an appreciative chuckle from his audience.

'Small? Don't you mean corrupt and contemptible?'

'You're shouting, Irène,' Simon said, as though the impropriety outweighed the theft.

'I'll shout from the rooftops if need be. It's Bella's picture of Papa and Maman, last seen in the Avenue Frochot salon.'

'I must correct you there,' Severin said. 'It was last seen in the Galerie Fischer in Lucerne. I bought it a month ago, along with that Nolde to your left. I can show you the sales notes.'

'I didn't suppose you sneaked back to Paris and prised it off the wall. Look!' She grabbed Simon's sleeve and dragged him to the picture. 'Don't you recognise it?'

'It may be a copy,' he said feebly.

'She's not Rembrandt!' She turned to Severin. 'What did you pay for it? And the Nolde? No, don't tell me! What do I know of the art world? No doubt it was a good deal. After all, such degenerate painters aren't wanted in Berlin.'

'We all like a bargain,' Severin replied equably.

'And the devil take everyone else!'

'You must have it. I shall be happy to return it to its rightful owner.'

One man clapped.

'Really, there's no need,' Simon said.

'There's every need,' Irène said. 'This isn't horseflesh. Tricking the sentimental British with tales of farmwork! It's ... I don't know the term for acquiring stolen property. Not to mention, replenishing the Nazi war chest.'

'Calm down, Irène!' Simon said. 'You're making a spectacle of yourself.'

Not only were the men watching keenly, but the commotion had prompted Marguerite and several of the women to breach the masculine enclave.

'I think you should leave,' Severin said to Simon.

'I'd like to take the picture,' Irène said.

'I'll have it sent to the hotel.'

'I'd prefer to take it now.'

'On the train?' Simon said. 'Look at the size of it!'

'We'll manage.'

'As you wish,' Severin said coldly.

'What on earth's going on?' Marguerite asked.

'Nothing, my beloved. Just a case of disputed provenance. Would you tell the maids to start serving? I hear stomachs rumbling like freight cars.'

As Marguerite shepherded her guests into the dining room, Severin summoned the butler to help Simon lift the picture off the wall. 'If you'll excuse me, I have duties to attend to,' he said, as the old man grappled with the frame. 'I'm sure Koehl will find you some oilcloth to wrap it in. You wouldn't want anyone to accuse you of stealing it!'

Desperate to leave, Irène insisted that there was no need for any packaging. With Simon taking the front end, she carried the picture to the station, resting it against her legs on the short journey to Cornavin. In the train to Lausanne, she propped it on the opposite banquette, gazing at the portrait as fondly as if her parents were sitting there themselves.

Returning to the hotel, she ignored the string of quizzical glances and declined the bellboy's offer of help. 'My husband and I are a team,' she said pointedly, sensing his silent fury. They manoeuvred the picture into the lift and down the corridor to the salon, leaning it against the bureau. Setting aside Simon's protests, she called the children out of bed to see it.

'Did Grandmaman send it from Paris?' Sylvain asked.

'Don't be an imbecile!' Simon said, then ruffled his hair contritely.

'No, darling,' Irène said. 'Though in a way, maybe yes. It's as if she wanted us to have it. First thing tomorrow, I'll ask the housekeeper to take down that gouache of the monks on the St Bernard Pass and put Grandpapa and Grandmaman in their place.'

'You do that,' Simon said sharply. 'And spare a thought for me. How am I ever to look Roland in the eye again?'

'Why look at him at all?'

'Fine words! But the war will be over – maybe sooner than you think – and there'll be massive reconstruction work throughout Europe. Which will need finance. I intend to grab a slice of it.'

'In partnership with Severin?'

'He still has many influential friends.'

'Next term I want to be a boarder,' Sylvain said.

'What new nonsense is this?' Simon asked.

'I don't like living in a hotel. I don't like hearing you argue.'

'See,' Simon said to Irène, 'your madness is contagious... That's it: a breakdown! I'll tell Roland you're suffering from a delayed reaction to the horrors we witnessed in France. Isn't that what happened to Leon after the trenches?'

Irène didn't answer, although she suspected that if anyone were suffering such a reaction, it was Simon. During a restless night nursing her aching shoulder, she again heard him crying out in his sleep. As he coughed and spluttered and writhed beneath the covers, his garbled words began to cohere: 'Mari... flames... forgive me...' Might the horrors have been the fire that consumed Salonica and the reaction been delayed for twenty-five years? But then why was he asking forgiveness of his sister if she'd died of influenza two years before? She got up and mixed a double dose of salts, in an attempt to ease her mind.

The following week, Simon made three trips to Geneva, assuring Irène that he had repaired relations with Severin. She presumed that the offer to pay for the picture, 'which he bought in good faith', had appeased him. Sylvain returned to school, although not as a boarder, and Clarice resumed her studies at the Conservatoire. She pined for Francisque, whose first letter from the École de Recrues, full of excitement at his new responsibilities, convinced her that he'd forgotten her. Meanwhile, Irène received grim news from Esther. They had barely renewed contact when she wrote that Felix had been killed in a bombing raid. Her own letter of condolence crossed paths with a second one from Esther, stating that Basil had been reported missing on a covert operation in France.

She was composing her reply, praying that, given the postal delays, her sympathy would be redundant, when she received a phone call from Hélène, who'd promised to notify her of the fostering arrangements.

'Try not to get too excited, but we may have located Annette.'

'Where? In Annecy?'

'No, here in Switzerland. In the Burgenspiral reception camp near Berne. I can't be certain because we don't have a surname, but she matches the description, doesn't speak and, crucially, never lets go of her hairbrush.'

'I can't believe it!'

'Best stick to that, at least until we can confirm it.'

'How did she cross the border?'

'You mustn't breathe a word of this – it's a total violation of Red Cross rules – but some of our relief workers in Lyon received intelligence of an orphanage in Charvonnex that was under threat. They informed the OSE – that's a Jewish aid agency – who extracted the children and led them across the Alps.'

'And she's unharmed?'

'They all are.'

'When may I see her?'

'I'm doing everything I can. But bear in mind that it may not be her. There are plenty of red-haired Jewish girls. She may have given the hairbrush to one of them—'

'Impossible!'

'Or it may have been snatched from her. Children can be brutal, especially when they've been brutalised themselves.'

Opting to say nothing to the family until she knew more, Irène walked down to the lake, the only place vast and impassive enough to contain her emotion. She felt grateful, excited and frightened in equal measure, but at her core lay a deposit of guilt: guilt that she'd broken her pledge to Bella and abandoned Annette in Annecy; guilt that, in her concern for Annette, she'd neglected Clarice and Sylvain; guilt that she'd lived comfortably at the hotel, while so many displaced women languished in camps.

Hélène was true to her word, calling at the Beau-Rivage Palace the following afternoon.

'I've brought someone to see you,' she said, as they met in the lobby. 'But she won't come inside. She appears to be terrified of hotels.'

'Annette!' Irène said, grasping Hélène's hand. 'Quick! She may run off again.'

'Take a deep breath!' Hélène said. 'She's with Emil Gruber from the ZLA. But I should warn you, when I told her that she'd be seeing the people who took care of her in France, she grew very agitated. I fear she may have had some bad experiences after you left.'

Trembling, Irène followed Hélène outside, where a stocky, middle-aged man stood with one arm wrapped protectively around Annette's chest.

'Annette . . . oh my darling! Annette!' Irène ran towards the girl, who moaned and squirmed under Emil's grip.

'Don't you remember me? It's Irène . . . Tante Irène.'

'Cellar!' Annette replied, spitting out the word.

'You're speaking! She's speaking,' she exclaimed to Hélène and Emil, who looked equally startled.

'Cellar!' Annette repeated.

'Oh my darling, it's so wonderful to hear your voice.'

'In the cellar . . . in the dark,' Annette said, struggling to articulate each syllable.

'Did you lock her in a cellar?' Emil asked, eyeing Irène warily.

'No! No, of course not. We didn't have a cellar. And even if we did . . . How can you think that?'

'Not you! Not her! Him, him, him!'

Two guests walked up the driveway, quickening their pace as Annette started to scream.

'Please don't do that!' Irène said. 'You'll hurt your voice . . . your beautiful new voice. Come inside! We can have something to eat. Cake.'

'I'm not sure that this was such a good idea,' Emil said to Hélène.

'She's confused . . . disturbed,' Irène insisted, her mind racing with dark conjecture. 'Don't you want to see Clarice and Sylvain?'

'Sylvain.' Annette clapped her hands. 'Sylvain!'

'They're upstairs. They'll be thrilled . . . overjoyed to see you.'

Clutching Emil's unengaged hand, Annette took a step towards Irène, who held back from hugging her, afraid of triggering another outburst.

'Come along then!' she said, with forced cheer, leading the group up to the salon. She opened the door to find Sylvain sprawled on a sofa, reading.

'Look who's here!' she said to him.

'Annette!' He jumped up, grabbed hold of her, and swung her in the air, before giving her the hug that Irène had withheld. 'Where did you come from then?' he asked, at which, in an abrupt change of mood, she dissolved into giggles.

'I told you everything would be fine,' Irène said to Hélène. 'She just needed time to adjust. I dread to think what she's been through.'

'What's all this racket?' Simon asked, walking in from the terrace, followed by Clarice.

'You found her!' Clarice said, rushing up to Annette, who allowed herself to be embraced, while her gaze remained fixed on Simon.

'I don't believe it!' he said, gulping. 'It's a miracle.'

'You! You put me inside the cellar.'

'What's this?' Clarice asked. 'She's talking!'

'She's talking nonsense,' Simon said. 'Did the Nazis lock her in a cellar?'

'You! You and the hotel man. You! In the cellar. In the dark.'

She broke away from Clarice, grasped Emil's hand and crouched behind his back.

'I don't know what you mean, Annette,' Irène said, fighting the urge to retch. 'But I promise you I'll figure it out. Now's the time for happy things. Let's order some cake and sandwiches. Then you can stay here. You can sleep with Clarice and Sylvain.'

'It's too soon to be discussing bedrooms,' Emil said, scrutinising Simon.

'There are no cellars here,' Irène said to Annette. 'Everywhere's lovely and light.'

'I want to go back!'

'You'd rather stay in the camp than here?' Hélène asked uneasily, Annette nodded.

'We can do jigsaws and make hand shadows,' Sylvain said. 'It'll be fun.'

Annette, still staring at Simon, shook her head.

'I think we should make a move,' Hélène said.

'If you don't like hotels, we'll get an apartment,' Irène said. 'Just the four of us . . . five of us.'

Annette, mute again, shook her head, as Emil ushered her to the door.

'I'll wait for you downstairs,' he said to Hélène.

'Not yet,' Irène said. 'Stay a little longer. You've had no tea . . . cake.'

'I'll call you in the morning,' Hélène said to her. 'We'll find a way forward . . . when Annette's more settled.' She looked at Simon, her eyes narrowing. 'When we've got to the bottom of the cellar.'

She kissed Irène lightly on both cheeks and followed Emil and Annette out, leaving the Silveras in stunned silence. Simon spoke first.

'The child's damaged . . . deranged. Who knows what happened after we left? I trusted Legrandin, but . . .'

The family couldn't be leaving if it weren't for him: Simon's words swept back through Irène's mind. She had assumed that he'd included Annette in the family, but what if she'd been wrong?

'Why are you looking at me like that?' Simon said, to either Clarice or Sylvain or both, since Irène couldn't bring herself to face him. 'None of you appreciate how much I do for you . . . the strain of being the one who always has to make decisions. You're all I think about - all I care about.'

'No more, Papa, please!' Clarice said.

'Stop shaking, Maman!' Sylvain said, clasping her as tightly as Emil had Annette.

'I'm just . . . I'm just . . . I must just lie down for a few minutes. My head's splitting. Please let me rest, all of you.' She finally glanced at Simon. 'I just need rest.'

She retreated to the bedroom, crumpling against the door, before standing up to lock it. She entered the bathroom, poured three - and then four - heaped teaspoonfuls of the bromide salts into a glass of water, drank it and lay on the bed. When, after half an hour, she found herself as agitated as ever, she measured out another dose.

7

BELLA

NICE, SEPTEMBER 1943

THE WHOLE OF Nice appeared to have taken to the streets to celebrate Italy's surrender. Music spilt from open windows and laughter rippled through the air like a wave of hope. Bella, buoyed by the elation of the crowd, danced the length of the Avenue de la Victoire with two elderly fishermen, a Tuscan anti-fascist, and a girl draped in the tricolour. In the early hours, she went back to her hotel accompanied by a young Neapolitan soldier with the face of Caravaggio's Bacchus.

Two days later, the Wehrmacht's march into the city cut short the revelry. With their battle-ready uniforms and flawless discipline, the Germans stood in stark contrast to the Italians, whose plumed helmets and casual manner had smacked of a comic opera. In what was no doubt a calculated ploy, the troops Bella encountered were courteous. Unlike the Italians, they didn't wolf-whistle and make lewd comments, and one, happily ignorant of her race, offered her his seat on the tram. That, however, was cold comfort when, with the war turning against them, the military command proved to be yet more ruthless than that of Lyon. The Italians, in a show of independence, had refused to hand over Jews to either the German or Vichy authorities. They had even mounted a guard in front of the synagogue in the Boulevard Dubouchage when it was threatened by the Milice. The Nazis stormed synagogues, disrupting services and arresting worshippers. Meanwhile, Milice thugs, brandishing submachine guns, raided hotels, pensions and apartment blocks in search of residents with Jewish-sounding names.

Bella had fled south in July. Hours after the swoop on the British agents they'd been harbouring, the Gestapo homed in on their network. She escaped, as did Bertrand, but Henri was captured while waiting for a contact in the Place Carnot. He was taken to the Hôtel Terminus for interrogation. He had told her quite soberly that he didn't expect to survive the Occupation, but that, at seventy-one, he'd had the best of his life and, if he were to die at the hands of the Nazis, he wanted his death to serve a purpose. Claiming to be a physical coward, he dreaded breaking down under torture and naming names. As a precaution, he always carried a cyanide pill. She prayed that he'd had a chance to swallow it before encountering Barbie.

She wished that Papa, who'd been dismissive of his younger brother, were alive to witness his courage. She trusted that, at the Liberation, his nephews and nieces would be alive to celebrate it. The ghost of 'Le pauvre Oncle Haim' had been permanently laid.

Marie-France, their network chief, warned her not to let emotion cloud her judgement. 'You're working to avenge a whole country, not just one man.' Bella acknowledged the advice, even as Henri's death steeled her resolve to resist. A marked woman in Lyon, she fled to an isolated cottage outside Pérouges, telling the villagers that she'd moved there after her husband and children were killed in the Allied bombing of Rennes. Over the next four months, she sheltered three British agents, parachuted into France with ammunition, explosives and instructions for the local maquis. During the long hours of waiting, they played cards, read poetry and danced to the scratchy tunes of the wind-up gramophone she'd found in the attic, which Ariel, the first of the agents, repaired.

The second agent, Gillion, sprained his wrist during a bungled landing and was confined to the house for a week while it healed.

She confided more in him during their short acquaintance than she had in some of her oldest friends, and even lovers. In turn, he revealed that his wife had been nearing the end of her term when he left London. He'd been offered the chance to wait for a later mission, but had told his bosses that he was fighting to create a world fit for his unborn child.

'If it's a girl, I promise we'll call her Arabella,' he said, as he waited for coded news from home.

'Good luck convincing your wife that we were just comrades-in-arms!'

Then by the most extraordinary chance . . . coincidence . . . serendipity (given the events of the past three years, she refused to credit providence in any particular), the third agent billeted on her was her nephew Basil. After a joyous reunion, in which her effusive endearments in front of his leader, Tyrell, and courier, Perry, brought a deep flush to his already freckled cheeks, he explained that he'd applied to be a pilot like his uncle – the brother she and Irène had dubbed 'the eyeglass' – but had failed his medical and been assigned to ground support. His commanding officer, learning that he spoke fluent French, dispatched him to the War Office as a candidate for SOE. He was accepted and given a brief training in Scotland, Manchester and London's Natural History Museum (on which unlikely setting he declined to elaborate), before his current deployment as a wireless operator. He'd informed his section head that he had family in France, but never in his wildest dreams had he imagined meeting his aunt.

While Tyrell translated the Marseillaise into Latin and Perry read a dog-eared crime novel, Bella and Basil exchanged family news. He told her of Felix's death in an airstrike and the devastating impact it had had on Esther. 'It was a shock for us all, since we'd supposed that the raids were over. I don't want to sound heartless, but I wasn't that close to my father. I hadn't thought Mother was either. I've always known that theirs was no love match. And though Father was never cruel, he wasn't the most sensitive or affectionate of husbands. Nathan called it a "cemetery marriage" – set in stone and yoked together eternally.'

Bella grieved for her sister more than her brother-in-law, whose crude advances to her during her parents' anniversary party still made her shudder. Esther had been wretched during the early years of her marriage, but after Nathan's birth, she no longer complained about Felix's faults, a change that Bella had attributed to loyalty rather than love. It was a comfort to learn that she had been wrong, even if Esther were suffering for it now.

'Shouldn't you have stayed in Didsbury to support her?'

'In case you've not noticed, there's a war on! I had a week's compassionate leave and organised the funeral. To complicate matters, they had a lodger who was also killed and whose husband was somewhere in the Mediterranean, en route for Sicily. With her home flattened, Mother moved in with my grandmother and her creepy companion, Flori. I just wish that Nathan weren't halfway across the world. Should anything happen to me—'

'It won't. You lead a charmed life. Look how you found your way here!'

'I know. But if it should, promise me you'll tell Mother how much I loved her. I'm afraid I've not always shown it.'

He stayed with her for two weeks while he and his team completed their mission, the details of which he never divulged, but, the day before they left, the main Lyon to Saint-Étienne railway line was sabotaged. They set off for Mont Pilat, where a plane from England was to fly them home. As they said their goodbyes, Bella impulsively unhooked the hamza from her neck and fastened it around his. Since then she'd had no word of him, which was only to be expected, but she felt in her bones that he was safe. His visit had made her realise how much she missed her family even if, like Basil himself, she hadn't always shown it. As the Nazi noose tightened, and she prepared to travel south, the urge to contact Maman consumed her, despite not knowing whether she was still living at Irène's or using her own name (she refused to contemplate her arrest or detention). For two days, she agonised over a message that would be both intelligible to her and opaque to the censors, before settling on 'After months of stalling, I agreed to have the operation. The doctor has confirmed my complete recovery and prescribed a period of convalescence in Nice.'

Unlike the many Jews who'd registered openly during the Italian occupation and were now living in terror under the Germans, Bella had the papers issued to one Laure Deferre in Lyon. She took a plain third-floor room in La Maison du Rivage, a small, rundown hotel in the Sainte-Hélène district and, after queuing for four hours in the draughty Passage Gioffredo, received a six-month residence permit from the Préfecture. She had few dealings with her fellow guests who, desperate to obtain visas from Cambodia or Mexico, the only countries still granting them, regarded any newcomer as a potential rival. The one exception was Asher Herzlich, a former journalist for the Austrian *Neue Freie Presse*, who'd fled to France after the Anschluss and who, on their first encounter, was at pains to emphasise that he was an émigré, not a refugee.

A precise, dapper man, he invariably sported a polka dot bow tie and cream linen jacket, which, although threadbare and soiled, imparted an air of Vienna's Café Central to the drab hotel dining room. Somewhat to Bella's surprise, given his employment by one of Europe's leading liberal newspapers, he was an avid reader of *Das Reich*. But as he raked through Goebbels' filth, he delighted in detecting signs of Nazi defeatism. Instead of crowing about the imminent victory, the arch-propagandist was now assuring his readers that their soldiers' blood would enrich the earth.

After three years of strained nerves, Bella spent much of September in a state of inertia. She toyed with resuming work, but she had no studio, no materials and no subject – at least none that lent itself to paint. A constructivist might respond to the wholesale desolation with collages of scraps and refuse, but her sensibility and practice were of a different order. Ruben had reported that Picasso was as productive as ever, but she wondered how other artists were faring. The only one she might consult was Matisse, a friend from Madame

Weill's gallery. Roaming the city's hinterland, she caught tantalising glimpses of the Regina Building and was tempted to climb the hill and knock on his door, but she knew that his health had been poor and his muse, model, manager and, if rumour were to be believed, mistress, the Russian Lydia, was fiercely protective of his privacy. She couldn't risk a rebuff.

In the second week of October, a new family arrived at the hotel: Yael Mantout, her eight-year-old daughter Noémie and six-year-old son Mathéo. After eight months' internment at Les Milles camp outside Marseille, Yael's husband, Zacharie, had been transported north and she and the children released. At first, they stayed with her sister and brother-in-law in Fréjus, but he sought payment in kind, 'if you catch my drift,' Yael said, with a pointed glance at the children. So, they moved further down the coast. She had no money, but Monsieur Courtois, the proprietor and a staunch anti-fascist, gave them bed and board in exchange for her help with the cooking and cleaning.

She was tormented by her husband's fate. 'Horrific stories circulated in the camp. A Belgian partisan told us how two escaped prisoners from Upper Silesia claimed that Jews sent there were being electrocuted.'

'Rubbish!' Bella said. 'I wouldn't be surprised if Goebbels planted the stories himself to scare us into submission. The Nazis may be monsters, but they're not mad. Why on earth would they murder able-bodied men and women whom they can put to work?'

Loath to accept financial help, Yael welcomed Bella's offer to watch the children while she carried out her chores. To Bella's surprise, the supervision restored her sense of purpose. They played games of Bataille and Vieux Garçon with a deck of cards that belonged to Madame Courtois (whose whereabouts remained a mystery). In a poorly stocked toy shop, she found a tin of thirty Caran d'Ache crayons and, lacking paper, they drew on flattened boxes, ledgers, old menu cards and Herr Herzlich's discarded copies of *Das Reich*. Scouring the flea market, she stumbled on a thousand-piece jigsaw of

'The Birds of France', which engrossed Noémie but bored Mathéo, who gloated when, with several pieces missing, the hoopoe's crown and kingfisher's plumage were left incomplete.

Both children bore the scars of their incarceration. Yael said that the one blessing of doing the laundry was the chance to change Mathéo's sheets every day. There'd been no bedding in the camp. At times, they slept on a thin covering of straw; at others, on bare planks. Mathéo was haunted by the memory. 'The cold was so cold . . . like icicles on my inside. Maman promised it was going to be better when it was summer, but it wasn't. Then there were the bloodsuckers that bit you and the roaches this big.' He extended his arms to their full span.

'Don't exaggerate!' said Noémie, who disliked being reminded of it.

'You didn't see the very worstest ones. And there was a smell like a smelly toilet all the time. And Maman's leg swollened up to this size.' He glanced at his sister before scaling down his gesture.

Yael made sure to spend two hours with the children before dinner each evening, Bella discreetly absenting herself, even when they begged her to stay. Once, when they refused to go up to the attic until they'd finished making finger puppets, Yael fixed her with a weary smile. 'I'd be jealous if I wasn't so grateful. The children love you. You're a natural.'

'I'm a novelty,' Bella said, feeling curiously moved.

'Have you never wanted a family of your own?'

'Maman would have liked it,' Bella replied, deflecting the question. 'Nothing would have made her happier than for me to be a Mother's Day gold medallist, proudly displaying my ten children and prolapsed uterus.' Yael winced. 'I jest, of course.'

Despite Monsieur Courtois's best endeavours, food remained scarce, and the children regularly complained of hunger. Bella supplemented their meagre diet with whatever she could find at the market, queuing alongside women whose main topic of conversation – and, it appeared, point of pride – was the length of time that they'd stood at the various stalls. Those with children were given priority so, as often as she could, she took Noémie and Mathéo with her, even though Mathéo, who'd lined up for scraps at Les Milles, struggled to make the connection between effort and reward. As they waited, she told them stories of 'Maryam the enchantress', who created such delicious treats that people felt full at the mere sound of them.

This morning, knowing Mathéo's sweet tooth, she described the *masapan manos* she'd baked for Esther's betrothal. 'I could nibble the fingers one by one, just like this . . .' She grabbed Mathéo's hand and pretended to gnaw at it, causing him to shriek with delight while their neighbours sniffed in disapproval.

'In the camp, one man was so hungry, he chewed his own hand,' Noémie said blankly.

'That's all in the past. You're safe now,' Bella said, wishing that she'd picked *rosquitas* or *ma'amoul* instead.

Persistence paid off, and she came away with a wheel of *banon* and a loaf of lumpy, adulterated brown bread, sufficient to quell any hunger pangs left after the lunchtime *bouillon perpétuel*. Walking back, they were waylaid by a red-faced, breathless Monsieur Courtois. Drawing Bella aside, he explained that the Gestapo had raided the hotel. All the guests had been arrested, apart from the Alsatian couple on the first floor, whom he suspected of being informants.

'What about Yael?' she asked, biting back a surge of panic as she smiled reassuringly at the children.

'Her too! I should have killed more of the bastards at the Somme. The last thing she said as they took her away was "Give my love to your friend and her children." She meant you.'

Standing on the busy street with a cheese that had started to run, Bella felt paralysed. It was too dangerous to return to the hotel. Yael would give her life for her children, of that she had no doubt, but how long would she withstand torture? Once again, she prayed that Henri had swallowed the cyanide pill. To her immense relief, Monsieur Courtois named a concierge friend, whom he was sure would hide them for a day or two. Like Yael, he assumed as a matter of course that Bella would take charge of the children. After years of striving to avoid any kind of domestic responsibility, she now had no choice but to embrace it.

Giving the fractious Mathéo a piggyback, Monsieur Courtois led them to a nondescript apartment block, where, leaving Bella and the children on the doorstep, he went inside to talk to his friend. Mathéo moaned for 'Maman' and even the docile Noémie bleated: 'I don't like it here.' At long last, Monsieur Courtois emerged with the friend, Madame Hubert, who, after scanning the street, hustled them into her parlour and informed them, without warmth, that they could stay for a maximum of two days. Brushing off Bella's thanks, she declared that she was doing it for Gilles, a salutary reminder that he had not only a first name but a private life.

Monsieur Courtois proposed to go back to the hotel to pack a suitcase with changes of clothes and toiletries. 'You'll find a pair of shoes in my wardrobe,' Bella said, steering him away from Madame Hubert, whose manner had done little to inspire trust. 'There's a bundle of cash in one of them. We'll need it.'

He left, promising to return in the evening, after which Madame Hubert showed Bella the rudimentary accommodation. 'You can sleep on the couch, Madame, and I'll put cushions on the floor for the children. I hope you don't expect food. It's not a hotel.'

'No, of course not. I've brought some bread and cheese for now.'

'That's for Maman,' Noémie said.

'She wouldn't want you to go hungry.'

'*Pain caca*,' Madame Hubert muttered, much to Mathéo's amusement, as Bella placed the loaf on the table.

After the simple lunch, she settled the children to rest, entreating Madame Hubert to watch over them while she went to the Villa Dupanloup.

'The Bishop's residence!' Madame Hubert said.

'One of the hotel guests told me that he – the Bishop that is

– has set aside a room for the Resistance, working secretly to save Jewish children.'

'Then it can't be much of a secret.'

'Herr Herzlich has his ear to the ground. Surely it's worth a try? What other hope do I have of finding somewhere for them? I'll be back before you know it.'

'My husband – God rest his soul – was a sailor, Madame. I've heard that one before.'

Wary of asking directions, Bella reached the villa by a circuitous route. She pressed the bell marked *Office* and was greeted by a glamorous blonde, whose peplum suit, silk stockings and immaculate pompadour instantly put her on guard. Asked to state her business, she replied charily that she'd heard of the diocese's relief work and had come about two homeless orphans. With a gentle nod, the girl offered her a seat and disappeared down the corridor, the clack of her heels amplified by the ghostly stillness. Moments later, she returned with an older woman, who ushered Bella into a fusty room, occupied by a round-faced, bespectacled priest. Introducing himself informally as Marcel, he asked bluntly what he could do for her.

'I'm afraid there's been a mistake, Father.'

'What? Oh!' He gave her a bleak smile. 'I'm no priest. Bishop Paul asked me to wear the soutane in case of unwelcome visitors.'

'He's taking a big risk.'

'He's a brave man.'

Marcel described how he'd approached the Bishop with trepidation. He was known to be a friend of Pétain's, having served under him at Verdun, and was reputed to have been his confessor. Yet he had protested against Vichy's antisemitic laws and, since the German occupation of the coast, had worked tirelessly with the Resistance to place Jewish children in convents, orphanages, boarding schools and foster homes. He had even provided church candles for use in Sabbath prayers.

'Isn't that something of a luxury right now?' Bella asked.

'Not for some people,' Marcel replied brusquely.

Chastened, Bella outlined Yael's arrest, which had left her the children's reluctant guardian. She stressed the urgency of finding them a safe home, since Madame Hubert's was only temporary. After noting down their particulars, Marcel went upstairs to consult the Bishop. Alone, Bella studied the sepia photographs of the Holy Land on the wall, which evoked bittersweet memories of Ruben. Marcel came back to report that the Bishop had made an emergency telephone call to the Abbess of a convent near Mougins. She had agreed to take in the children – or, for wiretapping purposes, to accept delivery of 'two stocks of holy oil' – the following morning. He jotted down the times of the buses, the designated stop of Font de Galou, and directions for the two-kilometre walk to the convent. He then filled out the children's file, explaining that it would be buried alongside several others in the garden, to facilitate reunions once their parents returned from Germany.

Humbled by his vestments, Bella kissed him lightly on the cheek and took her leave. She hurried back to the house, where Madame Hubert, tapping her watch, berated her for her timekeeping, as if it were still 1939.

'The children have been running wild. What if someone was to hear?'

'You've been most patient. But you needn't fret. We'll be off your hands first thing in the morning.'

Frantic with worry, the children wanted their mother. Bella's promise that they would see her soon drew a querulous 'When? Will it be longer than one day or two days or three days?' from Mathéo, who'd recently grasped the concepts of more and less, while Noémie murmured: 'That's what she said about Papa and he never came.'

Monsieur Courtois returned at dusk with a battered cardboard suitcase covered with half-torn stickers from the Hotel Clodio in Rome, the Hotel Minerva in Florence and the Hotel Luna in Venice. 'It was my wife's,' he said, hinting at another veiled history. Blushing furiously, he informed Bella that he'd packed a few of her 'feminine pieces', adding in a whisper 'as well as what I found in the shoe.'

'I can't thank you enough for all you've done for us. It may be a while before you're able to let my room. I wouldn't wish you to be out of pocket,' she said, seeking a formula that wouldn't insult him, as she peeled several notes from the bundle.

'No more of that! You've paid too much already,' he said solemnly.

Madame Hubert, on the other hand, was mollified by a five-hundred-franc note. As they said their farewells the next morning, she gave each child a chunk of bread rubbed in garlic for the journey. With Mathéo dragging his heels, they walked to the Avenue Fabron. No sooner had he boarded the bus than he threw himself down on the floor and refused to budge.

'Behave for your maman!' the driver said.

'She's not my maman,' he replied, to Bella's consternation.

'She's our aunt,' Noémie interjected nimbly.

Bella settled the children side by side on the seat next to her. As the bus drove off, Mathéo pressed his face to the window, gazing happily at the beaches and coves, and even the batteries and blockhouses dotting the coast. He lost interest once they wound their way inland, but Noémie relished Bella's commentary on the plain stone houses, whose earthy colours reflected both the landscape and their owners' lives. Bella felt a twinge of nostalgia as they entered Biot, where, in what felt like another lifetime, she and Fyodor Menshikov had spent a carefree afternoon, lunching in the Place des Arcades, roaming the cobbled streets and buying two cachepots from a testy ceramicist. The atmosphere today was less tranquil and, as they passed the old water mill, she quickly distracted the children from the sight of passengers off an earlier bus lining up outside the vehicle, while three German officers checked their papers. Had Mathéo been less dilatory, they might have been among them. In the row behind, one woman prayed the rosary and another thanked her *bonne étoile*, but as ever Bella refused to credit anything beyond chance.

They left the bus at Font de Galou, as instructed. She led the children down a narrow lane, lined with cypresses and scented with rosemary. Spotting two gnarled olive trees, Mathéo pressed his face against her waist, stumbling as he refused to look up.

'What's the matter, darling?' Bella asked. 'Are you tired?'

'He doesn't like seeing trees that are split in two,' Noémie said. 'Grandmaman told him how it happened whenever a naughty boy broke their hearts.'

Bella, no stranger to old wives' tales, searched for a corrective. 'Look at the cypresses over there, as straight as spires. That must mean they're proud of you.'

They trudged past a field of wilted lavender, which she pictured in its summer splendour, before coming to a tumbledown wall with two cracked granite gateposts, without a gate. On one, a faded sign in Gothic script marked the entrance to the *Convent and Orphanage of the Sisters of Notre Dame de Sion*. They proceeded up a mossy path, bordered by spent bougainvillea bushes, arriving at a long, squat building with small, barred windows, which might have passed for a prison were it not for the row of crosses on the front. Bella tidied the children, straightening Noémie's skirt and smoothing Mathéo's cowlick, before pulling the bell rope. After a lengthy wait, she was debating whether to pull it again when a peephole slid open.

'The door has a face,' Mathéo said.

It was a kindly face, with plump, rubicund cheeks. A moment later, the rest of the body was revealed: stout and stumpy in a white veil and grey habit, leaning on a rough-hewn stick.

'Welcome, welcome! I'm Sister Célestine. I've been greeting guests to our cloister for fifty years. May you find peace and solace within these walls.'

Unsure how much she knew about their visit, Bella thanked her and explained that the Mother Abbess was expecting them. Limping valiantly, Sister Célestine escorted them through a chilly passageway to the Abbess's office. The modest room, dominated by a large Empire desk and a bookcase crammed with files and ledgers, resembled Madame Weill's, except that the picture above the desk was a cheap copy of Rubens' *Massacre of the Innocents*, rather than a Suzanne Valadon *Self-Portrait*.

As Sister Célestine withdrew, the Abbess reiterated her welcome, albeit more gravely. An angular woman wearing a heavy pectoral cross on her grey scapular, she had an austere, aquiline face which Bella could picture stitched into a medieval tapestry. She invited them to sit, and Bella pulled up chairs for the children, steadying Mathéo, who dangled his feet and rocked. After asking the children their names and ages, which both whispered into their chests, the Abbess assured them that they were safe.

'We have thirteen children with us at the moment, so we're specially glad to have you.'

'When's Maman coming?' Mathéo asked, staring at Bella.

'She'll be here as soon as she can.'

'In how many days? In one day or in two days or—'

'You must be tired after your journey,' the Abbess interjected.

'No, I'm not,' Mathéo said.

'That isn't what you told me,' Bella said. 'And thirsty,' she added, fearing that the Abbess might overlook their bodily needs.

'I'd like a glass of water, please,' Noémie said, emollient as ever.

'I'll ring for Sister Angélique to take you to the children's block. But you'll want to say goodbye to Bella first.'

'Are you going away?' Noémie asked.

'I'm afraid I must.'

'No, you're not allowed!'

'I don't want to stay here without you here,' Mathéo said.

'I promise I'll ... see you again before too long,' Bella said, her voice wavering.

'No!' Mathéo clambered off his chair and clung to her.

'I apologise,' Bella said to the Abbess, as Noémie jumped up, echoing her brother's pleas. 'Though you must be used to it.'

'Most of our charges are brought here by their priests.'

'You'll make lots of new friends,' Bella said. 'You'll soon forget about me.'

'We'll run away to find you,' Noémie said.

As they tugged at her arms – and her heart – Bella remembered Esther's account of abandoning Basil at boarding school; which was absurd since she wasn't their – or anybody else's – mother.

'Where are you proposing to go?' the Abbess asked, which was something Bella had yet to decide. 'Is it safe to return to Nice?'

'Probably not,' she said blithely. 'But I travel light.'

'We have four guest rooms. They're basic but clean and bright. You're most welcome to stay here for the time being. You'll be able to see the children, provided you don't disrupt their routine.'

'Yes, yes!' Noémie said.

Bella felt an abrupt attraction to a way of life that couldn't have been more foreign to her. 'Are you sure?' she asked, and the Abbess nodded, with a trace of impatience. 'Then thank you, I shall, while I work out what to do next.'

'You promise?' Noémie asked.

'How could I tell a fib to the Reverend Mother?' she replied, with a grin.

The Abbess rang a bell, and a young nun appeared at the door.

'Sister Angélique, please take Noémie and Mathéo to the children's block and settle them before lunch.' She turned to the children. 'No nonsense now! You'll see Bella – or should I say Laure? – this evening.'

'I'm taking this with me,' Mathéo said, struggling to lift the case. 'Now you won't ever be able to run away.' He heaved it a few paces and then dropped it as they went out, leaving Bella alone with the Abbess.

'Those children love you.'

'They scarcely know me.'

'They know you better than you think,' the Abbess said, with a conviction which, in other circumstances, would have irritated Bella.

'I'm afraid I'll be an added burden on you.'

'It's our duty.'

'As Christians?'

'It's the duty of our Order. How much did His Excellency tell you about us?'

'I didn't meet the Bishop. Only Monsieur Marcel.'

'Then let me explain. We were founded exactly a hundred years ago with a mission to bring the Jews to Christ. Our founders believed that, through our prayers, our penances and our sacrifices, as well as our teaching, we could save them from eternal damnation.'

'If you've asked me to stay in the hope of converting me, I'm afraid you'll be sorely disappointed.'

'I expressed it badly. The past is the past. The Church has dishonoured itself with its persecution of the Jews over the centuries. You are our spiritual forebears. You are the people with whom God established His covenant and among whom He chose to become incarnate. And in the midst of the most brutal persecution of modern times, it's our duty to stand alongside you.'

'Still, I'd hate there to be any misunderstanding. I have a little money. I've always paid my way and I'd like to do the same here.'

'We're grateful for all donations. But what we'd prefer is for you to engage with the community, if not in the life of prayer then in other ways, such as helping in the kitchen or the garden.'

'I've never been known for my culinary skills and I'm liable to pull up your prize plants,' Bella said. 'But I'll be happy to peel vegetables or gather leaves.'

'Excellent. Then I'll call Sister Célestine to show you to your room. Meanwhile, I advise you not to say too much about the reasons for your stay. We recently had a visit from the Gestapo, who warned us that anyone caught sheltering Jews risked being shot. I have complete trust in the obedience of the sisters, but there are some who are less enlightened. When we took in our first Jewish child, Sister Hiliane raked through every hair on his head. It turned out that she wasn't searching for lice, but for horns.'

Sister Célestine conducted Bella to her room, which bore out the Abbess's description, its sole ornament being a macabre print of Jesus holding up His Sacred Heart. After unpacking her case, she lay on the chaste bed until she was summoned to the refectory for lunch, which was eaten in silence, while a silver-voiced nun read from the Latin Bible.

After lunch, the sisters spent an hour in work or contemplation, followed by afternoon prayer. Left to her own devices, Bella explored the convent, until the nuns filed out of the chapel. One, Sister Thérèse, introduced herself and asked if she would care to help her plant cauliflowers. Amused by the improbable request, Bella accompanied her, first to a ramshackle shed to collect the tools and then to the kitchen garden. As she hoed, composted, sowed and watered, she found herself using muscles that had lain dormant since she stowed away her easel. Although the dirt beneath her fingernails was earth, not paint, it felt good. Chatting more volubly than she would have expected, Sister Thérèse explained that she was one of the convent's five lay sisters whose temporary vows were renewed each year. She had embraced her calling late in life, after keeping house for her father, whose drinking had driven her mother to an early grave and estranged her eight brothers and sisters. Her candour so moved Bella that, ignoring the Abbess's advice, she shared some of her own story.

The bell rang again, and Sister Thérèse returned to the chapel for evening prayer.

'But it's only four o'clock!'

'Four thirty. You'll soon grow accustomed to our hours.'

Prayer was followed by Bible reading and the Angelus, after which Sister Thérèse who, either at the Abbess's behest or of her own volition, had assumed the role of Bella's guide, fetched her for collation. At the end of the modest meal, she escorted her through the cloisters to the children's block. They were admitted by Sister Augusta, who, with the curtest of greetings, led Bella up to the junior dormitory, which was eerily quiet given its occupants. Mathéo perched on the side of an iron bed, looking at a picture book with a stocky blond boy. Noémie eyed them guardedly from across the room. At Sister Augusta's summons, they walked ('Slowly!') to Bella, Mathéo refusing to let go of his companion's hand.

'I had an egg,' he said proudly. 'This is my friend, Pierrot.' He pushed forward the boy, who cast a doleful gaze at Bella.

'I don't have a friend,' Noémie said, 'but Sister Angélique says it takes more time because I'm older.'

'I'm sure that's true,' Bella said.

'Come and see my bed,' Mathéo said, grabbing her with his free hand. Bella glanced at Sister Augusta, who nodded her consent. 'We're not let to take our clothes off when we wash. I had to put the washcloth on the inside of my shirt.'

'You'll get used to it.'

'It's sticky.'

While deploring all forms of prudery, Bella acknowledged that, for once, it might serve a purpose in concealing Mathéo's race. Likewise, she was unperturbed when he showed her how to make the sign of the cross (albeit backwards) and Noémie described how Sister Angélique had taught them to pray for Jesus's protection. But her tolerance reached its limit three days later, when Noémie bolted from the children's block (an offence in itself) and, finding her in the herb garden with Sister Thérèse, sobbingly related how Sister Augusta had shown them a film of Jesus's torture and crucifixion.

'She said He was killed by the Jews, but I didn't kill anyone.'

Bella flinched. Somewhere she had heard those words before.

'Of course you didn't. He was killed nineteen hundred years ago by the Romans, not by a little girl who's never harmed a fly.'

'Only beetles,' Noémie replied, with a sniff.

Leaving her in Sister Thérèse's care, Bella headed straight to the Abbess, whose calming presence dulled the edge of her anger as she recounted Noémie's story. 'I'm indebted to you for offering us a haven – a sanctuary – and it's not my place to criticise your practices, but showing such a film to children – any child, but especially one who takes its guilt upon herself – strikes me as immoral.'

'I apologise without reserve,' the Abbess said immediately. 'It's to the Church's shame that it holds the Jews uniquely culpable for Our Lord's death . . . although, by the same token, it would make them uniquely eligible for His redemption. And where would that leave the rest of us?' She shared a shy smile. 'Sister Augusta is a devout doctrinaire. Every Friday, with the aid of an ancient projector and a bedsheet, she shows the film to help the children comprehend Our Lord's suffering.'

'Haven't Noémie and Mathéo comprehended enough suffering? In the camp, they saw men tethered to posts and beaten.'

'I can only ask your forgiveness and assure you that the film won't be shown again. I trust you're not regretting your decision to stay here. It's been a privilege for us to welcome you. I've been particularly pleased to see you at several of our offices. I know you're a mere observer, but I hope that they've brought some comfort.'

'Against all my expectations, yes,' Bella replied. 'Who wouldn't be moved by the singing? But it's more than that: there's a strength in such simple devotion.'

'Is that a polite way of saying simple-minded?'

'It might have been once, not any more.'

'We'll make a believer of you yet. Take note that I didn't say a Catholic!'

'Don't set your heart on it. I would never deny my Jewish heritage – except, of course, to the Nazis – but even as a girl in Salonica, I didn't feel drawn to it. I was the despair of my parents for honouring the Greek gods: Zeus, Hera and their fellow Olympians.'

'You believed in their divinity?' the Abbess asked, her brow furrowing.

'It wasn't so much that I believed in it as that I told myself I did. Whichever it was, they expressed a truth about the world that I didn't find in the Bible. I've never understood how any student of human nature – not only in these dark times, but at any time in history – could suppose that we're the creation of a single loving God.'

'Perhaps He has more faith in us than we have in ourselves . . . You're a painter.'

'How—'

'I'll come to that. Does your work always turn out the way you plan? Do you stick to a preconceived pattern or allow it to evolve?'

'I accept the metaphor but not the argument. The evidence is right here in front of you - or rather, behind you - in that *Massacre of the Innocents*. Throughout the Bible - the Jewish Bible - God inflicts floods and plagues and slaughters on both His own people and His enemies, but as I understand it - forgive me if I'm wrong - the birth of Jesus was meant to be the start of something new.'

'It was King Herod who ordered the Massacre.'

'But God was complicit. He sent His angel to warn Joseph to take his family to safety - at least according to Rubens. In another piece, he depicts them resting on the road to Egypt, while several angels look on.'

'I see why you have a reputation for irreverence.'

'You know more about me than I realised,' Bella replied. 'Not only my profession but my so-called reputation.'

'You told Sister Thérèse that you were Timarete.'

'But it was patently clear that she hadn't heard of me.'

'She hadn't, but I have. To be precise, of your pictures of the licentious rabbis. *Le Pelèrin* covered the controversy in detail. It must have been ten years ago.'

'Twelve . . . no, thirteen. I was trying to shine a light on religious hypocrisy. I thought it only right to do so within my own tradition. If I'd been Catholic, I'd have made them cardinals.'

'We've had a lucky escape,' the Abbess said, with a shudder. 'But I've been waiting for the opportunity to ask whether you'd paint something for us.'

'What? You mean a Last Supper for the refectory?'

'If you like. But there are other rooms. And other subjects. I was hoping for something from our joint tradition. Of course, it would require you to stay with us a while longer.'

'I reckon I can bear it,' Bella said with a smile. 'I don't know whether *Le Pelèrin* included illustrations. It's only fair to warn you that I have a distinctive style, which may not be to everyone's taste.'

'I have no doubt that you'll give us something splendid.'

Bella herself was beset by doubt, but she accepted the Abbess's proposal. The Nazis had taken so much from her – her family; her home; her name; her friends; her freedom – but they couldn't take her art. Nevertheless, there were serious obstacles to surmount before she could set to work, first and foremost being the lack of paint. So she prepared her pigments in the age-old way, using the materials to hand: chalk for white; charcoal for black; madder root for red. Ochre posed a particular problem. She scraped the rust from an iron grille but, however hard she ground, it remained lumpy. In the end, she replaced it with yellow, extracted from a clump of weld. She was equally resourceful in crafting brushes from various textures of hair – Noémie's, Sister Célestine's, and her own – which she attached to some of Sister Thérèse's plant stakes. Without linseed oil, she was forced to use tempura. Fortunately, the convent kept thirty hens, which were excellent layers, notwithstanding their Occupation diet.

To the unconcealed dismay of several sisters, the Abbess authorised Bella to paint the three empty bays in the chapter room. The subjects she chose were not only drawn from their joint tradition but also crossed cultural boundaries: Joseph interpreting Pharaoh's dream; the Moabite Ruth pledging loyalty to the Jewish Naomi; Solomon welcoming the Queen of Sheba to Jerusalem.

She started chronologically, with Joseph. With no paper for preliminary sketches, she outlined the composition directly on the wall, applying a yellow wash and filling in the figures in black. Working in tempura required speed, but she was so invigorated that she would have pressed ahead whatever the medium. Within four days, a youthful Joseph, his features and musculature delineated in white, stood boldly before a ceremoniously attired Pharaoh, framed by a frieze of seven lean and seven healthy cows.

Breaking the timeline, she turned next to Solomon's reception of the Queen of Sheba, ensuring that, unlike the many depictions of the scene where the King, either elevated or enthroned, dominated his guest, the two were given equal status. She was eager to emphasise the Queen's Ethiopian heritage, which, given the black-figure painting, had to be conveyed through her tribal robes and headdress. Five days later, amid fevered speculation from the sisters, who were banned from the room, she embarked on the painting of Ruth and Naomi. Depicting their asexual intimacy presented a challenge, and she abandoned her initial image of the two women comforting each other at Mahlon's death for one of them dancing together at the celebration of Ruth's remarriage. She was busy rendering Naomi's smile when she heard a hammering at the convent door.

Panicked by the thuds and shouts that followed, she scanned the room. The lattice windows were too narrow for escape and the only door led to a corridor, now resounding with barked commands. She heard the Abbess, summoned from her office, remonstrating with the intruders. As they drew closer, their exchange grew clear.

'We've received information that, in defiance of the Occupying Authorities, you're harbouring Jews on the premises,' said a man whose accent marked him out as French.

'What nonsense! Why on earth would I shelter the murderers of Our Lord Jesus Christ?' the Abbess replied.

Bella wondered who might have informed on them, since the only visitor during her entire month's stay had been the village priest, who came every morning to say mass. Her conjecture was cut short by armed Milice men herding the sisters into the room.

'Who's this?' their leader asked, pointing at Bella.

'Sister Laure is the convent artist,' the Abbess replied.

The man glanced at the paintings and snorted. 'Why's she dressed different?'

'To avoid soiling my habit,' Bella said, without conviction.

The leader instructed the Abbess to provide identity papers for each nun, and Bella prayed that she might evade detection in the gap between baptismal and religious names. The Abbess asked Sister Juliette, the mistress of novices, to fetch the documents, just as two Milice men ushered in Sister Augusta, Sister Angélique and the children, some looking scared and others bewildered, while the blond, blue-eyed Pierrot, with far less to fear than most, whimpered.

Bella willed Noémie and Mathéo to ignore her, but as soon as she spotted her, Noémie ran forward. Mathéo, not to be outdone, followed, shouting: 'Bella! Bella!'

'That's not the name you used,' the leader said to the Abbess.

'It means beautiful in Italian,' Bella interjected. 'You don't have to agree.' She forced a laugh.

'So you're Italian?'

'No,' she replied, mindful that, since their country's defeat, it was almost as dangerous for the convent to harbour Italians as Jews.

'What about them?' he asked, indicating the children.

'They're French.'

'Why are they clinging to you?'

'They're brother and sister. I've cared for them since their parents were killed.'

'Jews?'

'No,' she said, fighting back her scorn. 'In a fire.'

The Milice leader hovered over Noémie. 'How old are you, little one?'

'Eight,' she replied, looking at her feet.

'Then you must know your catechism.'

She shook her head.

'Of course she does,' the Abbess said. 'But she's too terrified to speak.'

'Go and stand by the door!' He signalled to one of his men, who wrenched the resisting child from Bella's arms.

'I must protest,' the Abbess said.

Turning his back on her, the man addressed Mathéo. 'What about you, my lad? Can you say your catechism, like a good Catholic?'

'He hasn't learnt it yet,' the Abbess said. 'He's five.'

'I'm six,' Mathéo said truculently.

'Well then, a big boy like you must know the Lord's Prayer. The special prayer that Jesus taught us. The most important prayer of all.'

Bella watched as Mathéo's eyes took on a determined glint. Or was that just her imagination?

'Come on,' the man said. 'Pray!'

'*Shema Yisrael Adonai Eloheinu Adonai Echad.*'

'Jew! I could smell it. Take them away!'

A second Milice man grabbed Mathéo, who wriggled and kicked. Several of the children screamed, in defiance of Sister Augusta's calls for quiet.

'This is wrong,' the Abbess said. 'They're children. What harm can they do?'

'They grow,' the Milice leader replied. 'Like weeds.'

Bella glanced at her unfinished painting. Ruth left her homeland for the sake of her mother-in-law. How much more should she do for two motherless children!

'Then you must take me too. They're my children.' She approached the man holding Mathéo. Shocked by her temerity, he released the boy, who fell sobbing into her arms. She hugged him, while leaning forward to clasp Noémie's hand. Affecting a broad smile, she turned back to the Abbess. 'Forgive me, Mother, I lied when I swore on the Bible that we were baptised. But rest assured, there was no sacrilege. I made certain that it was on the Jewish part.'

8

MADELEINE

PARIS, AUGUST 1944

TOO BULKY TO straddle a bicycle and too weary to walk, Madeleine resigned herself to taking the metro. In recent weeks, the timetable had been reduced and the passengers crammed in like cattle. On leaving work this evening, she arrived at Saint-Augustin to find the station itself closed. The city teetered on the verge of collapse, although it was hard to obtain accurate information without access to a wireless. She relied on Madame Chambert, who, tuning in to the BBC, reported that Allied troops had landed in Normandy and were rapidly advancing towards Paris. While too soon to hang out the bunting, it felt as if the Occupation were in its last gasp.

She had defied both Ruben's appeals and Madame Fabron's objections and carried on working, albeit confined to the storeroom, where her condition would not, in the latter's words, 'offend the customers'. Not that there were many left to offend. The officers and officials who'd opened accounts at the store were returning to Germany, while the collaborators and black marketeers, who'd plucked thousand-franc notes from wads of illicit cash, were lying low, doubtless rehearsing their alibis. The day would come when every Parisian who'd consorted with the enemy would be held to account. By way of reminder, the baby delivered her a sharp kick.

She lumbered slowly to the tram stop, which was as thronged as a bakery at dawn. Wary of the crush, she proceeded on foot towards Les Halles, where food supplies were so low that, even at the inflated prices Ruben was prepared to pay, she procured nothing but a loaf of potato bread, an overripe camembert, and a jar of meatless pâté which a soft-hearted profiteer produced from his reserve because 'the baby must be hungry too'. With aching calves and ankles, she crossed the river and headed down the Boulevard Saint-Michel to the Rue Racine. A stranger to the Left Bank when she'd moved into the Quai Montebello eighteen months before, she had soon grown to love it – and nothing so much as the view of Notre Dame that greeted her when she opened the shutters each morning. But they had been forced to flee the apartment after the concierge received a letter denouncing Ruben.

She entered the courtyard of their new block, only to be accosted by Bastien Chambert. In a world sullied by Nazi caricatures, she was loath to judge by appearances, but if ever a face betrayed character, it was Bastien's. Gaunt, sallow and pockmarked, he was the pettiest of criminals, peddling stolen goods, running errands for racketeers, distributing handbills for brothels – scorned as much by those he flattered as those he threatened.

'You'll wear yourself out shopping in your condition,' he said, eyeing her bags. 'I've told you before: anything you need, just ask Bastien. Special rates for friends.'

'Then I'll expect to pay full price.' She attempted to squeeze past him. 'Excuse me. As you so gallantly observed, I'm tired.'

'You shouldn't insult me. With the Americans on their way, you and your Jewish pals think you're safe. But I have it from an impeccable source that von Choltitz has a secret plan to take all the Jews hiding in the city . . . smoke them out like rats and space them round factories and airfields, so they'll bear the brunt of any stray bombs. And I could tell them where one Jew is hiding . . . oh yes, I could.'

'Let me through!' Pushing him aside, Madeleine hurried into the building and up the first flight of stairs, pausing on the half-landing to catch her breath, before plodding up the remaining four. Nothing - not hunger, not fetor, not fatigue - could induce nausea as surely as a brief exchange with Bastien. She didn't take his threats to heart. As Madam Chambert had pledged: 'I may be his mother, but he knows that if he utters one word against Monsieur Ruben, I'll report him for forging his medical exemption from the Forced Labour Service. Still, he's my son and the only one I've got.'

A sense of dread engulfed Madeleine and she clutched her stomach. How could such a good woman have spawned such an odious son? Like her own father, Monsieur Chambert had been killed at Ypres, but whereas her mother had turned against all of France's 'invaders' and railed at her daughter for living with a Jew, Madam Chambert reserved her hatred for the real enemies. Although her husband had been shot by a German cannon, she insisted that she would be as vehemently anti-Nazi if he'd been run over by a Peugeot.

Madeleine shuddered to think how they would have managed without her during the past few months. She'd pulled Ruben's rotten tooth in the spring, when the only available dental tools were pliers and brandy. With the aid of another bottle, she'd distracted two gendarmes during the building's solitary raid, enabling Ruben to escape down the service stairs. She had shown herself a true friend, looking in on him every day while she was at work. For all his complaints about her prattle, he admitted when pressed that he would miss her if she stayed away. Moreover, unlike his former concierge in the Quai Montebello or his mother's in the Rue des Martyrs, she refused to accept a centime.

Madeleine rapped three times on the apartment door, which Ruben swiftly unlocked.

'You're late. Where have you been? I was worried sick,' he said, wrapping her in his arms.

As he rummaged through her bags, she explained about the metro closure and her trudge to the market. 'It's a meat day, but there was no meat to be had anywhere. I managed to get us a mushroom pâté. And the man only let me have that because of the bump. If

I'd known, I'd have stuffed a pillow down my skirt last year.' She gave a short laugh, which he ignored.

'What about the books? I don't see any.'

'Monsieur Benoit wasn't there.'

'So why didn't you try elsewhere? God knows how many stalls there are on the quay!'

'I was frightened.'

'Of the bouquinistes? They're not informers. Butchers perhaps ... bakers, grocers, haberdashers, pharmacists, furriers perhaps ... silk sellers, definitely. But not bouquinistes. Or what hope would there be for the world?'

She didn't like to admit that, for once, her fears had been less of betraying him than of betraying her own ignorance as she ran through his reading list and the bouquinistes, who saw themselves as mentors as much as merchants, asked her opinion of earlier volumes in the *Jean-Christophe* sequence or novels by Balzac and Dumas that hadn't been made into films.

'How can you be so unfeeling? Do you have any idea what it's like for me, holed up in here day after day? I watch the clock and wonder whether the minute hand has moved. I watch a spider crawl across the floor and make a bet with myself how long it will take to reach the table or chair, and then crush it. I smoke my regulation one and a half cigarettes – you do know that my father owned a tobacco factory? Sometimes I think I should smoke my entire month's ration and then slit my throat.'

'I'm sorry,' she said, glancing instinctively at the bread knife. 'I promise I'll go back there tomorrow.'

'Why bother? I should give myself up to the Germans ... no, I should buy a gun and shoot at least one of the bastards before shooting myself. Just one and I'd have finally justified my worthless existence! You'd grieve for a while, but you'd get over it. You and the child will be far better off without me.'

'Darling, please, I can't listen to this right now! I'm exhausted.'

'Whose fault is that? I've begged you to stop working, especially for those crooks. It was madness even before you fell pregnant.'

Painful though it was to admit, she knew that the true madness would be to spend all day alone with him. She loved him (she had never needed to remind herself of it before), but it was increasingly hard to be with him. He had been living on his nerves for the past four years, first in the army, then in the prisoner-of-war camp and now in hiding. His world had steadily shrunk, until it was just these two small rooms, freezing cold in winter and stifling in summer. With the hunt for Jews – and the fears for their fate – intensifying, he'd not set foot outside since his mother's funeral in June the previous year.

She had died of pleurisy after six weeks in the Rothschild Hospital, the only one in Paris still treating Jews. Many of the patients were transferred from the detention camp at Drancy, while others, who entered of their own accord, were moved there at the first sign of recovery. Several were women in labour, and a nurse who befriended Madeleine confided that the high rate of stillbirths was due to babies being registered as dead and smuggled out through the neighbouring convent to prevent their falling into German hands.

'And the mothers?' Madeleine asked.

'They're just happy to know that their babies are safe.'

With armed guards stationed at the gates and patrolling the corridors, Ruben had accepted that it was too dangerous for him to visit and asked Madeleine to go in his stead. She readily agreed, but doubted that his mother would welcome the substitution. It had taken the Occupation for Ruben to introduce them and, after two years, Madame Carrache remained reserved. Ruben claimed that she was nervous, but Madeleine knew she disapproved of his living with a Catholic shop assistant, rather than one of the eligible Sephardim to whom, even in the midst of the Nazi persecution, she sought to match him.

On her first visit to the hospital, a guard detained her for questioning. Ruben had concocted an elaborate cover story in which she was his mother's maid who, in the absence of any living relative, had assumed responsibility for her former mistress. While saddened by the ease with which he had assigned her to domestic service, she played her allotted role. The official in charge, openly scornful of her misplaced loyalty, checked his list and confirmed, 'The patient Carrache is permitted a short weekly visit.'

Madeleine, expressly forbidden to venture beyond the ground floor, waited in the cluttered parlour which, despite the sunshine, felt cold and drab, the heavy bars on the grimy windows blocking out the light. She was shocked when, supported by an orderly, Madame Carrache shuffled into the room and sank into a chair, struggling for breath. After two years of persistent ailments, she had been dealt a crippling blow by the death of her old dressmaker, Madame Naar, severing one of her last ties to Salonica. Since then, she'd suffered acute chest pains, aggravated by a hacking cough. When the risks of her remaining at home outweighed all others, Maryam, at Ruben's behest, had brought her to the hospital. So far, her stay appeared to have been of little benefit, and Madeleine felt guilty for dragging her out of her bed. But as they clasped hands, her eyes glistened with tears, and in short tussive bursts she thanked her for coming.

'I owe you an apology.'

'For what?' Madeleine asked, flushed with embarrassment. 'Really, there's no need.'

'Yes . . . yes, there is. This may be my last chance to talk to you.'

'I'll come again next week.'

'To talk to anyone.' Gasping, she mustered her strength. 'When Ruben first told me he wanted to marry you, I admit I was angry: angry that he'd waited until his father was dead and he couldn't object . . . angry that he'd waited until the Germans were here and I couldn't object. But believe me . . . please believe me, I don't object any more. And I don't think Jacob would either. He'd—'

Her words were drowned in a fit of coughing.

'Would you please fetch Madame a glass of water?' Madeleine asked the orderly.

'It's not my job,' he replied, barely looking up from *Je Suis Partout*.

'I'm fine, really,' Madame Carrache said, grabbing Madeleine's hand to stop her protesting. 'Tell me about Ruben. Tell me about my boy.'

With a glance at the orderly, Madeleine assured her that he was well and described their trips to the Salle Pleyel to hear Alfred Cortot play Beethoven, which she'd found hard going, and the Opéra Comique to see Bizet's *Pêcheurs de Perles*, which she'd enjoyed far more. They continued their weekly cinema trips, most recently to see Michel Simon in *Au Bonheur des Dames*, which she'd loved, although Ruben objected to the liberties they'd taken with the novel, one of the many classics he'd been reading. He joked mordantly that, if nothing else, Hitler had allowed him to fill the gaps in his education.

She visited Madame Carrache on six successive Sundays, their conversation constrained less by the presence of the orderlies than by her increasing frailty. At times, every word she spoke seemed to scrape against her chest, which she pressed as though to hold back the pain. To spare her, Madeleine chattered away, passing on messages that Ruben had fabricated from his brother and sisters, which would never now be challenged.

'Such dear children,' his mother said distantly. 'I've been blessed with such dear children. And how's Maman?' she asked, catching her unawares.

'She's well,' she replied, flustered. To the best of her knowledge, Ruben's grandmother had been dead for twenty years. 'Though she's missing you.'

'No, your maman,' Madame Carrache said, with a chuckle which turned into a yelp.

'She's well too, I think,' Madeleine said, loath to admit the estrangement of which Ruben was the cause.

'Treasure her. You must treasure her. You only have one maman and—'

She succumbed to a prolonged fit of coughing, at which the orderly, looking more disgusted than concerned, summoned a colleague to help him take her back to the ward. The last Madeleine heard of her was a muffled howl as they hauled her up the stairs. The following Wednesday, the hospital rang her at the store (the only telephone number it had been safe to give), to say that she had died. Praying Jeannette hadn't overheard, she told Monsieur Fabron that it was her grandmother who had died. To his wife's visible annoyance, he gave her three days' compassionate leave.

She hurried home to break the news to Ruben, whose anguished 'No, no, no!' made her regret having shielded him from his mother's rapid decline. All the rage he had reined in for months – years – spilt out as he swept the crockery from the table and the pots from the rack. With wild eyes, he seized the wireless from the bread basket and hurled it against the wall. She pleaded with him to stop since, for all her anxiety each time he tuned into Radio London, she knew how much he depended on it. The outburst appeared to drain him and, after clearing the worst of the mess, she called Madame Chambert to sit with him, while she went to the hospital to inquire about the funeral.

Ruben wanted to keep vigil over his mother's body, and Madeleine suspected that, alone, she would have been unable to deter him. But Madame Chambert, older, more detached and a mother herself – though neither a contented nor a proud one – persuaded him that it would be the height of folly to risk his freedom by asserting a relationship which for months he'd striven to conceal.

'Do you call this freedom?' he asked, indicating the room.

'Yes, yes I do. And so would you if you were sent to Drancy.'

Armed with Ruben's instructions and a wallet full of cash, Madeleine headed to the hospital, where the superintendent outlined the authorised procedure, from which no deviation would be tolerated. A rabbi from the Ottoman synagogue in the Rue Popincourt would conduct a short service for a maximum of six mourners, after which the deceased would be buried in the adjacent Picpus cemetery. Madeleine returned home to report the ruling to Ruben, who blamed her for not insisting that his mother be interred beside his father in Montparnasse. She resisted telling him that it was only because she'd paid an extortionate fee that his mother had been allocated an individual plot. The common practice was for a communal grave.

Not even Madame Chambert could deter Ruben from attending the funeral. In a bizarre twist, his alias needed an alias, since the presence of the Catholic Jean-Marc Renaud at the depleted ceremony would have aroused suspicion. So, the following morning, he set out for the Rue des Saintes Pères to obtain an identity card in the name of a Jew (which the forger declared was a first), while she went to La Samaritaine to buy a scrap of yellow cloth. Sickened at propagating the stigma, she bungled the star. As ever, Madame Chambert came to the rescue. 'The thing to remember is that you're tricking the Boche twice over,' she said, deftly turning the handwheel on her ancient Singer.

Two days later, Madeleine and Ruben, now the tailor Elie Shalem, left home together, only to part on the Odéon platform, where she entered the second carriage and he the fifth. On their arrival at the hospital, a sluggish guard ushered them across the courtyard to an unfamiliar block. They were met by four grizzled men in shabby suits, who introduced themselves as the Chevra Kadisha, their attendance all the more valiant after their colleagues had been arrested at Madame Naar's funeral. Ruben shook hands with each in turn, his listless eyes misting over as they assured him that, despite the restrictions, they had been able to perform *taharah*. They entered the chapel, its ornate decoration in stark contrast to the crate-like coffin at the centre. She feared that its roughness would offend Ruben, but his gaze was drawn to a middle-aged man sitting beside it. He strode up and hugged him so warmly that she took him for his brother Leon, who had somehow made his way to Paris, but, after repeated embraces, he called her over and introduced her to his father's cousin Nissim.

'I'd no idea you were still in the city,' Ruben said to him. 'How did you hear about Maman?'

'From a doctor at the hospital. He recognised the name. Luna died here last year.'

'Luna died? I didn't know that. How didn't I know?'

'How can we know anything any more?'

'Luna died? I'm so sorry. She was a good woman.'

'It was a blessing,' Nissim said curtly, without clarifying whether that was on account of her own suffering or the world's.

After a further embrace, Ruben turned to his mother's coffin, bending to kiss it, before standing in silence to reflect, revere and perhaps even to pray.

The stillness of the chapel was punctuated by clomping as Maryam entered, her legs more bloated than ever. When she'd told her of Madame Carrache's death, Madeleine had urged her to mourn in private, avoiding the risk and strain of the funeral. Witnessing Ruben's joy on seeing her, she was grateful that she'd ignored her advice. They had barely exchanged greetings when the rabbi arrived. Looking relieved at the sparse attendance, he shook hands with Ruben and Nissim and, after a brief word of welcome, launched into a series of prayers or readings, of which all she could follow were the Amens. Addressing the two men, he asked whether either wished to pay tribute to the deceased. In a faltering voice, Ruben who, as far as she knew, had nothing prepared, faced the handful of mourners and declared that having such a gracious, loving and compassionate mother had been the greatest blessing of his life.

'She always put other people first: my father; her parents; her sister; her children, even when – at least in my case – we didn't deserve it. One memory must stand for so many. In Salonica, as Maryam will confirm, my brother, my sisters and I looked forward to her birthday almost as much as our own: not, as would have been fitting, to honour her, but because she gave us all presents – far more exciting ones than the soap and scent and scarves we gave her. "Why?" you may well ask. "Because," she said, "seeing my children happy is the best present I can ever have."'

The rabbi, looking anxiously at his watch, said a final prayer. At his signal, the four members of the Chevra Kadisha, whose presence had doubled the congregation, approached the coffin and, hoisting it onto their scrawny shoulders, carried it out of the building, across the grounds, and into the cemetery. Madeleine walked alone, behind Ruben and Nissim, who supported Maryam as they made their way past neat rows of tombstones, to a patch of grass where, alongside several recent mounds, a grave lay open. The Chevra Kadisha lowered the coffin on makeshift ropes, drawing back as the rabbi spoke a short prayer, before inviting Ruben to throw a clod of earth into the grave. He was followed first by Nissim, then Madeleine, and finally Maryam, who tottered perilously close to the edge.

After shaking hands again with Ruben, the rabbi turned to leave.

'What about the Kaddish?' Ruben asked.

'We have no minyan,' the rabbi replied.

'We must still say it.'

'I'm sorry, but it's forbidden under Halakha.'

'This is my mother!'

'*Yitgadal v'yitkadash sh'mei raba . . .*' Nissim's voice resounded through the cemetery. While the rabbi looked shocked, Ruben and three of the Chevra Kadisha joined in. At the end of the prayer, Ruben grasped his cousin's hand in wordless thanks.

'That was not appropriate,' the rabbi said, 'but then who's to say what is any more?'

He left the graveside, followed by the Chevra Kadisha. The others trekked back to the cemetery gate, where Maryam's knees buckled and she slid, almost gracefully, to the ground.

'You should have buried me with the Señora,' she said to Ruben, as he and Nissim struggled to raise her to her feet. 'I'm not worth a nail any more.'

'You're worth a good deal more than that to me,' he replied. 'And to Leon and Bella and Esther and Irène. The Boche are losing the war. Soon, we'll all be together again.'

'You must always be there for one another. That's what the Señora would have wished. "They may bicker and fight, Maryam," she'd tell me, "but it isn't serious. Even Ruben and Bella."'

Although she insisted she was only suffering from cramp, it was clear that she could no longer walk unaided. Madeleine felt impelled to articulate what the men were surely thinking. 'I hadn't wanted you to come today, Maryam, but I'm doubly glad you have. You're not well. You're in the right place here.'

'What?' Ruben exclaimed.

'Not *here* here,' Madeleine said. 'The hospital! She can scarcely move. How can she . . . how can you fend for yourself?'

'I'll manage,' Maryam said. 'If I go in there, I'll never come out.'

'Madeleine's right,' Ruben said. 'I wish more than anything that you could come back with us, but it isn't safe. You must be sensible.'

'Oh, that's too much to ask of an old goose like me,' Maryam said, as the men half carried, half dragged her back to the hospital. Madeleine offered to wait with her while she was examined, but the guard forbade it. So with a heavy heart, she left, promising to visit her very soon. She walked back to Daumesnil station with Ruben and Nissim, where, once again, she and Ruben were to occupy different carriages, while Nissim was to take a different line.

'Since you're heading east, I presume you're not in Passy,' Ruben said. 'Where are you living now?'

'I'd rather not . . . it's better not to say,' Nissim replied. 'Nor to know,' he added, in case Ruben were about to confide their address. 'But we'll meet when all this is over.' He kissed Madeleine fondly. 'Take good care of him.'

'I promise.'

They returned to the apartment, where Ruben tore off his yellow star so violently that he pulled stitches in his coat. She boiled some cabbage soup, but, despite years of shortages, he claimed to have no appetite.

'I was the only one . . . the only one of us five to be here . . . for all I know, the only one of us still alive,' he cried, as she cradled his head. 'And what good was I? I couldn't give her a dignified funeral. I couldn't bury her beside my father. We couldn't even say a proper Kaddish.'

'I thought you no longer believed in all that.'

'I believe in the tradition; I believe in the respect.'

His mother's death, amid the mounting cycle of arrests and disappearances, cast Ruben into despair. He refused to go out to a film or concert. He abandoned his evening walks, even through the mazy streets of the sixth. As the months passed, Madame Chambert urged Madeleine to take heart, reporting that the Germans were being pushed back on all fronts and would soon be driven out of France. But she saw little sign of defeat either on the faces of the Wehrmacht officers who patronised the store, or the posters of executed Resistance fighters pasted on the *colonnes Morris*.

Then one morning, as she was preparing to leave for work, there was an unexpected rap on the door.

'*Aufmachen!*'

'*Einen Moment, bitte*,' she replied, fighting to keep the panic from her voice. 'I'm just putting on my skirt.' She shoved the breakfast crockery into the sink, while Ruben bundled himself into the false chimney breast. With the panel slotted into place, she opened the door to find Helmut.

'You!'

'Who did you think it was? The Gestapo?'

'What do you want?'

'Aren't you going to invite me in?'

It was three months since she'd told him that she was pregnant: three months since he'd vanished from her life. While Madame Fabron upbraided her for driving away one of their best customers, she felt only relief to know that, whatever else might occur, she had escaped his clutches. Now, he was not only back, but in her bedroom, which she hadn't had time to secure.

'I see you wear men's pyjamas,' he said coldly.

'They're more practical. My nightdress is worn to a thread.'

'You should have told me. I'd have bought you something silky from the store. You could have shown me how it clung.'

It was plain that he knew Ruben was hiding and intended him to hear. This was what she had dreaded ever since he read the address on the denunciation letter. 'Let's go outside,' she said. 'The apartment is a shambles. If I'd known you were coming, I'd have tidied it.'

'You must be heading to the metro. We can go together.'

'No, it's my day off,' she said, impulsively.

'What luck! I'll take you for coffee.'

'I need some air,' she replied. If Madame Chambert were right about the imminent rout, this was no time to be seen fraternising with a Nazi. 'The Luxembourg Gardens are just across the road.'

She slammed the door twice for emphasis, fearing the conversation she would have with Ruben on her return almost as much as the one she was now to have with Helmut. But he remained tight-lipped as they entered the gardens and walked to the Medici Fountain.

'Disgraceful!' he said, gazing at the basin, choked with debris. 'Do you French have no pride?'

'What is it you want with me?' she asked, her nerves fraying.

'Is all going well with the . . . ?'

'Pregnancy? Yes, the baby's making its presence felt.'

'May I touch?'

'No!' She recoiled. 'You still haven't told me why you've come.'

'I had to see you.'

'Strange. That urge seemed to fade the moment I told you I was having your child.'

'Oh, the urge remained, just not the courage. But now that I'm returning home . . .'

'What?'

'We all are. Those of us who can. It's not yet official, but the Americans will be here in a matter of days.'

'So she was right!' Madeleine murmured.

'But I couldn't leave without saying goodbye. You are Paris for me.'

'Occupied and exploited? Tyrannised?'

'Must you?'

'Raped?'

'You can say that all you like, but your body didn't lie. Your lips . . . your heat . . . your juices.'

'If you're leaving, leave!' She turned towards a clump of trees. 'Thank you for letting me know. Now leave.'

'Wait!' He grabbed her wrist. 'We may never meet again.'

'You're not Charles Boyer and I'm not . . . not anyone,' she said, shaking him off.

'But you're carrying my child.'

'It's Ruben's child. He wants him. He'll care for him. He'll make a wonderful father. Can you bear that? A Jew raising your child.'

'Yes. Perhaps I shouldn't. But the child is still mine. Pure Aryan. If I believe in anything, it's the power of blood.'

'Even as your army is in abject retreat?'

'What if he asks about me?'

'He never will. He'll never know. And why *he*? It may be *she* . . . my daughter, Ruben's daughter.'

'I've always wanted a girl. My two sons . . . two scamps: it's been so long; will they even know me?'

'Will they know you for what you are? Will your wife know you for what you are?'

'You remind me of her so much.'

'So you've said. Repeatedly. I used to think it was to ease your conscience: I was so like her that you were barely betraying her. Until I realised that you have no conscience. So I decided it was to ease mine. To convince me that I wasn't taking her place so much as keeping it warm.'

'I have a present for the child. You don't need to tell him . . . or her . . . or Ruben, who it's from. I'd just like him to have something – a token – from me. Surely you won't deny me that?'

He handed her a small, unwrapped box containing an antique silver rattle. After a moment's enchantment, she pictured the two . . . three . . . four generations of the family from whom it had been pillaged.

'It's beautiful,' she said, flinging it into the basin.

'You heartless bitch!'

She hurried away, leaving him poised over the edge, trying to retrieve it.

She was determined to consign him to oblivion, but her memories proved too strong, drawing her back to their first meeting in Tissus de Lyon. Helmut had come to purchase a length of silk for his wife's evening dress. He had no idea of a pattern, other than 'something feminine', or of her style, since 'she looks good in everything'. After enthusing over each roll she showed him, he was no closer to deciding. Eventually, he asked which one she would choose.

'Oh, they're far too expensive for me, Monsieur,' she said, in the fawning tone Madame Fabron had ordained.

'But what if your boyfriend were to buy one for you?'

'I don't have a boyfriend,' she said sharply.

'Your husband then?'

'I'm not married.'

'So you're keeping your options open?'

'I could say the same for Monsieur,' she said, more pertly than she'd intended. 'Or have you found one you like?'

After further dithering, he picked a red and black organza print, which, being a Timarete design, was one of her favourites.

He returned the following week. Jeannette went to assist him, only to stalk back to the counter, where Madeleine was folding scarves. 'He wants you,' she said, with the contempt she reserved for men who were 'seduced by a pretty face'.

'Greetings, Mademoiselle,' he said, lifting her hand to his lips, which made her squirm. 'You may remember serving me last week.'

'You must forgive me, Monsieur. We have so many customers, it's hard to keep track.'

He glanced around the empty shop and smiled. 'I bought a piece of silk to send home to my wife.'

'I trust she was pleased with it.'

'I haven't heard yet. The French post is primitive. I'd like to get her something else. I don't know ... what about one of those scarves I watched you arranging.'

'Yes, of course. Do come with me.' She led him through the store. 'How would you describe her colouring?'

'Aryan. Blonde hair, blue eyes. Just like you.'

'Then maybe something in mint or lavender to complement her complexion,' she said, quickening her pace. 'Or else emerald or sapphire, by way of contrast.'

'Which would tempt you?'

'I never wear scarves.'

'Shall I show you her picture?' Without waiting for a reply, he took a small, overexposed photograph from his wallet.

'She's very attractive.'

'Are you fishing for compliments?'

'What?'

'You might be twins.'

Even if there were a resemblance, Madeleine knew that it would be superficial. A German official's wife wouldn't wear a turban because her hair was dirty and brittle. She wouldn't wash herself at a sink because there was no hot water for a bath or stand all day in shoes soled with cork or wood. She wouldn't return home each evening to a man who kept a packed bag by the bed ready for a swift escape. No, she would sport silk dresses and scarves from an expropriated store in a subjugated city.

He took even longer to select the scarf than the fabric, asking her to model several, while he adjusted the knots at her neck.

'Is everything to your satisfaction, Monsieur?' Madame Fabron asked as she approached.

'Perfectly. Mademoiselle has been most helpful.'

'If there's anything else we can do for you, just let us know,' she said, stepping back deferentially.

'There's nothing at all you could do for me, you old hag,' he whispered to Madeleine, who refused to collude in his mockery. 'But you, Mademoiselle, could join me for a drink after work.'

'I'm forbidden to meet customers outside the store.'

'Helmut,' he said, holding out his hand. 'There! Now I'm more than a customer.'

'Have you decided on a scarf? I've shown you almost our entire range.'

'Just one drink. You've no idea how lonely it is for a foreigner . . . how one longs for female company.'

'I understand that there are brothels catering exclusively to Germans.'

'Madame!' He summoned Madame Fabron, who scuttled over. 'Do you allow your staff to insult your customers?'

'Never. Not at all. What have you said, Madeleine? Apologise at once!'

'I simply explained that Monsieur Fabron wouldn't approve of me meeting a customer outside of work. He wouldn't wish the store to gain a reputation.'

'My husband is very strict, that's true. But I'm sure he'd make an exception.'

'There's no need, Madame,' Helmut said, scooping up a Dufy design of oak leaves almost at random. 'I'll take this one.' He paid for the scarf and left without giving Madeleine a second glance.

Exiled to the storeroom for the remainder of the afternoon, she left for home on the dot of seven. Turning into the Rue d'Anjou, she came face to face with a group from the Parti Populaire Français, the right-wing rabble with whom Bastien Chambert had allied himself, waving placards and chanting their slogan of 'Unity, Force and Honour!' She was gripped by panic as several broke ranks to jostle and taunt her. 'Don't worry! I'm right beside you.' A steady hand on the small of her back guided her through the mob, but, as she reached the Rue de Penthièvre, she realised that she had exchanged one peril for another.

'Thank you. I'm most grateful. I must just . . . What are you doing here? Were you waiting for me?'

'Of course not.' He held up the bag containing the scarf. 'I was bringing it back to change for the one with the tennis players.' She felt mildly reassured. 'But I insist on seeing you home. No arguments! There may be more demonstrators. Whatever you think, we Germans are gentlemen.'

Horrified at the prospect of his knowing her address, she told him that she lived with her mother in Belleville. He cleared a path for her on the station platform and claimed the only free seat in the carriage, although she would have preferred to stand. As he swayed on the hand strap above her, she steeled herself to ask the question that was haunting her.

'Are you Gestapo?'

'What?' He laughed. 'Do I look like . . . ? I'm hurt that you should even suppose . . . I'm a eugenicist.'

'A what?'

'The Deputy Director of the Institute for the Study of Jewish and Ethno-Racial Questions. Sorry it's such a mouthful! I was seconded here from Berlin three years ago to work with my chief, George Montandon, on the great exhibition of *The Jew and France*. Perhaps you saw it?'

'No!' She bit her tongue.

They arrived at Belleville, where she begged him not to escort her to her door, to avoid her mother's censure. She wandered the streets for twenty minutes, worried that he might have seen through her subterfuge, before taking a roundabout route to Goncourt for the journey home. Ruben greeted her with a barrage of reproaches, no less severe than those she had imputed to her mother.

'I worry all day long about what you're doing . . . who you're seeing. I know none of this is fair on you. I'm nothing but a dead weight. I couldn't blame you if you took a lover . . . but I couldn't forgive you either.'

'I have no lover but you. I want no lover but you. You have to trust me.' She clasped his hand between hers. 'Monsieur Fabron kept me back to change the window displays.'

'This is what the Nazis have done to me. They've made me someone else – not just a non-person but a cynical one . . . a jealous one. I'm Swann . . . ridiculous, self-deluding Swann.'

Returning from work the following evening, Madeleine made a detour to the Quai Montebello. She knew that it was a risk, but, on her last visit, there had been four letters of denunciation pinned to the door of their former apartment, and the concierge, impervious to both her hefty bribes and her assurances that the letters were not official, refused to tear down any others that might appear. She crept up the stairs, anxious not to alert the neighbours, only to find that her fears were well-founded.

No sooner had she approached the offending envelopes than Helmut bounded onto the landing.

'I thought it was you.'

'No! What are you doing here? Did you follow me?'

'I miss my wife. I miss her so much.'

'I'm not your wife!'

'What are *you* doing here?'

'It's my friend's apartment. I offered to water her plants while she's visiting her parents.'

'I'll help you,' he said, wedging himself between her and the door. 'Look, there's a letter for Monsieur Ruben Carrache. No, I tell a lie. It's about Monsieur Ruben Carrache.'

'Give that to me!'

'Why? It can't be your friend. You said *she*. But then Madame Fabron told me a different story. You may have refused to have a drink with me, but she was delighted to accept. It's remarkable how much someone will let slip after a couple of glasses of Cointreau.'

'What do you want from me?'

'This one looks more formal.' He plucked the second envelope off the door. 'Shall we open it?'

'No,' she replied dully.

'*To whom it may concern* . . . well, I'm concerned even if you're not.' He started to read. '"I know that it's the patriotic duty of every French citizen" – citizen is good, so we don't know whether it's a he-citizen or a she-citizen – "to report the whereabouts of Jews. The Jew Carrache who was domiciled at this address is now living at

4 Rue Racine, with his French whore, Madeleine Dubois . . ." Oh, that's not very polite! I thought you such a clean-living girl. "She should be questioned." On balance, I'd say that was a she-citizen, wouldn't you?'

'What do you want of me?'

'Who said I want anything? But surely, as a patriotic French citizen, it's your duty to find out whether this information is true? You know Paris so much better than I do. How far is the Rue Racine from here?'

'You told me that you weren't the Gestapo.'

'I'm not. But as a patriotic citizen of the Reich, I have my connections. Well-established connections. One word from me to my friends in the Avenue Foch and they'd descend upon – did you catch the address? – like a pack of wolves.'

'What do you want of me?'

'I want you! You're a beautiful Aryan woman.'

'I'm not Aryan; I'm French!'

'Why do you refuse to take pride in your race? Why do you debase yourself with a Jew?'

'And you're an honourable German man. Why do you debase yourself by hounding a woman who wants nothing to do with you?'

'There are forces more powerful than honour. Besides, I shall be purging you of your malady.'

He smiled like a doctor administering an injection. Would a eugenicist – an exhibition curator – have friends in the Gestapo? Could she afford to doubt it? In a film, this would be when Jean Gabin or Gary Cooper rushed to her rescue. But it was the real world, and Ruben's freedom – his life even – was at stake.

'And if I agree, you'll leave us alone?' she asked, staring at the floor. 'You'll forget him; you'll forget me.'

'There are forces more powerful than memory.'

'You swear?'

'I swear.'

'On your mother's life? No! On the Hitler oath?'

'I swear.'

'Then so be it.'

They walked through the musty, deserted apartment to the bedroom, which Ruben had deliberately left in disarray. As she gazed at the unmade bed, in which she had once known such joy, tears welled in her eyes.

'Your snivelling fools no one, Mademoiselle,' Helmut said, undressing as mechanically as in a barracks. She had no choice but to follow suit. She felt a trickle of shame as she glimpsed her shrunken breasts and bony hips in the glass, followed by a surge of scorn for her vanity and a perverse gratitude for the privations that had rendered her less desirable. He pulled her towards him, sealing his lips to hers and sliding his tongue into her mouth. He caressed her face and neck, breasts and belly. She attempted to detach herself from her body, looking down at the alien figure on the bed, but she remained trapped in her skin. She wanted him to maul her, nourishing her contempt for him, but he was surprisingly gentle. To compound her shame, when he entered her, she was wet.

His passion slaked, he longed to bask in her embrace, but she insisted on returning home.

'To the Jew?' he asked, his lip curled.

'To my Jew,' she replied, boldly. Desperate to wash – to sluice him out of her – she headed to the bathroom, only to find that the water had been cut off.

'Good!' he said. 'I want the smell of me – the smell of us – to linger on you.'

Shuddering, she threw on her clothes and hurried down the Boulevard Saint-Michel, where she was caught up in a small crowd, watching impassively as a gendarme led away an elderly Jewish couple. She told herself that she should be proud of having saved Ruben from a similar fate. But when she arrived home and he rebuked her yet again for her tardiness and neglect, before lapsing into sullen silence, all she felt was resentment towards him, hatred for Helmut, and, most of all, disgust with herself.

'There are forces more powerful than honour,' he had said. So it proved when, in violation of his oath, he showed up at the store three days later to buy a set of mulberry silk bedclothes, requesting that Madeleine deliver them to his apartment. She begged to be excused, but Madame Fabron was adamant. She took the metro to the Avenue Kléber, where the concierge refused to accept the parcel, insisting that Herr Winter wished her to bring it up herself. Lying in wait, he opened the door the instant she knocked. Threats and inducements on his side and appeals and accusations on hers were followed by a repeat of their copulation . . . coition . . . fornication . . . congress (eight years at a convent school had accustomed her to euphemism, but she refused to describe it as *making love*). Over the next four months, he engineered her return on six occasions; each time, the sheets, supposedly purchased for his wife, were laid, freshly laundered, on the bed.

In terms so opaque as to have been sinister, the nuns had warned their pupils that men were pawns of their passions. So what did that make her, as she found herself idly stroking his skin: his golden skin, so much smoother and clearer than Ruben's, which had grown dry and chapped? He caught her eye, and she dropped her hand, but the feeling remained. Had she secretly yearned for his touch? Was she pleasuring herself under the guise of saving Ruben?

She never considered that she might fall pregnant. She attributed her irregular periods and stomach cramps to poor diet and mineral deficiency, and her morning sickness to the stench of the closely packed metro. Ironically, it was Helmut who put the notion in her head, when he proudly remarked how his caresses had swollen her nipples. In an agony of apprehension, she saw a doctor who, holding a horn-like instrument to her belly, heard the baby's heartbeat and deduced that she was approaching her second trimester.

Never had she missed her mother more. In her absence, she turned to Madame Chambert, confiding the full saga of Helmut's assault. To her profound relief, her friend assured her that, far from betraying Ruben, she had made a brave and principled choice.

'Men think that they're heroes. If they only knew the truth.'

'Ruben must never find out. It would destroy him.'

'Are you absolutely sure the child isn't his?'

'Not unless I'm already eight months gone! We haven't made love' – she paused. In his case, the word was warranted – 'since his mother died. He tried . . . he tried so hard. It was as if all the life had drained out of him. Until it felt callous even to cuddle him in bed.'

'He'll find out soon enough. Nature's not good at keeping secrets.'

'What if . . . what if I get rid of it?'

'Don't say that! Don't even think of it!'

'What else can I do? Do you know anyone . . . anyone who knows anyone?'

'You'd be risking your life.'

'Not if she's competent.'

'Not just from the . . . procedure, but the law. Pétain has made it a crime against the state. On a par with treason.'

'My life's over anyway.'

'That's nonsense. You're young. You have years ahead of you. But if your mind's made up—'

'It is.'

'I may know someone. A retired midwife. But it won't be cheap. A retired midwife. But it won't be cheap. She'd also be one step away from the guillotine.'

'Please sound her out . . . please! As soon as you can. Which means telling Ruben. It's the only way to get the money.'

She dragged herself up to the apartment, where Ruben was engrossed in the second volume of *Jean-Christophe*. His rare good humour made her confession all the more painful. She repeated what she had told the concierge, leaving out the more intimate details. 'Whatever you may think,' she said, 'I did it for you.'

'Did I ask you to?' he replied, the anguish manifest in both his voice and eyes. 'Did it never occur to you that, given the option, I might have preferred to be arrested . . . I might have preferred to be shot?'

'How selfish of me to want to keep you alive!'

'No doubt it made a pleasant change. A real man whose flag flew high, not drooping at half mast.'

'I felt nothing. Like one of those Indians who sleep on a bed of nails or walk through fire.'

'Very prettily put.'

'It's the truth!'

'Is he handsome? I'm sure he's handsome. And virile? Well, he must be' – he clutched her stomach – 'to have given you a child.'

'It's not a child. It's a growth . . . a tumour to be cut out.'

'What?'

'Madame Chambert knows someone she thinks will do it. But she'll need paying.'

'No!' He paced the room. 'No, no! I won't allow it. It's far too dangerous. This happened because of me. I won't let you run the risk.'

'I won't be. The woman's highly experienced.'

'What if it stops you having more children? You'll make a splendid mother. Look at the way you've cared for me!' He laughed mirthlessly. 'I'm sorry for what I said. It was a shock. You must have this child. We'll be a family. I'll love it as if it were my own. It will be my own . . . Oh no! No, no! This man – this Nazi – he won't try to claim it for himself?'

'Quite the opposite. He has a wife and children in Berlin.'

'Then we'll have something – something good – to show for these wretched, wasted years.'

'Do you mean that? Honestly?'

'We have a future . . . a reason to carry on.'

'We'll be so happy, Ruben. I love you so much.'

Despite his initial response, she remained fearful that he would think better of it over time. On the contrary, his enthusiasm grew, until she wondered whether he had absorbed so much Nazi propaganda – Helmut's propaganda – that he felt unworthy of fatherhood.

He promised to love the child as his own, but what about her? What if it were a boy, one who bore such a strong resemblance to Helmut that she came to hate him?

She broke the news to Helmut the next time she was sent with a delivery. He glowered at her as though she'd confessed to giving him a disease.

'I intend to keep it.'

'So you should. When else will you have the chance of such a perfect Aryan child?'

'And Ruben will be the father,' she said defiantly.

'I can still arrange to have him arrested.'

'First, you'll have to find him. He's moved out,' she said, praying that he had forgotten the address.

'We'll hunt him down.'

But on the day he came to tell her of his departure, he didn't even search beneath the bed.

Events moved swiftly and, in the days after Helmut's visit, order in the city all but collapsed. Resistance leaders emerged from hiding and called for insurrection. Bus and metro drivers went on strike, followed by government officials, factory and shop workers, firemen, and even the police. Monsieur Fabron sent word to Madeleine that he was closing the store, but, in any case, Ruben forbade her to cross the river. Paris resembled a battleground, with barricades erected in streets and parks. Neighbours who had been too scared to talk to each other for years shared stories of the German retreat. Having finally ventured outdoors, Ruben witnessed overloaded Wehrmacht trucks heading east, the fleeing soldiers firing indiscriminately into the crowd. Regardless of the danger, people remained on the streets, watching the drama unfold as if on a screen.

Madame Chambert went to the town hall, which, like others throughout the city, had been taken over by the Resistance. 'Leftists, rightists, Gaullists, I don't know what they are, but I cried. Yes, even this tough old bird cried to see the tricolour flying in place of the swastika.'

That evening, she invited them for drinks in her parlour, along with Monsieur and Madame Grandjardin, their second-floor neighbours whom they knew only by sight, and a very subdued Bastien. They listened to the BBC announcement that Paris was liberated and church bells were ringing out across the city.

'Where do they get their information?' Ruben asked, over the thunder of bursting shells.

'They say that the Boche have mined bridges and planted explosives in the Eiffel Tower,' Monsieur Grandjardin said. 'They intend to destroy Paris before they leave.'

Madeleine was feeling increasingly uncomfortable. Although her calculations were of necessity imprecise, she reckoned that there were still three or four weeks before the baby was due. The spasms in her abdomen and ache in her lower back were symptoms of late pregnancy, aggravated by Madame Chambert's crossback chairs. Eager to escape, she stood up, only to find that her waters had broken.

'I'm so sorry,' she said, embarrassment deflecting the pain.

'Is it happening now?' Bastien asked, with a shudder. 'Not in here!'

'That's enough!' Madame Chambert said. 'Make yourself useful for a change. Go and fetch some towels.'

'I don't know where—'

'No, that's just the trouble. The top cupboard in my bedroom. Quickly!'

Madeleine wanted to return to the apartment, but neither Ruben nor Madame Chambert would let her brave the stairs. An acute contraction stifled her protests, and she allowed herself to be led into Bastien's room, which, much to his disgust, his mother declared to be the most suitable. With the turmoil on every corner dispelling any hope of reaching a doctor, Madame Chambert said that she knew a former midwife in the Rue de la Harpe and could send Bastien to fetch her. While he whined that she didn't care if he were shot by a sniper, Madeleine caught her eye and, realising whom she meant, shook her head. Madame Grandjardin, who'd been a Red

Cross nurse in the Great War, stepped into the breach. Madame Chambert and Bastien boiled water; Monsieur Grandjardin listened for news updates on the BBC; Ruben gripped Madeleine's hand, assuring her that the baby couldn't have chosen a more auspicious moment to be born.

Adrift on a sea of pain, she lost track of time, registering that it was morning solely by the light flooding the room. She cried aloud that she wanted to die and she would have done better to have had the abortion. In an affronted voice, Madame Grandjardin instructed her to breathe and push – as if she proposed to do anything else! – while Ruben told her how brave she was – as if she were a child to be humoured! She was pleading for deliverance when a long-lost sound silenced her. The air was filled with the clangour of church bells. She tried to recall the names of the nearby churches: Saint-Suplice, to be sure, and Saint-Joseph-des-Carmes. Was there a Saint-Ignace? The question carried her through another wave of pain.

'Liberation: the day we've been waiting for!' Ruben said, his words undercut by the crackle of gunfire. But as Madeleine felt the pain relent and her insides pour out of her, the only sound she could hear was a newborn's wail.

THREE

1

PASCAL

LYON, APRIL 1961

PHILOSOPHY, AS MONSIEUR Tournier had impressed upon the class at the start of *Primaire*, was the pinnacle of the French educational system. The *Bac Philo*, originally delivered in Latin, had been instituted by Napoleon in 1808. Though long since recast in the vernacular (he essayed a smile which no one returned), the study not only sharpened pupils' minds but distinguished them from other nations, especially the Anglo-Saxons, who favoured facts over ideas.

The philosophy paper would carry the most weight when they sat for their Bac the following summer and, to Pascal's disgust, Monsieur Tournier favoured grades over original thought. 'What the examiners are looking for,' he remarked, handing him a C for his essay on 'Morality in a world without God', is not Monsieur Pascal Carrache's musings on the subject – however ingenious they may be – but his analysis of Aquinas and Erasmus and Hobbes and Spinoza and Nietzsche, all of whom I trust even you, Monsieur Carrache, will admit have pondered it to more profound effect.'

For the past week, they had been considering the notion of truth. They'd compared Aristotle's view that honesty in word and deed was vital to the health of society with Aquinas's that it was vital to the health of the soul. They would shortly explore the opposing principle in Bentham's defence of lying for the greater good. This morning, they were immersed in Kant, whose essay 'On a Supposed Right to Lie' set forth the most uncompromising argument for truth-telling.

'For Kant, the duty is absolute,' Monsieur Tournier said. 'Even in his extreme example, when a murderer knocks on your door, demanding to know the whereabouts of his intended victim.'

'But that's inhuman,' Delphine Collet exclaimed, without raising her hand.

'He maintains the opposite: that a single lie, irrespective of the circumstances, is a diminution of humanity. Truth gradually disappears, not just as a general principle but as an empirical fact . . . You look bored, Monsieur Carrache. Perhaps you don't hold with empirical facts.'

'I'm sure that they have a place, Monsieur,' Pascal replied, trying to emulate the teacher's dry tone. 'But I set more store by the individual conscience. As Camus said on accepting the Nobel Prize: "I believe in justice, but I would defend my mother before justice."'

The mocking cheer that greeted his remark threatened his carefully cultivated pose of ennui. Sensing his discomfort, his best friend Thierry Palomer sprang to his aid.

'Surely we can't take Kant's argument seriously? He's simply playing with ideas. That's all very well on paper, but in the real world—'

'Ah, the "real world!" Remember your Plato, Monsieur Palomer . . . the allegory of the cave. Ideas - or forms, as Plato called them - are the ultimate reality.'

'That's just another idea . . . an idea about an idea, I grant, but still an idea,' Thierry said, in mounting frustration. 'What if Kant had been living here during the Occupation, and the murderer at the door was an SS officer searching for a Jew? Would he still insist on telling the truth?'

Several classmates - girls as well as boys - rapped their desks in approval of a point which, as the son of an executed Resistance hero, Thierry was singularly qualified to make.

'Let us strive to eschew sentiment,' Monsieur Tournier replied.

'But if you wish to pit Kant's universalism against your individual conscience, Monsieur Carrache, or your "real world", Monsieur Palomer, might I suggest that you – and, indeed, all the rest of you – switch on your radio or television apparatus this evening and every evening for the next few weeks, when both France 1 and RTF will broadcast regular bulletins from the trial of Adolph Eichmann. What's more, the proceedings will stand you in good stead for next term's discussion of Hegel and his contention that "History is a slaughter bench".'

Despite his instinctive resistance to extracurricular homework, Pascal resolved to watch the bulletins. He couldn't remember when he had first become aware of the Final Solution. In *maternelle*, he'd played games of Nazis and Maquis, but they might as well have been Cowboys and Indians. In *élémentaire*, he'd watched footage of the atomic bomb and regarded the destruction of Hiroshima as the greatest atrocity of the Second World War. In *collège*, he'd learnt about the six million murdered Jews, but such figures pertained to mathematics rather than history. Although he knew that among them were several members of his own family – his Grand-Oncle Henri, here in Lyon; his Tante Bella, Oncle Leon and Cousin Daniel, in concentration camps – he was little the wiser, since Maman had drummed into him that any mention of their fate would distress Papa.

Papa, in turn, had sought to cocoon his childhood, as he realised years later on recalling a visit to Gabrielle, the only one of his relations to have survived the camps.

'What's that?' he'd asked, pointing to the tattoo on her arm.

'A telephone number,' Papa said quickly. 'Gabi had no paper so she wrote it on her skin.'

Now he would have the chance to study the mindset of the man whose methods had reduced his fifteen-year-old cousin to a cipher.

Lessons over, he walked the few hundred metres home (the redundancy of his Mobylette fuelling his antipathy to the haut-bourgeois neighbourhood). He entered the apartment to find Berthe mopping the hall floor.

'Minuit had an accident,' she said.

'Minuit *is* an accident,' he replied, eager to share his distaste for Maman's overbred poodles.

'It was my fault. I had the radio on in the kitchen while she was scratching the balcony door.'

'It's never your fault, Berthe,' he said, whirling her around and pecking her cheek.

'What a liberty!' she said, shaking the mop at him.

'Urgh! Poodle piss, that's disgusting.'

'Get away with you! It's Sapoforme,' she replied, as he breathed in the synthetic pine.

He headed to his room with the usual, not altogether disagreeable sense that Berthe was the only member of the household who was genuinely pleased to see him. He flung his schoolbag on the floor and put Brassens' *Oncle Archibald* on the turntable. As anticipated, it drew Maman to the door within minutes.

She entered without knocking. 'Don't you think it would be polite to greet your mother when you come home?'

'But you're always telling me I have no manners, and I wouldn't want to contradict you,' he replied, wondering at his instinctive need to goad her.

'If you must listen to that disgusting man, have the courtesy to turn it down. It's not fair on Berthe.'

'She likes music. It's just about her only pleasure.'

'Not when it's a man who sings about a girl breastfeeding a kitten!'

'It's poetry!'

'It's perverse!'

Disinclined to argue, he asked whether dinner might be brought forward half an hour to enable him to watch the Eichmann trial on *Le Journal Télévisé*.

'Why on earth do you want to watch that?' Maman asked, strangely resistant to any reference to the Nazis, given how she'd outsmarted them during the Occupation.

'It's a philosophy assignment,' he replied, certain that that would clinch the matter. 'Of course, if Papa's not home, I can eat in the kitchen,' he added hopefully.

'Your father is always home by seven thirty and we always eat together. I'll ask Berthe to serve as soon as he returns.'

'Strange that he should be so late,' Pascal said, resenting her complacency. 'Paul Corbin says his father gets back from the factory at six on the dot.'

'It's different for the man at the top. Like the captain of a ship, always the last to abandon his post.' With a forced smile, she quit the room.

Pascal knew about Armande Bauchard, Papa's former secretary and long-time mistress, and both his parents knew that he knew, although nothing had been said, even after they found themselves in the row behind Armande and her mother at the Comoedia for a showing of Truffaut's *Les Quatre Cents Coups*. Papa visited her regularly after work, and Maman feigned ignorance as if they were back in the Belle Époque. With their marriage so passionless, he couldn't blame Papa for taking a lover; he sometimes wished Maman would do the same (although he swiftly suppressed the thought). The irony was that, with so few common interests, it must have been sex that brought them together. At forty-five, Maman was still a strikingly beautiful woman, and Papa, nearly two decades her senior, was in decent shape for his age. Their love had been strong enough to sweep aside the religious differences that, in Maman's case, had led his grandmother to disown her. Given the need for secrecy, the only witness to their early relationship was their Occupation-era concierge, Madame Chambert. On his visits to Paris, she'd told him of their mutual devotion, their courage in the face of constant danger and of Maman's sacrifice for Papa, on which she refused to elaborate, as if the memory were too painful. He had been born in her apartment and, as a child, he'd never tired of hearing her story of the bells ringing out across Paris at the very moment of his birth.

He could only suppose that the power of their desire had driven his parents to conceive a child at a time when, for all their losses on the battlefield, the Germans had intensified their grip on Paris. He could only suppose that their disappointment in that child as he grew up had fed their disappointment in each other. They barely conversed, at least not in Pascal's presence. Papa would return home in the evening and make straight for the whisky decanter, pouring himself a large tumbler, at which Maman would utter a routine 'Oh no, Ruben!' They would eat dinner, mainly in silence, apart from Midi and Minuit yapping for morsels from Maman's plate, at which Papa would respond with an 'Oh no, Madeleine!' After the meal, he would retire to his study with another large tumbler and listen to the latest Brahms or Bruckner recording, replacing the disc if there were even a minuscule scratch. Despite his subscription to the Salle Rameau, he rarely attended concerts, claiming that, having nurtured his love of music in hiding, he found the audience's presence a distraction. Pascal suspected that the true reason was his need to remain in control. Maman, meanwhile, would install herself in the salon for an evening of game shows, serials and gentle scolding of her dogs.

This evening, Papa arrived home at the usual hour and, ten minutes later, Berthe summoned Pascal to dinner. After a sorrel soup, which Maman pronounced 'too salty' and Papa assured her was 'just right', Berthe brought in the turbot, which Papa declared 'deliciously tender' and Maman 'rubbery', before complaining about the soaring price of fish.

Just when Pascal, who was mulling over a limerick about Margot the Turbot, thought he might escape any parental interrogation, Papa pounced. 'I gather we're eating early at the behest of your philosophy teacher.'

'Afraid so. To my mind, it's a deflection tactic. But with any luck, I might learn more than I do in class.'

'He's that bad?'

'His preferred method is to fatten us up with facts, ready for the examiners to gobble us up and spit us out.'

'Is that your excuse for doing so badly?' Maman asked. 'Madame Grosset told me that Édouard came second in the philosophy compositions while you dropped down to – I forget what – nineteenth or twentieth. I didn't know where to put myself.'

'How about under the dryer?'

'That's not clever,' Papa said.

'We can't all be Édouard Grosset.'

It was true that, having once ranked among the top three in every subject except geography, he'd slipped into the bottom ten, undergoing the ritual humiliation of standing before the class while his teachers belaboured him like drill sergeants. Even so, he suspected that his mother's chagrin had more to do with deferring to her hairdresser – a woman she tipped! – than with his academic decline.

'It's sheer indolence,' Papa said. 'You have a first-class mind and if you're not back in the top five by the end of term, there'll be no Lausanne – no Cannes – this summer. You'll be stuck here, working with a tutor.'

'That's just vindictive!'

'Because I want you to pass your Bac? Your entire future depends on it.'

'Why? I'm not Thierry planning to study law. I'm not planning to study anything. How often have you told me that I'll always have a job at the factory? I suppose I'll have to run it one day.'

'Just listen to him!' Maman said. 'It would serve him right if you appointed someone else.'

'Like Grandpapa with Oncle Simon at the bank?'

'You were there, I take it?' Papa asked heavily.

'No, of course not,' Pascal replied, conscious of having crossed a line. 'Anyway, who says I'll have a future after two years and three months of military service? I'll probably be blown up by an FLN guerrilla in Algiers.'

'Don't say things like that! You'll upset your mother. They may send you to teach in the mountains or some other out-of-harm's-way region. Which is another reason to work hard for your Bac.'

'Well, if I miss the bulletin, I'm bound to fail philosophy. Please may I leave the table? I don't want any cheese.'

'It's five to eight,' Papa said. 'There's no rush. In any case, I intend to join you.'

'We are honoured,' Maman said, her face falling. 'As long as you don't pass remarks.' She cut two slices of apple for her dogs. 'The girls and I look forward to a few moments' peace at the end of the day.'

Pascal repressed a scowl. Now was not the time to offend her. Ever since Monsieur Tournier mentioned the trial, he had hoped that, beyond the allotted task, he would learn more about his own history. He relished his dual heritage, not least because it legitimised his status as an outsider. Yet he knew next to nothing about Judaism. His mother wasn't religious, but the emblems of Christianity were everywhere: in Christmas presents and Easter eggs, in Joan of Arc and Notre Dame, and in the wealth of nativities, crucifixions and martyrdoms at the Musée des Beaux Arts. By contrast, apart from the odd Old Testament proverb and phrase, there was nothing Jewish in the general culture. Papa had studied Hebrew as a boy (he'd even celebrated his bar mitzvah, though it had been called something else), but he never went to synagogue and the sole remnant of his faith was his yearly fast on Yom Kippur, which felt as token as Maman's giving up chocolate or pastries for Lent (strangely, the one thing neither had renounced was renunciation). This would be his chance to redress the balance.

'I hope you're not expecting drama,' Papa said to Pascal. 'According to this morning's *Figaro*, yesterday's entire session was taken up with procedural wrangles.'

'But after that, there'll be witnesses. People will discover what the Jews suffered. Some of my friends have only a vague idea. They don't believe I'm Jewish at all. They think I'm making it up.'

'Why would anyone make up something like that?' Maman asked.

'They've seen that I'm not circumcised.'

'When? How? Did you hear that, Ruben? Promise me you're not doing anything filthy!'

'Yes, stripping off my filthy kit in the changing room... Honestly, Maman! Anyhow, boys talk about these things.'

'It was too soon after Liberation,' Papa said smoothly. 'I doubt that there was a mohel left alive in the whole of Paris. Besides, Judaism is carried through the maternal line. As you well know, your mother isn't Jewish.'

The meal over, they moved into the salon, Midi and Minuit trotting behind Maman to take up their privileged places beside her on the sofa. Papa switched on the television and settled in his usual armchair. Pascal sat at the back of the room and lit a post-prandial *brun*.

'You smoke too much,' Papa said.

'I'm honouring Grandpapa's tobacco factory and your ancestry.'

'Shush! You promised not to talk,' Maman said, as the credits for *36 chandelles* rolled across the screen, after which the announcer previewed next week's *Faire Face*, before introducing *Le Journal Télévisé*. 'You're in luck,' she added, on hearing that the presenter was Georges de Caunes, a favourite of *Télérama* and *Telé 7* ever since he'd begun to broadcast with his dog at his feet. 'He's the best.'

The main news item was of course Yuri Gagarin's historic space voyage, accompanied by the extraordinary images of the rocket blasting off and the earth through the window of his capsule. It was followed by a more mundane report on the refusal of the FLN to return to peace talks in Evian as long as de Gaulle insisted on including the rival Algerian MNA. At last, de Caunes introduced the opening day of the Eichmann trial, and Pascal got his first glimpse of the man himself, who, balding and bespectacled, with a pinched nose, thin lips and protuberant ears, bore little resemblance to the Nazis in films. Flanked by two guards, he sat in a glass cage, dressed in an ill-fitting dark suit, his mouth set in a faintly contemptuous smile, while the presiding judge read out the fifteen counts in the indictment, including Crimes against Humanity and Crimes against the Jewish people. Eichmann's defence lawyer challenged the jurisdiction of the court over crimes committed before the state of Israel was founded, after which the chief prosecutor, Attorney General Hausner, proceeded to refute his arguments slowly, meticulously (and somewhat tediously) for the rest of the segment.

'I hope your teacher is satisfied,' Maman said. 'I'm not sure what you were supposed to take from that.'

'I took a lot,' Pascal said, refusing to admit his disappointment.

'It may not have made for riveting viewing, but Hausner was right to devote so much time to asserting the court's legality,' Papa said. 'I've read several commentators, Jews as well as gentiles, who insist that Israel was wrong to breach international law in seizing Eichmann. No criminal act – however egregious – justifies another.'

'They must have studied Kant,' Pascal muttered sourly.

'Please! If you mean to chatter, go somewhere else. I'm trying to watch,' Maman said, as the camera cut to Thiais cemetery for the burial of King Zog of Albania.

Putting his finger to his lips in wry amusement, Papa led Pascal back to the dining room, where Berthe was clearing the table.

'We won't disturb you,' he said.

'No, Monsieur,' she replied wearily.

'You've never really explained to me why you didn't stay in Israel,' Pascal said, his mind fixed on the broadcast.

'It was so long ago . . . before there even was an Israel.'

'Aunt Esther told me you were determined to make a new life there. She quoted your exact words: "I want to till the soil and graze my flocks in the land of our fathers."'

'Really? I can't believe . . . though maybe I can. Trust Esther!'

'She made you sound like a modern-day Abraham.'

'That was half the problem. I was no farmer. A city boy, through and through, and a very privileged and pampered one at that! I'm not proud of it. I had no notion of what it was to lug heavy machines across swamps and hills when the mules refused to take another step, or to clear boulders from ground untended for centuries, and then plough it from dawn to dusk, before crawling back to camp for a bowl of bulgur – always bulgur – with the odd spoonful of lentils if we were lucky. Barely enough water to drink, much less wash in, with only an oil lamp in our tents and a single Primus stove between us all. And to think that my father brought electricity to Salonica!'

'You tried. At least you tried,' Pascal said, with unexpected sympathy.

'Yes, and I carried on trying, through recurrent bouts of dysentery (I sometimes felt that I was fertilising the fields on my own), and a spell in a Tel Aviv hospital with malaria. When I returned to the camp, I found the atmosphere greatly changed. Our leaders were Russian, inspired by Tolstoy as much as the Torah. They scorned our Arab neighbours, who'd welcomed us and helped us to settle. And for their part, the Arabs turned against us. There were three of us Sephardim, who tried to broker peace. We hadn't lived among Arabs, but we understood... we respected their culture. We wanted to build bridges, but our comrades preferred to build stockades. It may have been the Salonican in me (my best friend at school was a Turk), but I knew then that it wasn't the place for me. I went back to Paris, to the relief of my mother and the disappointment of my father, who, having bitterly opposed my going out there, was equally opposed to my giving up.'

'Have you ever wondered how your life would have turned out if you'd stayed?'

'Of course, though less so now. During the Occupation, I felt as if everything that was happening to me had happened because I'd left. I knew that the Nazis were persecuting me because I was a Jew, but, in my mind, it was because I was a bad Jew. Moses and the Israelites spent forty years in the desert; I ran away after eighteen months.'

Pascal couldn't remember when, if ever, Papa had talked to him for so long, let alone so intimately. 'After the war – when Israel was established – did you never think about going back?'

'By then you were born. It wouldn't have been right.'

'Because Maman isn't Jewish?'

'In part.'

'She could have converted.'

'Hadn't she done enough for me? Besides, despite everything that had occurred, I clung to my father's belief that there's more that unites people than divides them. It was important for me to stay here, in France: a French Jew . . . a Jewish Frenchman, put the emphasis where you will. A survivor.'

Over the next two months, Pascal watched religiously as *Le Journal Télévisé* broadcast nightly reports from the Eichmann trial. The Attorney General summoned a succession of witnesses, who testified to the horrors they'd endured. Pascal struggled to hold back his tears as a woman recounted hearing soldiers debate whether to kill her or her child first, before deciding on the child, whereupon she collapsed into the burial pit and was left for dead. A man described seeing his daughter selected for the gas chamber, craning forward until her red coat was no more than a dot. Another told how he escaped being shot alongside his comrades when the SS officer assigned to whip him enlisted him as his orderly. An artist sent to Auschwitz at the age of fourteen recalled how the ashes from the constantly belching crematoria were used to grit the icy roads around the camp. The camera repeatedly lingered on Eichmann, whose only response to the unrelenting testimony was to adjust his glasses or blow his nose. Yet for Pascal, the trial was less about the culpability of one man, or even a nation, than that of an entire civilisation.

At night, he was tormented by phantoms, so clearly conjured by the court testimony that his subconscious appeared to have played no part. He said nothing to his parents, who had both expressed misgivings about his 'obsession' with the trial, for fear that they would forbid him to watch the remainder. He was determined to discover more about the event that cast its baleful shadow over his life.

The questions that burned in his mind were those that the otherwise sympathetic Attorney General put to several witnesses: Why didn't you attack? Why didn't you revolt? Why didn't you resist? Despite feeling that someone who'd spent the war in the safety of

Palestine had no more right to challenge them than someone like himself who had yet to be born, he shared Hausner's disquiet. To lift his spirits one Thursday morning, he headed into the old town to inspect the plaque commemorating Oncle Henri. He knew little more about him than about the rest of his family, although when Oncle Bertrand died three years earlier and Sylvain confided that he and Oncle Henri had been more than just business partners, he suspected that there was an added reason for his ignorance.

'Sylvain had no call to gossip,' Papa declared, when questioned. 'It didn't stop Henri being the bravest man I've ever known.'

He explained how, during the Occupation, Henri and Bertrand had modified machinery at the factory to print *Combat*, the official organ of several Resistance groups, including the FTP, to which Thierry's father had belonged. Together with Tante Bella, they were members of an underground network which had been infiltrated by the Gestapo. For years, it was believed that Henri had swallowed poison, until Bertrand was contacted by a former boiler man at the Hôtel Terminus, who revealed that he had died under torture.

'God knows what he suffered!' Papa said. 'But he never breathed a name.'

Pascal gazed reverently at the grey plaque on the corner of the building, with its simple inscription:

> *To the memory of*
> *M. Henri Carrache*
> *1872 – 1943*
> *Died for France*
> *Victim of Nazi Barbarism.*

Having arranged to spend the free afternoon with Thierry and their girlfriends, Delphine and Fleur, he rode back across the river, finding them nursing their drinks outside the Café de la Cloche. He parked his Mobylette and joined them, kissing Delphine and

Fleur and shaking Thierry's hand. He ordered a croque monsieur and a *demi* and relaxed into the group.

Until recently, he had hidden his tangled feelings for girls – attraction, confusion and a touch of fear – behind a mask of indifference. Had he been more confident or athletic (which amounted to much the same), he might have mimicked his classmate Jules Fauquier, spinning a yo-yo under their chins and laughing at the stream of insults when he snatched it away. Everything changed after he entered the mixed Lycée du Parc. Paired with Delphine for a project on Paul and Camille Claudel, they sealed their friendship during a field trip to the Musée des Beaux Arts. He owed it all to Tante Bella. In the twentieth-century gallery, alongside works by her celebrated contemporaries, hung two paintings that Oncle Bertrand had found hidden in a storeroom. In parodies of the *Return to the Soil* designs mandated by Vichy, she'd portrayed a milkmaid masturbating a centaur and a farmer yoking his plough to two SS men. According to Oncle Bertrand, they were outlets for her self-disgust while executing the official motifs, and the last pictures she completed before fleeing Lyon. When he accompanied his parents to their unveiling, Pascal had been mortified by the centaur, staring at his feet while Papa proudly explained his sister's red-figure technique and Maman tried to steer him towards a Bonnard *Still Life*. With Delphine, however, he revelled in reflected glory. Over the following year, he bolstered his cultural credentials, taking her to hear Brassens at the Théâtre des Célestins and to several concerts during Les Nuits de Fourvière.

Although Delphine and Fleur had been classmates in *collège*, they'd not been especially close until they began dating the two best friends, and the newly formed couples became a loose-knit quartet. To Pascal's delight, his parents allowed him to invite the girls – unsupervised – along with Thierry, a regular house guest, to Bessenay on Ascension weekend. He was less surprised by Papa, who'd voiced concern that he and Thierry were 'like finger and nail', as though Oncle Henri's tendencies might run in the family, than by Maman, who, despite bemoaning her convent education, clung to its prohibitions. Yet, after speaking to both their mothers, she expressed confidence in the girls' good sense.

To Pascal's dismay, that confidence - at least with regard to Delphine - was not misplaced. Although Monsieur and Madame Dutoit, the caretaker and cook, had allotted the boys and girls to opposite wings of the house and no doubt been told to listen out for the slightest nocturnal creak, both he and Thierry padded across the second-floor landing minutes after their over-enunciated 'Goodnights'. Delphine unbuttoned her nightdress, letting him savour the soap-scented softness of her breasts, but forbade him from straying lower. For all that she was a dedicated Young Communist who derided bourgeois conventions, there were some that she refused to flout. From Thierry's exultant account the next morning, he discovered that Fleur had been more accommodating. Nevertheless, his 'I'm happy for you, buddy!' was sincere.

Since the beginning of the Eichmann trial, Pascal had missed only one edition of *Le Journal Télévisé*, when Delphine's parents invited him to the opera on her birthday. So he was outraged when, on Thursday 22 June, the third day of Eichmann's defence, Maman announced that they were expecting guests for dinner and would need the salon. Thierry, whose interest in the case had waned after the initial assignment but who continued to follow it out of loyalty to Pascal, invited him over. 'That is, if you can bear to slum it.'

'Your apartment isn't a slum!'

'I meant listening to it on the radio,' Thierry replied with a grin.

Encumbered by the large box of marrons glacés he took at Maman's insistence, Pascal trudged up the four flights of scuffed stairs, a climb he reminded himself that Thierry made several times a day, often with a full coal scuttle since there was no hot water in the apartment. He liked to pretend that Marion - unlike Maman, she dispensed with titles - chose to remain in the building where she'd lived during her cruelly truncated marriage, but he knew very well that her reasons were economic rather than sentimental. She managed a bookshop and every corner of the two cramped rooms was piled high with *Livres de Poche*, some dog-eared and tattered but all read, unlike the pristine first editions in Papa's study. Thierry slept on a divan, shared a toilet with neighbours on two floors and, as Maman was quick to observe, struggled with personal hygiene. Though by worldly standards, Thierry should have been jealous of him, it was the other way round. He longed for the casual intimacy that Thierry enjoyed with his mother. Whereas Marion and Thierry went out together, Maman gave Pascal money to go out with his friends.

'I take my hat off to Madame Palomer,' Maman said, after one of Thierry's visits. 'It's hard enough for two parents to bring up a teenage boy, never mind a woman on her own.'

'Why? What would you have done if Papa had died – or been deported?' Pascal asked. 'Consigned me to an orphanage?'

'Are you going to let him speak to me like that?' she asked Papa.

'Don't speak to your mother like that,' Papa said, as if he were already lost in Brahms.

While his parents and their guests sampled the traiteur's specialities, Pascal had two helpings of Marion's *pot-au-feu*, which she knew was his favourite. At eight o'clock, she turned on *Le Journal Radio*, which was dominated by news from the Middle East. A Jewish singer, unknown to any of them, had been shot dead in an Algerian market. President Nasser had nationalised the Al-Azhar university in Cairo. And, in Jerusalem, Eichmann continued his testimony. Pascal felt disoriented hearing clips of his voice without seeing his face, whose very impassivity hinted at the ease with which he had committed his crimes. His defence veered from the fatuous – claiming to have been a mere functionary with no power to disobey orders – to the risible: describing himself as an ally of Zionism, who, in 1938, had assisted Jews to emigrate from Austria.

'I understand now why they've put him behind bulletproof glass,' Pascal said. 'How can anyone listen to that without wanting to shoot him?'

'Carrache as Edmond Dantès,' Thierry said.

'I wish! But Eichmann is just one man. What about the thousands of Nazis still at large? My cousin Nathan says Buenos Aires is crawling with them.'

'What the world needs is justice, not revenge,' Marion said. 'I saw what happened here at the Liberation. Scores were settled: some fairly, others not. And it was the women who suffered most . . . the women who'd fraternised with the Germans - sometimes, it's true, for what they could get, but often as not for a little comfort . . . a little tenderness and, Lord knows, we all yearned for that. They were ready targets, to be shorn and paraded half-naked through the streets, some with babies at their breasts, some with swastikas scrawled on their skin. I'm talking about the poor . . . the humble . . . the powerless ones. The great ones, as always, escaped. Madame Chanel, who'd lived at the Ritz with an Abwehr officer, fled to Switzerland for ten years before returning to reopen her fashion house.'

'My mother wears Chanel,' Pascal said.

'I doubt she's the only one on the Boulevard des Belges. Then there's Arletty—'

'The actress?' Thierry asked.

'Is there another? It's much the same story. Though if I remember correctly, her lover was in the Luftwaffe. She was sent to prison, but no Saint-Lazare for her. It was house arrest in a private chateau. After a few months, she was released and resumed her career.'

'I had no idea,' Pascal said.

'You were a babe in arms. You both were.'

'They should all be punished, rich and poor. Kant may have been right after all. If one lie diminishes the store of truth in the world, so one act of collaboration - *horizontal* as much as any other - poisons everything. Those women didn't just dishonour themselves, they dishonoured France.'

'Only the young can afford to be so judgemental,' Marion said, although her tone was tender. 'I hope we can live up to your exacting standards.'

'Not mine alone,' Pascal replied. 'Those of six million others.'

Leafing through *Le Monde* the next day, he saw that Arletty was once again performing on the Paris stage, in *L'Étouffe-Chrétien* at the Théâtre de la Renaissance. Surrounded by such painful reminders, it was no wonder that Papa seldom returned to the capital. One inviolable obligation, however, was the *meldado* for his mother every 24 June. She had died in hospital – a rare occurrence for a Jew in 1943 – but the Occupation authorities denied her the right of burial alongside her husband. The first thing Papa had done at the Liberation – even before setting out to reclaim the family home – was to have her disinterred from Picpus cemetery and reburied in Montparnasse. Pascal, plagued with nightmares after reading of Armand Duval's gruesome exhumation of Marguerite Gautier in *La Dame aux Camélias*, was grateful not to have known about it until many years later, although Sylvain, who'd been present, assured him that it was both dignified and moving, especially when Papa sprinkled soil sent from the Jewish cemetery in Salonica on the coffin.

Every June, Papa invited his surviving family to join him for the ceremony. Tante Esther regularly flew in from England, but this year she was visiting Nathan in Buenos Aires, where they themselves were due to attend Katrin's wedding in December. Despite not being a blood relative, Oncle Simon never missed the chance to take part, nor, according to Papa, to remark how 'Maman' had always treated him like a son. To Pascal's disappointment, Sylvain and Annette had sent their apologies. As his only male cousin, Sylvain was the nearest thing he had to an older brother. He was fond too of Annette, even if he agreed with Maman that lunch would be more restful without her nonstop chatter. They harboured deep-seated grievances against Oncle Simon (which, as usual, no one would explain) and avoided his company as much as possible. In their absence, Pascal would have to make do with his two female cousins, Clarice and Gabrielle. Although both single women in their thirties, they were very different characters. Clarice was large, affectionate and spirited – she'd taught him to swim in her pool at Cap Ferrat and taken him up in a balloon on his fifteenth birthday. Gabrielle was earnest, sharp, and smiled only as a last resort. Whereas Clarice was demonstrative, Gabrielle was reserved. It took years for Pascal to understand why she flinched whenever he kissed her. Now that he did, he longed to hug her until she never felt afraid again. But she wouldn't let him - or anyone - that close.

This year, the *meldado* fell on a Saturday, so Pascal wasn't taken out of school, which, with the looming threat of the tutor, he claimed was a relief. On the early morning express from Perrache, he diligently read Livy's account of the Battle of Cannae until, both his parents having dozed off, he sneaked out of the compartment for a cigarette and a flirtatious exchange with a nurse from Gabon. Arriving in Paris forty minutes late, they headed straight to the cemetery, the taxi dropping them at the side gate on the Rue Émile Richard, where Remo, Oncle Simon's veteran chauffeur, was polishing the bonnet of a silver-blue Mercedes Adenauer.

'Only he would have the gall to buy a German car,' Papa muttered, as Pascal stifled an admiring whistle.

'Try not to pick a quarrel with him,' Maman said. 'Remember we're here for your mother.'

'I'm hardly likely to forget,' Papa replied testily. Although he professed to be on amiable terms with his brother-in-law, it was clear that he blamed him for Tante Irène's death, albeit not as directly as he blamed the Nazis for Oncle Leon's and Tante Bella's.

They walked down a sepulchral avenue, past rows of extravagant tombs and mausoleums. As they approached their destination, Pascal slipped down a narrow alleyway for his annual homage at the Dreyfus family tomb, its mound of remembrance stones, broken by a single misplaced geranium pot. He emerged to greet his cousins: one with a boisterous embrace; the other with a kiss that barely grazed her cheek. He turned to Oncle Simon, who startled him by clutching his shoulders and sniffing his hair and neck, until Clarice gently prised him away.

His Hebrew having grown rusty, Papa had engaged a rabbi to lead the prayers. Pascal recognised the distinctive cadences of the

Mourner's Kaddish, which Papa and Clarice tentatively echoed. Oncle Simon, whose Hebrew was fluent, remained mute, before blurting out a few garbled words of French, which sounded like 'sugar . . . sandwich . . . hotel'. With a sheepish smile, Clarice quietened him, while the rabbi and Maman looked bewildered, Gabrielle unperturbed and Papa irate.

The ceremony over, they headed for the traditional lunch at the Tour d'Argent. The restaurant held a particular significance for Papa, who'd lived a few hundred metres along the quay for more than three years during the Occupation but been banned from setting foot inside. For Pascal, the main attraction was the spectacular view of Notre Dame and the Seine and, since he could no longer command a window seat by virtue of youth, he was doubly grateful to Clarice for offering him hers. He gazed at the barges and boats chugging down the river while the others exchanged news.

'How's business, Ruben?' asked Oncle Simon, who had run one of the largest private finance companies in Europe. 'Workers behaving themselves? No strikes?'

'We enjoy excellent labour relations, thank you. And we're doing fine. We've just secured a highly lucrative contract to supply rayon to the J.C. Penney chain in the States.'

'Artificial silk?' Oncle Simon said. 'Henri would be turning in his grave.'

'Henri doesn't have a grave,' Papa said sharply.

'He has a plaque,' Pascal interjected, without looking round.

'Have you been watching the Eichmann trial?' Maman asked Gabrielle, the way that she might ask an Englishwoman if she'd met the Queen. 'Pascal has been glued to it.'

'No,' she replied.

'I don't know why they need to rake up all the unpleasantness,' Clarice said. 'The Mossad agents should have shot him in Buenos Aires. Don't you agree, Gabi?'

'No.'

Clarice looked stung by Gabrielle's rebuke, but she was soon distracted by Oncle Simon. Having unnerved the sommelier by vigorously shaking his hand when he brought the wine, he compounded his confusion by declaring that he wanted the Chenin Blanc with his foie gras and, as soon as he started to pour, pointing to the Saint-Julien. 'No, no, that's the white, you idiot!'

'Is he drunk?' Pascal whispered to Maman, who ignored him.

'The sun's so bright up here, it's impossible to see anything,' Clarice said, in an attempt to laugh off her father's eccentricity, as she did once again when the foie gras arrived and he scraped every pat of butter from the communal dish onto his side plate. But she could only watch in alarm when, brushing aside her 'What are you doing, Papa?', he strode to the adjacent table, where a bald, round-shouldered man sat opposite a large, ash-blonde woman flaunting an expanse of crinkled bosom.

'Excuse me, Madame, are you eating this duck?' he asked, in a voice that resounded through the restaurant. Pascal couldn't hear the softly spoken, no doubt perplexed reply, which tailed off when Oncle Simon grabbed her plate. 'Well, you shouldn't. You're too fat.' With a courteous nod, he brought the plate back to the table, picked up his cutlery and began to eat.

'Mercado!' Papa cried, as though the horror of the scene had transported him back fifty years, before rushing over to placate the affronted diners.

Clarice remonstrated with her father, who wolfed down the duck. Pascal glanced at Maman's stupefied face and feared he might burst out laughing. Only Gabrielle seemed unflustered, reaching for the wine to top up her glass.

Papa shook hands with the couple and returned to the table.

'Have you smoothed things over?' Maman asked.

'I told them he was on a day's leave from the clinic and offered to pay for their meal.' He stared in disbelief as Oncle Simon shovelled food into his mouth. 'Just what is going on?' he asked Clarice.

'Sunstroke. It must be. He's been acting strangely ever since the airport. We spent all yesterday afternoon by the pool. I told him to wear a hat.'

'Delicious! I'd like another,' Oncle Simon said, snatching Maman's bread roll to mop up the sauce.

'No, Papa, we must go now,' Clarice said. 'We're already late for the appointment.'

'What? With whom?'

'You wanted it to be a surprise,' she said, shrugging helplessly at Papa.

'Ah yes, of course. Trade secrets! Well, time waits for no one.' He slid back his chair. 'Goodbye, Madeleine, ravishing as ever.' To her visible surprise, he kissed her smack on the lips. 'Gabrielle, my dear.' He kissed the hand she thrust out to ward off a similar approach. 'Ruben, you're looking tired. I recommend retirement. A whole new lease of life. And Pascal, such a handsome boy. How old are you now? Thirteen?'

'In two months I'll be seventeen!'

'How your aunt would have loved you!' he said sadly. 'Wouldn't Irène have loved him, Ruben?' he asked, as Clarice led him away.

Papa, convinced that the entire restaurant was watching them, wanted to leave at once, but Maman insisted that they finish their entrées. Despite claiming her appetite was ruined, she ate all but one of her *coquilles Saint-Jacques*. The three adults mused over whether Oncle Simon might be displaying early signs of dementia, which Pascal, still smarting from the insult, considered self-evident.

'Poor man!' Papa said. 'I wouldn't wish it on my worst enemy.'

'Clarice is the one I feel sorry for,' Maman said.

'At least she has Sylvain,' Gabrielle said. 'Some of us have to deal with difficult parents alone.'

'Don't I know it!' Pascal said.

'Thank you,' Maman said, with a sniff.

'I didn't mean it.'

'You still said it.'

Oncle Simon's early departure spared them the annual battle when he tried to wrest the bill from Papa; although, given the two extra covers, Papa might for once have been willing to concede defeat. In the third of their traditions, they took a cab to the Rue de la Roquette, to visit the memorial to the Sephardi soldiers with whom Oncle Leon had fought in Flanders. As shoppers bustled past them, Papa told the familiar story of Leon's commanding officer commending his courage at the inauguration ceremony, and Gabrielle responded by recounting his visit to Vichy after Daniel's arrest, when that same officer promised to do everything in his power to secure his release. 'Maman was delirious with relief. But before anything could happen, Papa was also detained, and then me and . . . well you know the rest.'

They stood, rapt in recollection, only to be jolted by the jangle of a barrel organ.

'I know this tune,' Pascal said, humming it.

'It's Mozart,' Papa said. 'Figaro's march. Though I'm not sure who's massacring it more brutally. The organ grinder or you.'

'Is everything all right, Gabi?' Maman asked.

'Yes . . . no . . . I don't know. I feel sick, I'm sorry. Perhaps I've caught the sun too. Are you ready? May we go?'

No sooner had she spoken than she swept down the street, forcing them to keep pace. They parted company at Bastille where, refusing the offer of a lift, she descended into the metro, and they took a cab to the Rue Racine, for tea with Madame Chambert. With three of his grandparents dead and the fourth estranged, Pascal had designated her an honorary grandmother. He'd visited her regularly throughout his childhood and, unlike his parents, she had been happy to talk about life during the Occupation. Once, when he was five or six and the apartment vacant, she'd taken him up to the fifth floor to see where Papa had hidden. It was small and dingy but depressingly ordinary, with none of the alcoves or cubbyholes of his imaginings.

'Where's the bathroom?' he'd asked.

'There!' She'd pointed to the sink with a smile.

'And the toilet?'

'Two floors down. Not that your papa was able to use it.'

'So what did he use?'

'A bucket.'

'Did you have to empty it?'

'No, your maman did that.'

No wonder she had been so upset when he wet the bed.

Once he'd recovered his share of the family property, Papa offered to buy Madame Chambert an apartment, but she refused. She liked looking after her tenants and scoffed at the notion of retirement. As she later told Pascal: 'I'd have nothing to do all day but worry about Bastien.' She knew better than to say as much to Maman or Papa, both of whom loathed Bastien and called him her 'cross'. To Pascal, however, it was thrilling to know someone so disreputable.

'Let's hope Bastien doesn't grace us with his presence this afternoon,' Papa said, as the cab rolled over the Pont d'Austerlitz.

'Madame Chambert promised she'd do her best to keep him out of the house,' Maman said.

'She should keep him out of the house permanently. She deserves a little comfort in her old age.'

'She's his mother,' Maman said with a sigh, as though misery were the maternal lot. 'What other woman would have him?' She lowered her voice. 'She tells me he spends half his earnings in brothels.'

'What?' Pascal asked.

'It's very rude to eavesdrop,' Maman said.

'I'm sitting right here!'

'All the same.'

They entered the cluttered courtyard, where Madame Chambert greeted them as cheerfully as ever and led them into her parlour, where she'd laid out an assortment of pastries.

'You shouldn't have bought so many,' Maman said. 'I warned you we'd be having a large lunch.'

'I know someone who'll have a space for more.'

'No doubt,' Maman replied. 'He'd eat in his sleep if he could.'

'And still wake up fresh as a rose,' Madame Chambert said, giving Pascal another kiss.

'Is Bastien here?' Pascal asked.

'He's taking a nap. Saturday's the busiest day at the Puces. He starts setting up before dawn and hands the stall over to his partner after lunch.'

'I'll just say hello.'

'He won't thank you for disturbing him,' Papa said.

'He promised to look out for some 78s of Fréhel and Sablon for me. I'll go and check.'

'I'm putting the kettle on,' Madame Chambert said. 'Don't be long!'

Basking in his parents' disapproval, Pascal crossed the narrow hallway and knocked on Bastien's door. Ignoring the routine 'Scram!', he entered the rank room. Bastien, ashen-faced and acne-scarred, his hair thinning on top and straggling around his ears, lay on his bed, his hands clasped behind his head, exposing dark sweat patches on his shirt.

'Ah, the *Petit Prince*! How did I guess? What gives you the right to barge in here?'

'I was born in this bed,' Pascal said, asserting an interest if not a right.

'Tell me about it!' Bastien replied, with a grimace. 'We've never managed to get the stain out of the mattress.'

'You're disgusting!'

'It was your slime. What do you want from me? I'm a busy man.'

'Looks like it! No! What's this?' He caught sight of the large, framed photograph above the bed.

'Not what, who! A goddess! Why do you ask? It's hung there for years.'

'I've never noticed it before.'

'That's your lookout.' He scrambled to his feet. 'See, it's signed. *To Bastien, my brave thief. Fondest, Arletty.*'

'Did you meet her in prison?' Pascal asked, biting back his bile.

'What are you talking about? Oh . . . oh I see . . . You're one of those. For your information, I nicked the photograph from the front of a theatre where she was playing. I went back the following week and asked her to sign it. "You've got a nerve!" she said. Then she kissed me on the lips. These lips! She didn't care.'

'I can believe it.'

'I've known many women. You'd be surprised.'

'I would,' Pascal said, recalling Maman's remark in the cab.

'But no one's ever replaced her here.' He touched his heart. 'I've worshipped her ever since I saw her in *Hôtel du Nord*. I wasn't much more than a kid myself. I went back so many times the manager grew suspicious. So what? I can truly say, she's the love of my life.'

Had he been talking of any other actress, Pascal might have felt for him. There was something pitiful about a forty-year-old bachelor, still living with his mother, besotted with a figure – a flicker – on the screen. But this was Arletty, a Nazi collaborator.

'I've seen the film. She plays a prostitute. Typecasting!'

'You arrogant brat!' He leant towards Pascal, who braved his breath rather than give ground. 'You can barely even wipe your own arse and you think you know it all!' He gazed at the picture. 'You look at that face and you know that whatever she's seen – and she's seen a lot – and whatever she's done, at heart she remains pure ... unsullied.' He smiled maliciously. 'I recognised something of that in your maman.'

'Don't you dare talk about her!'

'That's what attracted me to her.'

'Stick to your Nazi!'

Wishing that he'd heeded his parents' advice and stayed in the parlour, Pascal moved to the door.

'You know what else I admire about her – Arletty, I mean, not your maman,' Bastien said, stopping him short. 'She never made excuses for herself. She was no Danielle Darrieux.' He affected a piping voice. "I was only twenty-three. I didn't know what was what when I accepted Goebbels' invitation." No matter that she'd been around film sets since she was thirteen! And what about that smarmy hypocrite Chevalier, who claims he was blackmailed into singing in Germany in order to save his wife? Arletty took what came to her, rightly or wrongly. And you know what she said to her accusers? "My heart is French, but my cunt belongs to the world."' Pascal watched in confusion as his eyes filled with tears. 'Which is why France still loves her.'

'Haven't you opened a paper . . . haven't you looked at the television over the past two months? Haven't you heard the accounts of what the Nazis did?'

'I was here. I know what we all did. Some closer than you think.'

'What do you mean by that?'

'Nothing. I promised my mother . . . Go on! Get out! Stop plaguing me!'

'Not until you take that photograph down!'

'Who the hell do you think you are?'

'A Jew . . . very well, a half-Jew, someone your idol's lover would have sent to a concentration camp.'

'Really? I wouldn't be too sure about that.'

'Oh yes, I'd have been classified as a *Mischling*.'

'Get out before I say something I regret.'

Pascal squeezed between the night table and the headboard to snatch the photograph, which slipped from his hand and crashed to the floor, shattering the glass. The blind fury on Bastien's face frightened him and he made for the door, only for Bastien to lunge forward and drag him back.

'Get off me!'

'You don't tell me what to do! Ever! All right? You little shit . . . so sure of yourself. A concentration camp, really? For the son of a Nazi?'

'You're hurting me!'

'Are you listening? Take a look at yourself! Such a pretty boy, with your blond hair and blue eyes. Where did they come from, eh? Not Maman and Papa.'

'My grandfather,' Pascal said, his breath ragged as Bastien loosened his grip. 'My mother's father. He died before I was born.'

'Convenient that! What about all the other blond-haired,

blue-eyed men who were in Paris nine months before you were born?'

'You're mad!'

'They weren't all having affairs with famous actresses.'

'You bastard!'

'That's rich coming from you. I'm afraid Maman had a taste for German sausage.'

Unable to think or speak, Pascal let out a guttural scream, at which Bastien hauled him onto a chair. Within seconds, Madame Chambert and Papa burst into the room.

'Have you been fighting?' Madame Chambert asked, taking in the disarray.

'You swine!' Papa said. 'He's just a boy.'

'I didn't lay a finger on him. I was telling your son – or should I say your stepson? – a few home truths he should have been told a long time ago.'

'Get out!' Madame Chambert said. 'Out of my sight!'

'It's the truth,' Bastien said. 'Something we're all very keen on until it slaps us in the face.'

'Out, now!'

'Very well, Maman. Anything you say, Maman!'

Bastien seized his jacket, pushed past Papa and stormed out of the apartment, slamming the front door. Madame Chambert stood wringing her hands as Papa steered Pascal into the parlour. He found Maman stock-still and stony-faced, as though she already knew what had happened.

'Sit yourself here,' Papa said, nudging him onto the couch.

'A nip of brandy?' Madame Chambert asked.

'No,' Papa replied.

'Just for me then,' she said, pouring herself a glass.

'Then it's true what Bastien said?' Pascal asked, finally finding his voice.

'What did he say?' Papa asked quietly.

'That you're not my father.'

Maman moaned.

'I am your father . . . I am your father. Never let anyone tell you differently!' He paused. 'Just not in every way.'

'And my real father—'

'Not *real*!'

'My *real* father was a German?'

'I never wanted you to find out like this,' Maman said.

'You should never have found out at all,' Papa said, glancing at Madame Chambert.

'He was your lover?' Pascal asked Maman.

'No, no, never! We'll talk about it when we're back home . . . when you've had time to recover.'

'When will that be? 1970?'

'I'm sorry.' Maman began to shake. Unbidden, Madame Chambert handed her the glass of brandy, which she drained in a single gulp.

'I am your father,' Papa repeated. 'I have been since the day you were born.'

'As if I really did come from a cabbage patch!'

'You're more than blood. We all are. To think otherwise is to think like them.'

'Then who was he – my father – if he wasn't your lover?' Pascal asked Maman. 'Oh no! Oh God, no! Were you a prostitute?'

'No!' Papa shouted.

'I can't bear it!' Maman cried, as Madame Chambert hugged her.

'Then what? I don't understand.'

'Don't make me . . . You tell him!' Maman said to Papa. 'Tell him everything! I won't listen.' She clamped her hands over her ears.

Papa took a deep breath. 'Your mother was forced.'

'You mean raped?'

'Yes,' Papa said in a whisper.

'My father was a rapist?'

'You're not him!'

'Just tell me the truth! Was he in the Gestapo?'

'No!' Maman said, her hands dropping to her lap. 'He wasn't

violent.'

'Then how . . . who was he? The truth!'

'He was a eugenicist,' Papa said.

'What?'

'A type of race scientist.'

'You were raped by a scientist?' His incredulity triggered Maman's tears.

'I know it makes no sense,' Papa said.

'No, it doesn't.'

'But then nothing made sense in those days.'

'Tell him everything,' Maman said. 'No, I will . . . no, I can't.'

Struggling to maintain his composure, Papa explained how the German – the only identity he would afford him – had been a customer at the Tissus de Lyon store. Obsessed with Maman, he discovered that she was living with a Jew and threatened to expose them unless she slept with him.

'So it was just once?' Pascal asked.

'Yes,' Maman said flatly. 'We made an agreement.'

'So he was an honourable rapist? I suppose I should be grateful for that.'

'I know how hard this must be for you,' Maman said, gingerly reaching out to him.

'Yes, hard!' Ignoring her, he threw off his jacket, tore off his tie and began to pull his shirt over his head.

'What are you doing?' Papa asked, his face etched with alarm.

'Who am I? Who am I?' he asked, as he wrestled with the fabric.

'You won't find out like that,' Papa said, grabbing him and pulling his shirt back down.

'Should I fetch a doctor?' Madame Chambert asked.

'What for?' Pascal said. 'Arsenic?'

'Stop it!' Papa said. 'You've had a great shock, but you must stay calm.'

'I'm perfectly calm, see!' He held out his arm, which scarcely trembled. 'I know I don't look like either of you. What about him?'

'I never met him,' Papa said.

'That's no surprise. I was asking her.'

'I don't remember,' Maman replied.

'The father of your only son? Was he wearing a mask?'

'I've tried to forget.'

'What about his name? You can't have forgotten that.'

'Helmut.'

'So you were on first-name terms?'

'He signed it in the store.'

'We'll need the surname if we're going to put him on trial. He may not be Eichmann, but, whatever Marion Palomer says, people must pay for their crimes. What was it?'

'Schmidt.'

'Oh, very good! Are you trying to protect him? Well, it won't work. I'll go to every race institute in Germany. I'll find him and shoot him dead. I'll avenge your rape. Why aren't you more grateful?'

'I want to die.'

'There are no longer any race institutes in Germany,' Papa said.

'So that makes everything all right? Or don't you want me to find him? Are you afraid of what he'd tell me? Was she no better than the rest? The women paraded through the streets, without clothes, without hair? Did you shield her? Did you?' He turned first to Papa and then to Madame Chambert.

'Your mother sacrificed herself for me,' Papa said, his voice breaking. 'I owe her my life.'

Pascal doubled over and vomited.

'I'm sorry . . . very sorry. I'll clear it up,' he said to Madame Chambert, wiping his sour mouth with his hand.

'Don't be silly,' she replied, throwing a cloth over the mess and passing him a napkin.

He heard the sounds but not the words as his parents talked to Madame Chambert. To his relief, Papa had refused to spend the night in Paris and they were taking the last train back to Lyon. At some point, somebody must have rung for a taxi, since one arrived to drive them to the station where, too overwrought to go to the buffet, they sat on a bench in the chilly concourse before boarding the train. After tersely greeting the elderly couple who shared their compartment, Pascal huddled in the corner, draped his jacket over his face and tried to reconcile himself to his new reality. He wasn't the first child to find out that his father wasn't his father, but how many bastards – an identity he tentatively explored – were the children of Nazis? Maman might have saved Papa's life, but she had blighted his.

'Is that why you hate me?' he asked her, sitting up abruptly and flinging his jacket to the floor.

'What do you mean? Of course I don't hate you,' she replied, glancing at their fellow passengers.

'Pascal, please,' Papa said. 'This is neither the time nor the place.'

'Because I remind you of the rapist?'

'Monsieur, kindly restrain your son,' the man said. 'My wife shouldn't have to listen to this.'

'Oh be quiet!' Maman snapped. 'You know nothing about it.'

'You see,' Pascal told him, 'during the Occupation, my mother slept with a German to save my father's life. I thought I was half-Jewish, but I'm half Nazi.'

'This is outrageous,' the man said. 'Come!' he urged his wife, who looked reluctant to leave. He heaved a small suitcase from the overhead rack and struggled with the compartment door.

'Can I help?' Pascal asked.

'No!'

Having wrenched it open, he took hold of his wife, who smiled apologetically as he dragged her out.

'I wish I could throw myself off the train,' Maman said.

'Try to rest, both of you,' Papa said. 'It's three hours until we reach Lyon. We'll talk tomorrow.'

They arrived home shortly before midnight. Assuring Papa that he wanted nothing to eat or drink, Pascal headed straight to his room. Exhaustion overwhelmed him and he fell sound asleep. Waking at dawn, he knew that he had to escape; the question was where. He couldn't trust any of his relatives, who, for all he knew, were complicit in the deception. His only hope was Thierry. Dreading further drama, he packed a small bag and left a note for his parents, telling them where he was going and asking them to respect his privacy. He crept out of the back door and into the service lift. Failing to balance his bag on his Mobylette, he lugged it to Massena, where, much to his surprise, he encountered Thierry and Marion setting out for early morning mass. If they were equally surprised to see him, they didn't show it. Marion gave him the key to the apartment and told him to make himself at home.

He had never before felt shame on someone else's behalf and, when Thierry later asked what was wrong, he found himself prevaricating. The closest he came to the truth was telling him that he wasn't the only one not to have known his father, but Thierry took it as a metaphor. Marion promised that he could stay as long as he liked, provided that his parents were happy and he was prepared to 'rough it'. His claim to despise the Boulevard des Belges felt increasingly hollow as he stood in line outside the communal toilet, stumbled on the dimly lit stairs, and slept top to toe with Thierry on the divan, trusting that his skimpily washed feet were less pungent than his friend's.

To avoid gossip, he and Thierry agreed to make their separate ways to school, taking only Delphine and Fleur into their confidence. The plan collapsed when Jerome Héroux rang Pascal at home and Berthe, poorly briefed, revealed where he was staying. Thierry, thinking more quickly than Pascal (who was barely thinking at all) told him that Madame Carrache had been quarantined for measles, which, when the news spread, had the bonus that several of his classmates gave Pascal a wide berth.

Though not ill, Maman was suffering, as Marion related when they returned home on Monday evening. She was roasting a veal shank, much to Thierry's delight.

'The fatted calf!' he said to Pascal. 'You should stay more often.'

'Well, it was his father who paid for it,' Marion said.

'What?'

'He came to the shop this afternoon. He insisted that the last thing he wanted was for me to be out of pocket and gave me some money for Pascal's keep.'

'And you took it?' Thierry said, frowning.

'Certainly. Though it's only a fraction of what he offered.'

'You should have taken it all,' Pascal said. 'Money! That's how he controls people.'

'Enough of that! We'll toast him at dinner. Then I suppose you'll want to listen to today's report from Jerusalem.'

'What? No, absolutely not! I hope they hang Eichmann and the rope breaks and he has to go through the whole thing again, feeling twice the terror. But he's not the worst offender. That title belongs to the eugenicists: the ones who propagated the theory of the master race . . . the ones who paved the way for the Nazis' crimes. They're the ones who should really be in the dock.'

The week wore on, and Pascal pretended not to notice Thierry and Marion's growing strain as they navigated the confined space. Term would end the following Friday. Having heard nothing more about a tutor, Pascal presumed that Maman still intended to take him to visit Sylvain and Annette in Lausanne, after which Papa would join them in Cannes. Appalled by the prospect of a family holiday, he contemplated hiding in one of the disused cottages at Bessenay, living on whatever he could forage from the land. He had no idea if or when his parents would demand his return. They had each called at the Palomers', leaving without protest when Marion relayed his refusal to see them. Then on Friday evening, while Thierry was changing for a party that Pascal had decided to skip, Marion answered the doorbell. Recognising Maman's voice, he was about to retreat to the bedroom when Marion turned back, looking pale.

'It's your mother. I know you don't want to talk to her, but I think you should. Truly.'

Perturbed by her tone, Pascal nodded, and Marion opened the

door wide. Maman entered and Pascal feared that he might faint. Instead of her usual immaculate coiffure, her hair was cropped almost to the scalp. He stared at her, aghast.

'This is what you wanted, isn't it?' she asked. 'For me to be punished. I've done it for you, Pascal. I love you. I always have. Are you satisfied now?'

2

NATHAN

BUENOS AIRES, DECEMBER 1961

B RING BACK EICHMANN!, *Long Live King Christ!* and *Death to the Jews!* had been scrawled on the factory walls within hours of the guilty verdict being delivered in the Jerusalem court. While stung by the sentiments, Nathan was convinced that they were a reflection less of innate antisemitism than of the blow to national pride. Ben Gurion's announcement of Eichmann's capture in May the previous year could not have been worse timed: an admission that Argentina's sovereignty had been violated just two days before the 150th anniversary of its founding. Although a diplomatic crisis had been averted, far-right groups had launched a string of violent attacks on Jewish schools and businesses, synagogues and cemeteries. That last was a perennial target, as though they not only wanted the Jews dead but were determined to keep them from resting in peace.

The factory bell signalled the morning break, and Nathan stood at his office window, watching his staff stream outside to bask in the brilliant sunshine and share gourds of *mate*. After twenty-five years in the country, he was still not reconciled to its bitter, earthy taste. A couple of spinners were taunting Benicio as he sprayed acetone on the wall. Might they be the culprits returning to the scene of the crime? It would be wise not to delve too deeply, especially given Uncle Ruben's imminent visit. Having spent the Nazi era in the haven of South America, he was acutely sensitive to any suggestion of denying his heritage. Yet he had no desire to put himself on the line for a faith as remote to him as his childhood. Did the workforce even know that he was Jewish? Henriques was not an obviously Semitic name. As his father had frequently reminded him, the first King of Portugal had been Alfonso Henriques. So the slogans were unlikely to be aimed at him, unless the perpetrators had so absorbed the prevailing rhetoric as to assume that every wealthy businessman must be a Jew.

Leaving work at the end of the day, he surveyed the newly scrubbed wall on which traces of red remained like bloodstains, as though the death threats in the graffiti had been realised. Despite being parked beneath the canopy of a giant ombù tree, his car was searingly hot. He wound down both front windows to drink in the breeze as he raced along the expressway, only to close them against the sickly-sweet stench of the slaughterhouses when he reached Mataderos. He crawled through the city centre to the Calle Uruguay, relishing the jacaranda blossom that adorned the street like a purple ruff. It was beginning to fall, and he prayed that it would last a few more days for his family's visit. Like any proud Porteño, he was eager to show them Buenos Aires at its best.

He locked the car and gazed at the house, its stucco freshly whitewashed in honour of Katrin's wedding. He opened the front door to find his younger daughter, Arabella, guided by her unerring instinct, waiting to greet him. She lurched towards him, a broad smile on her undersized face, her shoulders jerking and hands drawing figures of eight in the air. She toppled into his arms and he hugged her tightly before leading her into the salon where Margarethe, her mother Ingeborg, Mother and Katrin were scrutinising the reception seating plan. The bride-to-be walked over to him, kissed his forehead, pronounced it 'sweaty', and relieved him of her sister. He poured himself a generous glass of vermouth and took his seat among what Margarethe had jokingly called his harem until admonished by Mother, who claimed that, as a girl in Salonica, she had known of actual harems – 'where women were treated like slaves'. That seemed far-fetched in early twentieth-century Europe, but, with Margarethe piqued by the rebuke, he hadn't wished to force the issue. Tensions might have been eased had the women spoken the same language. But Margarethe spoke to Ingeborg in German and Katrin in Spanish. Katrin spoke to one grandmother in German and the other in English. Margarethe and Mother spoke in a mishmash of the former's fractured English and the latter's Ladino-inflected Spanish. And that was before any of them tried to converse with the Guarini-speaking maids. The only one who neither struggled nor complained was the one with no language at all. Instead, she banged a tambourine and shook a string of miniature bells which, to judge by her constant grins and giggles, filled her with joy.

Mother, as forthright as ever, held that Arabella lacked sufficient stimulation at home and should attend a paediatric day centre. The remark had deeply offended Margarethe and Nathan begged Mother not to repeat it. She stood her ground, insisting that the change would benefit his wife as much as his daughter. 'Seeing her every day, you don't realise how worn out she is.' Yet, while he had long been concerned about Margarethe's overprotectiveness, he knew that there were no circumstances in which she would entrust Arabella's care to strangers. She blamed herself for having volunteered to distribute food in the *villas* when she was three months pregnant. She subsequently contracted rubella and, although he assured her that she might just as easily have caught it from a sneeze on the Calle Florida, she spurned such specious consolation.

After the initial shock, followed swiftly by rage, bitterness and despair, Nathan had come to terms with Arabella's condition. He still felt moments of terror at the thought of her fate should the world sink back into barbarism, but, for the past sixteen years, she had brought him unexpected and inexhaustible delight. Chiefly, he cherished her bond with her sister. Many children would have resented the attention lavished on a younger sibling, but Katrin treated her with boundless tenderness, patience and, most precious of all, respect. She had wanted Arabella to be her flower girl, scattering rose petals in all her bittersweet confusion, but Margarethe, declaring 'she'd be lost . . . overwhelmed and make a spectacle of herself', dismissed it outright.

Arabella's condition – or, more accurately, Margarethe's response to it – had placed a permanent strain on their marriage. They enjoyed little privacy at night, thanks to her insistence on leaving their bedroom door open to listen out for the faintest whimper. For the main, they heard nothing but the tinkle of the bells Arabella clasped even in her sleep and which he trusted echoed the enchantment of her dreams. During the month of Mother's visit, that had been coupled with the muffled sounds of the BBC World Service, which, as her insomnia worsened, she tuned into until the early hours.

While she knew better than to complain about the radio, Margarethe didn't hesitate to voice her other grievances. 'You know I love having your mother here,' she said when, washed, brushed and cold-creamed, she slipped into bed that night.

'Yes,' he replied warily.

'But you have to talk to her. She's causing havoc in the kitchen.'

If Nathan were ever permitted to meet the therapist he paid so handsomely each week, he would ask him why his wife abandoned Spanish and reverted to German whenever she spoke of his mother.

'How? Is she mobilising the maids again?'

'That's not funny.'

Undeterred by the language barrier, Mother had ascertained that Mela and Yanina both had children living with their grandmothers in Paraguay. Horrified by the separation, she accused Nathan of exploiting their poverty and demanded that he bring the children over to Argentina. When he explained that the women were happy with their lot, earned far more than they would have done at home, and preferred their children to grow up within their own culture, she accused him of twisting the facts to salve his conscience.

'So what's the problem this time?' he asked Margarethe.

'Hands! As if we're not run ragged with only eight days till the wedding, not to mention your uncle and aunt arriving tomorrow, she wants to make some sort of traditional marzipan hands from Salonica. Hands ... more hands! What is it with her and hands?'

She had yet to forgive Mother for giving Katrin a small gold hand, an amulet to ward off the evil eye, which, as a rationalist, she should have abhorred, except that she'd received it from her own grandmother fifty years earlier. To Margarethe's distress, Katrin, whose faith had become a formality, had taken to wearing it in place of a cross.

'Hand? Foot? Breast?' he teased, as he leant across to caress his wife. Sensing her struggle not to flinch, he extricated himself as discreetly as possible. 'Why not let her make her pastries if it keeps her happy?'

'But it doesn't. She cooks a batch and they turn out wrong. So she starts again. She's commandeered the oven. We were lucky to have any dinner at all tonight.'

'Just be glad she's celebrating. Not that long ago she was vehemently opposed to Katrin getting married so young.'

'She wasn't the only one.'

'I wanted them to wait until they graduate.'

'It'll be four or five years ... more if they embark on doctorates.'

'I'm well aware of that! Mother's basing it on her own experience. She was nineteen when she married Father.'

'In very different circumstances. Anyone can see that Katrin and Stefan are head over heels in love. Besides, she grew fonder of your father over the years. Basil wrote of her desolation at his death.'

'A lot must have changed after I left. I suppose the war brought them closer.'

'It's a shame that she never married again or even met somebody else. How old was she when your father died. Fifty?'

'Forty-eight.'

'Only five years older than me.'

'So will you become a merry widow, on the hunt for husband number two?'

'I'll definitely keep all my options open.'

'Don't forget Basil died a few months after Father. You might move on from me, but if Katrin or Arabella—'

'No!' She rolled over and put a finger to his lips. 'Don't say it! Goodnight, *Liebchen*.' She kissed him softly on the cheek, turned on her side and switched off her bedside lamp.

Nathan yawned, laid his head on his hands and gazed at the ceiling. Late-night thoughts of Basil banished sleep as forcefully as the strongest *café negro*. While his own war effort had amounted to little more than chorusing the Marseillaise during cinema newsreels, his gentle, bookish brother had not only fought but, as he now knew, undertaken perilous missions behind enemy lines, the last of which proved fatal. Along with more than three thousand other combatants whose bodies were never recovered, his name was inscribed on the Brookwood War Memorial in Surrey. Nathan had flown to England to escort his mother to the unveiling three years before. Far from consoling her, the occasion had revived all her bleakest memories.

'It's my fault . . . my own selfish fault. If I'd allowed him to join you in Argentina when he asked, he'd be alive today.'

'He might still have signed up.'

'You didn't,' she replied, in a tone that was impossible to gauge.

After a fretful night, he came downstairs to find the household gathered for breakfast. Mother was reading the *Buenos Aires Herald*.

'Will it never end?' she asked, brandishing the front-page article on the new wave of antisemitic attacks.

'Don't worry, Granny,' Katrin said. 'We're fighting back. There's a demonstration at the university this morning.'

'Another one?' Nathan asked.

'It's not just against Tacura and their fellow fascists but against police apathy. Our rector is the President's brother and they still do nothing! Things have got so bad that some Jewish students have started carrying guns.'

'Guns! Are they mad?' Nathan said. 'Guns? I absolutely forbid you to go.'

'They won't have them today. They won't need them. There'll be thousands of us.'

'You might still get knocked and bruised,' Margarethe said. 'Need I remind you that you're getting married in a week?'

'Of course not. Besides, I'm going with Stefan.'

'I'd no idea that this country had grown so dangerous,' Mother said. 'You should think again about coming home, Nathan.'

'This is my home,' he replied, wearily. 'And what about British antisemitism? The Northern – that's a tennis club,' he explained to Margarethe, busy buttering a *medialunas*, 'bordered our garden in Elm Road. I was a decent enough player. But was I permitted to join?'

'That's as may be,' Mother said. 'But they don't paint swastikas on our gates. They don't chant *Death to the Jews*. They don't shoot schoolchildren.'

'One schoolchild! Which is abominable enough. But it doesn't justify your condemning the entire country. During the war, I was criticised for refusing to sack my German workers. I don't hold with collective guilt.'

'Then you're in the right place. Look at all the Germans they've allowed in here! I'm sorry, I didn't mean . . .' She turned to Ingeborg, who munched her toast obliviously.

'My father was a printer,' Margarethe said, with a strained smile. 'He had fifty thousand copies of the sharp attack Herr Mann had written on the Nazis printed with his own money! These copies were brought on ships back to Germany. It has made him many enemies, but he is standing for what he believed in.'

'Yes, of course, my dear,' Mother replied, flustered. 'I didn't mean families like yours, who've lived here for generations, but the ones who sneaked in after the war.'

'But not Stefan's?' Katrin asked Mother, who seemed intent on offending the whole table. 'I know that some high-ranking Nazis were smuggled here by the Church.' She glanced defiantly at Margarethe. 'But his parents were anti-fascists. Isn't that right, Papá?'

'As far as I'm aware, yes.'

Nathan had been troubled by Katrin's budding friendship with Stefan, whose father only left Germany in 1954. But Helmut was candid about his past, explaining that, while he'd worked for the Military Administration in France, he had served his country, not its ideology. His disillusion with his homeland had deepened on seeing former Nazis return to prominence, even at the heart of Adenauer's government. Matters came to a head when thousands of fascist sympathisers gathered at the gates of Landsberg prison to demand the release of jailed war criminals. He planned to emigrate, but jobs for foreign ethnologists were scarce. When a friend informed him of a vacancy at the ethnographic museum in Buenos Aires, he applied and, on his appointment, moved his family here.

He enrolled Stefan in the prestigious Goethe-Schule, whose pupils regularly restaged the battles of the 1930s, attacking local Jewish youths. According to Katrin, Stefan refused to take part or even fight back when confronted, determined to refute the notion of the master race. Doubting that he would exercise the same restraint in a just cause, Nathan secured Katrin's promise to quit the demonstration at the first sign of trouble. He then retreated to his study to make a series of phone calls to the factory and showroom, before leaving with Mother for the airport.

His family would be underrepresented at the wedding. Aunt Milly, who had yet to visit Argentina despite numerous promises, was stuck in Bournemouth, tending to his ninety-one-year-old grandmother. His cousins Gabrielle and Clarice were similarly tied to their ailing parents. Aunt Lily was a chronic hypochondriac, but Uncle Simon had recently been diagnosed with Pick's disease, a form of dementia hitherto unknown to Nathan. The medical dictionary detailed symptoms such as speech difficulties, mood swings, delusions, aggression and greed, all of which matched Clarice's account. She had taken him to live with her in Cap Ferrat, hiring three nurses in swift succession, each of whom quit after he crept into her bedroom during a siesta. Clarice downplayed his offences, but loss of inhibition was highlighted in the dictionary. She denounced the nurses' lack of professionalism, but, rather than risk a repeat, chose to care for him herself.

Sylvain, who, as expected, had excused himself from the wedding, maintained cynically – cruelly – that Clarice could now enjoy the martyrdom that had eluded her during the war. Moreover, it came coupled with the stewardship of Uncle Simon's vast fortune. In a letter addressed to the entire family, she wrote that, with her father's blessing, she was endowing a museum in Thessaloniki to honour its Jewish heritage. Nathan had welcomed the project and agreed to fly over for the opening, but Mother was outraged.

'She's so impetuous. What does she know of the heritage? She'd never set foot in Salonica until three years ago.'

'Thessaloniki,' Nathan had said, as irritated by her use of the old name as by her calculations in old francs.

'Your Aunt Irène would turn in her grave. She was the most level-headed of us all.'

'It's her father's money. She can spend it however she likes.'

'Money he made by leveraging my father's property.'

'You shouldn't make such allegations without proof.'

'Mercado was far too canny to leave tracks.'

Uncle Ruben, Aunt Madeleine and Pascal were the only Carraches to have accepted the invitation, which, in Nathan's view, stemmed as much from his uncle's desire to inspect his Argentine subsidiary as to attend his great-niece's wedding. He stood beside Mother in the arrivals concourse at Ezeiza, watching clusters of passengers file out, exhilarated and exhausted after one of the new nonstop flights from Paris. Finally, his relatives appeared, behind a Mapuche porter pushing a trolley, its five large suitcases filling Nathan with alarm. He hung back while Mother rushed forward to embrace her brother and sister-in-law.

'Your hair, Madeleine! Is this what's called a pixie cut?'

'So I'm told. Pascal thought it would suit me.'

'Count yourself lucky. Nathan never shows the slightest interest in the way I look.'

Nathan kissed his uncle and aunt and, catching Pascal wince at Mother's kiss, offered him his hand, which he shook listlessly.

'You look more like your father each time I see you,' Mother said to Pascal, although Nathan failed to detect the resemblance.

'No more of that, Esther,' Uncle Ruben interjected gruffly. 'Every boy likes to think himself his own man. Imagine if Tante Amada had said it to Leon or me.'

'I'm passing out with the heat,' Madeleine said, as Nathan led the way to the car park.

'According to the paper, the humidity today is seventy per cent,' Mother replied. 'Which is why I usually avoid coming in the summer – their summer, I mean. You swelter during the day; then, at night, you can't sleep for all the dogs barking when the thunderstorms hurtle across the Pampas. Don't forget to ask the chambermaid for ear plugs.'

'It's a five-star hotel,' Nathan said mildly. 'It's sure to be well insulated.' He drove down the expressway and onto the Avenida 9 de Julio.

'My goodness!' Madeleine exclaimed. 'I wasn't expecting this.'

'According to the *Encyclopaedia Britannica*, it's the widest avenue in the world. We Porteños are very proud of it.' Nathan ignored Mother's sniff. 'So take care only to cross at the lights,' he added, glancing back at Pascal, who seemed strangely subdued, no doubt from the after-effects of Dramamine.

'This is the Avenida de Mayo. Any moment now, you'll catch a glimpse of the Plaza de Mayo and the famous Casa Rosada.'

'It really is pink,' Madeleine said, as it emerged into view.

'It's reputed to come from pig's blood mixed with the whitewash, which certainly fits its history. A great deal of blood has been spilt in the square. Most recently, when air force bombers killed three hundred people and triggered Perón's ousting.'

'Isn't that a good thing?' Pascal piped up. 'He's a fascist.'

'Yes and no. He's not quite that easy to pigeonhole. True, his rallies sent a shiver down my spine ... blink and you'd think yourself in Nuremberg! But in this country, you learn not to cheer too soon. You never know what's round the corner.'

They arrived at the Alvear Palace hotel.

'I wish you'd change your minds and stay at Nathan's,' Mother said, as the porters fetched the luggage. 'It feels wrong that you should be in a hotel. And so extravagant!'

'Ruben doesn't like to be beholden to anyone,' Pascal said.

'You call your father Ruben?' Mother asked.

'It's the fashion among young people,' Madeleine said.

'I trust it's not one you'll adopt,' Mother said to Nathan.

'I'm not young.'

He left the visitors to settle in and drove Mother home, returning at eight o'clock to collect them for dinner and a tango show at El Querandi, where they were greeted by Margarethe and Katrin and introduced to Stefan.

'I'm afraid it's very touristy,' Nathan said, as they took their seats at a dimly lit table to the plaintive strains of a piano, violin and bandoneon.

'Well, we are tourists,' Madeleine replied. 'Besides, Ruben told me this was how you two met.'

'In the school,' Margarethe said, struggling with the French they were speaking for Madeleine's benefit. 'We were both – how does one say? – beginners.'

'Are you experts now?' Pascal asked, at which Katrin smiled.

'It's not a dance for old married couples,' Nathan said. 'Seductive but not romantic. You'll see.'

Like the many foreign visitors he had brought here over the years, Pascal and Madeleine were dazzled by the dancers' virtuosity but surprised by the studied disregard they displayed towards each other, even as their bodies were intimately entwined.

'It's as if the closer they get, the further they're apart,' Pascal said.

'This is true,' Margarethe said haltingly. 'The dance arose in – how does one say? – *ein Bordell*.'

'The same: a bordello,' Nathan replied. 'And not between the men and women, but among the men themselves as they waited to be summoned upstairs. Which is why there's such a tension: contemptuous faces, competitive feet.'

'When I was young, Buenos Aires was a byword for decadence,' Uncle Ruben said. 'If ever there were an Argentine ship in port, Bella would refuse to leave the house. She was convinced she'd be kidnapped and sold as a white slave. Do you remember, Esther?'

'Yes of course,' she said, her eyes glistening.

At the end of the evening, the visitors returned to the hotel. Katrin, who spoke to Pascal in English, her third and his second language, arranged that she and Stefan would pick him up in the morning, 'so long as you're cool with our little *Fitito*. We can show you the city, or just hang out in a café, whatever feels good.'

Margarethe was too focused on her French to notice Madeleine's pout when she proposed to take her shopping.

'We will be going to Calle Florida. There are many clothes shops, but also leather shops . . . art shops.'

'That sounds lovely, thank you.'

'There's even Harrods,' Mother said encouragingly.

Nathan, meanwhile, arranged to meet Uncle Ruben in the hotel lobby at eight thirty to drive him to the factory. He strove to contain his impatience during the forty-minute delay as his uncle called France and their subsequent ensnarement in rush hour traffic.

'And I thought Lyon was noisy,' Uncle Ruben said, amidst the cacophony of car horns, tram bells and taxi radios.

'All part of life's rich symphony,' Nathan replied, forcing a laugh.

He took advantage of the journey to report on the company's recent developments. He knew how hard Uncle Ruben had worked to relaunch the label in France after the Liberation. And while even the gravest abuses of the Perón regime paled beside the atrocities of the Occupation, he felt that he deserved praise for restoring the factory to profitability after the former president's fall. Perón was in exile in Spain, and it was illegal to utter his name or refer to him as anything but 'the dictator' (although scrawls of *Perón will return* were increasingly prevalent in the poorer barrios). Nevertheless, after many years of labour unrest, stagnant productivity and rising costs, the workforce was tranquil, output had increased and costs fallen. Aided by the tax breaks and credit facilities that the Frondizi government had offered to manufacturers of synthetic textiles, he'd boosted rayon production. And by founding mulberry plantations and silkworm farms in the Pampas, he'd streamlined the supply chain for natural fibre. The company had doubled its market share across Central and South America and, with the growing renown of local designers, he even envisaged expanding into Europe.

'Who knows? Maybe one day Tissus de Lyon will become a subsidiary of Hilos del Pampas,' he said, to avuncular amusement.

He spent the morning on the factory floor, guiding Uncle Ruben through the entire production process, from sorting the cocoons to storing the finished fabric. He introduced him to operatives from each section – reelers, twisters and spinners; dyers and weavers – before heading to the research lab to meet the team developing a new type of flame-retardant rayon. After a final stop at the design studio, he led him back to his office, running into one of the factory's therapists along the way.

'You have two therapists permanently on the payroll?' Uncle Ruben asked incredulously over lunch.

'That's the bare minimum. Anything less, and the staff would question my commitment to their wellbeing. The whole of Buenos Aires is addicted to therapy.'

'Why?'

'Ask a therapist! Margarethe has friends who take their holidays at the same time – and in the same resorts – as their therapists so as not to miss a single session. It's a second national religion. You know they've made the Virgin Mary an honorary general in the army.'

'You're not serious?'

'Cross my heart! They should make Freud her chief of staff.'

They returned to the city in the late afternoon. Nathan dropped Uncle Ruben at the hotel and drove home, where Margarethe was busy preparing a dinner for the Carraches to meet Stefan's parents. The former were the first to arrive, Pascal carrying a large parcel which he sweatily relinquished to Katrin.

'It's not your main present. That will come in an envelope,' Uncle Ruben said, as she tore off the brown paper to reveal an exquisite, illuminated parchment.

'It's darling!' she said. 'Thank you so much.' She gazed uncertainly from Pascal to Madeleine and Uncle Ruben. 'What is it?'

'It's called a *ketubah*,' Uncle Ruben replied. 'The marriage contract in which a Jewish husband sets out his obligations to his wife. This was my mother's. I can still see it, hanging in her bedroom, first in Salonica and then in Paris. When the Germans ransacked the house, they must have considered it worthless because, years later, I found it in the cellar, the glass and frame shattered but otherwise intact. I'd hoped to give it to one of my nieces, but since both seem destined to remain old maids—'

'Ruben . . .' Madeleine said reprovingly.

'I'm sorry . . . strong, independent women . . . I'm delighted to give it to my great-niece.'

'I shall cherish it,' Katrin said.

'We shall cherish it,' Stefan said.

'Do you think you should set out your obligations to me?' she asked him.

'With pleasure. As long as it's in a language you can't read.'

They kissed fondly.

'Do you remember it, Esther?' Uncle Ruben asked Mother, who was studying the *ketubah*.

'You keep asking me that! My memory's every bit a match for yours.'

'Then you must recall how you disapproved of it. Something

about its embodying male privilege or licensing male lust.' He laughed.

'Don't tease your sister,' Madeleine said.

'Utter drivel!' Mother said. 'I only wish I could call Irène and Bella as witnesses.'

'So do I. But I'm afraid you have to make do with me,' he said, tenderly taking her hand.

A silence descended on the room, broken by the banging of a tambourine as Ingeborg brought in Arabella. Nathan curbed a frown at her beribboned hair and ruffled, puff-sleeved dress, further evidence of Margarethe's attempt to infantilise their already backward child. It was clear from Pascal's expression that neither of his parents had warned him what to expect. Even so, his reaction was extreme.

'Why didn't you tell me about her?' he asked his father. 'Why is no one in this family ever honest?' He crossed the room to where Arabella was etching the air with what Nathan hoped were fantastical images, not random tangles.

'Gently!' Madeleine said, as he hugged her. But as soon as he released his hold, Arabella waved her string of bells in his face, a sure sign of favour.

She gurgled at him. Then, catching sight of the *ketubah*, which Katrin had propped against a chair, she twisted her head back and forth for a better view. 'Pretty, isn't it?' Pascal said, lifting it to show her. 'See all the birds and the flowers round the edges?' Arabella held out her hand and, before Nathan could stop him, Pascal passed it to her. It slipped from her grip, and she tumbled to the floor beneath it. She let out a faint groan as Margarethe and Katrin rushed to her aid.

'I'm sorry. So sorry,' Pascal mumbled. 'I didn't mean . . . I didn't think . . .'

'No worry,' Margarethe said, breathing heavily. 'Nothing is broken. Just a few bruisings.'

'I'm such an idiot!'

Arabella ceased groaning and, along with everyone else, watched as Pascal slapped his face with increasing force.

'Idiot! Idiot!'

'Stop that!' Uncle Ruben said, grabbing his hand.

'Arabella's made of rubber,' Mother said. 'Aren't you, angel?'

Pascal burst into tears. Madeleine moved towards him, taking his arm more tentatively than Nathan might have expected. 'There's no harm done,' she said. 'Even the contract-thing's undamaged.'

'I want to go home . . . to the hotel. Please!'

'We can't leave yet. It would be rude. We've come to meet Stefan's parents.'

'They'll understand,' Stefan said, looking embarrassed at the unrestrained emotion. 'You'll meet them another day. I can drive you and be back here in no time.'

'If you're sure it's no trouble,' Madeleine said uncertainly.

Stefan took Pascal to the hotel and Ingeborg took Arabella into the garden, where she scrabbled happily in the sandpit. Under the circumstances, Nathan chose not to wait for Helmut and Monica before opening the champagne, and he was already recharging glasses when they arrived. He effected introductions and hoped that he was alone in observing the lingering gaze Helmut cast at Madeleine, as though comparing her beauty and glamour with the matronliness of his wife.

Monica's lack of French and Madeleine's of German impeded fluid conversation. Moreover, Madeleine seemed barely to be listening when Margarethe translated Monica's greeting.

'Is all in order?' Margarethe asked her.

'Sorry, I was somewhere else for a moment.'

'We will speak French for Madame's sake,' Helmut said. 'My wife is very shy. She will be happy to sit quietly.'

'You have a fine accent,' Uncle Ruben said. 'Nathan tells me you were posted to France during the Occupation.'

'I hope he explained that I was attached to the German Institute in the Hôtel de Sagan. Very low-level. I ran language courses for the many thousands of your compatriots who wished to learn German. Clearly, Madame wasn't one of them.' He smiled at Madeleine. 'It's true that in my role I met people responsible for other aspects of policy, but I took no part in implementing it.'

'Though you did facilitate it,' Uncle Ruben said.

'I tried to facilitate understanding.'

'I can't help noticing the way you've been staring at my wife,' Uncle Ruben added, in a colder tone.

'Forgive me, I don't mean to be impolite.' He addressed Madeleine. 'But I feel sure that I've seen you before. Are you an actress? Or were you one twenty years ago?'

'No,' Madeleine faltered, as if she were the one speaking a foreign language. 'I worked in a fabric store.'

'Our parent company, Tissus de Lyon,' Nathan said.

'Tissus de Lyon?' Monica said, catching the name. She turned to Helmut. 'Isn't that where you bought me the silk for my kimono and the oak-leaf scarf?'

'I don't wish to disillusion you,' Helmut replied, 'but it was my secretary who bought them. I had no time to shop. You should be grateful.' He laughed and reverted to French. 'She had far better taste than me.'

'We speak enough about the past,' Margarethe said briskly. 'We look forward now. Old enemies . . . new friends. I wish to pronounce a toast.'

'I'm sorry,' Madeleine said, 'but I need to lie down. I feel rather dizzy. Too much champagne on an empty stomach.'

'I make the call for Mela,' Margarethe said. 'We eat at once.'

'I really need to lie down.'

'Is there anything I can do?' Uncle Ruben asked.

'I'm just a little light-headed. Please don't make a fuss.'

'You take our bed,' Margarethe said. 'Come, I bring you upstairs.'

'No, stay and see to your guests. Nathan, would you help me?'

'Yes, of course,' he said, sharing a baffled glance with Margarethe. With the usually poised Madeleine clinging to his arm, he moved towards the stairs, only to steer her to the study when she explained that what she really needed was to talk. She sank into an armchair before springing up to gaze at the garden, where, in the twilight, Ingeborg stood watching Arabella sprawl in the sandpit, trickling grains between her toes.

'Do you ever wonder what her life might have been like had she been born ten or fifteen years earlier and on another continent?'

'Every night,' he murmured.

Notwithstanding her sombre tone, he was quite unprepared for what followed. In a wavering voice and with her eyes still fixed on the window, she revealed that the man sipping champagne in the salon, the man to whom in less than a week's time he would be related by marriage, was a Nazi eugenicist who'd forced himself on her eighteen years before and fathered her son.

'Do you despise me?'

'What?' He blenched. 'No, never. Him, him!'

'We watched the nightly bulletins from the Eichmann trial over the summer. One moment that sticks in my mind is when the prosecutor asked a witness – a Pole, I think – why he didn't fight back. Pascal was outraged, but the question resonated with me. I was alone with that man more than once. I could have taken a knife. I could have . . .' Her voice trailed off into what felt like a silent scream.

'You're not a killer.'

'I should have made myself one.'

Eager to console her, he stood up and clasped her shoulders, only to recoil from her shudder.

'He can still be held accountable, if only by us. I won't have him in the house. I won't have him at the wedding . . . No, how can we even have a wedding?'

'You must. Stefan isn't his father, any more than Pascal is. The cruellest verse in that cruellest book is the one about children paying for their fathers' sins. Stefan and Katrin love each other. I've only seen them together twice, but it shines through. We can't destroy their happiness – to say nothing of Ruben's peace of mind.'

[431]

'Does he still believe he's Pascal's father?'

'He never has . . . He's lived with the shame – my shame, his shame – from the start. He hadn't met that man till now, though they were once – briefly – in the same room. But I could sense his unease when he saw him staring at me. Did he catch a glimpse of Pascal in his face? Because it's there. God knows, it's there.'

'I won't say a word – not a word, I swear.'

'Not even to Margarethe, nor to Esther . . . dear God, not to her! We'd barely stepped off the plane when she told Pascal how much he looked like Ruben. It was as though she was trying to convince herself, without knowing it.'

'Pay no attention to Mother. She tries to fit us all into boxes. And what do looks matter anyway? I see so much of Uncle Ruben in him: the same intelligence and integrity, the same refusal to suffer fools.'

'Now you're the one trying to convince yourself. The irony is that, if it wasn't for Pascal, I'm quite sure that Ruben would have left me years ago.'

'What nonsense! You saved him.'

'That's my point. Of course he was grateful. How could he not be? But gratitude isn't love. His uncle had left him his share of the factory, and we thought we'd make a fresh start away from the pain of Paris. Soon after that, he began to lead his own life, if you take my meaning.'

'And your life?'

'What did Margarethe suppose I'd most want to do in Buenos Aires? Like those women from the sixteenth I used to serve, buying the new season's silks when they'd barely unwrapped the old ones, my life is one long Calle Florida.'

'But you have Pascal.'

'And there's another irony. I was so terrified of hating him as a baby that at times I wouldn't pick him up, in case I felt the urge to drop him. Does that make sense to you?' Nathan said nothing. 'Good! It shouldn't. Yet for all the terror, my only urge – an abiding, unquenchable urge – was to shower him with love. Over the years,

I've been tough on him – not, whatever you might suppose, because I recognised something of that man in his wilfulness or bluster. No, I reasoned that if I was the one who set the rules and dealt the punishments, then he'd look to Ruben for affection and support. As his mother, I had an instinctive bond with him, whereas Ruben's would need to be forged. You can tell I'm no psychologist! Now that he knows the truth, he feels estranged from us both.'

'How long has he known?'

'Only since the summer. I'd deluded myself that he would never find out. He felt betrayed . . . confused . . . wounded . . . angry . . . I expected him to turn the anger on me, but he turned it on himself. He . . . it doesn't matter. He's seen several therapists.' Nathan cringed to recall how he'd mocked them to his uncle at lunch. 'He or perhaps they – it's sometimes hard to know who's talking – assured me that I'd done the right thing. "A child born out of hatred can still live in love."'

'Pascal said that?'

'Word for word. Which is when I realised he was parroting what he'd heard at the clinic. He's still very fragile. I dread to think what it might do to him to learn that that man is here.'

'Then he never must. If we appeal to Helmut's sense of decency . . .'

'I tried that once before . . . I knew I would never escape him, but I thought it would just be in here.' She tapped her head. 'I never thought I'd meet him again – let alone after flying halfway across the world, and in your salon!'

'He knew exactly what to expect. He must have made the connection the moment I told him that our parent company was French and mentioned Uncle Ruben's name. No wonder he was so keen to know which of my relatives were coming to the wedding!'

'So what does he want, apart from another chance to torture me?'

'What if it's the opposite: he's changed and he wants to atone?'

'Never!' Her features twisted in fury. 'He's incapable of remorse.

He was toying with me over again. The pretence that he'd seen me on stage! It's all part of some sick game.'

'So what do we do? Act as if nothing's wrong and wait for him to make a move? Or should we challenge him?'

'You're the only one who can help. You must find a way out.'

'Right now the best thing we can do is get you back to the hotel,' he replied, crushed by the responsibility. 'Stay here while I fetch Uncle Ruben.'

Nathan entered the dining room, where Mela and Yanina were serving pumpkin soup, and explained that Madeleine was still feeling out of sorts. Dismissing the clamour of concern, he advised Uncle Ruben to return to the hotel.

'Yes, of course. I thought she was resting upstairs.'

'But you've had nothing to eat,' Mother said.

'I'll have something sent up to the room.'

'And Madeleine needs her bed,' Nathan interjected.

'Do you have any pickled herring?' Helmut asked, with a supercilious smile.

'What?' Nathan snapped.

'At home, we swear by it when someone is feeling – what's the word in French? – *merry*.'

'Trust me, she's feeling anything but merry,' Nathan replied through clenched teeth.

He ran his uncle and aunt back to the hotel, wincing when Uncle Ruben commended Helmut's charm. Rather than return straight home, he took a drive along the Avenida Costanera to clear his head, but the shimmering darkness of the Rio de la Plata merely mirrored his confusion. He'd thought he had plumbed the depths of his family's wartime suffering, only to discover this new horror. He was seized by the desire – shocking in its intensity – to hurt Helmut, but his duty was to protect Madeleine and Pascal. Who could tell what Helmut would do when he came face to face with his son? And even if he did nothing, everyone there would be bound to detect the resemblance, which, now that he knew of it himself, was unmistakable.

'He looks more like you, Helmut, each time I see him.' Mother's voice rang in his head during another sleepless night.

At breakfast, blissfully oblivious of the spectre looming over them, Margarethe ran through the latest wedding preparations, reminding Katrin of their five o'clock appointment at the florists. After lengthy debate, they had settled on arrangements of white roses and cornflowers, the national flowers of England and Germany, for both the church and the bridal bouquet. Sensing Katrin's growing irritation with her mother's meddling, Nathan was struck by a possible – albeit extreme – solution to his problem.

'Remember when you told us that you and Stefan felt like eloping to avoid all the fuss?' he asked Katrin.

'What rubbish is this?' Margarethe said, narrowing her eyes at him.

'There's still time. You could fly down to Ushuaia . . . or take a boat to the Malvinas. They have a cathedral.'

'And what am I supposed to say to the 250 guests at the reception?' Margarethe asked.

'*Bon appétit?*'

'I'm not joking!'

'Neither am I.'

Katrin circled the table and kissed the crown of his head. 'Don't you want to give me away?'

'I just want you to be happy.'

'I am. Gloriously. Now I must dash. Stefan's picking me up in twenty minutes. We're meeting the Carraches at the hotel. While you were ministering to Aunt Madeleine last night, Helmut offered to show them round the Museo Etnográfico.'

'No, that's out of the question!'

'Why?' Mother asked. 'It's most generous of him.'

'What is there to see? Just masks . . . feathers . . . bits of bark.'

'You called it fascinating when he took us,' Margarethe said.

'For Buenos Aires, yes. But there'll be far more extensive collections in Paris . . . in Lyon too, for all I know. I've a better idea. I'll take them to Tigre. Arabella can come with us. She always loves it there.'

'Helmut will be offended,' Margarethe said.

'I'm sure he'll understand.'

He rang Helmut and, in as even a tone as he could muster, informed him of the change of plan. He asked to meet him the following morning at the Tissus de Lyon showroom 'to discuss a couple of issues that have cropped up'. Without missing a beat, Helmut promised to be there.

Madeleine, still feeling 'poorly', chose to remain at the hotel, so Mother took her place, sitting beside Arabella and Pascal in the back seat of the car, with Uncle Ruben in the front, for the thirty-kilometre journey. They met up with Katrin and Stefan at the harbour, where, after protracted haggling, Nathan engaged a boatman to take them on a two-hour trip around the delta.

'They may be dilapidated,' Mother said to Uncle Ruben as they cruised past a row of once-opulent mansions, 'but don't they remind you of the Campania?'

'It isn't good to dwell in the past, Esther.'

'I don't *dwell*, just pay an occasional visit.'

Back on dry land, Stefan led the main party to lunch, followed by a tour of the artists' quarter, while Nathan took Arabella for a cheese empanada and a donkey ride in the park. At three o'clock, they returned to the city, and at seven thirty, having exchanged his blazer and chinos for evening dress, he drove Mother and Margarethe to the Teatro Colón to join Uncle Ruben and Madeleine at a performance of *Salome*.

He was greatly relieved to see Madeleine, recovered and resplendent in an ostrich feather capelet over a sea-green taffeta gown. Leaving the others nursing their cocktails in the bar, he guided her through the gilded grandeur of the Salo Dorado. 'I must thank you again for yesterday,' she said, as they strolled along a colonnade, the evening sun streaming through the stained-glass dome to dapple her face. 'I daren't think how I'd have managed without you there. Seeing that man walk into the room, I panicked. Now I've had time to reflect on it, I realise he has far more to fear from me than I do from him. Ruben and Pascal know the truth; Monica and Stefan quite clearly don't. A few choice words about his brutality - his violation, as well as his murderous propaganda - and his whole world would crumble. Why should I lie low? I'm tempted to ask you to bring us together. Let me confront him! Let me bully and blackmail him the way he did me!'

The auditorium bell rang. 'We'll talk more in the interval,' he said, escorting her to their box. As it transpired, there was no interval. So, after leaving the theatre, he drew her aside as they walked to the car. 'I've arranged to meet Helmut in the morning,' he whispered, aware of Mother's quizzical gaze. 'I'll warn him that, should he say anything to upset Pascal, much less reveal their relationship, I'll denounce him to the museum. It's linked to the university, one of the few nominally progressive institutions in the country, and they won't take kindly to employing a former Nazi ideologue.'

'Perfect! The perfect plan. I knew I could depend on you.'

'If you like, why not come along?'

'Would that be wise?'

'You can eavesdrop from the secretary's office.'

'Just like old times,' she said wryly. 'I'm used to being hidden away at Tissus de Lyon.'

The next morning, with Madeleine in position, he waited in the manager's office for Helmut, who arrived on the stroke of ten. 'Come in!' he said coldly, disdaining the proffered hand.

'I see that Madeleine's spoken to you,' Helmut said, smiling at the naked rebuff. 'When does she want us to meet?'

'Why would she want to do that?'

'Surely you felt the spark between us . . . rekindled after all these years? She fled the room in case she betrayed it.'

Nathan stood transfixed by his arrant self-delusion.

'Aren't you afraid of betraying it - to your wife and son?'

'I'd never do anything to hurt them. I came to this country to protect them.'

'And wove a tissue of lies.' Galled by Helmut's pacing, he gestured to the armchairs on either side of a low smoked-glass table. 'Sit down!' He waited for him to take his seat before taking the other. 'You didn't work at a cultural institute in Paris but a race institute.'

'I dissembled out of necessity, not shame.'

'You were – perhaps still are – a eugenicist.'

'As I said, I'm not ashamed. It was my great good fortune to study anthropology in Berlin, when a ground-breaking scientific discipline was introduced at the Kaiser Wilhelm Institute. The Führer's election enabled us to put it into practice. I was privileged to play a part in developing our selective breeding programme. Then, in 1941, I was sent to Paris to educate the French about the Jewish threat.'

'And you had no qualms?'

'None whatsoever. I was – and remain – a dedicated champion of my race. My father alerted me to the Jewish plot for world domination, both at home and from the pulpit. He explained how Christ came to redeem the Jews, but they rejected him. It's in their nature always to want something more. Besides, how could a gospel of meekness and poverty appeal to such an arrogant, avaricious people?'

'Yet your son is about to marry my daughter.'

'If I'd set my face against it, I'd have lost both Stefan and his mother. It's not the first time I've had to swallow my principles.'

'And who knows? Soon you may have a grandchild with Jewish blood.'

'One quarter Jewish blood! The Führer permitted such *Mischlings of the second degree* to breed with Aryans, knowing that the purer blood must prevail.'

Soul-sick, Nathan moved to his desk and rang for coffee, as much for the distraction as the drink. Instinct compelled him to offer a cup to Helmut.

'Thank you. A pity it's not *mate*! I could demonstrate my newfound magnanimity by sharing your straw.'

'Are you trying to make me loathe you even more?'

'Your opinion is of no consequence to me. I'm simply speaking the truth . . . and highlighting the hypocrisy. Please spare me the cant that all human life is sacred! Even in America, that so-called bastion of equality, more than half the states had laws to sterilise the feeble-minded before we enacted ours. A procedure which, as I understand it, you've carried out on your younger daughter.'

Nathan jumped up. 'That's slander!'

'I apologise,' Helmut said coolly. 'I must have been misinformed.'

Nathan was horrified to learn that he knew of Arabella's hysterectomy. He had vehemently opposed the operation when Margarethe first broached it, accusing her of seeking to suppress Arabella's nascent sexuality, relenting only after she produced a raft of medical opinions confirming that their daughter would be unable to cope with the mental and physical impact of menstruation. Helmut's jibe inflamed his festering sense of guilt.

'Every expert agreed that it was crucial to her wellbeing.'

'Believe what you wish, but, in the Reich, we were more honest when we rid ourselves of "lives unworthy of life".'

'You're despicable!'

A salesgirl brought in a tray of coffee, laying out the cups with painstaking propriety, giving Nathan time to regain his composure.

'I should throw you out,' he said to Helmut, as soon as she left.

'You're the younger man. But I suspect that there's more you wish to ask me.'

'I take it that you didn't leave Germany because of the rallies outside Landsberg prison.'

'Correct! I left because of the communist teachers, who'd returned from exile. They should have been hanged as traitors, but, instead, they were indoctrinating my son, along with his whole generation, encouraging him to reject everything I hold dear. I'm not one of those romantics who believe that the Fourth Reich will be built on Argentine soil, who take heart from the waiters who click their heels and salute them at the ABC café. But I knew I'd find kindred spirits. And the perfect job opened up at the museum, which, in addition to its artefacts, holds the remains of many primitive peoples (Mapuche, Tehuelche, Quechua, to name but three), an unparalleled collection of raw material to explore.'

'So time and distance have done nothing to alter your beliefs?'

'Have they altered yours?'

'And you're not worried that I'll expose you?'

'Who to? Mossad? I doubt they'll risk another breach of Argentine sovereignty. I'm no Eichmann; you'd be hard-pressed to find any evidence against me. The head of the institute, George Montandon, was murdered at the Liberation, but I didn't even face one of the revenge hearings.'

'What if I tell Monica and Stefan?'

'True,' Helmut said with a sour smile, 'I wouldn't want that. But you won't. Even if you care nothing for the pain you'd cause them, you wouldn't wish to compromise Madeleine.'

'So what do you want from her? Haven't you done her enough harm?'

'You may scoff, but we were lovers, in the truest – the fullest – sense. The moments we shared are the most precious of my life. I need her to acknowledge that.'

'It's a fantasy you've fed yourself for so long that you've come to believe it. You have no—'

Madeleine's entrance arrested him mid-sentence, bringing both men to their feet.

'You've been spying on me!' Helmut said.

'I needed to remind myself of who you are,' she replied, with a confidence that reassured Nathan.

'I needed no reminder. I've never stopped thinking of you. Seeing you the other evening – barely changed (that's no empty compliment) – it was as if we were together again in Paris.'

'We were never together! You hounded me . . . intimidated me.'

'I would never have informed on Ruben. That was a ploy, to ease your conscience when you did what your heart – what every cell in your body – was telling you to do.'

He took a step towards her; Nathan moved to intercept, as Madeleine retreated behind the desk.

'You barely knew me. "Can I help you, Monsieur? A scarf . . . a blouse . . . a bolt of silk for your wife?"'

'I'll never forgive myself for abandoning you when I went back to Berlin.'

'You abandoned me, as you put it, when I told you I was pregnant.'

'I was in shock. I thought about you every day for years. In the midst of the hunger and the cold and the rats and the rabble, you were all that gave me hope.'

'What about Monica and Stefan?' Nathan interjected.

'You told me that we looked alike,' Madeleine said. 'Another lie.'

'That was true! She didn't always look like - what? - a burst balloon. You don't have to search hard to know why. When the Slavs entered Berlin, she was raped. Six . . . eight . . . more times than she could count or wish to remember. On the table, on the floor, against the wall, and all in front of my boys. Stefan was seven, but Jurgen - the elder - was twelve. He ran to his mother's rescue - kicking and punching and biting. So they shot him and went back to her.'

Through watery eyes, Nathan saw that Madeleine was similarly moved. For a moment, he feared she might take Helmut's hand, or even hug him, but he'd underestimated her resolve.

'I'm sorry - with all my heart - for Monica and Stefan and, of course, Jurgen,' she said. 'As well as for every other abused German woman and child. But there's more to rape than being pinned to the ground at gunpoint.'

'I realise that seeing me again the other evening was a shock. I should have prepared you. But the fact that we've found each other seventeen years and thousands of miles from where we left off proves that it's meant to be.'

'What more can I say to make him understand?' Madeleine asked Nathan, before redoubling her efforts. 'There was nothing between us; there is nothing between us; there will always be nothing between us. When I saw you on Sunday, I was terrified of what you might say: what it might do to Pascal; what Ruben might do to you. But then I realised you could never say anything, or else your wife and son would learn what you did, not just to me but at the institute. I've barely exchanged a word with Monica, so I can't tell whether she's genuinely ignorant of the man you are or has so little self-respect that she'll stay with you regardless. But I've spent enough time with Stefan to know that he'd cut you out of his life for ever.'

'I think we're done now,' Nathan said to Helmut. 'You'll see Pascal on Saturday, not just on opposite sides of the church but on opposite sides of the reception. I'd rather you didn't speak to him at all, but, if you must, please restrict yourself to pleasantries: the food; the heat; the Argentine football team . . . and "Doesn't Arabella make a beautiful flower girl?"'

'What?'

Nathan declined to elaborate on the scheme taking shape in his mind. 'Remember, he'll be flying back to France,' he said. 'Your life remains here in Buenos Aires.'

'If you have one shred of the affection for me that you profess . . . one shred of concern for the child you spawned,' Madeleine said, 'you'll heed that advice. Pascal doesn't have the slightest desire to know you. Discovering what you did to me very nearly destroyed him. It's been the worst six months. But he'll recover. His father and I will make sure of that.' She moved to the door. 'Thank you, Nathan. I'm most grateful for all your help. I know you're a busy man.'

She walked out, leaving Nathan with a stunned-looking Helmut.

'We'll meet again on Friday for the rehearsal dinner,' he said. 'My mother intends to treat us to some Sephardic betrothal delicacies. Then we're all set for the big day. I presume Stefan has told you that they're including the Seven Blessings in the ceremony.'

'I'm not religious.'

'Otherwise known as the *Sheva Brachot*. They're a key element of a traditional Jewish wedding – not that I'm an expert; the last one I attended was my Uncle Leon's when I was eight. Stefan chose them to honour Katrin's heritage. You must be very proud of such a sensitive son. They've asked the cantor from the Agudat Dodim temple to recite them. But don't worry, he doesn't have a hooked nose or puffy lips or any of the other distorted features you trafficked in at the institute.'

He ushered Helmut out and drove home to find Katrin in the kitchen, sampling Mother's first successful batch of *manos*. Whisking her into the salon, he outlined his proposal for a last-minute addition to the ceremony, in line with her original plan.

'It's wonderful!' Katrin said, planting a sugary kiss on his cheek. She immediately rang Señora Ortiz, returning with the news that the dressmaker would be happy to help and was free for a fitting at two o'clock. 'Now all we need is to convince Mutti.'

'Wish me luck!' he said, as he headed into the garden to tackle Margarethe.

She was sitting on the lawn, making a daisy chain for Arabella, who tottered up and rubbed herself stickily against him.

'Quite a coincidence to catch you doing this.'

'Really? Why?'

'Katrin and I have been talking and we're both resolved – with your blessing, of course – that Arabella should be a flower girl.'

'Must we go through all this again,' she asked, scrambling to her feet, 'four days before the wedding?'

'I'm sorry, but I realised this morning that it's not only right but imperative.'

'I thought you were going to the showroom.'

'I did.'

'Look at her!' She gestured to Arabella, who was shuffling after a butterfly. 'She can't keep still for an instant.'

'We'll be with her.'

'Besides, it's too late. What would she wear?'

'Katrin's spoken to Señora Ortiz, who can be here at two. And a flower girl doesn't have to be a perfect match for the bridesmaids.'

'So it's a fait accompli?' she said angrily.

'Not at all. You've shouldered the entire affair. It has to be your decision.'

'What about the basket? You haven't thought it through. How will she carry it?'

'We can tie a ribbon to her wrist.'

'And the petals? Even if she manages to take hold of them, she won't know when to scatter them. What if she throws them all over herself or tosses them in a heap?'

'I'll be two steps behind her. I can kick . . . that is tap them into place.'

'Very dignified, as you lead your daughter down the aisle!'

He cupped her face in his hands. 'Some things are more important than dignity.'

'I won't let you paint me as the villain of the piece.'

'I'd never do that,' he said, sensing her yield both to his argument and his touch.

'What about Monica and Helmut? Have you considered them?'

'Oh, most definitely! Trust me, all that matters is to remind people that Arabella is an integral part of this family. If she slips, we'll pick her up. If she wanders off, we'll bring her back. If she wets herself—'

'You see!'

'We'll dry her. If she's overwhelmed, we'll reassure her. She's our daughter . . . Katrin's sister. We must never be ashamed of her.'

'I'm not!'

'Or of ourselves,' he added tenderly. 'For once, we have the exact same usage. *Sie ist mein Stolz und meine Freude*: She is my pride and joy.'

3

GABRIELLE

GALILEE, MAY 1962

A FOX, OR it might have been a hyrax, scurried through the undergrowth. A frog, or it might have been a toad, croaked from a nearby stream. Crickets chirped and cicadas buzzed. As nature teemed around her, Gabrielle gazed across the cotton, wheat and sunflower fields, barely distinguishable in the gathering dusk, towards the bulbous slope of Mount Tabor. On evenings such as these, it was hard to believe that only twenty kilometres away lay the explosives-strewn border with Jordan, a nation with which Israel remained at war.

Aron, still spry despite having worked the farm since dawn, carried a tray of pomegranate and lime juice onto the verandah. 'Our homemade recipe from our homegrown fruit,' he said with a trace of self-mockery as he handed his guest a glass.

Gabrielle had been touched by his invitation to celebrate the fortieth anniversary of the moshav's founding the weekend before. At seventy-one, he was the last surviving member of the Salonican Three Musketeers. He had given up a comfortable life running his family's flour mill, the largest in the city, to carve out a living here. During every conversation about the past – and several about the present – hung the tacit acknowledgement that had Papa and Ettore, the Athos and Aramis of the group, accompanied him in making

Aliyah, the one would not have been gassed in Sobibor and the other shot in the Ardeatine caves outside Rome.

Aron had originally joined a kibbutz near Tiberias, but while his wife Mayra was happy to share her work and wealth with the collective, she refused to share the care of their children. So, with other disaffected kibbutzniks, they founded the moshav, upholding many of their communal ideals but placing the family at its core. A substantial gift from Aron's father enabled them to purchase the 1,800-dunam plot from the absentee landlords in Beirut. The existing tenants were delighted to receive compensation for abandoning the inhospitable terrain, only to feel cheated once the moshavniks had cultivated it. 'The Arabs are like children who throw away their broken toys, then want them back after they've been mended,' Aron said, an analogy that alarmed Gabrielle, although she refrained from challenging a man who had lost both his sons in the 1948 war.

In their impecunious early years, Aron supplemented his income by working on various infrastructure projects outside the settlement, leaving Mayra to oversee the farm. In time, he was able to devote himself entirely to the land, growing wheat, watermelons, green beans, white beans and, most gloriously, sunflowers, now in full bloom during Gabrielle's visit. While retaining charge of the chicken coop, Mayra was freed to become the moshav kindergarten teacher, sparing future generations the hour-long donkey ride to school in Beit She'an that her own children, Gidon, Gilad and Devorah, had made every day.

As if on cue, Devorah and her husband Lev strolled up to the house from their office in the converted cattle shed, which Aron had transferred to them when advancing years and the government's strict milk quotas made dairy production impractical. He had planned to pass on the farm to one or both of his sons, but Gilad had been killed in an ambush on a food convoy outside Jerusalem and Gidon two months later in the Egyptian attack on Nitzanim. They were commemorated in photographs, letters and tapes of Gidon's songs preserved in the moshav museum, where Mayra volunteered as a guide.

Gabrielle greeted the couple, who had been young newly-weds on her previous visit in 1949. She had never met Aron before then, but he'd featured so prominently in Papa's boyhood stories that she'd felt honour-bound to accept his invitation. Moreover, she felt estranged from a France, deeply scarred by the Occupation, a France that wanted to know nothing of her ordeal except that she'd survived. She had expected more of Israel, but found that it too had its own agenda. The only genocide story people were willing to hear was that of the heroic Warsaw Ghetto Uprising. An apologetic Aron explained that their priority was resisting present enemies, not revisiting the past. Even so, she was taken aback when Caleb, Gidon's eight-year-old son, pinched her Auschwitz tattoo and called her *sabon*. She didn't know the Hebrew word, but sensed its import when Aron slapped his face. At her insistence, he translated it as 'soap', begging her to excuse the boy, who shared the widespread belief that, while men like his father had died for their country, the Jews of Europe had acquiesced in their fate.

'Of course. I quite understand,' she replied, wondering if there were anywhere in the world that her suffering would be acknowledged.

Her tattoo came to define her after her release almost as much as it had in the camp. Maman claimed that it physically pained her to see it, demanding she cover it up even when alone in the garden. Oncle Ruben told five-year-old Pascal that it was a telephone number, as if she'd been picked up by a stranger in a bar. In Israel, when not the object of Caleb's hostility, it provoked suspicion. On a bus from Nazareth, she'd been humiliated by an old man who, after watching her cling to the strap, turned to his neighbour and asked in a German she'd learnt in captivity: 'Why is it always the young and pretty ones who survived?'

Hearing the story, Aron conceded that there were fools and knaves in Israel as anywhere else, but he maintained that the majority of his countrymen were honourable and sincere.

'We may only be six hundred thousand or so in a world of more than two billion, but for the first time in millennia we're strong.

Until you've experienced it, you can't know the joy and power of being surrounded by your fellow Jews.'

'I have experienced it,' she replied softly.

'No, for that you have to live here. Not just a two-week visit. I remember your grandfather. I admired him very much.'

'So did I.'

'He extolled Salonica as a model city, where Jews, Muslims and Christians lived together in harmony. Then what happened? The Empire collapsed, as empires invariably do. The Christians threw out the Muslims. And those who didn't actively collude with the Nazis when the Jews – my two younger brothers, their wives and children among them – were rounded up and deported, took the opportunity to seize everything they left behind, down to the very tombstones in the cemetery.'

The place where Gabrielle had been surrounded by her fellow Jews was Auschwitz. How much solidarity had she known there? From childhood, she had been taught by her mother's family to believe in the superiority of the French and by her father's in the superiority of the Sephardim, but in the camp she was soundly disabused. The French were scorned for betraying the Czechs, failing the Poles and abjectly surrendering to Hitler. Although a few of the Ashkenazi women admired her delicate features and soft skin, most spurned her, labelling her a whore even before she became one.

'What kind of Jew can't speak Yiddish?' a truculent woman asked, laughing when a *Kapo* beat her for failing to obey an unintelligible command.

Aron might have seen a proud, united people. She had seen a cluster of rival tribes.

She'd found a far deeper understanding of the camps on this, her second visit to Israel. The irony was that it stemmed from the trial of their chief facilitator. The survivors' accounts could no longer be dismissed as fantasies triggered by the shock of imprisonment and malnutrition. Television was banned here since, as Aron explained, 'the government considers it bad for our souls', but people listened to the radio broadcast, at their workplaces, in shops, even on buses, where Kol Israel blared out all day long. Aron himself had bought a transistor set to take with him into the fields. During the long proceedings, the nation had come to comprehend not just the enormity of what their fellow Jews had endured but that, far from acquiescing in their fate, they had been powerless to escape it. It wasn't only because Caleb was thirteen years older and a postgraduate student at the Weizmann Institute of Science that he would never repeat his slur, but because he knew that the six million dead had also paid a part in the foundation of the state. Their blood had given it legitimacy.

After a respite of several months, Eichmann had dominated the headlines again since Tuesday, when the High Court rejected his appeal against the death sentence. In a final attempt to escape the noose, he'd petitioned President Ben-Zvi for clemency. As the hoot of a barn owl added a shrill note to the dusk chorus, the conversation on the Sides' verandah turned, as Gabrielle pictured it doing in homes across the land, to the President's likely response.

'What would you have him do, Gabi?' Lev asked, deferring to her experience. To her surprise, she realised that she was indifferent to the outcome. Whether Eichmann rotted in jail or died on the gallows, all she wanted was never to have to see his face or hear his name again. Although she hadn't followed the trial in depth, she'd watched various reports over the spring and summer. What had offended her most wasn't Eichmann's aloofness from the witnesses or even his claim to the sanctity of his feelings, but his refusal to admit his own agency. In the camp infirmary, she'd observed a doctor – an inmate herself – substituting samples of her own blood for those of her infected patients, which, if analysed, would have led to their instant gassing. If someone struggling to heal the sick, without medicine and equipment, in overcrowded, filth-encrusted, rat-ridden rooms, could preserve her integrity, why couldn't he?

'To be honest, I don't know,' she replied. 'Maybe to show mercy would be the heavier punishment.'

'How?' Lev asked.

'He's still in his fifties. He'd have decades in prison to dwell on how his enemies showed the greater humanity.'

'No!' Mayra said. 'He gave up all claims to humanity when he sent six million innocent people to their deaths. He deserves none from us.'

'But how can hanging one man – however culpable – redress the suffering of a single victim, let alone millions?' Devorah asked.

'Just because there can't be justice for everyone doesn't mean that there should be justice for no one,' Aron said.

'Then perhaps we should regard it as hanging the symbol, not the man,' Gabrielle said. 'Will you excuse me? I don't wish to be rude, but my head is racing. I think I'll take a short walk before turning in.'

'Would you like company?' Aron asked.

'I have it,' she said with a smile, pointing to the stars.

Six million dead: the figure was almost as unfathomable as the billions of stars in an infinite universe. Why, among such a multitude, should she have survived? She'd been told countless times by well-meaning people that the question shouldn't be why she had survived, but why the others had died. And she knew that to search for any pattern – any purpose – behind her survival would be immoral, even obscene. Yet seventeen years on, when the horrors had been catalogued like exhibits in the Auschwitz museum, she continued to ask why women with husbands and children and fathers and brothers had been murdered but not her, who had no one to return to but a peevish old woman whom – she whispered it even to herself – she had begun to hate.

Shivering, although the chill wasn't in the air, she rejoined her hosts on the verandah before heading to bed. She opened Pagnol's *Le Temps des Secrets*, but his tender teenage recollections failed to engage her. All the talk of Eichmann had drawn her back to Auschwitz. Resistance, as she had previously discovered, was futile.

Her practised technique was to exhaust herself until sleep overtook her, and the dream world became her reality . . . the waking world merely a dream.

She had arrived at the complex in the dead of night, impounded in a cattle truck so acrid and cramped that even the bitter cold and shrieking guards afforded some relief. But the greatest solace came from the billowing chimneys, a sign that the rumours circulating in Drancy were as unfounded as they were preposterous. The inscription on the gates indicated, even to one with rudimentary German, that this was a factory where she'd been brought to work . . . How could she have been so naïve?

Herded into the camp, she waited in line on a gravel path while an officer, whose boots shone like mirrors in the floodlights, stood ramrod stiff on a step, whistling a Mozart march. As each new arrival approached, he wagged his finger to the left or the right, the very slightness of the gesture seeming to reflect the arbitrariness of the choice.

She was dispatched to the right, which, as she subsequently learnt, destined her for 'extermination through work'. First, however, all trace of her former self had to be erased. Although not even Maman had seen her naked since childhood, she was stripped and sent into a room full of men, one of whom shaved her head and another tattooed her as inmate 43,319. Years later, a cryptographer would tell her that it was a prime number, as if to make her feel special. The tattooist, who must have noticed her budding breasts and sparse pubic hair, braved a blow to whisper that she should give her age as seventeen. She did so, without understanding why, and was put to work on a building site, carrying bricks, mortar and sand, alongside Elena, a young woman from Salonica, who knew of her family. They became camp sisters, sharing everything from a slice of bread to a sliver of lipstick, to redden their cheeks before inspections. It was Elena who saved her when, consumed by despair, she proposed to fling herself at the fence, like a bird flying into a window.

'If you do, I swear I'll follow you. Do you want that on your conscience?' she asked. 'Though it might be worth it to know that the *Blockälteste* would be beaten.'

Gabrielle had laughed, sobbed and laughed again.

She stood up and paced the spartan guest room, longing to wander into the kitchen but afraid of disturbing the household. She peered out of the window, but the shimmering fireflies failed to ward off the gloom that once again engulfed her: the leaden skies and bleak huts, the stark uniforms and jutting bones, all seen through a cloud of ash, which seemed to be scratching her eyelids and clogging her throat even now . . . She grabbed the glass of water from the night table and splashed her face.

Salvation had emerged from the latrines, the one place where male and female prisoners crossed paths. Every day, desperate women would gather when the men came to collect their wastes, some for no more than a fleeting validation of their femininity, others in the hope of a trifling reward. Although the latrines themselves – planks with holes so closely spaced that every bowel movement was communal – had robbed her of her last shred of modesty, Gabrielle refused to believe that any man, however dehumanised, would be attracted to her emaciated, pustular carcass. But Elena, who urged her to use her one remaining power, cited the shepherds in the hills above Thessaloniki who made love to their sheep. Likening herself to livestock, she loitered in a murky corner and suffered a man with filthy hands to put them up her skirt. As she numbed herself to his assault, she wondered what Maman, who'd impressed on her the value of virginity long before there'd been any need, would think if she knew that she had traded hers for a potato.

One of the men she met took a fancy to her and, through the nefarious network that extended across the camp, secured her a place in the Kanada warehouse, sorting the luggage brought by new arrivals. She hesitated to take it since it meant leaving Elena, who warned her that, if she squandered the opportunity, she would not only never speak to her again but would report her to the *Blockälteste* for some bogus offence. She moved into a new block – one with basic sanitation – and swiftly discovered how to secure better rations and clothing for herself and her friends by bribing the guards and *Kapos* with the rings, watches, money and alcohol to which they themselves were denied access. Most precious of all was the sturdy pair of shoes that she salvaged from a consignment bound for the Reich. Years later, long after she'd accepted the loss of her father and brother, she was haunted by the fate of their shoes. Papa had been especially proud of his, which were custom-made by Aubercy to last a lifetime. The war may have been over, but, somewhere in Germany, someone with size 43 feet was enjoying its spoils.

The Mozart march resounded in her mind, its jauntiness a jarring accompaniment to her desolation. She found herself back in the camp infirmary since, although she had gained a little weight, her skin had cleared and her periods returned erratically, she'd contracted both typhoid fever and pneumonia. The guards left her behind when, faced with the inexorable Russian advance, they evacuated the camp and forced the wasted inmates to trudge westward through the brutal snowscape. Had she been with them, she would surely have perished, alongside Elena. Instead, she lay febrile and delirious without medical help, feeling nothing but gratitude when a fellow patient died and she could crawl from her bunk to steal an extra layer of rags. Eventually, the Russians arrived, and a Polish Red Cross doctor – his face at first another hallucination – administered a course of drugs that saved her life. What gave it meaning was his stray remark that he had a daughter just like her in Lwów. She was able to recover herself because she resembled somebody else.

Oncle Simon, who had contacts at the Red Cross headquarters in Geneva, set out to collect her, travelling across a devastated Germany where, according to Sylvain, ever ready to disparage his father, he used the opportunity to investigate the prospects for post-war reconstruction. He brought her back to Geneva, where he lived alone with Clarice, since Sylvain was at a boarding school in Lausanne. Their friend and neighbour, Marguerite Severin, whose immaculate clothes and coiffure appeared untouched by the war, took it upon herself to organise her schedule of doctors, nurses, nutritionists and even visits from her personal masseur.

'It does no good to brood on the past,' she said, presaging a host of well-wishers. 'You've been liberated.'

Not wanting to sound ungrateful, Gabrielle concurred. But Marguerite was wrong. Paris had been liberated. Oncle Ruben had been liberated. She had simply been released.

It was during her recuperation that she learnt the fate of her relatives. Tante Irène had died of an overdose, deepening the rift between her cousins: Clarice declaring it an accident and Sylvain deliberate. Tante Bella had been murdered in Auschwitz. 'If only you'd known, you could have looked out for her,' Clarice said, as if they'd missed one another at a party. She spoke briefly on the phone to Maman, who, having escaped arrest, proceeded to list the hardships she'd been left to undergo alone. They were both frantic for information about Papa and Daniel, which Oncle Simon promised he was exhausting every avenue to obtain. Later she suspected that he'd withheld the news of their deaths until the doctors confirmed that she was strong enough to survive it.

'They were gassed at a camp called Sobibor.'

'Where's that?' she asked, as though it mattered . . . as though anything mattered any more.

'In Poland, somewhere to the east of Auschwitz.'

'They must have been cold.' Her teeth chattered.

'Scream and shout as much as you like,' Clarice said. 'We're here with you.' But they weren't. They were here with her body . . . her shell, but her heart and spirit were with Papa and Daniel in Sobibor, with Tante Bella in Auschwitz, and with everyone in every camp waiting to take a shower.

As soon as the doctors pronounced her fit to travel, Oncle Simon arranged for Clarice to accompany her back to Marseille. After checking in at the Hôtel Beauvau, they headed to Panier, where Denise Fournier and her mother had concealed and coddled Maman in their tiny apartment for almost two years.

'No!' Maman screamed, when she entered the parlour. 'You're not Gabi. Gabi's cheeks were pink ... and plump ... and pink. And her hair! You remember her hair?' she asked, turning urgently from Clarice to Denise. 'Hair down to her waist. Hair she could sit on.'

'Maman ...' Gabrielle said, edging into the room.

'No, it's not you, you're an imposter,' Maman said, clinging to her in a flurry of kisses and tears that left her strangely – guiltily – unmoved. 'I won't ask any questions. They'll only upset you. And you mustn't ask any of me. Such loss! More than flesh and blood can bear. Denise and Clothilde have been so very kind, but ... but now I have you again. We have each other.'

Madame Fournier brought in the tea, whereupon Maman declared herself exhausted and retired to the room that Denise, squeezing into her mother's three-quarter bed, had relinquished to her. Over the first *navettes* Gabrielle had tasted in more than three years, Denise outlined what she knew of Maman's life since Gabrielle's deportation. Initially, she'd remained at the Villa Dahlia with Madame Esposito, assisting at the birth of her daughter, Daniela, in June, and distracted from her grief and terror by helping to look after the children, although, according to their mother, it was more often they who looked after her. In August, they were raided by the Gestapo, who, accepting Madame Esposito's story that they were a family of Italian refugees, gave them ten minutes to leave the house, which had been allocated to the Abwehr. A seamstress friend of Madame Esposito's took them in, but weeks cooped up in a basement room with the boisterous Antonio, bored Lucia and squalling Daniela left Maman's temper frayed to breaking. Madame Esposito, recalling her visit to Papa, appealed to Denise, who brought Maman here.

'We're forever in your debt,' Gabrielle said, aware not just of the danger and disruption but also the constant plaints and demands that she must have faced. 'Please don't pretend otherwise,' she added, as Denise made to interrupt. 'We'll take Maman with us to the hotel tonight. You can start to reclaim your apartment ... your life ... and, no doubt, your sanity.'

'There's one piece of good news,' Denise said. 'Since the Boche cleared off, the villa's been empty.'

'So we can go straight back?'

'Whenever you wish, and with far less trouble, I'm ashamed to say, than if it had been appropriated by the French.'

Although Maman insisted on throwing out all the bedlinen, towels and napery, having the carpets and curtains cleaned and even recovering the furniture, Gabrielle had to admit that the house itself was in good repair. The same couldn't be said of the garden, where the Germans had chained their dogs besides Maman's cherished dahlia beds, destroying the flowers that had given the villa its name.

'We'll get a gardener to do the spadework. Then in the spring, you can plant some tubers,' Gabrielle said hopefully, as she stood with Maman, surveying the ravaged borders.

'What do I want with flowers?' Maman asked. 'Your father and brother have no graves.'

Madame Esposito visited them regularly, before returning to Turin in 1954. Her husband had died in Mauthausen and she and her children were living with Enzo, a car mechanic ('I see the pattern!' she said, laughing). On their departure, Gabrielle gave him the cash to open his own garage, while Maman gave her the ruby necklace that Grandpapa Carrache had given her on her engagement.

'That was very generous,' Gabrielle said, unable to conceal her surprise.

'What's the point of keeping it in the safe?' Maman said. 'I've no reason to wear it any more. And you won't even wear that good luck charm your father gave you.'

'It's called a hamza. It's intended to ward off the evil eye. Enough said!'

'Perhaps it'll help you find a husband,' Maman said, reverting to her favourite theme. 'You're still young. It's not too late.'

Gabrielle refused to argue. How could someone who flinched at any mention of Auschwitz hope to understand? She wasn't afraid of intimacy. She had slept with several men since her 'liberation';

indeed, there was a period, thankfully of only a few months, when she'd slept with too many, as though she also needed a validation of her femininity. Although less squalid, the liaisons were no more meaningful than those in the latrines. One man, who called himself a healer, ran his hands over her chest in what she'd assumed was foreplay, before declaring that he'd exorcised her demons. Others sought to cannibalise her ordeal. On one excruciating occasion, Matthieu (or he may have been Maxime) introduced her to his parents, only to denounce them for serving German soldiers in their seafood bar while she was surviving on bread mixed with sawdust.

Maman's pressure on her to marry was coupled with a longing for her to have a child. But how to explain to someone who'd given birth in the American hospital in Neuilly, attended by a team of midwives, what she had felt watching the woman in the next bunk, who'd desperately hidden her pregnancy lest she be sent for 'special treatment', go into premature labour, gnawing on a broom handle so as not to alert the *Stubenälteste*? When the agony was over, Elena, lacking any form of blade, had bitten through the cord and, without a word being spoken, taken the stillborn child and buried him in the latrine, thereby completing the circle.

She felt utterly alone. Seeing Devorah with Aron brought home how much she missed Papa: her noble, gentle, wise, compassionate – and so many other things – father, who had made the world feel safe, an illusion for which he was not to blame. With the same ache, she missed Daniel, so passionate and funny and clever and kind, who'd lived life at twice the normal speed, whether eating or swimming or telling jokes or peddling down the Rue d'Endoume. Her relatives had rallied round her. She was particularly close to Oncle Ruben and Tante Madeleine, so it had both shocked and saddened her when they'd separated on their return from Argentina. The timing was odd, just a few months before Pascal was due to take his Bac, but Oncle Ruben assured her that the split was amicable. Pascal would live with his mother in the Boulevard des Belges and spend alternate weekends with him in Bessenay. Maman, who had been horrified when her brother-in-law married a 'shopgirl', declared that she wasn't surprised.

'Sure as sunrise, Madeleine has taken a lover. Blood will out.'

'For Heaven's sake, Maman! Haven't we had enough of that sort of talk? My guess is that, seeing Katrin and Stefan's happiness, they realised what was missing from their own lives.'

'Then why haven't you?'

Fractures were appearing across the family. Sylvain had been at odds with his father ever since his mother's death. It was only after Clarice begged him on bended knee – which she swore was no metaphor – that he invited him to his and Annette's wedding. Theirs was a romance to rival Dante and Beatrice's, at least in respect of their youth. Sylvain had been twelve and Annette six or seven when Tante Irène and Oncle Simon took custody of her. In the chaos of their flight from France, they'd been separated, but, by a quirk of fate, they were reunited in Switzerland. A Vaudois couple adopted Annette, but she and Sylvain kept in touch and, ten years later, the childhood friendship blossomed into love. In a break with family tradition, Sylvain became a teacher, returning to the school where he had been a pupil. Annette worked as a nurse before giving birth to twins, Louis and Max, whom Gabrielle struggled to tell apart.

Sylvain had not only resisted his father's presence at his wedding but refused his offer to pay for it, or anything else thereafter. In consequence, even before his current incapacity, Oncle Simon had lavished his fortune on Clarice, who, in Gabrielle's view, was unhealthily attached to him.

There had been no other man in her life since Francisque, a fellow student at the Lausanne Conservatoire, who left for military service swearing his undying devotion, only to bestow it elsewhere on his return.

Heartbroken, she renounced both love and music, applying herself instead to good works. For years, she was an active representative of the Jewish National Fund, hectoring family and friends to support reforestation in Israel. Gabrielle dedicated dozens of pines, acacias, cypresses and olive trees to the memory of Papa, Daniel and Tante Bella, before discovering that some of the plantations were in depopulated Arab villages. Clarice shrugged off her concern, but from then on she focused her fundraising efforts on Yad Vashem. Of late, she'd poured all her energy into the museum she was founding in Thessaloniki. To her dismay, the rest of the family hadn't greeted the news that it would be housed in her grandparents' former mansion with unalloyed delight. Headstrong as ever, she failed to appreciate that Tante Esther, in particular, would be deeply offended by her going ahead without consulting her.

In one of the newsletters she dispatched with increasing regularity, she credited Oncle Simon as the architect of the project, which, unless he'd initiated it several years earlier, strained credulity. Gabrielle had last seen him in August during a visit to Cap Ferrat. She had taken Maman, who was much exercised by the forest fires raging across the south.

'My friends the Leclercs – with Jeanette's eighty-year-old mother – had to shelter from the flames in their swimming pool,' she remarked.

'Eighty years old! Really? Eighty years old!' Oncle Simon laughed so hard that he wet himself.

'I'm very sorry,' Clarice said. 'It's one of the symptoms of his illness that he lacks empathy.'

'In which case, he must have suffered from it all his life,' Maman muttered to Gabrielle, as Clarice led her father upstairs to change.

While guarded about the rest of the museum's collection, Clarice had induced Gabrielle to donate two of Tante Bella's paintings. During his first visit to Marseille after her return, Oncle Ruben informed her that, in a will made on the eve of her flight from Paris, Tante Bella had named her her sole heir, not only to her Port-Royal apartment and portion of their father's estate, but to all the paintings and drawings left unsold at her death. Gabrielle was at once moved, honoured and perplexed. Tante Bella had been eccentric, but had she also been psychic? Had she foreseen that Gabrielle would share her plight yet escape her fate? Or had she simply set out to reward her favourite niece?

In Paris, Oncle Ruben introduced her to Berthe Weill, the gallery owner who'd first recognised Tante Bella's talent and later represented her work. She lived in a drab, cramped apartment on the Rue Saint-Dominique, a cruel twist for someone dedicated to the joy and expansiveness of art. After serving coffee in dusty cups, she recounted how she'd hidden there throughout the Occupation, with the aid of a trusted concierge. On the one occasion that the Gestapo searched the building, she had risen to her full height (all of one metre fifty!) and rained down curses on them, whereupon they turned tail and fled. 'They yelled "*Was für eine alte Hexe!*"– "What an old witch!"' she said with a cackle. 'Weak men pretending to be strong!'

Infirm and impoverished, Madame Weill could offer Gabrielle little practical assistance on managing the bequest, but she advised her to visit Marie Laurencin, with whom Tante Bella had studied and enjoyed a close bond. The painter welcomed her warmly, taking a rare interest in her recollections, not only of Auschwitz but of Drancy, where her friend Max Jacob had died. She arranged to return a stack of canvases that Tante Bella had left with her for safekeeping and introduced her to her dealer, Louise Leiris, who, despite expressing reservations about Timarete's work, agreed to represent her 'for sentiment's sake'. She went on to sell every picture in her 1950 exhibition (two of them to the government) before the official opening. Ten years later, she curated the retrospective at the Musée d'Art Moderne, sealing Tante Bella's reputation as, in the words of *Le Figaro*, 'one of the most original and accomplished female artists of the early twentieth century'.

According to Oncle Bertrand, who must have been the last family member to see her alive, Tante Bella devoted herself to textile design after leaving Paris. The revelation of her later paintings came from an unlikely source. Gabrielle's cousin Claude, who'd been sheltered by nuns in Bordeaux, had converted to Catholicism and joined the Sisters of Notre Dame de Sion. While not sharing Maman's outrage at her apostasy, Gabrielle had little sympathy for her vocation. Papa had taught her to respect other people's beliefs, but a belief in God appeared no more rational than a belief that the earth was flat or the moon made of green cheese. She knew about the rabbis in Auschwitz who put God on trial, found Him guilty and then, in a typical Jewish paradox, decided to pray. If that were true – and it struck her as overly neat – conditions in the men's camp must have been less brutal than in the women's, where it was a battle to summon the strength to wish one another goodnight, let alone engage in theological debate. The only God that made sense to her was Daniel's: a God who, in creating the universe, allowed His ambition to run away with Him. As it expanded into infinity, He lost control of its workings, becoming as powerless to influence it as mankind.

Claude, now Sister Théodore, was based in Saint-Omer, but the order had convents across France. Five years after taking vows, she was sent on retreat to Mougins, where she found murals in the chapter room whose unique style she recognised at once. Amazed, she questioned her fellow nuns and learnt that Tante Bella had indeed sought refuge there, accompanied by two young children. She explained the family connection to the Abbess, who invited Gabrielle to visit. Thrilled by this unsuspected strand to her aunt's story, she set off the following week. After spending the night in the village, she took a car to the convent. Dropped at a dilapidated gateway, she walked down an overgrown path bordered by clusters of pink and white bougainvillea to a stark, rectangular building. She reached for the bell rope, before spotting a tattered notice: *Broken! Please knock*. Following instructions, she waited several minutes before the door was unlocked by an elderly nun, whose cheerful countenance offset the cheerless setting.

'Welcome, welcome! I'm Sister Célestine. I've been greeting guests to our cloister for sixty years. May you find peace and solace within these walls.'

Her gnarled hands gripping her stick, she led Gabrielle with halting steps to the Abbess's office. After pouring her a specially blended honey and lavender tisane and delicious homemade *croquants*, the Abbess shared her memories of Tante Bella when, as a newly professed sister, she was assigned to the children's block. She then escorted her to the chapter room, maintaining a discreet distance while Gabrielle studied the three murals. Though at pains to conceal it, she was underwhelmed, attributing her disappointment to their poor condition. The makeshift pigments and lack of an effective varnish had caused the colours to fade and, in places, even flake off the wall.

'I'd be glad to fund the restoration,' she said.

'That would be most generous.'

'I know that my aunt's many admirers would welcome the chance to see them.'

'Which may be a mixed blessing,' the Abbess replied, as if weighing up the promise of goodwill offerings against the disruption to convent life.

Leaving Gabrielle to take photographs, she went to fetch two sisters who were eager to meet her. They arrived together, introducing themselves as Sister Thérèse and Sister Augusta, both of a certain age, albeit younger than Sister Célestine. The bright-eyed, apple-cheeked Sister Thérèse spoke first, describing how, although she had now taken perpetual vows, she'd been a lay sister at the time of Tante Bella's visit, appointed by the late Abbess to guide her through the convent regime.

'Not that she intended to stay. She was simply delivering the children to safety.'

'Or so she thought,' Sister Augusta said. 'But they were betrayed to the Milice—'

'Please, Sister . . .' Sister Thérèse said.

'By me,' Sister Augusta said, throwing down her stick and, with what looked to be an agonising effort, falling to her knees and kissing Gabrielle's feet.

'What on earth are you doing?' Gabrielle said, horrified. 'Stand up, please!'

'Not until you tell me you forgive me.'

'This is ridiculous,' Gabrielle said. She tried to extricate herself, but Sister Augusta clung to her ankles.

'Forgive me!' she said, turning atonement into coercion.

'I will . . . I do,' Gabrielle replied. 'Just stand up!'

Sister Augusta clambered to her feet. 'I was the one who alerted the postman,' she said. 'I knew he'd pass on the information to his friends in the Milice. But I never thought they would arrest the children.'

'So what *did* you think?' Gabrielle asked, discomfiture giving way to disgust.

'Please try to understand,' Sister Thérèse interjected, helping her fellow nun to a seat. 'We had very little contact with the outside world. No newspapers. No radio. Only what we gleaned from the villagers. Sister Augusta couldn't have anticipated what happened.'

'My heart was full of malice. She'd turned our blessed cloister upside down. We were no longer permitted to profess the truth of our faith.' She glanced at Sister Thérèse. 'Or so it seemed to me. Her very presence was a provocation. She changed the way my sisters acted and felt . . . and even prayed. We now asked God's grace on those who killed His Son without first asking Him to redeem them. I wanted her gone.'

'And dead?' Gabrielle asked.

'No, I swear. I thought they'd simply send her away.'

'When the Nazis were rounding up every Jew in sight?'

'I wasn't thinking clearly . . . and not about the children. We've heard nothing. We tried to get information from the Jewish agencies, but they had no record of them. Do you think that, by God's mercy, they escaped?'

'No,' Gabrielle said, recalling the guards who regarded themselves as honourable men because they conducted the children to their deaths with a paternal smile. 'There was no mercy.'

'They arrested the Abbess,' Sister Thérèse said. 'They brought her back the next morning, although she never breathed a word about her interrogation. Since then – for the past twelve years – Sister Augusta has fasted two days every week, taking nothing but a few drops of water. Even when she caught pneumonia and the doctor insisted that unless she ate she was at risk of death, she refused to renounce her penance.'

'And I recovered,' Sister Augusta said, with a trace of triumph. 'That must be a sign, mustn't it?'

'If that's what you choose to believe,' Gabrielle replied, grateful that she'd had the forethought to decline the Abbess's invitation to stay the night. 'I was brought up to respect untenable beliefs.'

A rap on the door jolted her from her reverie. Years, faces, rooms, paintings fragmented like ancient film stock exposed to the light.

'Come in!' she called.

'I was afraid I'd wake you,' Aron said, hovering at the threshold. 'But I felt sure you'd want to know. *Kol Yisrael* reported that Eichmann was hanged at midnight.'

Gabrielle's first thought was that it was strange news to receive in bed. 'So there was no clemency?'

'I know you had misgivings about the sentence.'

'Not now I've slept on it . . . or, rather, haven't. I had a fitful night.'

'Is it the mattress? We've been meaning to buy a new one.'

'Not at all. I couldn't be more comfortable. Truly. But our conversation after dinner stirred up too much.'

'I'm so sorry. We should have thought.'

'Believe me, there's no rhyme or reason to these things. I was clearing my head. I realised that, man or symbol . . . man *and* symbol, Eichmann had to die. And it was a quicker death than being gassed.'

'Yes.'

'A more dignified death than being gassed.'

'Yes.'

'So you see, the Jews are merciful.'

'I'll leave you to get ready. We'll be on the verandah.'

Last night, she'd regretted the memories of Auschwitz that disrupted her sleep. Now, however, she was grateful, since they rid her of any qualms she might have harboured about Eichmann's execution. She regarded him with particular abhorrence. Hitler and Goebbels, Himmler and Rosenberg, Streicher and the rest professed beliefs of the utmost depravity, but, from what she understood, they were sincere. Was it perverse to feel that Eichmann's opportunism made him the more culpable? She had watched a moment of his trial when he compared himself to Pontius Pilate, who'd been compelled to condemn an innocent man to death. She knew nothing about Judas Iscariot's motives – as far as she was aware, Sister Théodore, Sister Thérèse, Sister Augusta and the Abbess knew nothing about them either – except for the thirty pieces of silver with which Christian writers had sought to stigmatise him and, thereby, his entire race. But she pictured him as a man of principle, who held, rightly or wrongly, that his master had abandoned his mission. Yet Dante had placed him in the innermost circle of Hell and kept Pilate on the periphery. If she believed in Hell – and espoused Dante's eschatology – she would reserve its lowest depths for the functionaries, the accomplices, the timeservers: the Eichmanns.

She walked onto the terrace, where Mayra had laid breakfast. She devoured the eggs, cheese and labneh, cucumber, peppers and olives, figs and dates as voraciously as if she were preparing for a hard day in the fields, yet she still felt a gnawing sense of emptiness. Devorah and Lev, both heavy with sleep, joined them midway through the meal. Making no mention of the execution (no doubt at Aron's behest), they discussed their trip to Beit She'arim. Gabrielle was doubly grateful to be accompanying them since, with Aron and Mayra at work, it wasn't a morning she wished to spend alone.

Israel's tourist industry was expanding, and Lev was one of a new generation of officially accredited guides. He and Devorah had set up a bespoke travel company and invited Gabrielle to try out one of their first excursions. While aware that it was a practice run, she missed the 'luxury saloon cars' featured in Galilean Odyssey's glossy brochure. Instead, she jiggled about on the back seat of the moshav's rickety jeep, amid a lingering stench of silage and insecticides, compounded by the stale sweat of two soldiers they picked up outside Amos Camp. She'd noted that, no matter how late or busy he might be, Aron stopped for any soldier needing a lift, once driving twenty kilometres out of his way to take a young man with a forty-eight-hour pass to Haifa. She'd presumed that he pictured Gidon or Gilad in their place, but he assured her that every driver in the country would do the same. The men were skittery after a successful operation to capture two Jordanians who'd crossed the border and attacked a bus in Nazareth, wounding an elderly man. One whooped when the other spoke of how they'd 'neutralised the targets', drumming his feet on the floor, only to apologise profusely when Lev swerved. Gabrielle felt a surge of revulsion, followed by pity for both them and their victims.

She offered each of them a Gauloise, which they proclaimed so superior to their native Noblesses that, when Lev dropped them off outside Beit She'arim park, she gave them her unopened pack.

'Only one left till we return home,' she said to Devorah, as they hopped down from the jeep.

'How will you survive?' Devorah asked teasingly.

'I've survived worse.'

'Yes, of course,' Devorah said, blushing, as though Gabrielle's every casual remark led back to the camp.

The sweet scent of rosemary came as a relief after the pungency of the jeep. They walked down a wooded pathway to the entrance of the necropolis, where Lev's old university friend Noam Barak was waiting to greet them. One of the leading archaeologists at the site, he had promised Lev's clients access to areas normally restricted to the public. As he shepherded them down a stony track, he explained that it was the most extensive burial ground yet discovered in Israel. It dated from the second century CE, when Jews were forbidden to bury their dead on the Mount of Olives. Excavations began in 1929 and, to date, they had unearthed twenty-one catacombs, of which the largest and most spectacular had been dubbed the Cave of the Coffins. They began the tour there, passing through a semicircular arch and descending a short flight of steps into a large hall, its dankness a sharp contrast to the scratchy heat outside. Lit only by Noam's torch, they ventured into a maze of burial chambers. Although many of its 135 sarcophagi had been desecrated by grave robbers, several had retained their original carvings of animals, birds and fish.

'So much for *Thou shalt not make unto thee a graven image*,' Lev said, as Noam spotlighted a tomb on which a pair of snarling lions confronted each other.

'That's one of the many puzzles we're trying to solve,' Noam replied.

He beamed his torch on epitaphs from Antioch, Phoenicia, South Arabia and as far away as Mesopotamia. Poignant as it was to learn that, eighteen hundred years earlier, Jews of the Diaspora had brought their dead to be buried in their ancestral homeland, Gabrielle was most intrigued by the foreign origins of a tomb in another catacomb, adorned with Leda and the Swan on one side and Achilles at the court of King Lycomedes on the other. Noam recounted how some archaeologists maintained – perhaps for religious reasons – that the classical imagery had been chosen solely for its pictorial value. There was, however, substantial evidence, not least an elegy written in Homeric hexameter and alluding to Greco-Roman concepts of Fate and the Underworld, that pointed to a rich cultural fusion. Once again, Gabrielle's thoughts strayed to Bella.

They drove home to find Mayra, back from the kindergarten, watching for them on the verandah. Intercepting the jeep, she told Lev to drive Gabrielle straight to the administration office to return a telephone call from Clarice in Thessaloniki. With no private lines in the moshav, there were few local calls and, as Mayra's knitted brows attested, long-distance calls generally signified bad news. During the brief ride, Gabrielle also imagined the worst: Maman or Oncle Simon having had a heart attack or one of her cousins an accident.

Leaving Devorah and Lev in the jeep, she hurried into the office and introduced herself to a pretty young secretary, who offered her a seat while she put through the call. Plainly nervous, she glanced up from her typing every few seconds with a commiserative smile. Finally, the phone rang and, after exchanging a few words with the operator, she handed the receiver to Gabrielle as though it were a handkerchief to wipe her tears.

'Clarice?' Gabrielle asked.

'It's Clarice,' she replied, her voice distorted by static. 'How are you?'

'I'm fine. You called me?'

'Yes. We heard about Eichmann this morning. What's it like in Israel? Is there dancing in the streets?'

'Don't be absurd! Life goes on ... that is ... You didn't call me to ask about Eichmann?'

She looked incredulously at the secretary, who'd blenched at the mention of the name.

'No, of course not. I have the most extraordinary news.'

'Is everybody well? Maman? Oncle Simon? Tante Esther?'

'Wouldn't I have told you at once if there were anything wrong?'

Given Clarice's singular sense of priorities, Gabrielle wasn't so sure. 'Then why are you ringing? Presumably not just for the pleasure of hearing my voice?'

'I'm sorry. It's hard to hear you.'

'What is it you want?' Gabrielle sprang up and shouted.

'That's better. I hope you're sitting down. I've had a phone call from a woman in Athens who claims – wait for it! – to be your sister.'

'Did you say "sister"?'

'As I said, quite extraordinary. There's been a lot of publicity about the museum. Articles charting its progress. Interviews with me. The Carrache name is in the news.'

'You did say "sister"?'

'Yes! There's every chance she's an imposter, out for what she can get. But she says that she's Oncle Leon's daughter, Eleonor.

Her mother's name is Xenia – not very Sephardi! She saw one of the articles. Though I don't know why she didn't contact you directly. It's not as if there are that many of us. Remember Oncle Henri? He found plenty of Carraccis in Italy and Carrache may be a variant. Apart from that, there's a branch in Alsace and a few in New Caledonia, I think it is.'

Gabrielle tried to curb her impatience. 'Clarice, this call must be costing you a fortune! She said she was Papa's daughter! From when . . . where?'

'Don't panic! She told me she was born in Piraeus before the First War. So even if she is genuine, there's no danger that he was cheating on Tante Lily.' That was hardly her main concern, although she understood that it might be Clarice's. 'She gave me her address. Do you have a pen and paper?'

'I'll never take it down correctly over all the crackling. Will you wire it to me at home? I'm going back on Monday . . . maybe sooner.'

'Whatever you prefer. But please don't expect too much. I deal with Greeks all day long. She may smell money. Remember, you already have a sister.'

'I do? Yes, of course,' she said, recollecting their girlhood vows. 'Thank you.'

She returned to the farm in confusion, assuring Mayra that there was no family crisis, but waiting until Aron came in from the bean harvest to tell them both what little she knew.

'Xenia,' Aron said, after a moment's reflection. 'It's all coming back to me. I haven't thought about her in fifty years . . . well, maybe not quite that long. But it must be a good fifty since Leon and I went to the taverna.'

'Was she a waitress?'

'No, she was a rebetiko singer. Not really my thing, but your father was entranced. He became utterly obsessed by her. Looking back, we led such privileged lives. I never lifted anything heavier than a billiard cue! Time on our hands . . . money in our pockets. And Leon spent both on her. He neglected his friends. And I know there was tension at home. Then Italy declared war on the Empire and he was expelled from the city. It broke his heart to leave her. I thought he would ask me to keep an eye on her while he was away. But no!'

'Perhaps he didn't trust you with her,' Mayra said, with a wry smile.

'He wouldn't have trusted anybody, except maybe one of the Sultan's eunuchs. When he returned from Paris, she'd disappeared. I presumed she'd found another rich admirer, but he was convinced she'd been abducted by a *manga* – one of the bandits who frequented the taverna. It was in a rough area, by the docks.'

'Whatever possessed you to go there?' Mayra asked.

'It was fifty years ago! We were young . . . fearless. I thought Leon was mad to get involved with her in the first place. But he never lost hope of finding her. The last time I saw him was just after the war, when he came back to Salonica to resume the search. I tried to persuade him to move out here with us, but it wasn't for him. And despite all our invitations over the years, he never even came to visit.'

Aron's story lent weight to Eleonor's claim, as did her name itself. After a second sleepless night – although this one full of hope, not horror – she decided to cut short her visit. Promising Aron and Mayra to return soon, 'maybe even with my sister', she spoke to the resident travel agents and asked Devorah to change her flights.

She realised that it had been a mistake to telegraph Maman the time of her arrival when she found her in bed in the early afternoon, following what she described as a severe attack of angina.

'The doctor said that, with my weak heart, I needed a complete rest. You have so few pleasures. I refused to let him contact you on holiday. I didn't want you rushing home to look after me.'

'That was most considerate,' Gabrielle replied, reading her remark as: 'I calculated that, by giving you a few days' grace, I could make greater demands on you later.'

Even less sympathetic to Maman's phantom ailments than usual, she contacted the doctor, who confirmed her suspicions that she'd suffered a mild case of heartburn, most likely caused by an excessive consumption of peppermints.

Speaking no Greek, she asked Clarice to set up a meeting with Eleonor, which she did with admirable urgency. Within three days of returning from Israel, she left for Greece. Maman was furious, accusing her of gadding off to Thessaloniki to 'assist Clarice with her hare-brained museum'. Gabrielle chose not to correct her, although she was actually flying to Athens to meet Eleonor, and Clarice was coming to assist her. 'I'm not letting you go through it alone,' she insisted. On balance, Gabrielle was grateful.

Their rooms at the Hotel Grande Bretagne offered breathtaking views: hers, a panorama of Syntagma Square, framed by cypresses and oleanders; Clarice's a partial vista of the Acropolis. Its majestic prospect reassured her that the trip wouldn't be wasted, even if Eleonor turned out to be a fraud. They arranged to meet her and her elder son, Alexios, in the hotel's Alexander bar at six o'clock on their second evening. After her initial scepticism, Clarice was captivated by her uncle's doomed love affair, plying Gabrielle with questions about how Eleonor would look, as though she were an old school friend she'd rediscovered after twenty years. She, on the other hand, felt sicker than she had done on the plane.

At the stroke of six, a short, dark-haired woman in a pastel-striped dress and a tall young man in a shiny suit entered the bar. 'This must be them,' Gabrielle murmured to Clarice, who stood up and waved. With his hand on his mother's elbow, Alexios steered her to their table, where Clarice, eager as ever to dispel any awkwardness, hastily introduced Gabrielle and herself. Despite numerous instances – one in her own family – of children not resembling their parents, Gabrielle was disappointed to see nothing of Papa in Eleonor's heavy brows and sharp features. A glance at Alexios, however, revealed that the resemblance had skipped a generation. He reminded her less of Papa than of Daniel: the same hazel eyes, high cheekbones, broad mouth and strong jaw. There could be no doubt that he was her nephew... half-nephew... no, nephew. She refused to countenance fractions.

She signalled to the barman that it was safe to serve the champagne. He poured them each a glass, which they raised and clinked. 'Santé!' Gabrielle said, in response to the others' 'Τειά μας!' She sat back, happy simply to exchange smiles with her newfound relatives since, even had she spoken Greek, words would have been superfluous. Clarice, more fluent in the language than she had expected, questioned Eleonor about her mother, translating her replies for Gabrielle. Under normal circumstances, the protracted rendering would have irritated her, but now it gave her time to absorb what she'd heard.

Eleonor's account of her parents' meeting aligned in large part with Aron's. What she added was the story of her mother falling pregnant while Papa was in Paris. She caught the name Mercado and Clarice's flicker of embarrassment when she reported that they'd employed her father as a go-between.

'Why couldn't they write to each other directly?' she asked.

Clarice relayed the question to Eleonor. 'They were afraid her letters would be intercepted by Grandpapa,' she translated, 'and Oncle Leon's would get lost in the haphazard postal service. His silence when she told him about the baby drove Xenia to despair.'

'What was that she said about Mercado?' Gabrielle asked, hearing the name again in a sentence Clarice failed to translate.

'Nothing of any significance.'

'My grandmother suspected Mercado,' Alexios interjected in flawless French.

'You speak French?' Clarice asked, startled.

'Yes, Madame, I studied it at the university.'

'Why didn't you say?'

'I didn't wish to disparage your excellent Greek,' he said smoothly. He turned to Gabrielle. 'But since you ask, my grandmother suspected that Mercado was attracted to her himself... the sort of attraction that makes men hate the women they can't have.'

'Before you say anything else, I should tell you that Mercado was – is – my father,' Clarice said. 'Simon Silvera. Mercado was his childhood nickname.'

'I assure you I meant no offence. I'm just repeating the story I've been told – and that only recently. My grandmother refused to tell my mother anything about her father, except that he came from a great family.' Clarice shot Gabrielle a warning look, which she ignored. 'It was only this year when my mother cleared out her apartment before bringing her to live with us that she found the bundle of letters her father – your father – wrote to her from Paris. Perhaps she shouldn't have read them.' He muttered something to Eleonor, who toyed with her hair. 'But she did, which is how we pieced together the story.' He turned to Clarice. 'But if it distresses you, I'll stop.'

'Not at all!' Gabrielle said, frowning at Clarice. 'We want to know everything.'

'There's little more to add. Your grandfather paid her to leave Salonica and never contact his son again. My grandmother is an honourable woman, and I've no doubt that, having taken his money, she complied with his terms.' He failed to conceal a note of bitterness. 'She moved to Piraeus, where she brought up my mother in hardship. She continued singing, until rebetiko was banned by Metaxas . . . do you know who I mean?' Gabrielle shook her head; Clarice, still smarting from his insinuation about her father, didn't respond. 'Ioannis Metaxas, our ruler in the years before the war. He cracked down on what he regarded as immorality. All my grandmother's musicians had their instruments broken; some had their bones broken; one ended up dead. It was said that the Asfaleia – the secret police – were trained by the Gestapo. They certainly used the same tactics. But to give him his due – though it sickens me – he refused to surrender Greece to Mussolini, entering the war on the side of the Allies. After the country's defeat, my grandmother, who'd scratched out a living selling fruit and vegetables in the street, worked as a chambermaid in this very hotel, which was commandeered by the German General Staff. At great personal risk, she passed on information to ELAS, the armed resistance. After the war, she received a letter of commendation from the King.'

'She sounds an exceptional woman,' Gabrielle said. 'I'd very much like to meet her.'

'That's easily done. If you wish, you can hear her as well.'

'Does she still sing?' she asked, trying to mask her surprise.

'Most weeks, yes. She hasn't made discs or appeared on the radio, so she never became famous. But she's always had a loyal following. Now, it's bigger than ever.'

'And she lives with you?'

'My mother finally persuaded her. They've always been close.' He said a few words to Eleonor, who sat silently sipping champagne, allowing him to speak for her. 'My grandmother worked so that my mother could complete her schooling and train as a secretary. That's how she met my father. He was a court recorder and older – twenty-two years – but my grandmother urged her to marry him. For her, the important thing was that – as we say in Greece – he was "as steadfast as an anchor in the sea".'

'Has it been a happy marriage?' Gabrielle asked, sensing his prevarication.

'Has yours?'

'I'm not married.'

'Forgive me, I assumed—'

'That's fine.'

'Such a beautiful lady.'

'It's fine.'

'My parents have a comfortable life. And I think – I hope – they're happy with us. My brother Dion is in the army for another four months. When he's discharged, he'll study to be a vet. Years!'

'And you?'

'I work in a bank.'

'Like your grandfather.'

'Really? Yes, of course . . . the famous Carrache bank. Not

quite the same thing, I'm afraid.' For the first time that evening, he smiled.

'Does your mother know that my father – our father – was murdered in Sobibor?'

'Yes, Madame told her.' He indicated Clarice.

'Together with my older brother, your uncle.'

'No,' he said gravely. 'We didn't know that.'

'Please tell her that I'm very, very happy to meet her.' She emphasised her words by taking Eleonor's hands, which were surprisingly delicate. 'Now that we've found each other, I'm intending to learn Greek, so we'll no longer need an interpreter. We'll be able to talk. We'll be able to do so many things.' She took a deep breath and repeated the phrase she had practised carefully. 'Είμαστε δελφίνια.'

Eleonor laughed.

'Yes,' Gabrielle said, 'we're sisters.'

'If you'll forgive me,' Alexios said, 'I think you meant είμαστε αδέλφια: we're siblings. Είμαστε δελφίνια means we're dolphins.'

'Really? Oh dear! I thought I was doing so well.'

'You are,' Clarice said. 'I'm proud of you.'

'Besides,' Alexios added, 'in all our ancient myths, dolphins are symbols of friendship and good fortune.'

'Then I was right,' Gabrielle said delightedly. 'We're dolphins too.'

4

CLARICE

THESSALONIKI, MAY 1964

AFTER NEARLY FOUR years of planning, construction and curation, the Irène Carrache Silvera Museum of Ottoman Sephardic Life was set to open. A core team had been recruited for the initial three-day-a-week operation, and fire and safety officers had completed their final checks. The Minister for Northern Greece was due to cut the ceremonial ribbon on Thursday, with Bishop Panteleimon, the Mayor of Thessaloniki, and a host of civic dignitaries in attendance. First, however, Clarice faced a more daunting challenge, when her family gathered for a private view.

From her office in one of the former maids' rooms, she watched a gardener trimming the myrtle bush beside the weathered statue of Zeus and Ganymede. Whenever she worried about the large sums of her father's money that she'd poured into the project, she had merely to look at the elegantly restored grounds for reassurance. Moreover, although she would admit it only to herself, it was the right way not just to spend the money but to atone for it.

In light of the wholesale plunder of Jewish assets by the Nazis and their Greek collaborators, a case of false accounting twenty-five years earlier might have seemed inconsequential. Yet Clarice not only brooded on its consequences but suspected that Papa's guilt had hastened his dementia. When Grandpapa Carrache left Salonica, he had appointed him as his agent, with the promise that, in due course, he would be offered a position in Paris. Although the war curtailed his prospects abroad, the Great Fire in 1917 afforded him equal, if not better, ones at home. As Roland Severin revealed one evening in Geneva (thankfully, not in Sylvain's hearing), Papa had used Grandpapa's title deeds as collateral to buy tracts of land in the devastated city. Once the reconstruction plans were drawn up, he sold them at substantially higher prices, laying the foundation for his personal fortune.

'I thought I was a master of the game,' Roland had said. 'But your father could teach me a trick or two.'

'Not really,' Papa replied, torn between basking in Roland's praise and soothing Clarice's unease. 'In the aftermath of the fire, people were desperate. I supplied them with the means for shelter. When trading was finally authorised, I sold the land, redeemed the deeds and made – shall we say? – a handsome profit. That way, I didn't have to go to Irène's father cap in hand. No one was any the wiser. And no one lost out.'

That profit had long exercised Clarice and, having assumed control of his affairs, she'd resolved to make amends. Her first thought had been to compensate all of Grandpapa Carrache's heirs, but such apparent largesse would have raised questions, and the truth would only have compounded their prejudices against Papa. None of the family had considered him good enough for Maman. If, as Tante Esther always said, she was the most sensible of them, surely they should have respected her choice? She'd had a happy marriage that would have lasted to this day had she not misjudged her bromide salts. Which of her siblings could say the same? Oncle Leon and Oncle Ruben both married women with whom they had nothing in common beyond their children. And, according to Maman, Tante Esther picked feckless Oncle Felix simply because she liked the name.

Having been captivated by the childhood tales with which Maman had relieved the tedium of the Occupation, she had been saddened on her first visit to Thessaloniki in 1958 to find barely a vestige of the once vibrant Jewish presence. She felt a powerful - almost atavistic - urge to create a memorial to a community that had been all but erased. It would be more complex and costly than planting forests in Israel, but what better way to employ Papa's wealth? She deliberated for months over the form the memorial should take. With none of her family showing more than polite interest, she had consulted others, notably the local historian, Maurice Saltiel.

Maurice, who'd amassed a private collection of sacred scrolls, documents and ritual objects, had long striven to create a museum of Jewish life in the city, but the project had foundered for lack of funds. Although happy to furnish them, Clarice was determined to be more than just a donor. Maurice was adamant that, given the history, they must avoid an anthropological approach, which might evoke the Museum of an Extinct Race that Hitler had envisioned for Prague. The exhibits should exist in dynamic relationship to their surroundings, so their first task was to find a suitable building. They viewed a derelict synagogue, an abandoned slaughterhouse and a row of disused almshouses, none of which met their requirements. While seeking alternatives, Maurice mentioned that her family's former home, now converted into government offices, was up for sale.

They arranged to visit it out of curiosity, rather than any expectation that it might serve their purpose. Clarice was charmed by the ornate façade, notwithstanding the scarred, dirty stonework, blotched with lichen and moss. She climbed the three cracked steps to the portico, capped with a horn of plenty reminiscent of those on her grandparents' bedheads in Paris, and entered a circular hall. The vast, empty space was dominated by a sweeping marble staircase, while brightly patterned, broken-paned windows cast motley shadows on the sisal matting. All she knew of the house's history after her family's departure was that Papa had leased it to the British army during the First World War, and it was later requisitioned to accommodate Greeks forcibly repatriated from Anatolia. In the early 1950s, Oncle Ruben had attempted to reclaim it, only to be informed that, as one-time holders of Italian passports, the Carraches had been classed as enemy aliens during the Second World War - by which logic they would have been allied with the forces that sought their destruction. There was no recourse against such inanity, but, with the building vacant, Clarice resolved to buy it. Although Maurice, a socialist firebrand in his youth, was initially hostile to associating the museum with a family of notables, she convinced him that it would provide exactly the setting they needed. For her part, she would not only be restoring the house to the family but making the family the lens through which to examine Jewish Salonica.

For the past four months, she and Papa had been living on the top floor (which would not be open to the public), along with two nurses, whose services had become indispensable. Although stronger medication had subdued his more violent impulses - or, rather, the more violent symptoms of his illness - Papa's increasingly erratic behaviour required constant supervision. She herself struggled to communicate with him. When she'd told him the previous week that Yiorgos was driving her to the shops, he warned her to make sure that he wore a condom, because she wouldn't want to return with *a little baklava*. Was he punning on the chauffeur's nationality (for which, despite the coarseness, she should be grateful), or had he confused the alliterative *baklava* and *bébé*, the way, yesterday at dinner, he had done his couscous and *cuillère*?

Trusting that the family would make allowances for him, she headed to the Méditerranée to greet the first arrivals. Tante Esther, Nathan and Margarethe had flown from London, after spending a weekend in Bournemouth with Nathan's ninety-three-year-old grandmother. She found them taking tea in the hotel lounge. Tante Esther, finally reconciled to the project, hugged her tenderly.

'Thank you for all you're doing, my dear. I shall reserve judgement until I see the house tomorrow, but it means so much just to be back here. I'd never have dared come if you hadn't arranged everything.'

'And paid for everything,' Nathan said.

'Ignore him! He drank three whiskies on the plane. I didn't recognise anything on the way from the airport. Listen to me! There was no airport in my day. There were scarcely any planes. There was definitely none of this.' She gestured around the lounge, which, with its plush furniture, swagged drapes and towering pot plants, might have been that of any grand hotel across the globe, were it not for the large-scale sepia photographs of Macedonian peasants in traditional dress.

'Is everything on schedule for tomorrow?' Nathan asked. 'Sylvain hasn't cried off yet?'

'No, and if he does, I'll never forgive him.'

'What about my reprobate brother?' Tante Esther asked.

'Mother . . .' Nathan said. 'Remember what you promised!'

'He and Pascal are arriving at lunchtime.'

'But no Armande?' Tante Esther asked.

'No Armande,' Clarice replied. 'She didn't want to fly with ten-month-old Jacques.'

'What in the world was he thinking? Starting a second family at sixty-seven? Did you know that Katrin's pregnant?'

'No, that's wonderful news! Congratulations! When's it due?' she asked, turning to Margarethe.

'Oktober.'

'So I'll have my first great-grandchild when my brother's second son will be – what? – barely fifteen months old,' Tante Esther said with a sigh. 'I know you all admire Ruben's – how shall I put it? – his zest for life, but I beg to differ.'

'*Plus ça change*, Mother.'

'Very droll. Madeleine's the one I feel for.'

'I invited her,' Clarice said. 'I still think of her as family. And Oncle Ruben says that she and Armande are the best of friends.'

'Another thing that strikes me as unnatural, though I'm not allowed to say so.'

'She's too busy revising. She sits her Bac in June.'

'If she passes, she intends to go to university . . . read for a degree. She'll be over fifty,' Tante Esther said. 'I tip my hat to her.'

While chatting volubly to Tante Esther and Nathan, Clarice voiced her concern that Margarethe, with limited French, must feel excluded.

'Please no worry. I understand more than I speak. And it is a beautiful language. I am happy just to hear.'

Maurice Saltiel joined them at seven. Though aware that not everyone shared her love of surprises, Clarice had planned on not mentioning him to Tante Esther, eager to witness her astonishment at encountering someone from her distant past, but Maurice had insisted she warn her.

'The last time she saw me, I was a young man of twenty-five. She won't recognise me and we'll both be embarrassed.' Gazing at the bald, bent figure with liver-spotted skin and ill-fitting teeth, Clarice felt compelled to agree.

Despite her determination that the museum should commemorate the splendour of Jewish Salonica, rather than the horror of its extinction, it had been Maurice's wartime memoir that first brought him to her notice. It had caused considerable controversy on publication since, alongside its account of native complicity in Nazi plunder, a commonplace of occupied Europe, it highlighted the criminality of the mandated Jewish police who ruled the ghetto, demonstrating that the Gestapo was no aberration. Given the licence, there were men of every race and creed willing to humiliate, violate and torture for personal gain.

The final chapter transcribed Maurice's testimony at the trial of the police chief Vital Levy, which he discussed with Clarice the day after Eichmann was hanged. 'I know there are people - friends - who feel that justice has finally been served. But for me, that happened fourteen years ago, when Levy, the man who raped my sister and broke every finger on my father's right hand, faced a firing squad on Corfu.'

Smiling, he moved to Tante Esther, who stood up and embraced him. 'Maurice was the first man I ever kissed,' she said to Nathan. 'It created such a scandal.'

'On stage, I hasten to add,' Maurice said.

'I never knew you'd acted,' Nathan said to his mother.

'You don't know everything about me,' she replied skittishly, as though Maurice's presence enabled her to shed fifty years.

To Clarice's relief, neither Maurice nor Tante Esther alluded to his time in Bergen-Belsen. Instead, he told her how, on his return to Thessaloniki, he married Perla, the nineteen-year-old daughter of a coffee merchant, in one of the twenty-five weddings that took place among the decimated Jewish community in 1946.

'As far as I remember, it was never spoken out loud, but we felt an almost biblical injunction to be fruitful and multiply, even if, at sixty, my natural inclination was to remain unattached. The following year, my son, Veniamin, was born, although, with no mohel in the city, it was another year before he could be circumcised.'

'And Perla?' Tante Esther asked.

'She died giving birth to our second son, Matthaios. She wasn't strong... I'm sure I don't need to elaborate. I've raised them alone. There are no Jewish schools left here, but I taught Hebrew at two of the Greek private schools, and I started to write. Now at my advanced age, I have a new career running a museum.'

'What about your boys?' Nathan asked.

'Veniamin is seventeen and Matthaios fifteen. Both still studying, though neither is a scholar. They're closer to each other than they are to me.' He rubbed his shoulder with a grim smile. 'It's not just my body that bears the burden of my past.'

The family fell silent. Tante Esther closed her eyes, as if to contemplate that past, before asking with uncharacteristic hesitancy: 'Did you ever hear from... hear anything of Leah?'

'Who's Leah?' Nathan asked. 'You've never mentioned her.'

'She was your mother's great friend,' Maurice said.

'And Maurice's colleague. We lost touch when she was transferred to a school in Demotica. I never understood why the Alliance moved her when she was doing so well here.'

'Under pressure from your father. He had a lot of influence with them. And he was worried about her influence on you.'

'It was Papa?'

'Yes, of course.'

'Papa?'

'Surely you knew?'

'No wonder she didn't reply to my letters. Papa . . . How long did she stay there? Was she still there during the war?'

'Unfortunately, yes. By then, the town was part of Bulgaria. But it was close to the Turkish border, so it was the one area of the country that the Germans kept under direct control. And in 1943, the entire Jewish population – all seven hundred of them . . . small enough for a single transport – was brought here and interned in the ghetto. Among them, Leah, her husband and two daughters.'

'So she married?'

'To the director of the school. Which is why they stayed. They were only with us for three days. We talked and talked. I can't pretend it was just like old times. She'd changed, as no doubt had I. But we reconnected amid the turmoil. And she was deeply moved to see girls whom she'd taught, some who'd worked as secretaries and dressmakers, some as shopkeepers, and two even as teachers. No factory workers or maids. She told me that, whatever the Nazis did to her, they couldn't take that away.'

'Then she knew what lay ahead?'

'I presume so. We none of us spoke of it . . . I don't know whether that was to sustain ourselves or one another. My last words to her were "Don't wait so long to come back next time." I'm still waiting.'

'But you came back,' Nathan said.

'It may sound shocking to say that it was my good luck to go to Belsen. But when the alternative was Auschwitz . . .'

'It's my fault that she ended up there,' Tante Esther said.

'Honestly, Mother!'

'If she'd never met me, then Papa wouldn't have pressed for her to be transferred.'

'In which case she'd have stayed here and still have been deported.'

'No, in the twenty years in between she'd definitely have been posted elsewhere – to a school in Bagdad or Beirut or Constantinople or Smyrna, Rabat or Casablanca or Tangiers . . . somewhere – anywhere – she'd have been safe from the Nazis. But because of me . . . Excuse me, I must wash my hands.'

Gloom descended on the group. Maurice apologised for any distress he'd caused, and Nathan was quick to reassure him. Clarice found herself babbling in broken English to Margarethe about the photographs in this week's *Paris Match*. After several minutes, she wondered aloud whether someone ought to check on Tante Esther.

'A good idea, thank you,' Nathan said, keen to delegate the task. So she made her way to the ladies' lavatory, where she discovered her aunt standing at a basin in an unforgiving light.

'It's ridiculous of me to get so upset about someone I haven't seen for more than fifty years,' she said, dabbing her eyes. 'But Leah was very special. She brought me out of my shell.'

'I lost touch with all my old friends when we fled Paris.'

'I'm going to tell you something I've never told a soul.'

'Really?' Clarice asked apprehensively.

'I kissed Maurice in the play, but I would far, far rather it had been Leah. Do you understand?'

'Yes, of course. There would have been no unsettling emotions. Not to mention, no scandal.'

'No, that's not what I meant,' Tante Esther said sadly. 'Never mind. It's too late anyway. Let's go back.'

Clarice knew exactly what she meant and felt both pity for her repressed desires and resentment at the assumption that, as a forty-year-old spinster, she secretly shared them. What did it matter if Tante Esther thought her naïve or even obtuse? Far better that than to become the repository of unwelcome confidences.

They went in for dinner, at the end of which Yiorgos dropped

Maurice off in Ladadika before taking Clarice home. The next morning, they retraced their route. Leaving Margarethe to explore the shops, Maurice escorted Tante Esther, Nathan and Clarice herself to the Mikra military cemetery in Kalamaria. As they drove through the city centre, Tante Esther grew despondent at her failure to locate the familiar landmarks of her childhood.

'That's one thing we can't blame on the Nazis,' Maurice said. 'After the Fire, the city was rebuilt on a different grid. So much of what you remember went up in smoke. Most of the synagogues, together with schools, libraries, clubs, theatres. Only the churches were spared, which you might say was a taste of things to come. Perhaps the Lord was sending us a sign? In which case, we were blind to it.'

'What about the mosques?' Tante Esther asked. 'I knew there was something missing this morning – no call to prayer!'

'And there hasn't been for forty-odd years. The Nazis left us one synagogue – the Monastir – if only because the Red Cross used it as a storehouse. But the Greeks didn't leave the Muslims a single mosque. Some were turned into churches, others into shops, offices, the archaeological museum and the Alkazar cinema, where I've seen many fine films (ironically, several in Turkish). They tore down the minarets and, with the exception of the White Tower, which would have provoked an international outcry, they've tried to eradicate every remnant of the Ottomans. The city's as Orthodox as it was at the height of Byzantium.'

'So Papa's cosmopolitan ideal is no more,' Tante Esther said.

'Along with the fraternal ideal and the egalitarian ideal and the ideal of proletarian solidarity,' Maurice replied bitterly.

Aunt Esther's discomfort increased as they drove down Egnatia Street. Having once bordered the ancient Jewish cemetery, it now adjoined Aristotle University. Groups of students wandered through the campus, either uninformed or unconcerned about what lay beneath their feet.

'All four of my grandparents – your great-grandparents – were buried there,' Tante Esther said to Nathan and Clarice. 'Three of them after we moved to Paris. Where are they now?'

'That depends on your view of the next world,' Nathan said.

'Let's stick to this one.'

'Their bodies were desecrated,' Maurice said, matter of fact as ever. 'Gangs of Greeks, convinced that we buried our dead like the Pharaohs, raked up their remains. Some even pulled the gold teeth from their jaws.'

'All the teeth I remember were white.'

'Friends of mine ran from grave to grave as fast as the workmen were digging them up, desperate to retrieve their relatives. What for? Where to put them? They weren't medical students needing skeletons.'

'Perhaps we should change the subject,' Clarice said to Maurice, who, sitting next to Yiorgos, was oblivious to Tante Esther's grief.

They reached the military cemetery, its uniform rows of upright headstones a stark contrast to the disordered tombs in Maurice's photographs of the ravaged Jewish cemetery. With the graves arranged sequentially, number 1757, that of Second Lieutenant Basil Henriques, was easy to find. Whether by accident or design, it was situated on the right-hand side of the cemetery facing the Stone of Remembrance, rather than the left, facing a large cross. The grass pathways were pleasantly soft and springy, but, without so much as a pebble to lay on the grave, Nathan went to collect stones from the roadside.

'My husband came here with his parents and sister at the end of the First War,' Tante Esther said to Maurice. 'But, with Nathan still a toddler, I stayed at home. Perhaps if I'd accompanied them, I'd have been better prepared for what the city has become. At least I'd have encountered it gradually.'

'Were you close to your brother-in-law?' Maurice asked.

'Only in retrospect. We named our second son Basil after him. He died in France in 1943. His body was never recovered.'

'I'm truly sorry.'

'Thank you.' With a wan smile, Tante Esther surveyed the cemetery. 'All these young men. So much promise squandered.'

Nathan returned with four stones, one for each of them to place on the grave. They then drove back to the hotel, where, after a light lunch, Maurice left for the museum and the family moved into the lounge. Tante Esther ordered a *café turc* and Nathan, more alert to local sensibilities, a *café grec*, which arrived looking identical. They had scarcely taken a sip when a receptionist ushered in Oncle Ruben and Pascal.

The last time her aunt and uncle had seen each other was at Jacques's circumcision, when Tante Esther made no attempt to hide her disapproval of her brother's geriatric paternity. Clarice prayed that the intervening months had mellowed her.

'Esther, my dearest sister, you look radiant,' Oncle Ruben said, as though no harsh words had ever passed between them.

'And you look worn out. I suppose it's only to be expected. Or do you leave your new wife to get up for the two o'clock feed?'

'I gather I'm still in disgrace.'

'How you live your life is your own affair.'

'May I have that in writing?'

'And you, Pascal?' Margarethe interposed. 'What do you feel about it, having a small brother?'

'I prefer to think of him as my godson.'

'How admirable!' Tante Esther said. 'Not to mention prudent, given your father's age.'

'I'm not Methuselah!'

'I'm so glad you were able to come,' Clarice said to Pascal. 'Your professors didn't object to your taking time off?'

'They're fairly relaxed. And I wanted to see where Ruben spent his dissolute youth.'

'If only,' Oncle Ruben said.

'I trust that one thing you'll teach your godson is to call his father Papa!'

'Mother, please! They've only just walked in,' Nathan said, with unusual vehemence.

'How's Maman?' Tante Esther asked Pascal. 'Is she enjoying her studies?'

'She's panicking about the exams, but her tutor's sure she'll get a *mention bien*. She's applied to read sociology at the ENS de Lyon. Given that, after graduation, I'll have a two- or three-year internship, we should finish at around the same time.'

'Don't take too long,' Clarice said. 'If all goes to plan, I'll need an architect to design a café for the garden.'

'That's far too lowly for Pascal,' Oncle Ruben said. 'He's busy sketching futuristic cities.'

'He'd do well to start here,' Tante Esther said. 'Anything would be an improvement. You won't recognise it, Ruben. Great sprawls of office and apartment blocks. Where are the elegant villas, the acacia-lined avenues, the secret gardens?'

'I thought you believed in change,' he replied.

'In society, yes . . . in people and institutions. But not places: places should remain the same.'

Nathan and Margarethe went to visit Hagia Sophia, while Yiorgos drove the others to the Campania. Tante Esther and Oncle Ruben both fell silent on glimpsing the house.

'I feel as if I've tasted the madeleine,' Oncle Ruben said finally.

'What's this about Madeleine?' Tante Esther asked.

'Not our Madeleine . . . Proust's.'

'I've always meant to read him but never had the time.'

'Some of us had too much.' They got out of the car. 'Shall we go inside?'

'No, not yet,' Tante Esther said. 'Give me a moment to get my bearings.'

'Then let's stroll round the garden.'

As he took her arm and led her through the side gate, it was clear that, whatever the strains placed on it, the bond between them was inviolable. Clarice wished that the same might be said of her and

Sylvain. Their relationship had been permanently soured after he accused her of using Papa's illness as 'a path to sainthood'. It was profoundly unjust of him to attack her for doing her duty when he had shirked his. Moreover, if he were as devoted to Maman's memory as he professed, he ought to thank her for safeguarding it from any gold digger who might seek to usurp her place.

Accompanying Pascal into the house, she saw at once that Sylvain and his family had arrived. One of her nephews was hopping from seashell to seashell on the mosaic floor, while the other was clambering up the newly installed ticket desk.

'Careful with that, Max darling,' she said, swooping him off it.

'I'm Louis,' he replied.

'And I'm Max,' Louis said, shuffling towards her and yelping as she scooped him up for a kiss.

'I'm too old to fall for that. And please don't play your tricks on Grandpapa. He'll only get in a muddle.'

'But he's older than you,' Louis said.

'That's why.'

'Who are you?' Max asked, eyeing Pascal.

'I'm Pascal. A sort of cousin.'

'Why's your hair like a girl?'

'Because my girlfriend likes it.'

'Where are Maman and Papa?' Clarice asked.

'Up all the stairs,' Max said.

'Shall we go and find them?'

As they each held out a hand to her, Clarice felt the familiar pang that she was no more to them than an aunt. They climbed the stairs to the top-floor kitchen, where Bierta, the Albanian maid, was serving coffee and pastries to Sylvain and Annette. Clarice gave Sylvain an awkward hug and brushed her lips across Annette's cheeks before asking whether they were happy with the hotel. She'd selected the Astoria as both suitable for children and shielded from Tante Esther's censorious eye. Sylvain assured her that it was perfect, and Annette congratulated her on the transformation of the house.

'You weren't supposed to look round till later.'

'Don't worry, the doors downstairs were closed,' Sylvain said.

'But you peeped,' Max said.

'Traitor!'

'Everything's so precious,' Annette said. 'I'm terrified of the boys breaking something.'

'We don't break any somethings,' Max said.

'I have one word for you: gramophone.'

'I take it you've not yet been to see Papa?' Clarice asked.

'We were waiting for you,' Sylvain said. 'He does know we're coming?'

'He's been told, which isn't necessarily the same thing. If you've finished here, I'll take you. Come on, you two,' she said to the twins. 'Shall we go to see Grandpapa?'

'I don't want to,' Louis said.

'You shouldn't turn them against him,' Clarice said to Sylvain.

'He did a good enough job of that himself last summer.'

'He shouted at Louis,' Max said.

'He shouted at Max,' Louis said.

'He's a poorly man. When he shouts, you have to understand that he's actually shouting at himself.'

They crossed the corridor to Papa's room, where he was doing a wooden jigsaw puzzle with the nurse.

'Hello, Papa,' Sylvain said, putting a hand on his shoulder.

'I know you,' he replied listlessly.

'It's Sylvain.'

'I know you!' After a brief glance at him, he returned to the puzzle, trying to force a piece that wouldn't fit.

'It's your son, Papa,' Clarice said, tears welling in her eyes. She grabbed Max's hand and pulled Louis away from Annette. 'And here are your grandsons.'

'Why are there two of him?' Papa asked, staring at them in confusion.

'They're twins, Papa,' she said, wishing that Annette would stop dressing them alike. 'Don't you remember, we spent a day with them in Lausanne last year? Now they've come to see you.'

'Give them some money,' he said testily. 'A thousand francs. Would you like a thousand francs?' he asked Louis. 'Give them some money!'

'They don't want money, Grandpapa,' Annette said. Having resolutely refused to call him Papa, she had found a way to address him through her sons.

'You!' Papa said, registering her presence. 'Have you come to torment me?'

'Maman!' Louis cried, running back to her, while Max stared at his grandfather with terrified fascination.

'Papa!' Clarice said, taking his arm as he half rose from the chair.

'I didn't mean to abandon you. You were having a seizure. I had to lock you up. I had no choice.'

'At last!' Sylvain said triumphantly. 'After all these years, he admits it.'

'What seizure?' Annette asked. 'I couldn't speak, but there was nothing else wrong with me.'

'No, Papa,' Clarice said. 'You explained long ago that it must have been Monsieur Legrandin.'

'I went to fetch a doctor. There were people everywhere running from the fire. I was afraid one of them would break in.'

'I don't like this,' Louis said.

'Don't be frightened,' Clarice said. 'Grandpapa's just having a bad dream.'

'I didn't know that the flames would spread to Kamara. You were my sister and I loved you, no matter what.'

'Sister?' Sylvain said to Annette. 'He thinks you're Mari.'

'Yes, yes . . . Mari, my sister!'

'Then you weren't the first,' Sylvain said. 'He must have locked his sister – his simple-minded sister – in her room and left her to burn to death.'

'No!' Clarice shouted.

'Mademoiselle, would you please take the boys downstairs . . . outside . . . anywhere,' Annette asked, at which the nurse led the agitated children away.

'You've no right to say that,' Clarice said to Sylvain.

'I didn't; he did!'

'He's raving, Sylvain,' Annette said softly. 'He thought she was me.'

'Since coming here, I've studied the history,' Clarice said. 'Thousands of buildings were destroyed, but not a single person was killed. Listen to your wife! He doesn't know what he's saying.' She gazed at Papa, who, deaf to their dispute, stared intently at the puzzle.

'He's a murderer, and you refuse to see it. Why won't you open your eyes?'

Bierta knocked on the open door and hovered at the threshold.

'Begging pardon, but there's more people have arrived. Enrik . . .'

'Henriques,' Clarice said.

'That's right,' Bierta said, smiling. 'Shall I bring them up here?'

'No! No, thank you.' For a moment, Clarice had forgotten about her cousins. 'Tell them we'll be straight down.' As soon as the maid was out of earshot, she turned to Sylvain. 'Please don't say anything about this . . . this nonsense. Everything's jumbled in his brain. We don't even know when Mari died. I've searched the records. Nothing!'

'Very well. But I'm doing it for you, not for him.'

'Leave that for now,' she said to Papa, who was twisting a jigsaw piece between his left index finger and thumb. 'We're going downstairs. Tante Esther and Oncle Ruben are here to see you.'

'Hand me my bottle!'

'Has he started drinking?' Sylvain asked, recoiling.

'No, his bottle of eau de cologne! It's the same whenever anyone comes. You two go down. I'll see to Papa. Just promise me you won't take anything he says to heart.'

She was dismayed that Sylvain could think something so wicked of Papa. Before he returned to Lausanne, she planned to give him the names of specialists in Geneva and Nice, able to explain the neurochemistry of Pick's disease. Her immediate task, however, was to ensure that his rancour didn't spoil the tour for the rest of the family.

She knew that many – if not all – of them had grave reservations about the viability of a Jewish museum in a city where so few Jews remained to support it. But, to her mind, that made its establishment even more urgent. Securing her grandparents' house had given it both form and context. It consisted of three discrete sections: the first, a recreation of a notable Sephardic family home at the turn of the twentieth century; the second, a multifaceted display of the family's history and religion; and the third, an introduction to its individual members.

With a wealth of archival photographs, they had been able to reproduce the furnishings of the reception rooms. The only authentic pieces were a gilded mahogany Empire desk in Grandpapa's study and a Louis XV bergère in the morning room, both of which her grandparents had taken to Paris and Oncle Ruben had recovered after their wartime removal to Germany. To fill the gaps, she had brought many of the finest antiques from their house in Geneva and employed agents to scour auctions and salesrooms across France. She had also contributed several paintings from Papa's collection, including Tante Bella's portrait of her parents, which, though painted long after they moved away, featured prominently in the salon.

The historical display was housed in the rooms once occupied by Oncle Leon. The first portrayed the family's fortunes over the centuries since their expulsion from Spain. Oncle Henri's exquisite genealogical charts hung alongside Renaissance prints of both the ducal palace in Milan, where the family first entered the historical record, and wills, deeds and marriage contracts from Modena and Livorno, where they settled before moving to Salonica during the sultanate of Mahmud I. A photograph of the tobacco factory, showing a youthful Simon Silvera overseeing two rows of seated cutters, was mounted between those of six old women in their Sabbath best on the steps of a Carrache almshouse and a less well-groomed group of Russian immigrants outside their newly built shacks in Vardar. Opposite that was the framed capitulation certificate which had rendered such philanthropy possible.

The second room was devoted to the family's religious heritage. Photographs and engravings of the Italia Yashan Synagogue, together with the architect's drawings for its late-nineteenth-century refurbishment, lined one wall. A vitrine on another held holy books, among them a sixteenth-century Torah scroll from the demolished Sicilia Yashan Synagogue, which, with none of the congregation left to claim it, Maurice himself had preserved long before there was any prospect of a museum. Two additional vitrines contained ancient ritual objects, many acquired from Jews fleeing Morocco: a nine-branched and a seven-branched menorah, a shofar, a yad, kiddish cups and seder plates. Most precious to Clarice were the only actual Carrache items: Oncle Leon's tallit and tefillin, which Gabi had found, hidden in a rock chamber beneath the Villa Dahlia.

The third room had sparked Clarice's one serious dispute with Maurice. She had conceived it as a museum of Ottoman Sephardic culture, concluding with the Greek annexation of the city or, failing that, the Great Fire. He, however, was determined that it should acknowledge the Nazi annihilation of that culture. After a heated debate, he came up with a solution that worked for them both. There were no yellow stars, broken tombstones or other emblematic objects but, instead, a pitch-black empty room, where the nightmare of deportation and imprisonment was evoked by sounds: screeching trains; barking dogs; howling babies; and, most hauntingly, the relentless commands of *'Schneller, schneller, schneller!'*

'My one condition is that we post a notice on the door forbidding entry to anyone under ten,' Clarice said.

'If only Hitler had shown such sensitivity,' Maurice replied.

The final part of the museum occupied the first floor. Inspired by Maman's stories, Clarice had realised that many pivotal aspects of the period could be explored through her own family. Each of the seven available bedrooms could be used to showcase activities in which its occupant took part. So Grandpapa and Grandmaman's depicted officialdom, councils and charities; Oncle Leon's, the Young Turk movement and insurrection; Tante Esther's, political meetings and popular theatre; Oncle Ruben's, Zionism and sport; Maman's, traditional folklore, wisdom and remedies; Tante Bella's, the arts and cultural exchange. Clarice had allotted the spare room to Papa, an honorary Carrache, constructing a replica of his father's silk farm to represent the city's cottage industries, which, in one of his rare lucid moments, he'd insisted she labelled as a hobby.

With most of the original objects either dispersed or destroyed, Maurice had recruited a team of scouts to track down suitable substitutes. The resulting exhibits comprised citations and invitations; photographs, posters and playbills; scripts and speeches; banners and pennants; footballs and trophies; buttons and armbands; amulets, talismans and potions; costumes and uniforms of all sorts; and, in Tante Bella's room (the most heavily insured), a first-century terracotta head of Dionysus and a fifth-century red-figure pyxis. Gabi had presented two small Timarete studies of Mount Olympus, painted in Paris from memory but vividly capturing the familiar view.

Casting an anxious glance at the bedrooms as she passed, she steered Papa down to the salon, where her family and Maurice were waiting.

'Good to see you, Simon,' Oncle Ruben said, extending his hand, which Papa ignored. 'Is he worse?' he asked Clarice.

'I should have warned you. He only answers to Mercado.'

Papa smiled on hearing the name.

'I thought he considered it demeaning.'

'Not any more, apparently.' She turned to the others. 'Apologies for the delay, but I hope you've had a chance to look round in here. So what do you think? Tante Esther, you're the expert.'

'I don't remember each stick of furniture, but the arrangement feels right. Has everything been here since we left?'

'Sadly, no. That would have made our lives a lot easier,' Clarice said. 'They're similar pieces procured from all over France. We've worked from a newspaper feature Maurice found in the archives.'

'*Le Journal de Salonique*,' Maurice said.

'Brilliant!' Oncle Ruben clapped his hands. 'Grandmaman Regina and Tante Amada routinely maligned Maman for allowing photographers into the house. If only they were here to eat their words!'

'Is that picture of the grandparents by Aunt Bella?' Nathan asked.

'Yes. She painted it in Paris, but it felt right to include it. Papa bought it during the war. It had been looted by Rosenberg's thugs and put up for sale in Lucerne. It was his last gift to Maman.'

'I remember her hanging it in the hotel,' Sylvain said. 'It made her very happy.'

'Thank you, Mercado,' Tante Esther said to Papa, who grinned.

Clarice took them on a tour of the small salon, dining room, morning room and study, before moving to the kitchen which, having been scarcely altered in fifty years, had required minimal restoration.

'This was Maryam's domain,' Oncle Ruben said. 'Stirring, chopping, whisking, kneading, terrorising the younger maids.'

'She certainly terrified me . . . those teeth!' Sylvain said. 'Why didn't Grandmaman do something about them?'

'She tried,' Aunt Esther said. 'She offered time and again to take her to a dentist. But Maryam flatly refused.'

'Why?'

'She was afraid of gas.'

A silence fell over the room.

'I wasn't supposed to set foot in here,' Oncle Ruben said, eventually.

'Why?' Pascal asked. 'Did you sneak food?'

'Thank you for that! No. It wasn't a boy's place.'

'In other words, it was a man's world,' Aunt Esther said.

'The food thief was Bella. Pastries, cakes, comfits. She had a sweet tooth.'

'Maman was always worrying about her weight,' Aunt Esther added.

'I don't recall her being fat,' Nathan said.

'You wouldn't. She slimmed down once she started painting.'

'The artist's diet,' Pascal said. 'Perhaps we should patent it.'

Clarice checked her watch. 'If you've seen enough in here, we can move on to the historical section. Where are the twins?' she asked Annette. 'It might not be suitable for them.'

'The last I saw, they were in the garden, running your father's poor nurse ragged.'

'You have the joys of a hyperactive four-year-old to come,' Sylvain said to Oncle Ruben.

'I've had a taste of them already,' he replied, with a smile at Pascal.

Clarice led them through a latticework door into the first historical room. While her family gravitated towards the displays of letters, documents, seals, coins and, most eye-catching, Grandmaman Regina's betrothal ring, crowned with a miniature Solomon's temple, she studied two photographs of the Fire, the impact of which had been troubling her ever since Papa's mention of Mari.

'Am I right in thinking there were no deaths in the Fire?' she asked Maurice pointedly.

'There are no records of any.'

'Did you hear that?' she asked Sylvain.

'Although of course they may not be exhaustive.'

'And did you hear that?' Sylvain asked Clarice.

'What's this?' Nathan asked, pointing to a large iron key, twice the size of his hand.

'It's the key to your maternal grandmother's family home in Córdoba,' Maurice replied. 'Passed down through the generations. On her deathbed, your great-grandmother Falcona entrusted it to her maid to give to your grandmother when she came back, which of course she never did. Hannah brought it to Clarice when she heard about the museum.'

'I would not want to carry this in my purse,' Margarethe said.

'Many Sephardim cherished their house keys in the hope that one day they would be able to return to Spain,' Clarice added.

'Many Palestinians do the same now,' Nathan said.

'Must you?' Aunt Esther asked.

Oncle Ruben took her hand and ushered her into the second room. 'I'd like to go to a Sabbath service while I'm here,' he said, inspecting the Torah scroll.

'I'll be most happy to take you,' Maurice said. 'Though you may be disappointed. We've only the one synagogue, the congregation's small, and we no longer have a rabbi. But apart from that . . .'

'What's this yad thing? Is it a backscratcher?' Pascal asked, staring into a vitrine.

'No,' Maurice said, chuckling. 'Though it would do the job. It's used to point to the text during the Torah reading, so that we don't touch the parchment. Didn't you use one at your bar mitzvah?'

'I didn't have one.'

'Pascal's mother isn't Jewish,' Oncle Ruben said.

'He could convert,' Maurice replied. 'After all, he bears the name Carrache. But it's none of my concern . . . Please, come this way.' He gathered everyone in the corridor. 'This third room needs no explanation,' he said, opening the door to the darkness. 'So I shall leave you to experience it for yourselves.'

Clarice remained outside, waiting for people to emerge. The first to do so was Pascal, wide-eyed and gasping.

'Would you like a glass of water?' she asked.

'It's fine . . . I'm fine. A bit claustrophobic, that's all.'

She wondered whether they should post an additional warning, as she watched the others come out slowly, sombrely, with Margarethe, the only non-Jew, wiping her tears.

They made their way upstairs where, after explaining the principles behind the selection, Clarice invited them to walk around the exhibits at their leisure. She fretted needlessly over Tante Esther's and Oncle Ruben's responses to the rooms that bore their names. Tante

Esther, having examined the playbills and photographs, costumes and props, from several Socialist Federation productions, smiled as coyly as an ingenue when Maurice translated an *El Avenir* review of her 'elegant and assured' performance as Marianne in *L'Avare*. Oncle Ruben, having examined a faded football shirt, scrutinised a photograph of the Maccabi team in 1911, thrilled to recognise two Ukrainian brothers who'd played alongside him.

'For the life of me, I can't remember their names.'

Bierta approached Clarice with the news that her last cousins had arrived.

'Cousin!' she replied, more sharply than she had intended.

Leaving the others to explore, she went downstairs to welcome Gabi, who had brought Eleonor, her husband Dimitrios and mother Xenia. Although she wasn't close to Aunt Lily, she couldn't help feeling a pang of resentment on her behalf to see how at ease Gabi was with Eleonor's mother. At the same time, she struggled not to feel resentful to see how at ease she was with Eleonor herself. After everything she had been through, Gabi deserved her share of happiness. Yet she seemed to forget that, had Clarice not set up the museum, publicising the Carrache name, Eleonor would never have found her.

The rest of the family came down in a cluster, congratulating her and greeting Gabi. As only Pascal had met Eleonor and Dimitrios – on a study trip to the Parthenon the previous autumn – Gabi effected introductions. Tante Esther shook Xenia's hand guardedly and Oncle Ruben more warmly, but, faced with this short, deeply lined, dark-skinned woman with garishly dyed hair, it was evident that, even allowing for the passage of time, they were taken aback by their elder brother's choice.

'I'm very ...' Oncle Ruben began in Greek. 'I'm sorry,' he said to Clarice, 'I've forgotten the little Greek I knew. Please tell Madame how happy I am to meet the love of my brother's life.'

She turned to Xenia, but the newly fluent Gabi anticipated her, translating first Oncle Ruben's remark and then Xenia's reply. 'She thanks you but denies that she was the love of Papa's life. After all, he was married to Maman for many years.'

'One doesn't rule out the other,' Aunt Esther said. 'No need to translate that!'

'She also says how grateful she is to Clarice for inviting her.'

'Nonsense,' Clarice said. 'She's Eleonor's mother. And Eleonor's practically family.'

Just as the stuttering conversation stalled, the twins rushed indoors, closely pursued by the nurse.

'Take off your shoes please!' Clarice shouted, spotting their footprints on the mosaics. Daunted by the unfamiliar faces, they ran to Annette. 'Shoes!' Clarice repeated.

'It's only mud. It'll brush off,' Sylvain said, bristling at the slightest criticism of his sons.

'And there's no point in them taking anything off,' Annette said. 'It's late. Time for these monkeys to get ready for bed.'

'No, no, Maman!' they cried with one voice.

'Yes, yes. Now kiss everybody goodbye.'

With moues of disgust, they raced to the door, shouting 'Goodbye, goodbye, goodbye' and giggling.

'Yiorgos will drive you back,' Clarice said. 'But first the boys must say goodbye to their grandfather. Where is he, by the way?'

'He must have stayed behind in one of the bedrooms. I wasn't keeping track,' Sylvain said. 'What on earth . . . ?'

Clarice followed his gaze to the landing, where Papa was clinging to the banister as if to a lifeline.

'What is it, Papa?' she asked, hurrying towards him.

'What's this?' he replied, looking at the stairs. 'How do I get down?'

Clarice felt a surge of despair, followed by warmth, as Gabi stepped behind her and clasped her shoulders.

'Go and help your father,' Annette said to Sylvain. 'I'll see you back at the hotel.'

She dragged the protesting twins out as Sylvain guided Papa down the stairs.

'How lovely to see you, Oncle Simon,' Gabi said, kissing him on both cheeks. 'It's Gabi,' she added, as he failed to respond.

'It appears that you now have to call . . . oh, what does it matter?' Sylvain said.

'Hello, Mercado,' said Xenia, who had only ever known him by that name. 'Xenia . . . Do you remember me?'

'I have an excellent memorial. I speak five . . . what is it I speak?' he asked Clarice.

'Languages, Papa.'

'I know that. You don't need to remind me.'

'I must have changed a lot since we last saw each other. But then, to be frank, so have you.' Xenia stared at him intently. 'But your scent. I'll never forget that scent.'

'What's she saying?' Aunt Esther asked Gabi.

'She's remembering his scent.'

'I'm not surprised. He's always drenched himself in the stuff. We used to find it suspicious.'

'You told me Leon wished to have nothing more to do with me,' Xenia said, which Gabi translated with a note of bitterness. 'I'm quite sure now that that wasn't true. Gabi told me how he came looking for me after the war. Why would he have done that if he cared nothing for me? I ought to hate you. Then again, if I'd registered Eleonor's Jewish father, who knows what she might have suffered under the Nazis? So perhaps I should thank you after all. Thank you, Mercado. Thank you.'

Papa smiled, as though her gratitude were unequivocal. Clarice wanted to speak up for him, but she remained bewildered by his remarks about the Fire. She no more believed that he'd murdered Mari than that he'd abandoned Annette. While his actions might seem questionable to those who didn't understand him, it was clear to her that he'd tried to protect his sister from marauders, just as he'd trusted the hotel manager to look after Annette. And if he'd concealed Xenia's pregnancy from Oncle Leon, he must have thought he was acting in his friend and future brother-in-law's best interests.

Had he married Xenia, a gentile rebetiko singer, Grandpapa Carrache would surely have disinherited him.

Deputing the nurse to take Papa upstairs, she led the way into the dining room. 'We'll have a second tour for latecomers after dinner.'

'Not for me, I'm afraid,' Xenia said. 'I used to dream of seeing inside this house, but I'll have to save it for another occasion – if there is one.'

'Whenever you like,' Clarice replied. 'But must you really rush off?'

'When I knew I'd be back in Salonica for the first time in years, I contacted some old friends. They've invited me to sing in their taverna.'

'A concert! In that case, we must eat at once.'

Reverting to French, Clarice explained that she'd planned this one last meal before the dining room was given over to the museum. She directed Tante Esther and Oncle Ruben to either end of the table, telling the others to sit where they liked. They split into separate pockets of French and Greek speakers, with Margarethe attaching herself to Dimitrios, who'd learnt German during the war. Xenia sat next to Maurice on Oncle Ruben's right, with Clarice on his left. She'd enlisted the chef de cuisine at the Mediterranée to prepare a selection of traditional Sephardic dishes that could be made at the hotel and served by off-duty waiters. Although she protested that 'We weren't provincial. Maman had a copy of *Le Guide Culinaire*,' Tante Esther was as excited as Oncle Ruben to rediscover childhood favourites: stuffed grape leaves and aubergines; haminados eggs; *bourekas*; cheese and lamb *sambusuk*; baba ghanoush; shakshuka; sumac chicken and couscous; and to finish, honey-baked apples, *marochinos* and rose-flavoured *tishpisti*.

'I wish I felt that nostalgic for our childhood foods,' Sylvain said to Clarice.

'We grew up with rationing. Maman was kidnapped, trying to buy eggs.'

'What was that?' Aunt Esther asked, pausing her conversation with Pascal. 'Irène kidnapped?'

'It's a long story,' Clarice replied.

Before she could elaborate, Oncle Ruben stood up and tapped his glass.

'I hope you'll bear with me while I say a few words, especially those of you who don't speak French. There was a time in my youth when, as Esther will recall, I studied the Torah religiously.' Pascal laughed. 'No pun intended. In one of his last speeches to the Israelites, Moses warned that, if they displeased the Lord, He would scatter the tribes across the face of the earth. I don't know what we did to displease Him, but the Carraches have definitely been scattered - and worse - and it's thanks to Clarice that we're together once more in our old home.'

'Hear hear!' Nathan said, only to be shushed by Aunt Esther.

'I was sceptical when she embarked on such a quixotic project. I don't know how representative our family was of the notables in Salonica, let alone of Sephardim more generally, but we had a story, and this museum goes some way towards telling it. If that strikes a chord with the visitors, it will be down to her. So, I ask you all to raise your glasses to Clarice.'

Clarice looked away as her name resounded down the table. Having wished for recognition, she was embarrassed to receive it. 'And Maurice!' she said. 'He did most of the groundwork.'

'And Maurice!' Oncle Ruben proposed a second toast.

'We really must go,' Xenia said to Clarice. 'I've eaten so much, I'm afraid I'll burst out of my costume.'

'Please tell her I think it's amazing that people still want to hear her sing,' Oncle Ruben said to Maurice.

'I'm not sure that would be very tactful,' he replied.

'I mean . . . wonderful that she remains in vogue.'

'It's found a new audience,' Xenia said, as Maurice referred instead to her 'timeless music'. 'Students . . . young people seeking a bridge to the past. Traditionalists complain that it's lost its way . . . too eager to please . . . had its balls cut off.'

Blushing, Maurice rendered the phrase as 'emasculated'.

'But I sing in the same way I always did. I'm too old to change.'

She stood up, followed by Eleonor, Dimitrios and Gabi, who explained to those at the far end of the table that they were heading to the taverna.

'I'd like to tag along,' Pascal said, 'if that's all right.'

'Me too,' Nathan said. 'Will there still be seats?'

Gabi muttered something to Xenia, who laughed. 'She says it's a large room and eight years since she sang here, so yes.'

'Let's all go,' Oncle Ruben said, a suggestion received politely by Tante Esther and enthusiastically by everyone else.

'Yiorgos has left,' Clarice said, 'but we can ring for cars.'

'Telephones throughout the city, Esther,' Oncle Ruben said. 'That's one change you must applaud. Remember when ours was installed? Maryam used to pick it up as though it was about to explode.'

'Don't mock me! They all mocked me,' Aunt Esther said to Sylvain. 'Ruben, Bella, even your mother.'

The call was made and, twenty minutes later, the cars arrived to drive them to Ano Poli, dropping them at the end of a narrow, cobbled street.

'What's that?' Aunt Esther asked, as they passed a wall dotted with inscriptions. 'It looks like Hebrew.'

'I'm afraid it is,' Maurice said. 'We saw where the Jewish cemetery was razed to the ground. The Greeks recycled the tombstones throughout the city: to repair the church of Agios Dimitrios, to lay the courtyard of the National Theatre, to build the university, to reinforce dance floors and even to line latrines.'

'No,' Aunt Esther said, shaking her head violently. 'No, I don't . . . I won't believe it.'

'Come away, Mother,' Nathan said. 'Don't upset yourself.'

'Whose stones are they?' Aunt Esther said, peering at the worn wording. 'They might be your grandparents'. This morning I was upset that I couldn't pray at their tombs. Who knows? Maybe I'll have the opportunity now, here in the street, or perhaps when I go to the lavatory.'

'Don't, Mother, please,' Nathan said, taking her hand as she started to weep. 'You've known worse. Basil never even had a grave.'

Clarice doubted that would be much consolation.

'But he lives on,' Oncle Ruben said. 'In those of us who knew him. And through us, to those who never knew him. His ideas live on; his example lives on; above all, his sacrifice lives on, or else we wouldn't be standing here today.' He opened the taverna door. 'So let's go inside and celebrate the life he preserved for us.'

'I don't know that I can.'

'Of course you can. Or Xenia will be hurt. And she's endured enough at the hands of this family.'

As they entered the harshly lit taverna, Aunt Esther glanced first at the floor, an expanse of green and white chequered tiles, then at the walls, bare brick, adorned with old copper pots and pans, climbing plants with withered leaves, and framed photographs of unsmiling men in fishermen's caps. Satisfied that there was no sacrilege, she followed Oncle Ruben through a fug of cigarette smoke to three tables that the waiters had pushed together without making a corresponding adjustment to the puckered oilcloths. A waiter took their drinks order: tsipouro for Dimitrios and Pascal; brandy for Oncle Ruben; retsina for the rest of them. The clatter of cutlery, whirr of overhead fans, and blare of piped music conspired against conversation, and they sat in companionable silence.

The performance began – half an hour later than scheduled – when a bouzouki player, guitarist and accordionist stepped onto the intimate stage and struck up a vibrant trio. As the final notes faded, the bouzouki player warmly welcomed Xenia, who'd come to them 'directly from the Klimataria in Athens'.

Dressed in a red tunic and black pantaloons, she joined them on the stage. Thanking the audience for their kind reception, she fizzed with the energy of a woman twenty years younger. 'It means so much to me to be back in the city of my birth, the city where I first made music and where I learnt this opening song, 'Mi Chika Flor'. The lyrics are in Ladino, and I sing it for my friends, my new friends, whom I hope I can call my new family.' Several heads turned towards the Carraches as prime candidates for the compliment. 'The song is very simple. All you need know is that a man is begging a kiss from his love, his little flower. If she denies him, he will despair.'

> *Tus dos lavyos kero bezar,*
> *Rogo, ninya, no me refuzar.*
> *Yo dezeo abrasarte con amor, mi chika flor,*
> *adorarte siempre con kalor.*
> *Vaz a ver si se amar,*
> *Siendo tu sola, me supites enflamar.*
>
> *Ven atcherkar, no me agas sospirar, mi chika flor,*
> *Si no, me vaz a desesperar.*

Clarice looked around the table. There were French speakers and Greek speakers and English speakers and German speakers, all listening to a song in a language that was once to be heard in every taverna, café, shop and marketplace in Salonica, from the Konak to the docks, but had now fallen silent. Yet, as Xenia sang, it lived again. *Love*, *flower*, *flame* and *despair* were words that transcended Babel, while Xenia's voice transcended language itself. Clarice heard the plea of the enraptured lover, saw the smile of his sweetheart, and prayed that she would grant him the coveted kiss.

ACKNOWLEDGEMENTS

FOR HELP AND advice on matters great and small, I would like to thank Philip Arditti, Philippe Bertrand, Rupert Christiansen, Bruce Hunter, Rivka Isaacson, Liane Jones, Alain Lizotte, Eleni Maniaki, Jane Mays, Peter Otto, Adam Samson, Boyd Tonkin and Jenny Topper.

I owe particular thanks to my new publishers, Chris and Jen Hamilton-Emery, and to Robina Pelham Burn for her editorial expertise.

Many books informed the writing of this novel. Among the most informative and insightful were:

Adler, Jacques, *The Jews of Paris and the Final Solution*, Oxford University Press, Oxford, 1991.
Amipaz-Silber, Gitta, *Sephardi Jews in Occupied France: Under the Tyrant's Heel, 1940–1944*, Rubin Mass, Tel Aviv, 2000.
Benbassa, Esther and Aron Rodrigue, *Sephardi Jewry: A History of the Judeo-Spanish Community, 14th–20th Centuries*, University of California Press, Oakland, 2000.
Drake, David, *Paris at War: 1939–1944*, Harvard University Press, Cambridge, MA, 2015.
Fleming, K.E., *Greece: a Jewish History*, Princeton University Press, Princeton, 2007.
Frenkel, Françoise, *No Place to Lay One's Head*, trs. Stephanie Smee, Pushkin Press, London, 2018.
Kundahl, George G., *The Riviera at War: World War II on the Côte d'Azur*, I.B.Tauris, London, 2017.

Langbein, Hermann, *People in Auschwitz*, trs. Harry Zohn, University of North Carolina Press, Chapel Hill, 2004.

Lipstadt, Deborah E., *The Eichmann Trial*, Bravo, London, 2011.

Marrus, Michael R. and Robert. O Paxton, *Vichy France and the Jews*, Basic Books, New York City, 1981.

Mazower, Mark, *Salonica: City of Ghosts*, Alfred A. Knopf, New York City, 2005.

Minerbi, Sergio, *The Eichmann Trial Diary: A Chronicle of the Holocaust*, trs. Robert Miller, Enigma Books, Littlehampton, 2011.

Naar, Devin, *Jewish Salonica: Between the Ottoman Empire and Modern Greece*, Stanford University Press, Stanford, 2016.

Poznanski, Renée, *Jews in France During World War II*, trs. Nathan Bracher, Brandeis University Press, Waltham, MA, 2001.

Rein, Raanan, *Argentine Jews or Jewish Argentines?*, Brill, Leiden, 2010.

Romero, Luis Alberto, *A History of Argentina in the 20th Century*, trs. James P. Brennan, Pennsylvania State University Press, University Park, 2002.

Ryan, Donna F., *The Holocaust and the Jews of Marseille*, University of Illinois Press, Champaign, 1996.

Schwarz, Urs, *The Eye of the Hurricane: Switzerland in World War 2*, Routledge, London, 1980.

Sciaky, Leon, *Farewell to Salonica*, Haus Publishing, London, 2007.

Sebba, Anne, *Les Parisiennes: How the Women of Paris Lived, Loved and Died in the 1940s*, Weidenfeld and Nicholson, London, 2016.

Semelin, Jacques, *The Survival of the Jews in France, 1940-1944*, trs. Cynthia Schoch and Natasha Lehrer, Oxford University Press, New York City, 2019.

Zuccotti, Susan, *The Holocaust, the French and the Jews*, Basic Books, New York City, 1993.

I am indebted to Robin Buller for sharing with me her doctoral thesis, *Sephardi Immigration in Paris 1918-1945*.

This book has been typeset by
SALT PUBLISHING LIMITED
using Neacademia, a font designed by Sergei Egorov for the
Rosetta Type Foundry in Czechia. It has been manufactured
using Holmen Book Cream 65gsm paper, and printed and
bound by Clays Limited in Bungay, Suffolk, Great Britain.

CROMER
GREAT BRITAIN
MMXXVI